THE PATIENT

An unputdownable psychological thriller
with a breathtaking twist

E.V. SEYMOUR

Previously published as *Beautiful Losers*

JOFFE
BOOKS

Revised edition 2023
Joffe Books, London
www.joffebooks.com

First published by Midnight Ink in the US in 2016
as *Beautiful Losers*

This paperback edition was first published
in Great Britain in 2023

Cover art by Nick Castle

ISBN: 978-1-80405-782-7

For Ian

BEFORE

He knew in an instant that something was wrong. He could see it in their faces, the way they looked at him, with pity.

The surgeon, a short, overweight man with a bald shiny head, briefly closed his eyes. The rest of the team watched with haunted expressions, the sense of collective unease palpable.

Someone coughed. A combination of phrases spilled into the room, disjointed, so that he was given the impression of listening to a master of ceremonies with a faulty microphone. *Unfortunately . . . unable to correct . . . difficult . . . given the nature of the injuries.* He blocked them out, ignored the hushed tones, the guarded looks, focused instead on the pale-washed walls, the smell of surgical alcohol, the rotating blades of the fan.

Silence spread through the room like an uncontrollable forest fire.

Wary, they huddled together, waiting for him to speak. He spoke, all right. He could barely control his anger.

"Things like this don't happen to people like me. Do you know who I am, for Chrissakes? Do you understand the fucking consequences?" His protest tumbled out in a jumbled heap, the slurred words falling from the gap where his lips should have been. There was no pain. The morphine took care of that.

That's when he began to feel scared.

Perhaps it was the residue of the medication. Post-operative, he was still light-headed, his concentration and coordination impaired. He had a nauseous sensation in his stomach, a hangover from the anaesthetic. Yes, that was it. Once he'd recovered, things would be fine. He couldn't expect miracles at this early stage. He needed time. That was all. They were probably talking to the wrong guy, the bad news meant for some other poor bastard. He voiced as much.

"I'm sorry." The surgeon's eyes were open now, his look direct. "There is no mistake."

A plain-looking woman dressed in a white coat talked about physiotherapy. She had a voice like a cracked plate and kept touching her mouth with the fingers of one hand. Her sensible flat shoes shuffled. Dead giveaways.

He lost all sense of time. People came and went. Anxious conversations burbled around him. Drugs administered. Tubes adjusted. He was constantly checked as if on suicide watch.

Finally, he asked to be left alone, insisted on it. They shambled out, worried about lawsuits, he suspected, as well they might be. Very slowly he got out of bed and tottered towards the only mirror in the room. He'd always loved them, photographs too. Anything that reflected his powerful good looks. And now . . .

His heart filled with razors of ice. Spots, like tiny tropical fish, darted before his eyes. He wanted to throw up. *Oh Christ*, he thought, stunned by his reflection. *Oh Jesus fucking Christ.*

A tight surgical cap clung to his skull. Tubes poked out from behind each ear. He inclined to the right, the once arresting features bloated in a way that was not simply post-operative. He was prepared for the bruising and swelling, but the skin on one side, where it was not discoloured, had the dead appearance of a waxwork. His left eye sloped and would not shut even though the lid drooped. The full lips had lost their shape and form and curved down in a permanent expression of disdain. A persistent ball of spittle hung like a cobweb in the corner of his mouth. He attempted a pose and failed, the message from his brain defeated by the catastrophic trauma to the facial nerve. And only months before he was at the top end of the face business in an industry dominated by colossal egos fuelled by vanity and rewarded with obscene amounts of money.

His hands stumbled over his injured features but there was no sensation. It was of no consolation that only one side was afflicted. In fact it was worse, one half mocking the other. He tried to avert his gaze, but found himself riveted, compelled to look. In his misery he felt powerless to turn away from the monstrous, unforgiving reflection staring back at him. And always the permanent, sad reminder of how he used to be.

Someone once told him that the face was the centre of humanity, every emotion reflected there — in the eyes, the slant of the mouth, the density and colour and texture of the skin. All he saw was terror, a savage fear of being ugly in a society that prized beauty, a dread of being unloved and worthless in a world where youth, or the appearance of it, was king.

They'd told him his injuries could be corrected. They'd said his new look would kick-start his career. After all the allegations, all the bad publicity, it was his chance for a brand new start. Like a fool, he'd believed them. He'd *trusted* them.

Fury and frustration built inside. He wanted to smash up the room, to shatter his image, to tear down the walls. He could do it. He still had a powerful body, beautiful even. But he no longer had a face to match. His throat wrenched open with dry sobs. Too late he realized how he'd relied on the eyes of others to define him. Now he was one of the ugly people; it didn't matter how kind he was, how good a friend, he would never be admired, envied and adored. Instead . . .

As the light in the room faded, casting his face into pale luminosity, his rage boiled and cooled, replaced by a cold, ruthless anger. It nestled in his gut, slithered through his veins and coiled around his heart. Just as well, he thought, because with born-again certainty he knew that nobody would love him now.

CHAPTER ONE

"I look hideous."

"In what way, exactly?"

"Isn't it obvious?"

"Not to me," I said with a smile.

The young woman in front of me sighed. "Look at my nose, it's huge. Everyone stares at it. My skin's a disaster, pitted and uneven. My eyes, well . . ." She shrugged. "Enough said."

I couldn't see much of my client's face. In spite of the July heat, a woollen hat obscured the brow. Dark glasses concealed her eyes. A hoodie, with the collar zipped up tight, hid most of the lower half of her features. Her GP's referral notes read *anxiety state/depression, abnormal concern with appearance/BDD*, or, as it was known by its full name, body dysmorphic disorder, a condition defined as a morbid preoccupation with an imagined defect in appearance. My working day usually revolved around women with anorexia or bulimia nervosa, both disorders highlighted by the patient's disturbed attitude to body image, which was why, even though the young woman sitting opposite suffered from neither illness, she'd wound up at the Bayshill Clinic.

"Would you like to show me, Lisa?"

"You'll be shocked."

"How about you unzip your jacket?" I flicked a lock of blonde hair behind my ear, wondering if she'd notice. She didn't.

My client nodded reluctantly. "See," she said, defiantly sticking out her jaw. "I'm grotesque."

Apart from the skin looking a little reddened, either from repeated attempts to cleanse it, or because of contact irritation with wool, there was nothing out of the ordinary about the texture. If hypercritical, I'd say that Lisa's nose was slightly large by comparison to her mouth, but it was an extremely minor flaw by anyone's standards.

"Take your shades off for me?"

Lisa complained but, persuaded by another warm glance from me, did as she was asked.

Nice eyes, I thought. They were brown and almond-shaped, not dissimilar to my own and I'd always thought my eyes my best feature.

"Thank you." I smiled encouragement, eager not to trivialize the young woman's beliefs. "How much would you say you think about your appearance?"

"Every nanosecond of the day."

"Do you find you're constantly checking mirrors?"

"Any reflection really."

I made a note. "How long would you say it takes to put your make-up on? From beginning to end, washing, cleansing, moisturizing, right to the last flick of lip gloss."

"A couple of hours, excluding the time I spend on facial exercises."

"And taking it off?"

"An hour, maybe more."

"So your appearance dominates your life. Would that be a fair description?"

The brown eyes glanced away. "I have no choice."

"Have you always felt like this?"

"For ever."

"Has the way you feel interfered with other aspects of your life?"

"I can't go out, if that's what you mean."

"So what do you do on your own?"

She chewed her bottom lip and averted her gaze.

"Do you look in the mirror?" I asked tentatively.

"Uh-huh."

"Do you think the mirror lies?"

Lisa looked up and stared at me with hard eyes. "Never."

"You sound very certain."

"Fuck's sake, it's the truth."

I let it go, unchallenged, and made another note. "This obviously causes you a great deal of distress."

Lisa's face darkened. "Sometimes I think I'd be better off dead."

"Ever attempted suicide?" I deliberately kept my expression and voice neutral.

She shook her head.

"You never think about it?" I enquired softly.

"Only in an imaginary way. Not for real, I guess."

Another note.

"If you had one wish, what would it be?"

Lisa's face lit up with a broad smile. "Easy."

I beamed back. "Go on, tell me."

"I'd have surgery."

Against every instinct, I maintained my smile. "It's a bit radical, isn't it? You're only nineteen."

"Be worth it."

"But it would still be the same you inside the skin."

Her eyes lost their lustre. Her mouth turned down in disappointment.

"All right," I said gamely. "Tell me how surgery would make your life better."

She lit right back up. "People wouldn't stare at me anymore. They'd like me. I could go back to university, finish my course, get a decent job. I could have friends, a proper relationship."

"Do you reckon that people don't like you based on the way you look?" Without warning, something chimed deep down within me. I cut off the sound before it had a chance to reverberate.

"Get real. It's obvious, isn't it? If you look pretty, people think you're good. If you're ugly, like me, they think you're bad."

"And what do you think?" I inclined my head, allowing the young woman a full view of the left side of my face.

Lisa leaned forward then back. "That's different."

"Is it? Tell me why."

A knock on the door saved Lisa from explanation. Jane, the clinic receptionist, glided in with a mug of coffee and a brown paper parcel. "Apologies for the interruption, Kim. It came by courier for you this morning. Express delivery." She placed the package on my desk. "Thought it might be important."

I squinted at the label, *To Kim Slade*, and pushed the parcel aside. "I wasn't expecting anything." Jane gave a mild shrug and left, quietly closing the door behind her. I sneaked a sip of coffee and returned to my client, spending a couple of minutes outlining my proposals for next time and agreeing the number and frequency of future sessions. Firmly zipping up her hoodie, Lisa reached for her sunglasses with obvious relief and fled.

I put my notes aside, grabbed my bag and was almost out of the door when I remembered the parcel. Padded, a label in the left-hand corner stating *Fragile*, it sat squat and faintly accusing. Tough, it could wait. But, then again, it might be . . .

The thought scarpered. It would only take moments to open, no harm in it. No harm at all. Nothing to worry about, I told myself.

So why was my heart racing?

Taking a pair of scissors, I snipped away the tape to discover a thick layer of bubble-wrap. Carefully unravelling the protective covering, I removed the object and stared at it, my own reflection gazing back in puzzlement and, yes, rising fear.

Oval, set into an attractive stained-glass surround, the mirror reminded me of something similar I'd seen in one of the chi-chi shops in Salcombe, Devon. I checked the wrapping for a note of explanation, or a clue about its source, but there was nothing. Sitting back down heavily, the leather of the chair let out a squeal of protest.

Heat fled across my cheeks. My mouth felt full of mud. Sweat broke out above my upper lip and underneath my arms. Why a mirror? I tried to hang on to my rational self, the one I adopted for clients, the one I used for self-preservation.

Irresistibly drawn to the glass, I studied my appearance: dark eyes, full mouth, the way my straw-blonde hair fell in layers down to the jaw line, the better to conceal the pink puckered skin on the left side of my face. Apart from a couple of memorably humiliating incidents, I didn't generally find my disfigurement a stumbling block. Okay, so I never got *the look* from passing handsome strangers, which was fine by me. But, generally speaking, once I got to know people, men seemed fascinated while women viewed me as less of a threat.

"Fuck it," I cursed out loud. "The bastard has struck again."

CHAPTER TWO

Georgia's reaction startled me.

"You should take it seriously, in case."

"In case of what?"

"It turns nasty." Georgia crossed her arms. She had a no-nonsense look, which I imagined wasn't the one she used in the consulting room.

"Are you serious?"

"For God's sake, Kim, we're in a dodgy business. We rummage through the emotional rubble of people's lives and sometimes those people are, frankly . . ."

"Mental? Is that what you were going to say?"

"I was going to say disturbed."

"Thank God for that."

"Actually, I was going to say mad as a box of frogs." Georgia grinned. "Sorry."

I let out a laugh. Deep down, I hoped it would ease the tension. No chance. I glanced around the bustling bar. A wave of pain rolled across my shoulders.

"Seriously," Georgia said. "You know the dangers."

"We trade in secrets and taboos, both come with a price tag."

"And remember the price tag can be damned expensive."

"You mean transference?"

"It happens more often than you think."

True, clients could sometimes become fixated on their therapists. But I was no longer working in the kind of areas that invited that particular problem. My present clientele consisted of terrified young women under the age of twenty-five whose only goal in life was to defy it. They were too self-consumed to pose a threat to me — or anyone else, for that matter.

Georgia picked at her salad. "Christ, I hate lettuce," she said morosely. "How come you manage to stay so slim?"

"Genes and nervous energy. At this rate I'll be the diameter of a pencil."

Georgia raised a smile and munched thoughtfully. "Do you think it's linked to the mysterious chocolates?"

I absently ran a finger down the scar tissue on the side of my face and thought about the accompanying message. Made up from assorted pieces of newsprint, the crazy arrangement of letters had set my teeth on edge. It simply said: *BEAUTY QUEEN*.

"I like chocolates, as you well know." Georgia patted her ample tummy. "But if someone sent me a huge box with an anonymous note attached it would frigging freak me out." She forked in another mouthful of lettuce. "You kept the note as evidence?"

"I shredded it."

The fork hovered in midair. "You did what?"

"I know. I'm an idiot. Honestly, Georgia, I thought it was a one-off."

Georgia was having none of it. "This speaks of progression, a pattern. First the chocs and now the mirror."

I averted my eyes and took another bite of sandwich in a bid to distract Georgia, who was homing in on me like a guided missile. I was troubled enough already. I didn't need any help from Georgia.

"Anything else you'd care to share, Kim?"

"Not especially." I reached for my glass of water, flashed a smile and asked Georgia about her forthcoming holiday in Italy.

"Is this the technique you usually adopt with clients?"

"I prefer waterboarding," I said, flashing a weak grin. "Stop evading the question."

"Pot, kettle and black."

"Okay, Miss Marple," I said, with a huge sigh. "For three clear months after Chocciegate, nothing happened. Any unsettling feelings evaporated until . . ." I stalled. Stuff like this didn't happen to people like me. I couldn't get my head around it. For fuck's sake, who would want to pay *me* this level of attention? Georgia didn't say a word, didn't fill in the gap, simply looked, rapt, all eyes.

I cleared my throat. "Then three weeks ago, there were a number of silent phone calls to the landline in the flat."

"Jesus. You never said a word."

"Well . . ."

"What did you do?"

"Ignored them." In denial, I'd poured myself a drink, I remembered.

"Really?"

"Really."

"Did you check the number?"

"Withheld."

"You haven't reported it to the phone company as a nuisance call?"

"I tried. It didn't get me very far." Georgia looked as if she couldn't trust what she was hearing. "I hope you don't stare at your clients like that," I said.

"This is you and me," Georgia flashed back. "I don't normally conduct one-on-ones in a bar." She took a thoughtful bite of chicken. "Are you usually this cool under pressure?"

I forced a smile. Internally, I was quaking, although pressure wasn't new to me. Pressure is waking up in the morning and finding the ground from underneath you gone. Pressure is being trapped in a home life of testosterone, competitiveness, raised voices and barked commands. Pressure is being teased at school because you're the only kid in the class whose mother doesn't exist. Pressure is being talked about because your face looks funny. This, on the other hand and make no mistake, was abuse of power, a form of control and potentially criminal. Chest-deep in the past, I almost missed Georgia's next question.

"Does Chris know?"

"Sure."

"And?"

"Obviously he's worried."

"*Worried?*"

I let out a giddy laugh. "Will you stop repeating everything I say?"

"Is it any wonder?" Georgia said, not a bit apologetic. "I suppose you blinded him with science."

I'd blithered on about the ways in which people indulge in inappropriate behaviour to disguise fear and hurt, some more extreme than others. I'd assured him that it was my profound belief that the nastiest exterior cloaked a good person. What I didn't tell Chris: making silent phone calls was sometimes the precursor to something far more serious.

In the absence of a reply, Georgia pressed me about my anonymous caller. "You say no words were spoken?"

I shook my head. No threats. No demands. I should feel relief. I felt nothing of the sort. Deep down, I knew this had a personal dimension. I dreaded to think what Chris would make of the mirror.

"Want my professional opinion?" Georgia said.

"Nope, but I expect I'm going to get it."

Georgia pushed away her plate, leaned slightly forward like a judge summing up a case for the jury. "Slotting the mirror into a clinical context, anorexics and bulimics are as much governed by mirrors as they are scales. When an emaciated anorexic regards herself, she only sees a distorted, overweight version."

"While BDD sufferers stare with the firm hope that their appearance will somehow be acceptable to them, a hope that's always dashed," I chipped in.

"Right," Georgia agreed. "Ergo: the mirror is significant. I reckon it's one of your clients."

I shook my head.

"No?" Georgia had a shrewd gleam in her eye.

"Making silent phone calls isn't a female pursuit. Women are too verbal, too language orientated."

"You know as well as I there are exceptions," Georgia said. "Whoever it is, what's the motivation? Is this person reaching out and saying they too have been scarred in some way, that they . . ." Georgia broke off, embarrassed, and splayed the fingers of her right hand as if they would do the talking for her.

"Are like me," I finished off the sentence. Scarred on the outside. Scarred on the inside.

"Sorry." Georgia's eyebrows drew together in apology.

I didn't speak. An unexpected flash of anger banged between my ears. How dare this person take a pop at me and upset my life?

Georgia tried a different tack. "Have you pissed off anyone, inadvertently or otherwise?"

"Not that I'm aware of. Confrontation isn't really my thing." *Passive aggression*, Chris had flung at me once, which I thought mighty unfair because that was more his line.

"So you've absolutely no idea who it might be?"

I'd spent oceans of time trying to figure out the personality, attempting to identify an obsessive theme or signs of psychoses, but there was so little to go on and no real indicators. "There's no face on which to focus, no clue to identity, no idea what this individual might be capable of, from which direction he'll come, whether he'll lose interest or step it up."

"He? You're really set on it?"

"Oh yeah, this is a guy, all right." Everything about the situation told me a man was involved.

"Go to the police, Kim."

"With what? It's not as though I've been followed or anything like that."

"Would you know if you had?"

She had a point. Terrified at the prospect, I'd started imagining all sorts. Glancing over my shoulder had become second nature. So far, thank God, it had yielded no results.

Georgia glanced at her watch. "Bugger! I've got to go." She gathered up her belongings and gave me a hug. "Just make sure you keep a note of the calls and detail anything else that happens. Then, for God's sake, Kim, go to the police."

CHAPTER THREE

I stepped out into the sunshine, tilted my head to a sky the colour of French navy and willed myself to feel better. Whatever was happening to me was only upsetting if I allowed it. Tonight, I'd drive to Devon and see Chris, and all would be well again.

I set off down Montpellier Walk, bars on one side, gardens with bandstand on the other, music from a brass band in full spate competing with the low growls of Ferraris and Aston Martins. The leafy promenade stretched out before me like a wide street in a continental city. Cheltenham at its finest: smiley, glossy and wealthy.

Ellerslie Lodge, a pioneering fifteen-bed residential home, housed thirteen- to eighteen-year-old anorexic girls. Either they'd recently come out of hospital or were trying the Lodge as a last ditch attempt before it was deemed necessary to remove them to a more clinical setting.

Splitting my time between Bayshill Clinic and Ellerslie, an eight-minute walk away, allowed me a degree of professional latitude. At Bayshill, a white stucco double-fronted house that could easily pass for an insurance firm or design outfit, the atmosphere was serene and calm. Ellerslie was generally messier, the client's higher maintenance, the vibe highly strung. I actually preferred the latter because it represented more of a challenge. On a purely practical level, it offered a pragmatic solution to the perennial "Cheltenham" parking problem. Unlike Bayshill, the Lodge had extensive parking facilities, and I parked my silver Mini there every Monday morning and picked it up every Friday after work.

Cathy Whitcombe, the senior nursing sister, greeted my arrival with a friendly smile. Her kind face and easy-going manner often lulled people into falsely thinking that she was a pushover. "All quiet on the Western front. Ellen's settling in well."

"The girl from Stroud?"

"She seems to have chummed up with Kirsten."

"Brave," I said with a laugh. Argumentative by nature, Kirsten was one of my more tricky clients. "So who am I seeing this afternoon, Cath?"

"Ellen, Carla and Lauren. Before you do, could you pop into Jim's office? He's got a proposition for you." Cathy wore a wide smile.

Jim was our resident psychiatrist and my boss. "What sort of proposition?"

"PR and media."

I groaned inside. I'd already taken part in a television discussion for the BBC in which I'd talked about the work carried out at the Lodge. The episode had been the most knicker-wetting experience of my life, and that was saying something. The unscheduled mention of my facial disfigurement by the presenter had felt like random violence. I didn't relish the idea of another stint in front of the camera.

"Is he in his office?"

"Knee-deep in referrals."

I crossed a large, comfortably furnished hall that smelled of polish. A deep-seated sofa ran the length of a wall hung with watercolours of beach scenes. Magazines lay in a lazy heap on a coffee table. A spectacular arrangement of flowers sat on a pillar near the wide, sweeping staircase, the effect undeniably welcoming. The same could not be said about

Jim Copplestone's office; it bore all the hallmarks of a student squat.

Jim glanced up from a pile of medical literature. He oversaw my cases from a medical perspective and took care of the few clients who displayed more complicated and serious disorders requiring drug intervention. With his long dark hair, streaked with grey, he had the louche exterior of an out-of-work session musician — one of the reasons, I suspected, for his popularity with the girls.

"Just the woman," he beamed.

"I gather you want to twist my arm."

"A finger perhaps, nothing more. It's a phone-in programme, BBC Radio Gloucester. They're after a general discussion to highlight the problem of eating disorders. Apparently it's come back into vogue."

I pulled a face.

"Mine is not to reason why," he said, "but anorexia just got sexy again."

"Terrific. I'll make a note to tell my clients."

"Now, now," he said with a chuckle. "Think of it as a wonderful opportunity to enlighten listeners. Honestly, Kim, it's a great vehicle to highlight eating disorders."

"How come you're not doing it, then?"

"They prefer a woman."

"*They* being the same people who think anorexia is sexy?"

"The audience we're trying to reach."

"Cool. I'm fine with that." I recognized when I was snookered.

"Good," he said conclusively.

"Not so fast. What's in it for me?" I threw him a playful smile.

He slowly reached up and put his hands behind his head. "You drive a hard bargain, Slade. What would you like?" Leaning back expansively in his chair, the curve of his lips suggested that he was open to offers. *You old flirt,* I thought. Jim's company and office banter made me feel briefly normal again.

"A couple of bottles of decent wine?"

He flashed me an expression of mock disappointment. At least I thought it was.

"You're a terrible woman."

"Ha-ha. When am I expected?"

"Monday, at noon. I've got the name of a contact here, somewhere." Jim plunged his hand helplessly into an overflowing in-tray.

"You'll be there all day. Catch me later." Anxious not to be late for my first appointment, I left him to it.

CHAPTER FOUR

No wonder the girl had gone off the rails.

I closed the door on the last of my clients. For weeks I'd been working with a girl called Lauren: see-through skin, sunken body, fear personified. After careful probing, one event stood out as a major contributory factor: her mother had abandoned her. And I knew only too well her sense of betrayal.

I updated the notes on my laptop, picked up my bag and walked across the hallway to Jim's office. The door was closed, an envelope taped to it with my name scrawled across. I peeled it off, shoved it into my briefcase and stepped outside. It had gone half past four and most of the girls were in the dining room having tea before they got on with homework before dinner.

The air throbbed with compressed heat, the flickering sun above my head sucking the moisture from anything that moved. Eager to sit in the climate-controlled interior of my car, my feet crunched across the gravelled drive with a quick step, my eyes squinting at the shining streak of melting silver.

Until my gaze zoomed in on the windscreen.

Halted in my tracks, I narrowed and refocused my vision, unsure what to think or do. Nervously, I glanced over my shoulder at the Lodge's solid Regency architecture. Should I go and find Jim? Indecision engulfed me. Sweat prickled my palms. My chest tightened as if there was not enough room inside for my stuttering heart. Although I tried to hang on to my intellect, calm deserted me. I instinctively knew that what I was looking at was part of a warped pattern of behaviour. And, if I did go back for Jim, I would have to tell him about the other things. It would blow it up and into the open. It would be like admitting defeat. It would confirm I had a serious problem.

Jumpy as hell, I advanced slowly, eyes scanning the surrounding streets, watching for sharp and sudden movement, anything or anyone that didn't fit, but all I saw were office workers and passers-by. Listening for an unexpected noise, the scuffle of footsteps, the only sounds were the steady drone of traffic, the chorus of car horns and sirens, and the screech of seagulls.

Reaching into my bag, muttering curses under my breath, I scrabbled about and gathered together a wad of tissue. My jaw set, I leaned across the windscreen, recoiling at the glassy eyes, the blood seeping between its open jaws, the tail curled and entangled in the windscreen wiper like a serpent waiting to strike. As I placed my hand over the dead rat, it felt alarmingly warm, soft and fresh to touch. Oh. My. God.

Repelled, I attempted to get enough purchase to pick it up. Finally, I gripped hold and flung it into a nearby hedge.

"Didn't know you were a litter lout."

I wheeled round. "Christ, Jim, you shouldn't creep up on people. You nearly gave me a heart attack."

"Sorry, I came to check you got my message. What on earth are you doing?"

Cold slithered up my spine in spite of the soaring heat.

"Kim, are you all right? You've gone quite pale."

"It's nothing."

Jim crooked his head. "Problem?"

I tried to get a handle on my breathing. Pressing a hand to my chest, I cracked a smile. "Some idiot mucking about."

He studied me quizzically. I couldn't fathom either what he was thinking or what I should say. "I'll see you next week," I finally blurted out, escaping into my car, the clean and welcome smell of leather and car freshener enveloping me.

Starting the engine, I yanked the seatbelt across and looked dead ahead. A tap on the window made my insides twist. Jim was madly gesticulating. I pressed the switch to open the window. He stooped so that his face was level with mine, his breath hot on my skin. "Give my love to Devon and have a good weekend."

I did my absolute best not to react. *He stopped me simply to say that?* Nodding dumbly, I wished him well too.

As I drove out onto the main road I was forced to face one inescapable fact. Someone knew which car I drove.

Someone had targeted me.

CHAPTER FIVE

Packed with screaming kids newly escaped for the holidays, cars littered the motorway. For the first hour my eyes flickered to the rear-view mirror. As a precaution, I frequently changed lanes and tried to apply reason to something I felt entirely unreasonable about. I'd received no threats, I doggedly reminded myself as I pulled into the outside lane. The rat was simply one of those things that happen in urban environments. Could have been one of the girls at the Lodge. Could have been guys out for a night of booze and cheap jokes. Could have been *him*. I clamped down on my jaw, outraged.

Around Bristol, there was the inevitable stretch of roadworks. Once past the bottleneck of traffic, and against a thumping track from an old Red Hot Chilli Peppers album, the tension began to ease. I smacked my foot on the gas and felt the gravitational pull that only a fast car can produce. My thoughts eventually turned to Chris, his mane of dark hair, piercing blue eyes, the way he could floor me with a smile. Originally my lodger, ours was only supposed to be a temporary arrangement. It was no use getting suckered in by his electric blue eyes, his mysterious manner and the lure of a man of deep complexities.

But I had.

He knew more about me than any other human being. With him, I felt warm, relaxed and loved. He knew about my late father, about my eldest brother, Luke, who lived in the States. About Guy, my other brother, killed in a freak motorbike accident years before. Chris understood that the job in Cheltenham was my way of escaping beaches enshrined in too much history, that my new life up country was an escape from my past and my ghosts. In essence, he got me.

And I got him.

Intending to break with Devon and move on, with the arrival of Chris in my life, I'd wound up with a foot in two camps. That was almost four years ago.

Traffic clogged the narrow lanes. The sun lay low in a bloodshot sky. I was on the home stretch, intimately familiar territory and, more than ever, I felt relief that I still had a hideaway. The person dogging my footsteps might be able to exert influence in Cheltenham, but not here.

* * *

Cormorants Reach overlooked the river at Goodshelter. My father's last home, it was where we Slades gathered for family get-togethers and more recently for funerals. I knew every stone, lintel, cob wall, exposed beam and dark recess. I knew its secrets. Without warning, the fabric of the building rattled with ancient arguments, slamming doors, bunched fists and my tears. Startled by the memories, I banished them to the outer reaches of my consciousness.

At the sound of my arrival, the front door swung open, Chris's tall frame captured in a swathe of golden evening sun. Displaying a deep umber tan, he was wearing a brilliant white open-necked shirt tucked into faded denims. His feet were bare. The sight of him made my stomach jitter. I felt hopelessly happy, and the anger and fear that had assailed me disappeared. Seconds later I was enveloped: his lips on mine, his arms holding me tight.

"Better unpack the car," I said, drawing away.

"Leave it." He hooked me with his eyes and instantly I understood what he wanted, what he needed, what we both craved.

He took my hand and led me up the narrow flight of stairs to our bedroom. There, he slowly undid the buttons of my shirt, taking his time as though he'd meticulously planned the moment in detail, slipping it off and throwing it across the end of the bed. He kissed the top of my high breasts, my mouth, the base of my throat, tracing the ragged line of scarred skin from the outer edge of my left cheekbone to the hollow of my collarbone. I flickered with wanton desire.

"You're beautiful," he whispered. And I knew that he meant it, that in his eyes I really was.

He stripped off while I hastily undressed. Then he scooped me off my feet and carried me to our bed.

He kept his eyes open. He always did. I'd once wondered if it displayed a lack of trust, something with which I was familiar, or was connected to men's endless visual capacity for sexual pleasure. His warm hands slid slowly over me, reacquainting with my body, as if he wanted to explore every inch. I felt dizzy and shameless. We tasted and touched each other, and I told him explicitly what I wanted and what I wanted to do to him.

Soon I was burning with heat. His eyes locked onto mine, the expression indecipherable. In that fleeting moment of time I realized that however long we stayed together I would never truly know him. I sensed that his feeling for me was based more on biological need, on sex and lust, than love. Perhaps this was the way it was meant to be. Perhaps. The thought that you can't be truly intimate with someone you don't really know entered and, as quickly, exited my fevered mind. Too soon I saw his expression change.

Yet still he watched.

Afterwards we lay in bed and I asked what sort of a week he'd had.

"Fairly bloody."

I let out a whistle between my teeth. My own school days were detestable. I rarely spoke about them because, by comparison to Chris's childhood, I'd led a charmed life. His was a textbook case of brutal, abusive father and drunk, incapable mother.

"When school feels irrelevant, kids don't give a fuck," he said. "Trouble is, I kind of get it."

"That was different," I reminded him. "You were trapped in the care home system. No wonder you were an angry kid."

"Angry and criminal."

"Criminal?" It came out strangled. Chris had never mentioned this before. In fact, he'd revealed little about his past other than the odd highlight. I tipped up on one elbow.

He overwhelmed me with a big smile. "Don't worry. I wasn't an axe-murderer or anything. A bit of stealing, that's all."

"How much is *a bit*?"

"Food, booze, cigarettes."

"You don't smoke," I said, amazed.

"Everybody smokes at fourteen."

"I didn't."

"That's because you were holed up in a convent."

I let out a giggle. "It wasn't a convent, Chris."

"Might as well have been, from what you've told me."

A bleak vision of metal beds, green walls and linoleum-covered floors, cold and clammy underfoot, swam before my eyes. I thought back to forced walks in pairs — *in crocodile*, as it was termed — on sheep-shit-laden hills, twice-daily assemblies, supervised reading on Sundays, the slow and deadly crushing of identity. Most searing of all, I remembered the feeling of abandonment by those I loved.

Jettisoning the thought, I asked if there was anything else I should know about.

"I had a penchant for spraying public property with graffiti."

"Goodness," I said with an uneasy smile, "were you ever caught?"

"Not once. And how was your week?" he asked, without breaking a beat.

I told him about the radio programme.

He braced, no doubt concerned about the unwanted attention it might invite. I couldn't blame him.

"It's good publicity for the Lodge," I said a little defensively, "and a great vehicle for highlighting eating disorders," I added, thieving a line from Jim.

"I thought the press did a pretty good job. You can't read anything these days without stumbling across 'My Bulimia Nightmare'. The media's full of it."

"The media is also responsible for messages that reinforce the idea that young women can only be happy if they're thin as a blade," I said, unable to dampen the furious passion from my voice, something that had occasionally got me into trouble. Too intense, too strident — *give it a rest*, I'd been told.

"It's okay, you don't have to preach to the converted." He ran his fingers over my bare arm.

I chewed my lip. "Sorry, I feel so strongly about it."

"I'd never have guessed," he said with a dry smile.

I flashed an awkward smile in return, climbed out of bed and walked along the short landing to the bathroom, where I had a pee, washed my hands, cleaned my teeth and returned to the bedroom. Chris glanced up, hurriedly switched off his laptop and set it on the bedside table.

"Everything okay?" I climbed back into bed.

"An email from a supply teacher."

"On a Friday night? Must be conscientious."

He flicked a dismissive smile. "Nothing important."

I wrapped myself around him. His back felt strangely resistant.

"Any more calls?" He sounded deliberately casual.

I pulled away, sensing where the conversation was heading and powerless to prevent it.

"No."

Alarmingly, he turned over to face me, trapping me in his gaze.

I ran an index finger lightly across his chest. "But there have been a couple of developments."

CHAPTER SIX

I expected a spate of protestations, questions and demands. I'd have put money on Chris exploding in anger.

"Maybe it's someone having a laugh." Even to my ears, my voice sounded thin and unconvincing. In spite of what I knew I didn't want Chris to believe that I was at risk. "There haven't been any threats," I pointed out, catching the too enthusiastic note in my voice.

Chris's continued silence zapped my confidence.

"OK," I backed down, "the mirror *was* a bit cranky."

"And the rat?"

"Okay, okay," I said, caving in under Chris's stare. "A prank in bad taste?" I willed us both to believe it.

"Kim, you know that's not true."

Yes, I did.

He finally fell asleep with his back facing me. I wrapped my arms around him, hoping that he didn't fall into the twilight zone of waking nightmares. Sometime in the early hours I found myself on my stomach, Chris lying on his back awake beside me, gazing up at the play of moonlight on the ceiling. I wondered whether he was thinking back to the childhood he never had, the home he never slept in, the mother and father significant only for their absence in his life.

Sometimes he came across as detached — not cold exactly, but as if he wished to keep himself boxed-in from the outside world. It wasn't that unusual. Often people fled to Devon to escape from something. Recently, when he was unaware of me watching him, I'd noticed a haunted look in his expression. Oddly enough, I'd caught it again that evening: when I returned from the bathroom and he put his laptop away.

* * *

We decided to have brunch in Salcombe. The sun floated high above, its rays squinting through the trees as we followed the coastal road from Goodshelter river to the palatial homes that studded the hillside at Mill Bay. A strong smell of seaweed scented the air. Heat-haze settled on the land above the water. There was no breeze though the familiar noise of clanking halyards filled the river.

By the time we reached where the road split, the top route leading back up towards Holset and Gara Rock, Chris was talking about getting a new car.

"I fancy something more sporty."

"Anything in mind?"

"Mazda MX5."

"Colour?"

Chris burst out laughing.

"Colour's important," I teased.

"Black."

"A nightmare to keep clean."

"But very sexy." He gave my arm a delicious squeeze.

We took the narrow lower route to the ferry and could hardly move for people and boats with trailers and yapping dogs. Women with deep tans, discreet tattoos and expensive hairstyles talked in superior accents and brandished their designer-clad children as though they were Olympic medals. Men brayed into mobile phones. Adolescent girls and boys walked four abreast, yelling beautifully articulated obscenities and screeching with laughter before romping off across the burning sand. It set me thinking. Who were these people? What did they do when they weren't having fun? Where did they live when they abandoned their summer nests? I swallowed hard. The noise and chaos grated on my senses. The beach suddenly felt a very unsafe place to be. Apart from the melanoma-inducing rays of the sun, the hidden dangers of the water, the lethal mesh of fisherman's lines extending along the shore, the carelessly abandoned glass bottle or jagged can, it was the perfect spot for abduction. No CCTV. Swathes of open ground. Easy prey. Concealed by the crowd, nobody would notice.

"Are you all right, Kim?" Chris's eyes expressed concern. "I thought I'd lost you there for a moment."

"Admiring the view," I stuttered, grabbing his hand. "Daydreaming."

The queue for the ferry stretched back almost the length of the jetty. We crossed sand the texture of icing sugar and took our turn, me leaning into Chris, basking in the sunshine, desperate to shake off my unexpected fit of nerves. Whoever it was could chip away my confidence in Cheltenham, but not here. Not on my patch.

Ten minutes later, we were sitting in the bleached wood interior of a café, devouring American-style muffins, poached eggs and cappuccinos. Andy Johnson, Chris's best friend and colleague at the community college, popped in to join us. He sported a mop of ash-blonde curly hair that hung, leonine, over his forehead. With his big, slightly spatula nose, and his wide mouth, often as not, drawn back in a grin, he looked like a jolly rugby player. His blue-green eyes reminded me of the ever-changing colours of the river outside the cottage.

"So, how's life in Chelters? You must find us yokels a bit dull by comparison." Never one to resist poking fun, Andy exchanged his Devonian accent for cut-glass Home Counties.

I wiped crumbs from my chin and leaned in close to Andy's large happy face. "I'm more Devonian than you are." I prodded his thick chest with a finger. "You're practically a grockle."

Andy had to laugh at that. His family had moved to Plymouth from Cheshire. Mine were born and bred in the South Hams.

Retreating to a favourite and irritating tack, Andy said, "Don't you find the 'separate lives' thing a drag?"

"Leave it out," Chris said dismissively.

Andy flicked a cheeky smile. For an unnerving second, something in the gesture reminded me of my brother Guy. I stuck out my tongue. Undeterred, Andy continued, "I don't understand why you two don't get on, do the decent thing and tie the knot."

"We're perfectly happy as we are, thanks." I laughed but in truth I felt defensive. "I get to do my thing. Chris gets to do his. And we have a fantastic time together. It's perfect."

"Must be a stressor getting your stories straight," Andy joked, taking a deep slurp of coffee. A layer of foam coated his upper lip.

"Fuck off, Andy." Chris's accompanying smile lacked warmth, I thought.

"It's about trust." I hated the prim catch in my voice, not least because trust remained my weak spot. When you're nine years old and your dad pops you on his knee and warns you never to trust anyone in case they hurt you, it has an effect — even when your adult brain tells you it's bollocks.

I glanced warily at Chris. The thought of him playing away had never crossed my mind, for which, I supposed, I was a tad naive. A good-looking guy, working in an environment with a number of attractive women, he must get tempted. Devon was no different to any other place except that its peculiar geography and social structure provided a particularly rich playground for inappropriate liaisons. I pushed Chris's shady Friday night email from my brain with a hefty shove. Shifting the spotlight, I asked, "How's *your* love life these days, Andy?"

"Sweet, as it happens." Enthusiasm lighted his features.

"Go on. What's her name?"

"Jen. She's a sports instructor at Totnes Leisure Centre."

"And?" Chris said. "What's she like?"

A dreamy look stole over Andy's face. "She's got a lovely arse."

I burst out laughing.

"What kind of a statement is that?" Chris asked.

"A bloke's," I said with a dry smile. The backdrop to conversation at home during the blissfully long school holidays was football, cars and women, especially women.

Andy looked at both of us with a wolfish grin. "Her hair's kind of light brown . . ."

"He always goes for light brown," Chris interjected, taking a drink.

"You're right," I said, remembering a number of Andy's old flames. He picked up and dumped girls with the same alacrity public officials awarded themselves fat pensions.

"And brownish eyes," Andy continued.

"When do we get to meet her?" I said.

"Give the poor girl a chance. I don't want you two lovebirds frightening her off."

The discussion descended into general gossip, something for which Andy had a natural talent, and chat about films, Chris's big passion.

At Andy's suggestion, we agreed to continue the conversation at the Fortescue, a pub popular with locals and yachties alike.

"You two go on ahead," I said. "I want to pick up goodies for tonight."

"Tonight?" Chris said.

"Claire and Charlie's. Dinner, remember?"

His face briefly clouded. "Of course," he said, thumping his forehead with the palm of his hand. "Stupid of me." He forced a smile.

"You okay with it?" I rippled with anxiety. I couldn't possibly change the arrangement now.

"Sure," he said bullishly. "No problem."

I sauntered slowly in the direction of Island Street, nodding and smiling to people I knew, stopping briefly to talk to a local musician. Devon, or to be more specific the South Hams, had not only become a refuge for ordinary people, but a chosen sanctuary for the cool and trendy. Pop stars, actors and influencers had moved and set up camp in droves. It often didn't take them long to move back.

After buying chocolate truffles and cheese from a local deli I returned to the pub. Packed and sweaty, the bar enveloped in a boozy glow, there was no sign of Andy or Chris so I ordered a tonic water with lots of ice, swiped a spare newspaper from the bar and sat down near a window. Chris appeared a few minutes later.

"Where's Andy?" I asked.

"Had to go. Jen phoned from Aveton Gifford. Not sure what the problem is."

"Must be keen if he can pass on a pint of beer. Is he bringing her here?"

"Didn't say."

"Think she's a keeper?"

"God, Kim, that's jumping the gun. Let's hope she lasts longer than the last one. Are you all right for a drink?"

I lifted my glass, gesturing that it was full. Chris pushed his way to the bar, ordered a pint and settled himself back down.

"What time are we expected tonight?" he asked.

"Seven thirty for eight."

"Know who else is going?" He viewed me over the rim of his glass. It was asked as a casual aside but I knew that the question carried hidden meaning. Chris was not what you'd describe as a social animal. Ever the shrink, I put it down to his fractured upbringing.

"Haven't a clue."

He didn't say anything. I leaned forward, squeezed his knee. "Relax, it'll be fine."

He nodded, as if grateful for the reassurance, took out his phone, checked it.

"Are you expecting a message?" I asked.

He slipped it back into his pocket. "No."

"Right," I said, perplexed.

It wasn't long before he became lost in thought, hunched over his beer, unreachable. A gloomy look had taken up residence. "What are you going to do, Kim?"

So we were back to that again. For a few moments in time I'd blissfully forgotten. I took a sip of my drink to give me time to think. Meeting Chris's brooding expression, I said, "I don't have a clue who's responsible. It's not as if I've been assaulted. I haven't even been spoken to."

"He left a fucking dead rat on your car."

I flinched, caught the startled expressions of an elderly couple at the next table, and flashed an apologetic smile.

"I don't like it," Chris muttered. "It feels all wrong. It feels dangerous."

"At least the focus is in Cheltenham, not here."

"Maybe it's someone you work with."

I pinched with alarm, my mind immediately fixing on Jim Copplestone. He *was* a flirt. He'd half frightened me out of my wits the way he'd crept up on me. But wasn't it too obvious? And in any case, I really couldn't believe it. Jim would never take such a risk. His reputation was at stake. He had too much to lose.

"That's ridiculous," I said.

"Is it? And all that publicity stuff they keep asking you to do."

"What's that got to do with anything?"

"It puts you straight into the spotlight. Maybe that's how this creep hooked onto you in the first place."

"The TV thing?"

"Exactly. Honestly, Kim, you should go to the police."

"Funny, that's what Georgia said."

"You spoke to Georgia?"

The accusing note in his tone took me aback. "Well, yeah. Is that a problem?"

"You should be careful who you discuss this with."

"Oh, come on. We trained together. We go back years. She's a good friend."

"I know," he said, "but the fewer people in the loop, the better."

I wasn't sure about his logic and uneasily let it go.

With the sun streaming through the window, his skin was bleached of colour. He tapped a finger on the table. "It's vital you find out who it is."

I downed my drink and made a silent vow. My face, my life; Chris was right.

CHAPTER SEVEN

"More pudding?" Claire smiled, spoon poised.

Claire Lidstone was the kindest, sweetest human being I knew. We'd been firm friends since primary school and had continued our friendship despite me being sent away to school.

I passed my plate.

"I can see your work doesn't interfere with your appetite." Gavin Chadwick's laugh was light. His expression seemed to say, yes, the story behind your face is intriguing but I'm too polite and sophisticated to ask or stare. He had receding hair, which he swept back from time to time, and a face that exuded ruthless intellect. He wore a crumpled linen suit, the collarless shirt beneath oozing shabby chic. Throughout the evening I'd caught myself watching the criminal defence lawyer with a professional eye. Deferential to his hosts, he gave every appearance of clear interest in his fellow guests, but the sense that he was commanding the situation was crystal-clear. Maybe my observation was unfair. Maybe I was tired and strung out.

Claire's husband, Charlie, topped up everyone's glass and sat down next to me, his large frame, clad in a check shirt, solid and dependable. More used to seeing him in mud-spattered jeans and Wellington boots, I couldn't remember ever seeing Charlie make such an effort to look smart.

Lottie leaned tipsily towards me with a lop-sided smile. She had large brown downturned eyes that made her look vulnerable. "I think it's wonderful what you do."

"She's not a neurosurgeon," Gavin barked, as though apologizing for his wife's gushing manner.

I spotted the flex in Chris's jaw and caught the tail end of Claire's anxious frown. Gavin settled himself in his chair as though preparing for an entertaining debate. "How do you regard the current trend for counselling, Kim?"

This felt like the conversational equivalent of a light starter. Sooner or later, he'd be dishing up the main course. "Depends what you mean."

"Do-gooders."

Oh God, is that how you view me? I thought with a shudder. Heavens, I was too knackered for this. Time to go for the line of least resistance. "Naturally, I'm not too impressed with enthusiastic life coaches who take a six-week course and then start mucking about with people's psyches," I said with a dry laugh.

"That's my point," Gavin said, his smug smile exposing small, pointy teeth. A sudden image of the dead rat flashed through my brain. "We live in a society where everyone feels the need to use a life coach or counsellor, whatever the situation. We seem to have become a nation of losers."

"For God's sake, Gavin." Lottie gave an embarrassed laugh and looked apologetically around the table. "You're not addressing the witness stand now."

I said nothing, believing that my silence should move things along to the next topic. Plunging my spoon into a wildly elaborate chocolate confection, I pushed in a mouthful. Gavin, apparently, wasn't done.

"The point I was endeavouring to make," Gavin said, "is that therapy and the mental ailments that supposedly afflict us are a uniquely Western problem. In the Third World people are too busy surviving and searching for enough to eat to indulge in psychological nonsense. These girls you treat make self-obsession a luxury."

I countered with a thin smile. "Nothing glamorous about starving yourself to death."

Chris, I noticed, was staring at Gavin Chadwick with cold, murderous eyes. I understood; he was feeling protective of me.

"I'm not being personal, you understand," Gavin said, in a sneaky attempt to reassure.

Dabbing at my lips with a paper serviette, I gave him a straight look. "You appear to be asking me to rubbish my own profession."

"I'm asking you to defend it."

Why? I longed to slink off home, run a hot bath and, snug and warm, head off to bed with Chris. Judging by the expressions of my friends around the table, *sock it to him* seemed the prevalent mood. I couldn't tell what Chris was thinking. Disturbingly, he refused to meet my eye.

"Surely, you get where I'm coming from, Kim?"

That was the point. I didn't. Here I was, supposedly having supper with friends, and this man had singled me out. In the same way, and in spite of quietly minding my own business, a stranger had also selected me for special unwanted and unwarranted attention. What had I done to deserve it this time? Was it me? Was this *my* fault?

Pressing down hard on my nerves, I treated Gavin to my warmest, most confident smile.

"Never mind me," I said gamely. "I'm fascinated to know how lawyers make the moral leap to defend a guilty client."

"Atta girl," Charlie muttered under his breath.

"Everyone's entitled to a defence, guilty or otherwise," Gavin replied.

"But surely when a client has committed a serious crime . . ."

"Like murder or . . . ?"

"Stalking." I have no idea why I said it. The word simply fell out of my mouth. I didn't dare look at Chris. "How does the lawyer square it with his sense of morality?"

"He doesn't," Gavin replied. "Morals are irrelevant. In fact, it could be argued they're dangerous."

"How do you work that out?" Claire interjected.

"If a lawyer takes a moral stance, he's in effect making a judgement. That would be fatal. He's not there to judge. If he thinks his client is guilty, he'll advise him to plead accordingly. Simple as that," Gavin said. "The lawyer's duty is to uphold the law, to work within its constraints, to see that it's correctly applied . . ."

"What about miscarriages of justice?" Chris cut in. We all looked at him, the growl in his tone loud enough to be heard in the next county.

"It happens," Gavin conceded, raising his glass to his lips, "but that's not usually our fault."

Chris let out an exasperated laugh. "Whose fault is it, then?"

"Miscarriages usually happen because of problems with chains of evidence."

"You mean the police are to blame?" I said, surprised.

"More often than you'd think."

"No wonder cops have such a low opinion of lawyers," Chris said.

"On occasion the feeling is mutual," Gavin countered. "A police officer doesn't have the onerous responsibility of representing a client."

"For which the lawyer is paid handsomely," I pointed out.

Gavin's disappointed expression suggested mine was a cheap shot, which I guessed it was.

I scraped up the remnants of my pudding, wishing I'd asked for a bigger portion. Licking my spoon, I watched Gavin watching me. He had that predatory smile on his face again. Irrationally, I wondered if this was exactly the type of guy who might harass me: someone who took advantage of the law to aid and abet him in his pursuit. Perspiration gathered in my armpits.

"Cheese and biscuits, anyone?" Claire piped up with a tight, anxious smile.

The consensus was that everyone had eaten enough.

"Coffee, then?" Claire practically squeaked.

I pushed back my chair. "I'll give you a hand." As I clambered to my feet, my knees clanked together.

"Jesus," Claire fretted, kicking the door shut behind us and leaning hard against it. "All I can do is apologize."

"Don't be soft." My accompanying laugh was tinny. "Do you think I was rude?"

"Not at all, he really seemed to have it in for you."

I quaked with misgiving.

"I thought Chris was going to hit him," Claire continued.

"Thank God he didn't," I said. "Our lawyer friend would have had him in court quicker than you can say 'Gav'."

"That depends on whether the witnesses were prepared to give evidence," Claire said with a tight smile. "I, for one, would have denied all knowledge."

It really was only a lively exchange of views, I told myself. A bit of sparring. Nothing to it. "Where did you find them — under a rock on the beach?"

Claire groaned. "Charlie's idea. They met at the amateur dramatic society."

"I didn't know Charlie was still into all that."

"Frankly, it's a pain. There's enough to be done on the farm without him disappearing for rehearsals, but you know Charlie."

I did. Charlie the unstoppable. "I wouldn't have had Chadwick down as a wannabe actor."

"Oh no," Claire said. "He's helping with set design."

"You mean carrying props?"

"Probably." Claire giggled.

I tried to join in. Somehow, I couldn't.

"Are you okay, Kim?"

"Sure." It shot out a little too quickly.

"Problems at work?"

Chris's voice drip fed in my ear: *You should be careful who you discuss this with.* "No more difficult than usual," I bluffed. Claire eyed me in a way that suggested I wasn't entirely believed. "How on earth did you make that fabulous-looking pudding?" I asked, changing the subject.

"Impressive, wasn't it?"

"A masterpiece."

Claire's eyes sparkled. She looked exceptionally pleased.

"Don't tell me. You bought it."

"I invested half the weekly housekeeping in a cookery delivery service."

"Brilliant. Does Charlie know?"

Claire's eyes rolled in amusement. "What do you think?"

"Payback for indulging his acting ambitions?"

"Nothing malicious about it."

The word "malicious" froze the smile on my face.

"Hey, things all right?" Claire touched my arm; the fun of the last few moments smashed into pieces and littering the floor with emotional debris.

I tensed and lied. "Good. Everything's good."

CHAPTER EIGHT

We got up late and ate bacon sandwiches.

"Fancy a ride out?" Chris suggested.

This was code for a spin on the motorbike, a Triumph Tiger Explorer. It had taken Chris a couple of years to persuade me to ride pillion. After what happened to my brother Guy, I hadn't been keen, but eventually he'd won me round. The first time I'd stepped on board I'd found it exhilarating and quickly became a convert. Taking instruction from Chris, I'd even ridden it illegally myself when we'd ventured out to Dartmoor on the more lonely roads where motorists were rare.

It was too hot to bother with leathers so we grabbed our helmets and set off, Chris's muscular body upfront, me in the perfect sightseeing position with a warm wind against my face. Journeying into Kingsbridge, we looped round to Modbury, finally finishing back at the river, where we took off our boots and ambled barefoot, skimming pebbles, a bright sun perforating an ocean of blue sky.

A bleep from Chris's phone signalled a text message. He checked the caller and returned the phone to his pocket.

"Aren't you going to read it?" I said.

"I did."

"Who was it?"

"Someone trying to sell me loft insulation."

I chewed my bottom lip, uneasy. We walked some more. Chris was first to break the silence. "Why did you mention stalking last night?"

For God's sake. "What?"

"When you argued with that jumped-up creep, you mentioned stalking."

The sudden note of accusation attacked me like a random blow from behind. "Look, Chris . . ."

"Who the hell did he think he was, going after you like that?"

"He wasn't that bad."

"Yes, he bloody was. What got me: the fact he's the outsider. We've all known each other for ages — you and Claire go back almost thirty years. Then Mr Prick, the lawyer, turns up and starts mixing it."

"Probably in his genes." I really wanted to play it down, forget about it. It was Sunday, for God's sake. One more day before I had to drive back.

"You mean there's a genetic code for arrogant prat?"

I glanced across, caught his eye and felt a nervous ripple of mirth bubble up from inside.

"What?" His face cracked into a smile.

"You." I shook with helpless laughter. He melted into a broad grin and pulled me towards him.

Later, back home, things got strained. The landline went. Chris tore into the sitting room and snatched it up. With my forthcoming birthday, it was just possible that Chris was planning a surprise, but something caught my ear, the tone, or a slight catch in Chris's voice. Against my better nature, I found myself eavesdropping.

"It's rather awkward to talk." Chris's voice sounded unnaturally quiet. "I appreciate how you feel about it . . . yes, of course . . . I realize that . . . yes, but I can't bear to have her hurt, you understand. Look, I have to go . . . What? The usual routine, I guess . . . Yes, now I really have to go. It's not a good time. See you on Monday. Cheers."

Chris ambled back into the kitchen. I issued a breezy, questioning look. "Andy," he explained.

"What did he want?"

"Checking up on dates for parent–teacher evenings. He seems to have lost his sheet."

"Funny, I thought he'd have it all itemized on his laptop."

"You know Andy." Chris's accompanying smile was lame.

I did, which was why I didn't buy it.

Later, while Chris sat at the kitchen table marking essays, I opened a crisp white sauvignon and drank while I cooked. The cottage was as quiet as air. On impulse, I went over to Chris and slid my arms around his neck. He carried on marking. My mouth nibbled the top of his ear.

"I have to get these done," he said pointedly.

"Not now." I laughed, tousling his hair.

"For God's sake, Kim." He pulled away. Something deep inside me froze. A memory of rejection, long buried, threatened to push through into the past. I smothered it. He touched my arm. "Sorry, babe, the heat is making me crabby."

I drew up a chair and forced a sympathetic smile. "Are you okay?" It sounded ridiculous — *of course* he wasn't. And neither was I.

He rubbed his eyes and fixed on the papers in front of him.

A rush of irritation coursed through me. Whoever was playing with my life was having a destructive impact on both of us. "What if I tried to get a job closer to home?"

Chris started. "Doing what?" We both knew that Bristol, almost a hundred and twenty miles away, was about the nearest I could get for my particular line of work. He put his pen down. "Is this because of what's happened, or because that's what you really want?"

Stomach creasing with embarrassment and disappointment, I backtracked quicker than a politician exposed in a fierce debate. "It was only an idea. I haven't thought it through. Silly of me."

He leaned over and crooked a knuckle under my chin. His eyes were level with mine. Blood and heat surged through my temple. The rest of me was cold.

"I don't want you to rush into changing everything for the wrong reason."

"I understand. I expect he'll eventually lose interest and go away." I didn't believe a word of what I said.

The knuckle tightened. A tense expression entered Chris's face, but it was gone so quickly I thought I'd imagined it.

"Think about any decision carefully, yeah?" He inclined towards me and lightly kissed my forehead.

My heart pounding in my chest, I replied, "I will."

CHAPTER NINE

And I did. All the way in the car early the next morning, I thought of nothing else. I told myself that Chris was protective of me. He didn't want me to make any decisions based on a knee-jerk reaction. I'd grown up under the guardianship of men, so this type of response was normal to me. In a more sober frame of mind, I was also disconcerted by my off-the-wall suggestion. It wasn't like me to be impulsive.

I arrived back in Cheltenham shortly before eight in the morning. Home there was a second-floor apartment in Lansdown, a short hop from Montpellier. Built in the Regency style, offering large, airy rooms and an ornate wrought-iron balcony, it was indistinguishable from originals that populated the town. I loved it for its grandeur, even if parking was a nightmare. Instead of leaving the car at the Lodge as usual, I parked at a meter nearby so that I could drive the short eight-mile journey to Gloucester for the phone-in later.

As I entered the stucco-columned entrance, I bowled into Lizzie, my downstairs neighbour, on her way out to work.

"Hiya! Any luck with the sale?"

Lizzie smiled and tossed her butter-coloured hair over her shoulder. She had small feline features and a suspiciously slight build. "We had a couple round at the weekend but I'm not sure if they were that interested. The fact that it's a ground-floor flat put them off. People worry about security. We've got more viewers lined up this week, so fingers crossed."

"As long as they're nice quiet types," I teased.

Lizzie shot a smile. "We'll do our best to vet them."

I dashed upstairs, bubbly inside. I convinced myself that it was due to natural apprehension about the radio show, when in reality it was fear of the unexpected. Had there been any silent phone calls, any messages? Listening hard for the telltale beep of the answering machine, I let myself in, relief seeping out of me on seeing everything the way I'd last left it. To be really sure, I walked through the narrow hall with its large gilt-framed mirror, into the sitting room and dining area with golden-coloured walls, silk drapes at the windows, elegant cream leather sofa.

My territory reclaimed, I sat down and glanced up at the limited-edition print cresting the feature marble fireplace. Entitled *Beautiful Losers*, the work portrayed a tense drama played out between two men and a woman. Heavily atmospheric and sinister, it was a fine example of Jack Vettriano's style. I often sat and mused on the relationship between the man standing and the man who sat with a weary expression smoking a cigarette. And what was the exact nature of the relationship between the woman and the two men? Had they been lovers? What was going through their minds?

And what type of man had left a dead animal pinned to my windscreen? What kind was vying in the most bizarre fashion for my attention?

I ran a bath and chose what to wear. I often dressed casually for work and wore jeans. Pure psychology. With a young clientele, I didn't want to "get down with the kids", yet neither did I wish to come across as too far removed from them. But today I could dress in full authoritative mode, albeit unseen by the listening public. I decided on a peacock-blue sleeveless dress and high heels.

On the point of sinking into a foamy layer of bubbles, the phone rang. My watch told me that it was before nine. Probably Chris checking that I'd arrived back safely. Stepping out, I grabbed my robe and padded through to the sitting room, leaving a trail of damp, soapy footprints. I waited, hand hovering, unsure whether to pick up. *Oh, damn it,* I thought, snatching up the phone.

There was no familiar voice, nothing other than the faint noise of someone breathing. Instantly, my pulse rate stammered as though I'd popped amphetamines. My legs trembled and I felt mildly sick. In spite of an instinct to slam down the phone, I gathered up every bit of courage and forced my mouth open. The voice that emerged didn't sound like mine.

"Look, whoever you are, this isn't going anywhere. I don't know why you're doing it, but it's not welcomed. Please don't contact me again. Ever."

I hung up, instantly regretting my actions. I should have ignored it. I shouldn't have engaged. If only I hadn't been so rash. And then the cold thought entered my mind that the caller had waited for my return, seen my arrival, knew that I was there and pounced. *Christ,* I thought, *he's watching me.* Scared, I crossed the room, briefly scanned the street, wrenched the curtains closed then returned to the bathroom and locked the door after me.

As I sank beneath the surface of the water, a question torpedoed me. Could it be Phil, my ex-husband?

I hadn't given him a thought in years but this was exactly the brand of obsessive behaviour he'd indulged in. He'd almost broken me with it. But that relationship was years ago when I was young and gauche and inexperienced. It couldn't have any bearing on the present, could it? Why would Phil crawl out of the pit to intimidate me now, after all this time? More likely, he was exercising his jealous streak on another poor woman. Still, I was forced to consider as I reached for the soap, was it possible? And if so, what could I do about it? The last I'd heard he was in Canada.

Twenty minutes later, my scars itching, a sure sign I was upset, I carefully applied camouflage cream, eternally grateful that the titanium dioxide, acting as a high-density primer, managed to mask most of the discolouration. Lightly dusting my skin with finishing powder to make it waterproof, I applied make-up to the rest of my face, leaving my lipstick until after I'd had a late breakfast — not that I felt much like eating — then clipped on a pair of gold earrings. Halfway through a miserable slice of toast, the phone rang again. Leave it, I thought, taking an insistent bite. It kept ringing. Ignore it. Still it rang. *Mustn't* touch it. The caller rang off.

The toast hovered in midair. Rooted, I regarded the phone as if it were primed to detonate. Can't breathe in. Can't breathe out. Willed the thing to stay silent, to shut up. He *knows* I'm sitting here like this. He *knows* that I'm waiting. The phone started up again: it blared, deafened, screamed. Oh God, anything to shut off the bloody noise . . .

"Piss off!"

"I'd no idea you swore with such vigour, Kim."

"Jim," I spluttered. "I'm terribly sorry. I thought you were someone else."

"They must have upset you a great deal to elicit such a florid response so early in the morning."

"It's a private matter." Jim was smart. He'd piece it together with the "litter" incident. "Nothing I can't handle."

"Glad to hear it," came the disbelieving response.

Stomach squirming, my professional persona had slipped and I hated looking out of control, especially in front of Jim Copplestone. How had things spiralled so quickly? Why hadn't I simply let both calls go to voicemail?

"About this morning," he said. "All set?"

"Looking forward to it."

"Good, thought I'd give you a tinkle to wish you luck."

"Thanks." As I signed off, Chris's words reverberated. *Maybe it's someone you work with.*

CHAPTER TEN

"As already stated, eating disorders are not about food."

"But isn't that a contradiction?" Imogen Kulp, an American presenter, had a businesslike manner and machine-gun delivery. "If you're a sufferer the whole focus is on food, surely?"

"Only in so far as it's symptomatic of the disorder," I explained. "The weight loss is what catches our eye."

"So anorexia's not a slimming disease?" Kulp said.

"Too blunt a description. It's what's going on in the sufferer's mind that's the crux of the problem. The restriction of food is a genuine expression of chaos."

Kulp addressed the listeners. "We will, of course, be giving out a list of contact numbers for those seeking help, or you can visit our website for information after the programme. Right, we have another caller on the line. Kyle Stannard wishes to pick up on the issue of body image. What's your question, Kyle?"

"How does your expert feel about the use of plastic surgery to correct conditions like body dysmorphic disorder?"

Kulp pulled a face. "I fear this is going outside our sphere of discussion." She looked meaningfully at me. I gestured that I was prepared to take the call. Kulp nodded for me to go ahead, a silent moment of conspiracy between us.

"For the listener, I should explain that sufferers of BDD have an obsessive preoccupation with an imagined defect in appearance, most usually on the face. It's very distressing and the condition can persist for years. Patients literally feel repulsive."

"And surgery?" the caller persisted.

"Preliminary clinical reports suggest that surgery does not benefit patients. Either the patient remains focused on the perceived defect or they simply move on to another physical feature. So, no, I'm not in favour of it."

"Not in any circumstances?"

Kulp drew a finger underneath her throat. I raised both eyebrows in a *let me just wrap this up* gesture. "It's true that plastic surgeons can significantly improve the lives of those injured in road accidents or suffering from serious burns, but . . ."

"Are you speaking from a personal perspective?"

I mentally skidded to a halt. He might as well have pressed needles into my eyes.

"You've had plastic surgery, haven't you?" the caller persisted.

Shock shot through Kulp's expression. She shut down the fader, cut off the caller and pushed a glass of water in my direction. "Maybe plastic surgery would be an interesting area for discussion on another occasion, Kyle," she said, her voice as smooth as warm caramel. "Just to remind you, folks, we have Kim Slade, a clinical psychologist specializing in eating disorders, on the line. We're standing by, ready and waiting to take your calls."

The rest of the phone-in took place in a haze. I operated on autopilot, reeling off facts and statistics, promoting Ellerslie Lodge, recommending forms of treatment and various organizations and associations. The whole time my brain snagged on the sole male caller: Kyle Stannard. He'd talked for such a short interval yet I remembered every nuance of his voice. Low in timbre, precise, educated, without distinguishing accent. I estimated he was in his thirties. He didn't sound weird. On the contrary, he seemed lucid and rational, but his remark about my face set off alarm bells. *Was it him? Was Kyle Stannard even his real name?*

Kulp wrapped up the programme. "That's all we have time for. Our thanks to Kim Slade for joining us this morning. It's twenty-nine minutes past midday." The programme faded out to the sound of Roy Orbison's "Pretty Woman".

"That went well. Pity about the weirdo. We're usually a little better at screening them out, but you did good. You okay?" She shuffled some papers.

"Fine," I said tightly.

"Say," Kulp said, ghoulish fascination in her eyes, "how *did* you get those scars on your face?"

CHAPTER ELEVEN

On the short journey from Gloucester to Cheltenham, I stuck my foot down. The gears meshed as the car surged along a nice straight stretch.

People were rarely so direct. Of those bold enough to ask, I'd witnessed every type of reaction, from shock or ridicule to repulsion. Special camouflaging make-up had improved dramatically but it was never entirely successful. Sometimes people came straight out with it, as Imogen Kulp had done. Sometimes I found myself taking the initiative by getting the subject of my scars out of the way so that I could move on. I'd largely come to terms with the fact that people were curious, and I'd discovered that, by adopting a dismissive tone, the questioner felt less awkward. If I made out that my injury was no big deal, they tended to do the same. But if pressed, as sometimes happened, I always gave the same answer. "An accident when I was little."

My mind flicked back to a vagabond home life, to housekeepers who came and went, some only lasting a couple of days, a mother who wouldn't stay, random women who fancied their chances with my father to the extent that I never knew when I came home for the holidays who would be in the house. I remembered arguments fuelled by heat and passion and hard drinking, of me shouting loud to be heard above the clamour of men and noise. I thought about my parallel existences, the buttoned-up schoolgirl and the wayward daughter, rules and routines versus domestic mayhem. I recalled having to behave like a man at home to survive, and like a good little girl at school. Frequently, I got it mixed up, got it all wrong. As a grown-up, I'd adapted, done everything to shake off the traces of my past. Professionally, I pulled it off. Personally, I sometimes failed.

I overtook three cars at warp speed. However much I tried to lose myself, I couldn't shake off the growing sensation of rage. I felt infected by it. Attempting to grab a slice of perspective, I persuaded myself that it was only human to feel rocked by unwanted gifts and silent phone calls, but no amount of psychological trickery helped. Every lucid argument I could come up with turned to dust in my hands. Despite my determination not to be fazed, to tell myself that strong emotional reactions were normal given the circumstances, I found myself checking the rear-view mirror, wary of any vehicle following too closely. I did more than flinch when a black-clad motorbike rider roared past.

I felt hunted.

Driving into Cheltenham's one-way system, my mind clamped onto Kyle Stannard. Whoever he was, he had a certain amount of knowledge about what I did and who I was.

Time to find out about him.

CHAPTER TWELVE

"*Kyle Stannard, one of the highest-paid international male models, critically injured in street brawl.*"

"*Male model for Quartz Agency rushed to London hospital with serious facial injuries.*"

"*Was Kyle Stannard singled out for his good looks? Police are looking into . . .*"

I stared at the straplines and the photographs of Stannard in his prime and felt something inside me wither. I had no doubt that this was the man who had called the phone-in.

How bad were his injuries? Had he made a full recovery? If not, I recognized his plight and his longing for the time before, when he was whole. Horribly, in his mind, did he think it bound us together?

With a cold and outwardly calm voice, I pressed the intercom, signalling my readiness for the next client.

* * *

That evening, I went out to friends for dinner. Molly and Simon Fleming lived in what had once been a tumbled-down house in leafy Pittville, the place previously split into flats and let to students.

Molly kissed me exuberantly on both cheeks. Dark and flashing, with a temperament to match, she had the held-together stance of a Flamenco dancer. I handed her a bottle of wine.

Sunshine from a declining sun bounced off a single chandelier in the hallway. The staircase, which was wide and thickly carpeted, seemed to stretch up to the heavens.

"Thought we'd eat outside," she said. "Go on through. Simon's already out there fixing drinks."

French windows opened out onto stone steps that led down to a tiny, enclosed courtyard where hanging figs adorned one wall. Simon was engaged in easing a cork from a bottle. He glanced up and flashed a brilliant smile of greeting. As blonde as his wife was dark, he had deep smoky-blue eyes, good looks and, as a former paratrooper and fitness fan, a strong and athletic body.

Following a satisfying pop, he filled three glasses and handed one to me.

"So, how's life in Civvy Street?" The bubbles prickled my nose. I stifled a sneeze.

"Plenty of cut and thrust." A mesh of lines crinkled the corners of his eyes.

Simon's career had been chequered since leaving the armed forces. He'd recently joined a firm of up-market estate agents.

"Molly will be pleased." I knew she'd worried about the inherent dangers of army life.

"Yeah," Simon said with little enthusiasm.

"Still finding it difficult to adjust?" Once, in an intoxicated moment, he'd described himself as a killing machine. Not much scope in civilian life for people like him, he'd told me. I'd thought little of it at the time. Now . . .

"So-so," he said with a grin. "What about you? How's tricks?"

"I'm fine — all good."

"And Chris?" Simon was polite, the tone casual, but the way in which his eyes fixed on mine, the way his hand gripped his glass suggested that he felt anything but indifference. He and Molly had met Chris twice on one of Chris's rare forays to Cheltenham. They'd got on superficially, though it was clear there had been no great meeting of minds. I had to admit that Chris wasn't especially easy-going, his intensity one of the things that attracted me.

"He's well, thanks."

There was a pause, a few beats too long. I opened my mouth to plug the gap. Simon was already ahead of me. "Kim, what's wrong?"

Was it that obvious? Was I going to spend the rest of the evening lying to two of my oldest friends?

Molly joined us, scooped up a glass and caught the off-key mood. "Anything wrong?"

Simon fixed his full magnetic gaze on me.

"I suppose," I said, clearing my throat, "I've got a problem."

CHAPTER THIRTEEN

"Basically, you're being stalked."

Simon's cold observation elicited a protest from Molly.

"A bit strong, isn't it? I mean, in some ways, it's rather flattering."

We both looked at Molly as though she'd offered to take her clothes off and run naked down the Promenade, blasting out "Rule Britannia".

"Well, I'd find it exciting to have an unknown admirer." Molly's lips curved into a generous smile and she ran the tip of a painted fingernail along her husband's arm.

"A heavy breather, a guy who doesn't have the balls to make anything other than anonymous contact? A dead rat?" I said.

"The rat is probably some kid's idea of a prank," she said.

I quelled a response. Hadn't I used the same duff explanation to Chris?

"C'mon, Molly, you know better than that," Simon said. "Going back to the radio phone-in, Kim. Do you think it was him?"

"I wasn't certain this morning. After checking out Stannard, I'm prepared to suspend disbelief." A picture of

Stannard before the attack blazed in front of my eyes. He'd bucked the current trend for androgynous chic, nothing skeletal and hollowed-out about his features. With film-star good looks, he was the kind of man who, whether eighteen or eighty, would remain handsome. In the space of minutes, all that had changed. "The fact he was injured explains the connection," I said.

"It doesn't mean he and the stalker are one and the same," Molly pointed out.

"Agreed, but, clinically speaking, he ticks the right boxes."

"Why didn't Stannard cloak himself in anonymity, then?"

I couldn't answer. Simon stroked his chin. "What does Chris think?"

Chris didn't know about the latest development, but I didn't tell Molly and Simon this. "That I should go to the police."

"He's right."

"Georgia said the same."

"Then get on and do it," Simon said.

"What else does Chris say?" Molly glanced at Simon in a way that made me suddenly defensive. "I mean how does he *feel* about it?"

"Upset, annoyed, concerned." I didn't say he was edgy and that it was starting to turn our relationship upside down. I didn't admit he was behaving in a distinctly clandestine manner.

Molly touched me lightly on the back. "Couldn't he come up and stay with you, sweetie?"

"He has a job, Molly."

Molly arched an eyebrow. "What about those fantastically long holidays he gets?"

"They're not that long," I said, chippy. I didn't add that it was almost impossible to winkle him out of Devon. In all the time we'd been together, he'd stayed at the flat no more than a dozen times. "Anyway, I go back every weekend and, in a few weeks, I'm taking a break."

Nobody spoke for a moment. I sensed that this was due to an abundance of caution, rather than an absence of something to say.

"It's important you report it, Kim," Simon said. "I don't understand your reluctance."

Because it's like saying: *Hey, you've got me. I'm afraid. You win.* Any adversity in my life I'd overcome in my own way, on my own terms. And what would the police do about it? In spite of legal changes it took time for law to filter through and translate into action. It would more likely be a case of take a statement, make enquiries and "see you later". There was also a more obvious reason.

"Stalkers are pretty resistant to changing behaviour," I said. "It may make matters worse."

"How?"

"It will wind him up, Simon," Molly said in exasperation.

I agreed. I had to find another way, I thought darkly. I needed to slide into his slipstream and channel him away, to somewhere the bastard couldn't reach me.

Simon was adamant. "That's no reason to hold back."

"I'm with Kim," Molly said. "If you think this bloke's a really serious proposition, then I say leave well alone."

I appealed to the line of least resistance, which, in this case, was Molly. "It's not as if I'm a celebrity or a politician, or anyone in the public eye, for God's sake."

Simon rested a hand on mine. It felt warm and clammy. He gave me an apologetic smile. "You know as well as me you don't have to be. I'm sure your bosses will understand, if that's what's bothering you."

It wasn't. Well, not much. "If I bring this out in the open, I'm playing into the guy's hands. I'll be feeding his sense of self-importance."

"Treat him like a two-year-old throwing a tantrum," Molly said, heading off a furious look from Simon. I couldn't tell whether it was because Simon disagreed, or because she'd touched on a raw subject. The likelihood of the Flemings ever having children of their own was a rare possibility.

"Ignore him?" Simon flashed, his jaw set.

Caught in domestic crossfire, I topped up everyone's glass. Molly, who'd fallen silent, looked pensive. "You don't think it's Phil, do you?"

"He had crossed my mind," I confessed, "but why pop up now, out of the blue?"

"Ex-husbands are usually top of the list." There was a cold edge to Simon's voice. "Do you want me to talk to him?"

I was astonished. It had never occurred to me that Simon might still be in touch. I said as much. He looked suddenly sheepish. "The odd telephone call, nothing more."

"What's he up to these days?" I wanted it to sound casual. It sounded anything but.

"IT consultancy and stuff," he added vaguely.

"Last thing I heard, he was working in Canada."

"He's back in the UK."

I did my best to hide my shock. "When?"

"A few months ago."

Holy crap. "Do you know where he lives?"

"Not exactly, but I can track him down." Simon's eyes had turned a dangerous shade of cobalt. Alarmingly, I instantly saw what Simon meant about him being a "killing machine".

"I don't know." Part of me was uncomfortable with the prospect of Simon pulling strings on my behalf, the other part bewildered. In the space of a couple of minutes I'd decided that Stannard, then Phil and now Simon was my stalker.

And I still couldn't explain Chris's uncharacteristic behaviour.

"Think about it." Simon raised his glass. "In the meantime keep everything this guy sends, dead animals included. He hasn't sent you shit or dirty needles, has he?"

"Simon!" Molly burst out.

"Has he?" Simon persisted, ignoring his wife.

"No," I replied.

"Good. Anything you receive, bag it. Keep a note of times when you think you're being followed, drive-bys, anything out of the ordinary. Let your phone pick up all your calls and get a new unlisted number for anyone else to make contact. Has he called you on your mobile?"

"No."

"When he does, change it."

"*When?*"

"Keep a phone with you at all times, especially at night, and make sure you use your entry phone. Does the flat have an alarm system?"

I shook my head.

"Have one installed or get a big dog."

"Don't be daft, Simon. I—"

"And get a personal alarm for yourself. They make a hell of a racket and can buy valuable time in a tricky situation. If you think you're being followed in the car, drive to your nearest police station. Whatever you do, don't drive home or to a friend's house."

My head spun. Simon's advice made absolute sense, but I couldn't help think part of him was getting off on the excitement. "This sounds so extreme."

"They're basic precautions. If he gives up and goes away, that's great, but you can't afford to take that gamble. In the meantime you have to reclaim control by taking steps to protect yourself. Do you understand?"

I nodded. Control was good. Control equalled survival.

Molly threw me a solicitous look. Turning to her husband, she said, "What if that fails?"

Simon smiled with a salute of his glass. "I hear Devon's a jolly nice place to live."

Later, Simon accompanied me home. We walked companionably, arm in arm, the route lit by streetlight and the glow of distant shop fronts.

He was in his element. "You need to be on the alert for anything different, anything out of place, something that doesn't feel right."

"How will I know?" Drink had loosened my defences.

"You're the psychologist," Simon said, with a light laugh. "You're paid to pick up on things."

It wasn't the same. I was accustomed to working in a controlled environment, in a partnership with my clients, in which we worked together. By contrast, my stalker held all the cards, called all the shots. This individual had entered my life and latched on with the tenacity of an incurable disease.

We rounded a corner and crossed the road. Regency buildings towered impressively in the moonlight.

"I'll be all right now." I meant it. My fiercely independent and maverick streak had come to the fore.

Lizzie's place was suffused in a comforting glow and the main entrance lit up with spotlight, but Simon insisted on seeing me to my door. "Another tip," he said as we went inside the communal hallway. "Always opt for the stairs. Wherever you are, you don't want to get stuck in a lift with Mr Creepy."

Mr Creepy. I snuffed out the soubriquet as I snapped on the bedroom light. Staying alert was second nature to Simon; soon it would be second nature to me. I realized that I had to wise up and wise up quickly.

Drawing the curtains, I plumped down on the bed, kicked off my shoes and went into the kitchen, bare feet slapping against the cool tiled floor. I filled a glass of water and took a deep drink. Perhaps I'd call Chris.

A glance at my watch revealed that it was well past midnight. However much I wanted to hear his voice, it was probably not a good idea. Once, I wouldn't have hesitated. Once, we would have been on the phone for hours. Only a day apart and we'd be telling each other how much we missed being together. Once, Chris would have signed off with "I love you." I hugged the memory tight, felt it wriggle in my grasp and flee.

Drained, I walked over to the sitting-room window and kinked back the curtain. At night, Montpellier's stylish shops, bars and beauty salons lost definition. The roar of traffic dropped. The road melted into the blackness. Without warning, I caught a faint outline, a sudden movement. I craned forward, strained my eyes. Nothing.

Apart from the reddish glow of a cigarette.

I stood perfectly still, mesmerized. I squinted, trying to make out a face, but it was swathed in a spooky haloed moonlit glow. Was it him? Could he see that I was watching him watching me? Something buckled inside. Was this the ultimate connection?

Silence roiled around me. Shaken, I retreated behind the drapes, rested my head against the wall and closed my eyes. Heart clattering in my chest, my skin crawled with goosebumps. Make notes, Simon said. Log times and locations. *Think. Use your mind. He wants you to see him because it's critical to the game.*

I clenched both fists, willed myself to confront the fear writhing inside me. Whatever happened now I would not walk away. I would not let it go. I would not be beaten or evicted from my life.

I snatched back the curtain. Whoever it was had vanished.

CHAPTER FOURTEEN

"So, how are you feeling today?" I asked.

"All right."

Kirsten Matherson was plucked from obscurity at the age of twelve to begin a fledgling career in modelling. So far so inoffensive. Then came the hitch: the agency in question didn't like the naturally occurring changes in the girl's body shape as she reached puberty. By the time she was fifteen, Kirsten had resorted to a combination of starvation and laxatives to fulfil the skeletal proportions required by her employer. Three years later, her physiology screwed up, anorexia nervosa had ravaged her. Thin, wispy blonde hair clung to her skull for dear life. Luminous dark eyes dominated her face. Transparent skin stretched over her cheekbones. In spite of the heat she wore a thick sweater. When she hitched up the sleeve to scratch her arm, it had a fine covering of downy hair, like pelt, the body's response to low body mass. She sat perched on the edge of the seat, hands resting in her shallow lap.

"Cathy says you're doing well, eating more, and I gather Jim's cut down your drug treatment."

"Yeah."

I scanned the notes. "You've put on a couple of pounds. Does that bother you?"

"No."

"Not frightened?"

"Not especially."

"That's good. What about the exercise regime?"

"Nothing more than a walk in the grounds."

I smiled approval. Kirsten shifted position, listless, her focus on a faraway point beyond the room or even the building. I attempted to coax her.

"Last time we spoke, you said you were interested in textiles, fashion design."

"I wouldn't be good enough."

"Why not?"

"Haven't got the right qualifications."

"Then get them."

"I *said* I'm not clever enough." Perfectionism was a hallmark of the condition so I wasn't surprised.

"I'm not a good person." Her mouth pinched into a thin, brittle line.

"Who says?"

"I *know*."

"Is this about not wanting to take risks, about fear of failing?"

She eyed me with sullen dislike.

"Kirsten, who are you letting down exactly?"

The door flew open. "Sorry to interrupt," Jim burst in, unusually brisk, "but I need you to come with me, Kim."

I suppressed a streak of irritation. "Why?"

"There's something you need to see."

"Can't whatever it is wait?"

"Frankly, no."

I stifled a huge sigh. "Excuse me a moment, Kirsten."

Spotting an opportunity to escape, the girl got to her feet and began to shamble out of the room. Jim raised the flat of his hand. "Stay here, please, Kirsten."

"Fuck's sake."

"Don't you 'fuck's sake' me," Jim bellowed.

I stared. Whatever the provocation, Jim never swore at clients. Kirsten plumped back down.

"What's this all about?" I hissed, following at speed. He didn't reply, simply stalked in the direction of the common room. At his approach a gaggle of girls scattered. Clocking me, they burst into laughter, hands smothering their mouths. Cathy crossed the hall out of nowhere and shooed them into the garden. I knew sickeningly that I was the figure of fun.

Jim entered the common room, shut the door behind us and pointed in the direction of the computer screen. I approached and, winded, stopped. It was hard not to fasten on the image of a semi-naked woman wearing a black suspender belt and stockings, back arched, one hand cupping a breast, knees splayed, revealingly wide.

"Christ Almighty! I don't understand. How? Who?" I spluttered in confusion.

"Emailed from an anonymous source."

"What?"

"Apparently, it's perfectly possible."

"But . . . but . . . " I protested. "It's not me."

"It looks like you. I mean . . ."

"It's my face," I snapped. "Some crank has done this." Before Jim could protest, I launched forward, hit delete.

"That wasn't very smart," he muttered.

If I'd had my way, I'd have emptied the trash and yanked the plug and cable out of the back of the computer. Simon's warning to "bag anything" bashed my ears. Immediately, a light went on in my head. According to Simon, my ex was back in town and Phil's area of expertise was IT. *Shit.*

I sat down with a thud. Jim grabbed the back of another chair and parked it in front of me. We were eyeball to eyeball.

"Honestly, Kim, what you do in your downtime isn't an issue here."

I gaped at him. "It's a manipulated image, fake news!" I shouted. "I didn't do it. It's not me." Hot tears of shame and anger sprang down my cheeks. Jim gallantly pulled out a clean handkerchief. I took it, blew my nose vigorously and let out a wail. "Oh God, how many girls saw it?"

"That doesn't matter now."

"*Doesn't matter*?" More unsettling, I had an uncontrollable urge to waste the person responsible, to really hurt them. Unfamiliar with such extremes of emotion in myself, I felt as if my mind had split in two.

"I have a first-class honours degree in damage limitation," Jim said, clearly trying to calm me down. I didn't want to be calm. I wanted to shout, scream and yell. I wanted it to stop. "Sometimes stuff happens, Kim."

I clenched my teeth. On the emotional spectrum, I was probably hitting around nine or ten.

"Clearly, there are sexual overtones."

You don't say. I was heartbroken. How could someone do this to me at my place of work? How could some sick bastard undermine me in this way? I'd worked so hard to succeed and build a professional reputation, to be good at my job. When everything else was going to rat shit, work had always provided a solid ballast to my life. I enjoyed my work at the Lodge and at Bayshill. I liked the people and the clients. And now this? Suddenly, every obstacle I'd overcome, every achievement and success felt worthless. The stranger with malice in mind was threatening to rip away everything.

How could I stop him?

Jim continued to talk. "Could it be an old lover, perhaps? Someone scorned?"

Like Phil, I thought again, but didn't say.

"Yeah?" Jim said, spotting recognition in my eyes.

"Leave it with me. I'll check it out." This was better, I thought, this was a positive step.

"Because if it's a creature from your past, we'll prosecute."

"Prosecute?" I said, aghast. "I'd have to go to court."

"And we'll back you all the way."

I couldn't think of anything worse than a public court case. "What about the publicity?" Then another possibility grabbed me, an easier possibility, a possibility that didn't pack an emotional punch, one that made sense, and one that did not require legal or criminal intervention, or a jury staring at a grotesque replica of myself. I shuddered at the thought of some techie police officer mining the computer and retrieving what I so wished was irretrievable.

I looked Jim in the eye. "It could be one of the girls. You know how highly strung they can be, that they don't always appreciate support." I failed to curb the expectant note in my voice. "Obviously, if that's the case, I wouldn't dream of . . ."

Jim shook his head and held my gaze. Energy sapped, horribly weary, I crumpled. The thought of disclosing all to Jim and, by default, Cathy did not appeal. None of this was my fault, yet I felt inexplicable shame. How could I treat my clients in the future, knowing what they'd seen?

"I'm not technologically adept," Jim said, "so I don't know how easy or difficult it is to post an image like that. I'm pretty certain the police have dedicated officers who—"

"No!" I burst out, alarmed that Jim had given voice to my most immediate fear. "Absolutely no way."

"Kim, I appreciate—"

"You don't. You can't. I feel violated."

"But it's not *you*." Jim grabbed hold of me by the shoulders. "You said so. It's just a picture."

"If it's *just* a picture," I said, "why are we sitting here having this conversation? It's got my head on it, my face, my —" I struggled to get it out — "scars."

Jim let out a slow breath and dropped his hands. "All right, I respect your wishes, but if anything else happens, we're going to revisit it. Deal?"

I felt like I was driving a trade-off with Mephistopheles. "Deal."

"On one condition."

I inclined my head.

"You tell me everything."

"There is nothing to—"

"Everything," he said through tight lips.

CHAPTER FIFTEEN

I emerged an hour later, the afternoon sessions postponed, the day wrecked. Was this a warm-up and preliminary to violence? Was he plotting something truly awful? I nibbled thoughtfully on a nail. *Call Chris*, I thought, *tell him what happened*. Something inside snagged. Assailed by a paralysis of confused feelings, I settled into a slow trudge. Familiar streets that usually brought a smile to my face felt blighted. Buskers sang out of tune. When Connor, a homeless old guy and permanent fixture near the smarter shops, called "Hello" to me, I almost passed him by.

"Sorry," I garbled.

"You all right, Kim?" Connor looked up at me from his pole position on the pavement. I'd slip him the odd sandwich and hot drink and we'd struck up a rough kind of friendship. He'd hit hard times two decades before when his business failed, his wife left and he'd been done for assault. After a short spell in prison he'd wound up on the street. What was supposed to be a temporary event had turned into a lifestyle. How easily one's life could change, I thought grimly.

"Lost in thought, nothing more." I pulled out a couple of two-pound coins from my bag and pressed them into his hand. His skin was the colour and texture of bark. The tang of unwashed clothes and stale urine hit my nostrils full force.

"God bless you," Connor said.

Crossing the road to the apartment block, Lizzie was up ahead. She spun around, a mass of smiles. "We've got someone lined up for a viewing. Cash buyer. Apparently the area's perfect and there's no problem with the flat being ground floor. Looks promising."

"Good for you." At least something was going right for somebody. "Have you found anywhere?"

"We don't dare. You know what it's like. You're afraid to get excited because you know it could all fall through in an instant. It's such a stressful experience."

"I'll be sorry to see you go but hope it all works out."

Remembering Simon's advice, I checked for shadows that didn't exist, eyes swivelling to all corners of the sunshine-filled staircase. Bunch of keys digging into my palm and at the ready, I heard the landline phone beeping as soon as I stepped inside.

Catching sight of my reflection in the hall mirror, I noticed that, in the space of twenty-four hours, I'd developed lines. My skin looked waxy. My eyelids drooped. Fear, I thought. How come he'd so easily knocked the fight out of me?

I slumped down on the sofa, eyeing the phone. I didn't know how long I stayed like that, watching the flashing light, listening to my own shallow breathing and the insistent cheep of the messaging service. In the end I got up, crossed the floor and went for it.

There were two messages. The first from Chris: "Away for a couple of days escorting a grubby group of year-eights to Huckham for a 'team-building' exercise." This raised a smile. Chris was sceptical of using corporate terms for school activities. "If you can't get hold of me, it's because communications in the wilds are poor. Best if I give you a call as soon as I get back. Lots of love." I felt a mixture of warmth at his endearment and disappointment at not being able to talk to him. Fed up, I listened to the next message. "Hi, Kim, it's Simon. Sleuthing on your behalf has paid off. Phil is working in London. Do you want to talk?"

You bet. As soon as Simon picked up, I came straight out with it. "Give me Phil's number."

"Has something happened?"

I hesitated, foolishly revealing the lie, and made a mental note to get better at deception. "I simply need to rule him out."

"Is this a good idea?"

"Yes."

"Only, then he'll know that I've given you his number."

"Is there a problem with that?"

"Tell you what. I'll phone him and explain."

"Explain what exactly?"

"Look, Kim. I'm in the middle of something right now. Give me five minutes, and I'll call you back."

"With Phil's number."

"Yes, all right."

"You promise?"

"You have my word."

Frustrated, I headed to the fridge, took out a bottle and poured a small glass of wine. Taking it over to the window seat, I sat down and stared outside. Rather than dropping away, the temperature had reached new levels of humidity. You'd have to be suicidal to venture out there, I thought.

Twenty-five minutes passed. I drained the glass and poured another. My stomach jittered at the thought of speaking to Phil after all this time. I reminded myself that I was intelligent, a shrink, for God's sake, impossible to be pushed around, let alone manipulated, and yet my marriage had once reached a point where I felt that I couldn't breathe without permission. A chill tiptoed along my spine. Was there something about me that invited that kind of attention? Was it *my* fault, a defect in my personality? Was it happening all over again, only this time with someone I didn't even know? Even if Phil were guilty, he wouldn't admit it, not on a telephone, not ever.

The phone rang shrill. I picked up. "Hi, Si."

"Kim Slade?"

I frowned and tried to connect the voice to a face. The caller had a precise and controlled way of speaking. "Who is this?"

"We haven't met."

I reached for a connection: male, low pitch, cultured tone. Then it walloped me.

"You," I gasped.

"I contacted the phone-in."

"You also concocted that vile computer image."

Kyle Stannard didn't speak for a beat. I couldn't work out whether it was confusion or manipulation. "The pornographic one," I insisted.

"Are you mad?"

My responding laugh was hollow.

"Why would someone do something like that?" he said.

"That's my next question."

"Kind of embarrassing, I guess."

"Not for someone like you, *I guess.* Isn't that the sort of thing you get up to on photo shoots? Drugs and sex and rock and roll?"

"Your information is out of date." Stannard's voice was as cold as chilled water. "I left the game some time ago."

"So what *game* are you playing now?"

"I haven't a cl—"

"You admit you sent it?"

"I already told you, no."

"Why are you following me, standing outside my flat, sending me —" I faltered — "things?"

"Kim, I'm not."

"Don't you dare use my name."

"Why not? That's what you're called."

Smart mouth. I tried to grab on to the remnants of my composure. "What do you want, Mr Stannard?"

"Your professional help."

"I only treat women with anorexia." Which wasn't true, but hey.

"I saw you on that television programme."

So that's how this all started.

"I really admire your style and courage."

Flattery will get you nowhere.

"We're two of a kind, you see. I thought we might meet informally for a drink — unless, of course, that might upset your boyfriend."

"I don't do drinks with clients." I sidestepped the issue of boyfriends.

"Well, I'm not strictly a client, am I?"

No, you're a stalker.

"There's a terrific little cocktail bar off Cambray Place."

"Which bit of my answer don't you understand? I only work in a limited sphere. You need a different sort of professional." *Someone who can cure your delusion.* "I can give you names."

"Make an exception for me."

"No."

"You're supposed to help people, aren't you?" The tone rattled with threat and accusation. "Why won't you help me?"

Cut the call. Now. Hang up. Just do it.

"People generally do as I say. I've waited a long time to find the right person."

"I'm not the right—"

"And I always get what I want."

My vision snarled. The walls slurred and blurred. "Then I'm sorry to be the first to disappoint you."

"I don't do disappointment, Kim. Not in my vocabulary." He hung up.

CHAPTER SIXTEEN

"So, what's the problem?"

My stomach flipped. It was the following morning and I'd barely slept.

"Hi Phil," I said politely. "Thanks for calling me."

"I haven't heard from you or your lawyer in ten years."

I tried to laugh. It came out mangled. "Are you well?"

"What is it, Kim? I'm a busy guy, stuff going on." His tone implied that he'd been doing fine until he heard I needed to speak to him. After the call from Stannard the previous night, the conversation with Phil seemed like a pointless waste of everyone's time, but now he'd phoned I thought I might as well cover all the bases. "Have you visited Cheltenham lately, or attempted to look me up?"

"Are you cracked? Why would I do that?"

"It doesn't matter, a long shot."

He let out a chill laugh. "You must be really in the shit."

I privately agreed, said goodbye and instructed the receptionist at the clinic to hold off all calls from anyone she didn't immediately recognize without first checking with me. I made the same arrangement with Cathy Whitcombe at Ellerslie Lodge.

I saw three clients. The hours passed with the same gait as a dying snail.

At lunchtime, Chris called. Giddy with relief, I told him about the phone-in. I told him about Kyle Stannard. I didn't tell him about the pornographic image.

"He's clearly kinked. Go to the police. They can do him for harassment."

"He denies everything."

"He threatened you."

"But it will be my word against his. It's not as if I recorded the phone call."

"Do it, Kim. It will frighten him off."

"Will it?" Somehow I didn't think so.

"This is ludicrous," he burst out. "If you do nothing it will continue. Now he's got his hooks into you, he's not going to go away." Chris was silent for a moment. "Is anything else wrong?" There was a peculiar catch in his voice.

"Not really."

"Something's up," he said, wary.

"I've already messed up once this morning."

"Oh?"

"I got Phil to phone me."

"Okay." He took it a lot better than I'd expected. "Why did you do that?"

I pulled a face. I could hardly tell Chris about the IT connection. "Because he's nasty enough to pop back out of the woodwork."

"Got you."

"Anyway, it's not him," I said briskly.

He thought for a moment. "Why not get Simon to find out about Stannard?"

"Like what?"

"Where he lives, what he's doing with his life. Stalk the stalker?"

"I'm not sure that's a good idea."

His momentary silence gave the impression that he was cross with me for not agreeing to his suggestion.

"You're interested in him, aren't you?"

"Who?" I said, bewildered.

"Stannard."

"That's rubbish," I said hotly. "I don't give a damn about him."

"He intrigues you."

"That's utter crap. Look, I have to go. I'll be late."

Chris wasn't easily dismissed. "What are your movements for the rest of the day?"

"Why do you want to know?"

"Keeping tabs."

"I'm at work, Chris."

Rattled, I left the clinic and stepped outside onto a cement drive. It felt hotter than ever. The air tasted of diesel and petrol fumes. En route, I called Simon, told him I'd got nowhere with Phil and, reluctantly heeding Chris's suggestion, asked if he could put his soldierly skills to good use.

"You want me to check out Kyle Stannard?"

"I can hardly check him out myself. It would show unhealthy interest."

"Damn right. Leave it with me. I'll do my best."

I crossed the road, each step marred by my last conversation with Chris. What if . . . no, don't be stupid, how could I entertain something so bizarre, monstrous even? It had to be Stannard. I was sure of it. Everything relied on Simon getting the evidence to prove it.

Keen to get out of the heat, I skirted the entrance to the Lodge and walked around the back to the parking bays. Jim's Morgan convertible, highly polished in racing green, glinted in the strong sunlight. The Mini should have been next to it. Except there was no car, only empty space. I raced up and down, checking, running through events in my mind. Yes, I'd driven the car there after the phone-in. Yes, I'd parked it here, right here. But it had gone. Fear flared and expanded into panic.

I tore back inside and spoke to Cathy.

"Are you sure?" she said.

"You can't mislay twenty-eight grand's worth of vehicle by accident."

"True."

"Cath, I'd be grateful if you didn't tell Jim. At least, not yet."

She cast me a sympathetic look, paused and then took charge. "You give the police a ring. I'll take a walk outside." To be honest, I could have kissed her.

It took me five minutes to get through and explain my predicament. I was told I could expect someone to be with me later.

"How much later?"

"Can't really say, madam."

"Will it be today?"

"Possibly not. I'm sorry, but we're dealing with a major incident. Is this the best number to call you on?" I confirmed it was. Frustrated enough to kick something, I sat down hard and rested my head in my hands. Stannard had taken a step too far. He had committed a criminal act. I brightened. *Hello*, I thought, *this is a good thing*. Whereas before I had nothing really concrete to go on, now I could hand the police a solid piece of evidence and press charges.

The door to my office swished open and Cathy appeared. "Found it."

"What? Where?"

"Good news: it's tucked under the shade of a plane tree. Bad news: it's parked on double yellow lines in Vittoria Walk and you've picked up a parking ticket."

I stared, mystified. "Is it all right?"

"No dents, no scratches, good as new." Cathy looked at me uncertainly. "Are you sure you didn't leave it there? You've got a lot going on right now."

I covered my emotions with a weak smile. "You're right. My mistake. What an idiot. Thanks, Cathy. You're a star."

CHAPTER SEVENTEEN

The car was exactly where Cathy said it was. No marks. No signs of abuse. Wondering madly if the vehicle might be booby-trapped, I crouched down and peered underneath, except I had no idea what I was looking for. Using the remote, I opened the driver door. Gingerly, I climbed inside, my stomach catching at the thought of Stannard sitting in my seat, his body on the cream-coloured leather, hands on the steering wheel where mine rested. I examined the ashtray and glove compartment, searched for notes and gifts, but there was nothing. Even the air smelled undisturbed. There was no telltale scent of aftershave or cologne. How had he got in?

I drove back to the Lodge, re-parked the car, tore off the penalty notice and returned to Montpellier on foot.

The insane heat had died down. People were sitting at outdoor cafés and wine bars for early-doors drinks. The streets felt relaxed. Adopting a siege mentality, I popped into a delicatessen and bought salami, Parma ham, a slab of waxy Gran Padano cheese, purple-skinned olives, sun-dried tomatoes, artichokes marinated in olive oil, two bottles of Barolo and two bottles of creamy-dry sparkling white Prosecco. Minutes later, I was toeing open the door to the apartment, arms aching, chin resting protectively on the wine, my first thought to get the Prosecco chilled as quickly as possible. It wasn't until I'd stashed the food and was coming out of the kitchen that I noticed the single typed A4-sized brown envelope on the floor poking out from underneath the door to the apartment. I stood anchored to the carpet. Had it been there all along and I'd failed to spot it? From that distance I could make out that there was no stamp, no postal markings, only my name typed on the envelope in capitals.

Wary, I picked it up and ripped it open. Inside was a single sheet of white paper.

> THANKS FOR THE LOAN OF YOUR GORGEOUS SET OF WHEELS. (I WAS TEMPTED TO SPEND THE NIGHT IN IT — ONLY JOKING!!) NO, REALLY, IT WAS VERY GOOD OF YOU TO LET ME BORROW IT AND I JUST WANTED YOU TO KNOW THAT YOUR KINDNESS IS APPRECIATED. WHY ELSE WOULD I SEND YOU CHOCS? SORRY ABOUT ROLAND THE RAT — MY IDEA OF A JOKE. TALKING OF WHICH, IS THERE ANYTHING ELSE YOU'D LIKE, SOMETHING MAYBE TO TURN YOU ON? YOU LOOK SO GOOD NAKED. HAVE A THINK BECAUSE I'M NOT ENTIRELY SURE WHAT YOUR TASTES ARE IN THAT DIRECTION. I HAVE MY OWN IDEAS, OF COURSE, BUT I DON'T WANT TO SPOIL OUR RELATIONSHIP BY OFFENDING YOU. DON'T WORRY ABOUT LETTING ME KNOW. I'M NEVER FAR AWAY AND, ALTHOUGH I'M NO SHRINK, I CAN READ YOUR MIND.

Hurling the printed sheet of paper onto the coffee table, I scooped my keys back up and raced out of the flat. Taking the stairs two at a time, I tore off towards a small garage and lock-up in Lansdown, heart lifting at the sound of heavy rock music, which signified they hadn't yet packed up for the day.

I stood for what seemed an age as a mechanic in a maintenance pit finished working on an SUV. Another young guy, an apprentice maybe, poked about in the innards of an Escort. Patches of oil spread over the ground, rainbow-coloured in the late afternoon sun.

My focus fell on scrap metal and tyres, monkey wrenches and jacks. Nobody paid me attention. Finally in frustration, I approached the mechanic buried underneath the SUV and shouted a loud "Excuse me!"

The guy clambered out, wiping his oily hands on dark blue overalls. The top three buttons were undone, exposing an expanse of ghostly white skin. His head was shaved, pouched eyes narrowed to slits.

Staring hard at me, he addressed the young guy. "You going to be there long, Mark?"

"Nah, almost done."

"The bloke wants to collect in twenty minutes." He looked me up and down and pulled out a packet of cigarettes. "Now, what can I do you for?"

I began hesitantly. "I wondered if you could help me."

"Maybe, maybe not."

This wasn't quite the response I was after. I suppose showing up out of nowhere seemed strange. I began again. "My name's Kim Slade. I live over there," I said, waving my hand in the general direction of home. No idea why I'd done that. He couldn't have looked more disinterested if he'd tried. I couldn't blame him. It seemed like all the norms of social interaction had deserted me. "I'd like to pick your brains," I said, getting to the point.

He let out a short earthy laugh. "Sounds nasty." His hands shook when he lit up.

"The thing is, you see, someone moved my car."

"Vehicle theft is pretty hot around here."

"It wasn't stolen."

"A joyrider?"

"Maybe," I said, evasive. Admitting to it being taken and left a couple of streets from where I worked would sound plain weird.

"Out of interest, what sort of motor?"

"Mini Cooper S."

"Nice. Do much damage?"

"That's the point. There's not a scratch on it, so how would a stranger get in, do you think?"

He blew out a big cloud of smoke, some of it gusting my way. "He got in the same way as everyone else, darlin'. He had the key fob."

"But that's impossible."

"You sure you didn't leave it lying around?"

"Certain."

"You didn't leave it inside the motor?"

"Of course not."

"Amazing how many people do," he snickered. "Isn't that right, Mark?" He looked across at the young apprentice.

"Yeah, too right — although it could have been cloned."

The thought had never occurred to me. "How does that work?"

The apprentice answered. "Thieves can pretty much copy a key fob signal while you sleep."

I felt as if I'd swallowed stones. "From your bedroom?"

"Anywhere close by. There's an app, see. All kinds of devices can pull signals from key fobs. Basically, tea-leaf takes a copy, opens the car and off he goes."

The mechanic eyed me in a way I couldn't quite fathom, took a drag of his cigarette, narrowed his eyes against the smoke. "Have you reported it?"

"Nothing to report." I met his eye.

Two thin streams of smoke drifted out of his nostrils. "Villains in the old days would break into a car and hot-wire it. Now it's all digital, way more easy."

"And there's really no other way?"

He scuffed the ground with his boot, jettisoning a cloud of dust.

"Not that I can think of," he said, slow-eyed.

* * *

Fizz seemed the most inappropriate drink — this was hardly a celebration — but I opened a bottle anyway and poured a glass. Someone may have copied my key fob. But then someone else held a spare: Chris.

Glugging steadily, I picked up the letter and flopped down with it on the sofa. Unlike the pasted-together note attached to the chocolates, the script was more specific, the thrust personal, sexual and delusional, and language familiar. A stranger reading it could be forgiven for thinking that there was a pre-existing relationship.

Shit.

There must be some kind of mistake. Chris wouldn't do something like that. Didn't stack up with the Chris I knew.

But what about the one I didn't?

Plenty of youngsters went off the rails and became well-adjusted adults, I reminded myself, which meant that Chris, with his troubled past, was innocent and had taken no part in moving my car. Deliberate, a classic piece of manipulation, Stannard had to be behind the Houdini trick. How he'd got copied my key fob I hadn't yet worked out.

I finished my drink, helped myself to another — even though I knew it wasn't a great idea — sat back down and took a deep swallow. Immediately, my mobile phone blared. Fired up with booze, I picked it up, spoiling for a fight.

"Hello, is that Kim Slade?"

"Yes!" I snapped. "And before you utter another word—"

"It's Police Constable Cunningham. I understand you reported a missing vehicle this morning."

I sat up straight. Making a conscious effort to formulate the words in my brain before they poured out of my mouth, I said, "It's been found."

"Oh good," he said, in a way that suggested he was keen to cut the call and avoid a mountain of paperwork.

"Thing is," I said. "I'm being stalked."

CHAPTER EIGHTEEN

Telling the police was every bit as bad as I'd expected. It was like climbing a mountain with a grand piano strapped to my back.

PC Paul Cunningham had an open and trusting face, like a cherub. The accompanying officer was an altogether different proposition: older, short hair the colour of old mercury fillings, his face and manner worldly. He had a firm handshake and introduced himself as PC David Grant.

I invited them to sit down. Grant took out a notebook. Cunningham told me to take my time. It was the sort of thing I might say to a client. It felt strange to be on the receiving end. Having exchanged the wine for water, I took a sip and began to speak. I believed that once I got going, it would be easy. It wasn't. At the mention of the pornographic image, a host of questions ensued. I couldn't imagine what it must be like to be a rape victim.

Cunningham sucked the end of his pen and addressed Grant. "Posted from a site, do you reckon?"

"Then dumped."

"Dumped?" I said.

"Taken down. Technology now means that someone can send anonymous emails that self-destruct in twenty-four hours. Gives us no time to trace the source, let alone the person responsible. Have you received any personally abusive communications?"

I shook my head.

They fired more questions. When I'd finished, they did a recap.

"You're a psychologist," Grant said, scribbling a note.

"I know what you're thinking, but I've never met this guy professionally or in any other capacity."

"Stannard?"

"Yes."

Grant looked perplexed. "Then how come you're sure it's him?"

I looked from one to the other. "Of course it's him. He's the guy who called the phone-in. He pestered me at home. He was very clear about not taking no for an answer."

"But he denied sending the image," Grant stressed.

"Because he's lying."

Both men exchanged glances.

"Look, I'm not trying to stitch the evidence together." I flicked a nervous smile. "However you look at it, Stannard's the only rogue element. My life was going along nice and smoothly until this random stranger crossed my path. What are you suggesting, that it's someone else?" I stared at them incredulously. Out of nowhere, a voice inside whispered Chris's name. I silently told it to fuck off.

"We're not suggesting anything," Grant said. "We're simply asking questions."

I did my level best not to visibly bristle. I didn't quite pull it off.

"How did this man you allege you've never met get hold of the key fob?"

"Maybe he has contacts, maybe he stalked me and copied it when I wasn't looking. I don't know." I knew I wasn't making sense and yet felt incapable of clarity. All at once I felt about eight years old, trying to stand my ground against my father.

"Any sign of break-in here?" Cunningham glanced around the room.

I shook my head.

"And Stannard hasn't made direct contact with you since you told him you wouldn't meet?"

"No."

"And that was yesterday?"

"Last night, yes."

His expression suggested it wasn't much to go on. Heat spread up my neck and marched across my scalp. I felt as if I'd come out in hives.

"Can I see the letter again?" Grant asked.

I showed it to him, watching his face for a response. He gave a brief nod and looked at Cunningham. Excluded, I found it impossible to read either of their expressions.

"Unsigned," Cunningham said.

"Does it make a difference? He's hardly going to sign it 'yours truly', is he?" I said with a stupid smile. "It's Stannard, I'm sure of it."

Cunningham's face bore the mark of diplomacy. "He looks a fair possibility from what you've told us."

Hurrah.

"Have you shown the note to anyone else?" Grant asked.

"Nobody."

They discussed escalating the issue. "Could put a call in, I guess," Grant said, to appease me. Lifting prints off the note was floated as an abstract idea.

"He'll have worn gloves," Cunningham said.

"Is there a way you can track where the paper came from?" I asked.

Cunningham shook his head slowly. "It's bog-standard photocopier paper. It could have come from any number of computers."

I ran my fingers absently through my hair. "Might you get someone to profile the text?"

"'Fraid not. We don't have the resources on site," Grant said. "Cuts to funding and suchlike," he added with a withering look. He waited a beat. "The letter suggests you already have a relationship."

"That's what he wants you to think." *Come on, guys. Funding has nothing to do with brain function, does it?* I looked at them imploringly, desperate to get them onside. "Could you run tests on the car?"

Grant pulled a face. "From what you've said, there's nothing to really 'test' for."

"How about you track Stannard down and pay him a visit?"

Neither looked convinced.

Grant spoke, "If he lives outside Gloucestershire, we'll have to alert another constabulary."

"Oh," I said, spirits crushed. Did they think I was making it all up? For a brief, insane moment, I wondered if I were delusional. Is this how stalking works? Bit by bit, you're very slowly taken apart until you're so reduced you don't know what it is true and what is false, who's okay and who definitely isn't.

Cunningham waved the note. "Can we keep this?"

I consented with an eager nod.

"You say you split your time between Devon and Cheltenham?"

"I work here but drive down every weekend."

"And nothing's happened there?"

"No."

"Interesting," Grant said.

I smiled. *Interesting* was good.

"Do you have a boyfriend or partner, Miss Slade?"

"He lives in Devon."

"Name?"

Would they try to force Chris into the jigsaw? Should *I* be forcing Chris into the picture? Oh God. Chris had mentioned criminal behaviour. Would he be on a database? *No, silly*, I thought, *he said he was never caught.*

"Miss Slade?" Grant pressed.

I reluctantly told him.

"What's his occupation?"

"He's a teacher." Surely, this would count as someone who was fine and upstanding?

"And how long have you been together?"

"Over three years, nearly four."

"No previous relationships that might be tied to what's happening now?" Grant's look was steady. They definitely weren't buying the Stannard theory.

"I was married and divorced ten years ago. My ex-husband, who I never see, is not part of this."

"Are you sure?"

"I've already spoken to him."

"Better have his name," Cunningham said breezily.

"Is it strictly necessary?"

"To be on the safe side."

I reluctantly gave it.

"Do you use social networking sites — Twitter, Facebook, Instagram and so on?"

I shook my head. I recognized the dangers. Besides, the eternal pursuit of *moi* didn't do it for me.

"Anything else you've missed?" Grant said.

"Nothing I can think of. But there's something I wanted to ask."

"Fire away."

"If you discover who's doing it, can you stop it?"

Cunningham looked to Grant, who let out a breath.

"It depends on how fixated he is, doesn't it?" I said, grim.

"Worst case scenario, it can go on for years."

I felt undone.

"If we have enough evidence, a custodial sentence can be imposed, but it won't necessarily stop the most determined in the long term," Grant said.

I wasn't sure I appreciated his honesty. "And what are the chances of him turning nasty?"

Cunningham again looked to Grant. I waited expectantly.

"Most stalkers are not physically abusive. From what you've said there isn't a great deal to worry about, if I'm honest."

I should have felt reassured. I didn't. My dismay turned to frustration. "Can you be sure of that?"

Grant looked stung. "Look, there's an increased tendency towards extreme violence in cases where celebrities are involved, and with stalkers who've had a previous sexual relationship with their victims — ex-boyfriends and husbands, for instance."

"So the chance of me being open to attack is small?"

"Without strong evidence to suggest otherwise, yes."

There was a note of censure in Grant's voice. To be charitable, given the little they had to go on, I understood his caution. Just.

Sensitive to my frustration, Cunningham said, "We take this sort of thing very seriously. Rest assured that your complaint will be fully investigated." He ran through the same list of precautions as Simon, adding that I should alert neighbours, friends and people I worked with to what was going on, if only to act as witnesses should something happen. "Try to alter your daily routines where possible."

"That's going to be difficult."

"Under no circumstances meet Stannard or anyone else you suspect," Cunningham emphasized. "Don't pick up the phone — ever — before checking the caller number. Get a male to leave a recorded message on your main line, stating that you can't come to the phone at the moment."

"Don't say you're not at home as that might leave you vulnerable," Grant added. "If by accident you pick up and it's him, keep calm. Don't engage. If you come face to face with your stalker, don't confront him, walk away, preferably to the nearest crowded area. If you're in fear of immediate threat, call us."

He said that they would give me a log number to quote so that, if I needed to alert them to any fresh developments, my call would come straight through. "We'll take a quick look round the flat, check your security, if you don't mind."

I didn't and watched as they examined the windows and doors, paying particular attention to the wrought-iron balcony.

"It looks pretty secure," Cunningham said. "But you could do with a proper alarm system."

Mirroring Simon's advice, I remembered.

"How long have you lived here?" Grant said.

"Six years."

He looked around admiringly and turned his attention to the painting. "I see you're a fan of Vettriano."

"I like the drama, the suggestion of tangled relationships, the thought that you're not quite sure what's going on beneath the surface."

"Art imitating life."

After meeting the unwavering expression in his eyes, I walked with them to the door. "Is this a common problem?"

Grant answered. "Stalking is one of the fastest-growing crimes."

"Any particular reason?"

"Access, opportunity, the explosion in communication technology and social networking," he said. "Whether it's press and the power of digital technology, or a public eager to know the latest, we all think we can have a slice of other people's lives."

CHAPTER NINETEEN

I watched the sky change from gold to pink to indigo. I'd finished off one bottle and opened another and felt stone cold sober. I tried to process what I was supposed to do and how I should behave. There were so many "do's and don'ts", so many rules in a game alien to me, a contest where the goals were not clear. It felt as if my life had suddenly changed and I realized how much I'd taken normal freedoms for granted.

Pouring the fresh glass of wine back into the bottle, I made coffee. Part of my job was to remember what was said in front of me even if it made little sense at the time. Grant's observation about Devon stuck in my mind. He'd described the lack of incidents there as "interesting". I assumed he meant that Stannard hadn't yet worked out where I disappeared to at weekends. Perhaps it was only a matter of time. Or was Grant suggesting something else? Was it possible that my two worlds were not as compartmentalized as I believed?

I took a shower, washed my hair vigorously, lavished my skin with lotions and painted my toenails a defiant scarlet. I didn't phone Chris. After the spat that morning I decided to leave it. If I were honest, I still needed time to process and eliminate my darkest thoughts. A call from Simon came through on the landline as I was climbing into bed. I picked it up as soon as I heard his voice and told him about the car and the subsequent visit from the police.

"What were the cops like?"

"Like cops."

"Were they sympathetic?"

"As much as they could be, if that's what you mean — told me all the same stuff, gave me the third degree, offered good advice."

"They're taking it seriously?"

"Sort of, although they don't appear to think Stannard a contender."

Strangely, Simon didn't respond.

"Why the call?" I said.

"I've found out about our man."

"That was quick."

"Easier than you'd believe; Stannard is in my current line of work."

"He's an estate agent?"

"Property developer. By all accounts, he's quite a sharp operator. Must be doing all right as he hoofs around in a Maserati. He specializes in old houses, does them up, full architectural spec, and sells them for a profit. He's got offices in Imperial Square, all very respectable."

My eyes widened. "That's close. Where does he live?"

"Wellington Square."

One of the most expensive areas in town.

Simon cleared his throat. "There's something else you should know." I sensed where he was heading and felt utterly powerless to prevent it. "There's no easy way to put this," he continued. "Stannard got himself involved in a fight."

"Resulting in serious facial injuries."

"You knew?"

I took a breath. "Did it leave him disfigured, Simon?"

"Not half."

A sour taste bubbled up from the back of my throat and engulfed my mouth. I didn't speak. I couldn't.

"Are you still there, Kim?"

"How serious?" I murmured.

"Right side of his face is fine."

"Left side?" I absently touched my skin, feeling the jagged ridge of scar tissue.

"A surgeon apparently cocked up what was supposed to be reconstructive surgery. He cut through a facial nerve. Stannard successfully sued the arse off him."

I didn't know what to say that wasn't blindingly obvious.

"Are you all right?"

I snorted. "I'm swell."

"Shall I come round?"

I mumbled that it wasn't necessary.

"Sorry to be the bearer of bad tidings. Try and get some sleep. Anything else I can do, let me know."

There were three other occasions that I could remember when I'd been advised to get some sleep. After Guy's fatal road accident, the night my father died, the time I'd tracked down my mother and received a miserable audience. Each had been moments of high emotional drama. Sleep had evaded me then as it did now.

As I'd feared, my disfigurement was the connection.

I touched my face, felt the smooth, uninjured skin, then traced the line of raised scar tissue, the secret area where my hair refused to grow but was cleverly concealed by an excellent haircut. I ran a finger along where the lobe of my left ear should have been, hidden by day with a large clip-on earring. The physical trauma — the nightmare of changed dressings and skin grafts — remained deep in the past, buried. The emotional scars had closed over in a way I didn't quite understand. Friends suggested my father's sturdy influence. Others said that the character-building attributes of boarding school had stood me in good stead. I agreed with neither because only I could know that certain wounds never heal — that, by nature, I would always be drawn to the dark side.

I did my best. I played a part. I managed to fool myself in the same way that I fooled others. Sometimes, I even forgot my losses and my perpetual mourning for a life not of my choosing. I was the first to admit that nobody likes a person who wears grief like a second skin. It's wearing and boring and tedious. Smiley is best so smiley is what I did. Mostly it worked. My only certainty was that, in a society where a disproportionate value was weighted on looks, I'd managed to overcome prejudice and find my own niche. Stannard wasn't so lucky.

In spite of what Stannard was doing, part of me felt pity. What had happened to him was catastrophic. I could understand his need to reach out, but he didn't want my help. He wanted a connection. He saw me as a soulmate. It all made perfect sense. And yet . . .

I leaned back on the white fluffy pillows. It didn't entirely gel. The Stannard of my imagination was a social misfit, a loner, sadly inadequate, not some clever-dick property magnate with oodles of money. And another thing, how in his busy schedule did he find time for his stalking activities?

The flat seemed a mass of noise in the silence. Pipes creaked. Air vents opened and closed. Fridges and machinery hummed against the low background noise of communal apartment living. I craned for the sound of incursion — the scrape of a key in a lock, the spring of shoes on thick carpet, the "bump in the night". At seven in the morning, a dog outside yapped, the boiler inside kicked in. I twisted and turned. Sometime later I must have dozed off, Simon's words preying on my mind: *not half*.

CHAPTER TWENTY

"Kim, are you up to speed?" Jim said.

I blinked. "Absolutely."

Having arrived bog-eyed for work, I'd spent the first hour slumped gratefully in a staff meeting while Jim held forth about schedules, treatments and budgets. As soon as he'd finished I made a silent exit. Jim had other ideas. He marched straight into my office without knocking.

"About yesterday."

Fuck. "Cathy told you?"

"The police."

I attempted a concise reply but couldn't quite manage it. It all came out in a jumble. Stannard the stalker, Stannard maybe not the stalker.

"The poor guy had botched surgery." As soon as the words left my mouth, I realized that Stannard had done a number on my emotions.

"Poor guy?" Jim sneered. "He's not the Elephant Man. Don't you see? Whatever the man's agenda, guilty or innocent, he's playing on your sympathies, manipulating your good intentions."

I looked at him squarely. "His surgeon botched his reconstruction." I'd had an excellent plastic surgeon. My father had seen to that.

Jim didn't say anything for a moment. I could almost hear the electrical activity whirring behind his forehead.

"Setting aside Mr S., I'll see what I can dig up about . . ." he hesitated, choosing his words with care, "the sort of person we're dealing with, from a psychological perspective."

"A loner, obsessive, delusional," I said. "Anything else you can bring to the trauma table let me know."

Jim arched an eyebrow, opened his mouth to speak and clearly thought better of it.

"I've let Cathy know my schedules at Bayshill and vice-versa," I said, businesslike.

"Good. We'll do our best to screen things from this end. Whatever else, for God's sake, Kim, try not to dwell on it. If you need my help in any way, or if you're finding work difficult, let me know. You've got a holiday due, haven't you?"

"Can't come soon enough." With Chris, the Chris I snuggle up to on the sofa, the Chris who likes Led Zeppelin and U2, the Chris who can talk to me for hours about Shakespeare's characters and make them sound like fun, *the Chris who has a criminal past and a childhood of neglect.* I silently admonished myself for being so ridiculous.

My last patient was a bulimic forty-year-old woman with a long history of the disease, terrible teeth and bad breath. Afterwards, I fled from the Lodge with an unshakeable determination to concentrate on the weekend ahead. And that meant food.

Charlie and Claire were coming to dinner. I'd already devised a menu, the finale a sumptuous confection of Cornish cream and raspberries glazed with a thick layer of sugar — an excuse at last for the purchase of a kitchen blowtorch. Maybe I'd go the whole hog and buy a couple of other items on my wish list. I suddenly felt the pull of serious culinary retail therapy. A sucker for cooking gizmos, I browsed kitchen shops in the way most blokes walked around car showrooms. Besides, I was glad to be *doing*. If I kept active and my brain busy, I didn't have to dwell on the other stuff.

With the sun right overhead, I could feel the tension draining away as I walked along the street. Hope and the prospect of serious downtime made me giddy.

After a brief dalliance with a four-slice glacier-blue retro-style toaster, I homed in on a fabulous set of kitchen knives with rock-hard titanium blades. They weren't on the list, and I already had a decent number in both homes but found the temptation irresistible. There was something about blades which I supposed was a bit kinky. I liked the weight and feel of the handles. I admired their versatility. Sleek and unyielding, knives required skill and dexterity. With a knife in your hand, you were invincible. To fully persuade myself of the wisdom of an entirely unnecessary purchase, I imagined the ease with which I'd be able to bone out a piece of meat, slice and pare an overripe fruit, fillet a sea bass, *defend yourself*, a small voice in my brain interposed.

You could never have too many, I concluded, doggedly hefting the block and taking it to the counter. Next, I turned my attention to a chrome-plated blowtorch. According to the blurb on the box, it skinned, seared, toasted and glazed — a sexy and serious piece of kit. With a flame temperature of 1500 °C, it was potentially lethal. I wasn't good with fire, and it would require a degree of nerve. I'd have to be super careful. Still, it was a steal.

Laden with two heavy carrier bags, I lumbered back towards the Promenade, pausing now and then to window-shop. Close to a department store and about to cruise down the classy row of designer shops, I felt as if something inside had tightened like a screw. I stopped, caught sight of my own tortured reflection and spun around.

There were hundreds of shoppers in a multitude of colours, attitudes and moods. But was Stannard among them? Screwing my eyes tight against the sun, I scanned faces and bodies, of every creed and colour — my instincts on full alert. Young couples walked hand in hand. A tanned businessman carrying a briefcase brayed loudly into a mobile phone. "Close the deal, for Chrissakes, or we're fucked . . ." Mothers chastized children. Adolescents cheeked parents. Small boys with streetwise faces and pierced ears careered dangerously in and out of the crowds on skateboards. An old woman dressed in an oversized man's jacket shouted obscenities at the sky. A young man, darkly handsome with a short beard and glossy hair, shimmied along in a beautiful scarlet dress and white pumps. The place crawled with humanity in all its variety and complexity, and Stannard was out there somewhere. I *sensed* it.

Alarmed, I crossed over to the other side of the square, picked up pace. A small crowd of Japanese tourists, hanging around outside Waterstones, made it almost impossible to pass. I squirreled my way into their party and, on impulse, hitched a glance over my shoulder, above their heads, and cast a long look back. The place seethed and, among the ocean of people, one man stood out from the crowd. Wearing dark glasses, his face was canted permanently to the left. The newspaper he held in his hand, as if to protect his face from the harsh rays of the sun, gave him a slightly lop-sided appearance. As he drew close with a purposeful stride, I could see that he was tall, probably over six feet, his body spare and toned. Every inch a businessman, he wore black tailored trousers with sharp creases, a short-sleeved ice-blue linen shirt and a dark silk tie. *Was it him?* I angled my head to get a better view. My palms stuck to the plastic bags as I dumped them and pulled out my phone, the log number taped on the back in case of emergency.

I held up the mobile to check the signal, which was good. He came closer still. I could make out a fine head of hair, dark, thick and straight. In spite of the sunglasses, the side of his face on display was lightly tanned. From the bit I could see, he had a strong jawline.

Now he was only a dozen or so shop fronts away. Tourists scattered. Still he kept moving. As if breaking out of a trance, I glanced anxiously around, getting my bearings. Stay in a public place, the police said. Don't confront him. Walk away. Phone.

He was looking straight at me. That's when he took off his sunglasses and let the newspaper slide.

My breath hitched inside my chest. Couldn't breathe in or out. I felt as if I were dying.

One eye, including the brow on the left side of his face, sloped disastrously so that the region around his long slim nose was overcrowded. The mouth, which was wide and generous, curved down in a perpetual expression of displeasure as if he were the victim of a serious stroke. Perversely, the skin was smooth, too smooth, for it looked inert, plastic. There was no evident scarring or puckering, no signs of fire, only blotchiness along the hairline like you see in skin that has been surgically treated. The area below the cheekbone caved in. From his fixed expression, I guessed that all involuntary movement was severely restricted. It was like looking at a death mask, except the eyes were too bright. Almost a deep shade of topaz, they burned with an amazing intensity, lighting up his features.

Twenty paces away and counting, I knew I should turn and run but couldn't. I stood rapt and rooted, like the princess in *Sleeping Beauty*, knowing the spindle was to be avoided at all costs, that it was dangerous, but unable to prevent disaster. With this man, I felt that same inexplicable fascination. More than that, I shared a strange affinity with him.

"Kim." There was desperation in his eye.

The spell broke. I plunged my phone into my pocket, gathered up my bags and took two steps backwards.

"Stay away from me."

"I simply want—"

"Piss off, you bastard." I looked round, tried to catch the eye of a well-dressed woman walking past. The woman shook her head minutely and carried on as if I were trying to sign her up for a donation. I turned my gaze to two barefooted young men with dreadlocks. Same response. I was in a public place but nobody wanted to know. Nobody wanted to get involved.

Stannard spread out his hands inches away from me. I registered the plea, yet my heart was like stone and I turned on my heel. At the sound of my name, I shoved the bag from my right hand into my left, pulled my phone from my pocket and made a big gesture of putting it to my ear. Smart footsteps behind, I sped up, the shopping like lead weights, so that I listed to one side, like a small boat caught in a storm. A blare of car horn, then a cyclist zipped past and with a torrent of expletives almost knocked me flying. I didn't care. Stealing a feverish glance over my shoulder, I saw Stannard left behind.

Unappeased, I broke into a trot, ran past the imitation Trevi fountain, crossing the road at the lights, and let myself be swallowed up by a crowd moving in the opposite direction. Weaving and zigzagging across the pavement, I did my best to break up my outline so that I'd be less obvious to him, and thanked God for shade as I passed a row of parked cars beneath a canopy of trees. The operator picked up my call as the Queens Hotel reared into view. I rattled off the log number and explained the situation. Asked if he was still in pursuit, I looked back. By now I was level with Montpellier Gardens, where people were spread out among the flower-beds, eating sandwiches and sunbathing. I thought my heart would give out at the sight of Stannard only a short distance away, no break in step, no increase in pace, simply a dogged determination to get to me.

"He's still in pursuit," I bellowed above the sound of a jazz collective playing "Mack the Knife" against a background of cosmopolitan sprawl.

"Where are you exactly?" the operator said.

I gave the location.

"Can you make it to your destination?"

"I think so. I don't know."

"We'll send a patrol car. It may take a few minutes."

Breathlessly, I gabbled a brief description of what I was wearing. I broke into a jog, felt the pull on my muscles. My shopping weighed a ton and I could taste car exhaust and benzene. Sweat bubbled out of me. My chest heaved. A group of students shambled towards me, threatening to slow me down. I cannoned through them, prayed for the police to hurry. Risking another glance back, I stopped short.

He wasn't there.

Rooted, lungs bursting, muscles screaming, heart pounding, I combed the street again, scoping the other side, narrowing my eyes against the fierce glare of afternoon sunshine. He could be inserted anywhere, supposedly soaking up the sun in the gardens. My breath erupted in short and painful bursts.

I had no time to consider. A patrol car pulled up.

PC Grant stuck his head out of the window. "Want a lift?"

CHAPTER TWENTY-ONE

I described what happened. Grant drove back into town and made a quick fruitless search of the side streets, then drove me to the Bayshill Clinic.

"I think it's time we had a chat with Mr Stannard," Grant said, before dropping me off. "We'll make it plain that his interest is not appreciated."

I couldn't ignore the warm thrill of righteous vindication. At last I was being taken seriously; someone was listening.

Triumphant, I phoned Chris. It was supposed to be easy. A quick call to tell him what happened — say it was being dealt with, that I was fine.

"Christ, I could kill the little shit for this."

"But it's all right now."

"It isn't, is it?"

Disappointment descended like smog. "It's a whole lot better than it was."

"What are you doing?"

Why the inexplicable switch from Stannard to me? Guarded, I didn't immediately reply.

"Are you going back to the flat, coming home or what?"

I fizzed with irritation. "I can't jump ship. I've got clients, Chris."

"You'll return same as usual, then?"

"Yes."

"You'll come straight back?"

"Is there a problem?" *Why?* was what I really meant.

"Of course not."

"Good," I said, briskly ending the call.

* * *

Kirsten Matherson's parents were waiting for me. They seemed brittle. I wasn't sure whether there was an internal issue, or it was my fault for being late. I apologized unreservedly.

Tall and graceful, Mrs Matherson had straight blonde hair, cut super short. She wore a dress of palest green that fitted her lithe figure perfectly. By contrast, her husband was thickset, barrel-chested, and his jacket looked like it was a size too small.

They sat down and I brought them up to speed on Kirsten's progress. Marie Matherson seemed relieved by the improvement in her daughter's condition. Frank Matherson merely grunted. Hard to say whether it meant approval. It occurred to me that he'd been strong-armed into making an appearance.

Striking a neutral tone, I looked at Marie and said, "I gather she's interested in fashion design."

"I've tried to encourage her, but she undervalues her abilities."

"That's extremely common in anorexics," I assured her. "There's a tendency to focus on negatives. It's connected to a general problem of low self-esteem."

"Are you saying it's our fault?" Frank burst out. His neck flushed red.

"Not in the least," I said, startled by his hostile tone.

"I hold that damned modelling agency responsible for this," he roared.

"Please, Ken," Marie warned.

"You should never have got her involved."

I watched the minor domestic drama unfold. Frank clearly blamed his wife, which was interesting but unproductive. I tried to reset the conversational temperature.

"I see you have two sons."

"What's that got to do with you?" Frank snarled.

"I'm trying to help, Mr Matherson," I said, handing him a straight look.

Attempting to head off further confrontation, Marie cut in, "They're quite a bit older than Kirst."

"How have they reacted to their sister's condition?"

"They're concerned, of course," she said with an earnest smile. "They're working abroad at the moment."

"So they're shielded from the problem."

"To a degree."

"That might be a good thing. Having an anorexic in the family can make siblings feel powerless. It stirs up all types of diffuse emotions, like anger and guilt."

"Guilt? I've never heard such crap in all my life," Frank roared, jumping to his feet. "Come on, Marie, I've had enough."

Embarrassed, Marie glanced at me in apology and stood up.

"The only people who should be feeling guilty," Frank said, as a final fuck-you, "are those bastards responsible for our daughter's illness."

With that, he ploughed out of the consulting room, his wife following in his wake.

Shaken, I was almost out of the door when the police called.

"We picked up Stannard," Grant announced. "I'm afraid he checks out, Miss Slade."

My stomach gave a sickening lurch. I put a hand to the wall to steady myself.

"What was his defence for this morning's episode, then?"

"There's no law preventing two people from having a conversation. He maintained you'd made the first move."

"He said that?"

"According to Stannard, you were waiting to speak to him outside the bookshop. He said you looked deliberately in his direction and that you waved to him."

"That's ridiculous."

"*Were* you looking for him?" The serious note in Grant's voice made me suddenly feel as if I were the problem.

"I thought he was following me."

"So you admit you looked."

"I admit nothing."

"Calm down, Miss Slade." He spoke in a way guaranteed to wind me up. "I'm trying to get a handle on what actually took place."

Confidence disintegrating, I apologized. Was I wrong about all this? Was my hypervigilance making me see things that didn't exist? The more rational I tried to be, the more irrational I felt. "I'm certain Stannard deliberately followed me. Does he deny the other things?"

"Yes."

I throbbed with confusion. Either Stannard had done a good job selling his side of the story, or I was genuinely losing it. A brief silence signalled stalemate.

"Whatever the ins and outs, Stannard knows we've marked his card," Grant assured me. "He says he intends you no harm. I believe he's genuine in that regard. I think he really believed because of your . . . how can I put it? Er . . . shared difficulty . . ."

"My face is not a difficulty," I said bluntly. Hell, what happened to the change in public opinion following the Paralympics? What happened to the new attitude towards disability and disfigurement?

Grant coughed as though he had a hairball in his throat. "He must have been a good-looking man before his accident. I only meant that he's a victim."

I thought I was going to choke with frustration. Stannard's manipulative ability to engender pity meant he would always have the drop on me. "I was forgetting," I said with a cynical laugh, Gavin Chadwick's opinions bashing my ears, "we're all victims nowadays. We're all flaming losers."

"There's no need to adopt that tone."

My cheeks burned red. I tried to strike a more conciliatory note. "So that's the end of the matter, is it?"

"I'd say so," Grant said crisply. "It's really unlikely he'll bother you again. I think in his own way he's sorry for any misunderstanding."

CHAPTER TWENTY-TWO

Rattled after a God-awful conversation with the police the day before, Kyle Stannard felt relief the police officer had defied expectation and shown himself to be a reasonable and intelligent human being. He'd listened intently while Stannard explained that he was doing nothing wrong and merely going about his normal everyday business. Too bad, Kim Slade had reacted with hysteria. Perhaps she wasn't the woman for him after all.

With no case to answer, Stannard walked away unscathed. It did not stop him from making contingency plans. Always paid to have your back covered.

Adept at compartmentalizing, Stannard pushed the matter from his mind and concentrated on his next acquisition, a six-bedroom pile on the Evesham Road in need of considerable refurbishment. Due to discuss details with the owner, he knocked and waited on the threshold.

Heather Foley welcomed Kyle Stannard into her home with a frozen smile. It was an expression he'd witnessed on numerous occasions and no less tiresome and infuriating for it. Rarely vocalized, analysis of what the hell had happened to him always followed the initial shock. Stannard was something of an expert at reading all those pesky questions that hovered in the beholder's mind: could his face be due to an invasive illness? Was it a form of palsy that explained the dent in the lower half of one cheek? Was the general sloping appearance of his features due to a stroke? A terrible road accident might be responsible. Among the sophisticated, *poor man* seemed to be the consensus, followed swiftly by *how brave*. Among the ignorant, *freak show*. Whatever the attitude, most deemed it best not to look and made every effort to avert their eyes. Stannard had lost count of the number of conversations he'd engaged in with people who stared only at their feet.

"Thanks for seeing me at such short notice," Stannard said, shaking her hand, "I really appreciate it."

"Would you like coffee before we start, or afterwards?"

"The house first, if you don't mind. I see it was built in the mid-nineteenth century," he said, alluding to the plaque attached to the northern side of the building.

"Yes," she commented cheerily.

She started off with the dismal mausoleum of a kitchen, its size its only advantage. A trellis of rusting pipework poked out from a recess housing a decrepit-looking Aga — hard to imagine it was an iconic range cooker and much desired for that reason. The whole room needed knocking down and rebuilding, Stannard thought, gesturing for them to move on. Mrs Foley quickly led him through to what she called a utility room but in reality was a store that used to be the maid's quarters. Stannard gave it a cursory glance and walked to the back door that opened out onto a courtyard.

"Would you like to see the garden?" she asked.

"Later," he answered decisively.

She walked him back through the long dark hall to a cluster of rooms. The sitting room was comfortable. Then there was the study, a darkly masculine chamber. Stannard already knew that there was no Mr Foley with which to contend. According to his enquiries, Mr Foley had run off with his secretary, resulting in his wife receiving the house in the divorce settlement. This told Stannard two things: Mrs Foley was emotionally vulnerable and she was looking to maximize her asset. Consequently, his observations were brief and he spoke little. Feigning disinterest was the best means to drive down the price. Not very nice, but he was a businessman, a certain amount of ruthlessness part of the deal.

Wittering to fill the conversational void, Mrs Foley crossed to the other side of the large polished wooden-floored hall and threw open the door. A cascade of brilliant sunshine cast him into the light. Like a vampire after sun-up, he shot a hand to his face, automatically shielding his bad side with the set of details in his hand. Straightaway, he was catapulted to another time: streetlight shining, fists defending, body falling and then crack after crack to his head, his nose, his cheeks, his teeth. He remembered masked faces, shouted voices, the sensation of drowning in his own blood as his features were eviscerated. Jesus, it was all he could do now to contain his breathing and not let out a scream.

"Sorry," he muttered, complaining about low blood sugar.

Acutely embarrassed, Mrs Foley pretended not to notice. She twittered something about the glorious weather they were enjoying and walked in ahead of him in a poor effort to protect him from the blatant sunshine. Stannard followed, silently cursing his brief, terrifying and disjointed sortie into the past. The flashbacks were getting worse and yet he still couldn't piece together what happened.

In the middle of the floor, a shiny grand piano sat like a large black carrion crow.

"Do you play?" Stannard asked, eager to embrace the present.

She grimaced. "It belonged to my ex."

"Would you be prepared to sell it to me?"

She smiled graciously. "That depends."

He nodded. They had a deal. He'd noticed the ripple of excitement in her voice. From there, it was a whistle-stop tour through the remaining rooms downstairs and then up a long sweeping staircase to those upstairs, including a bedroom where mushrooms were growing through the ceiling.

She started to rattle an explanation but he cut across her.

"Once the roof's fixed it won't be a problem. The details suggest you have a cellar."

She assured him she did. "You can access it from both the hall and the garden."

"I'd like to have another walk around the house on my own before we venture outside. Is that all right?"

Eager to please, she smiled approval. "I'll make coffee."

A quarter of an hour later, they were sitting in the drawing room. Stannard was careful to hide behind his sunglasses, sparing Mrs Foley further embarrassment, but in reality a pretence so that she couldn't read his eyes.

"You have a genuinely lovely home," he said, making her smile warmly. "Thank you for sharing it with me. It must be quite a wrench to leave."

"One has to move on."

One certainly does, he thought. He raised the cup to the good side of his mouth. There was a brief awkward silence, punctuated by the clatter of fine china.

When he finally spoke his voice assumed a hawkish tone. "You realize that neither of us are going to be happy with the deal."

She gave him a sharp look. He turned the good side of his face towards her and attempted a smile. "We are both grown-ups. When I buy a property I want to pay the lowest price I can. You, as the vendor, want the highest you can get. Somehow we have to meet in the middle so neither of us comes away disappointed."

"Or feeling short-changed," she added sharply.

"I find the opening up of honest dialogue the key to successful negotiation," he continued smoothly. "If there's something you're not happy with when we come to crossing t's and dotting i's, you must let me know. I'll do the same."

He studied her expression. She seemed mesmerized by the prospect of a deal. This was it, he read in her eyes, the moment she'd been waiting for. Her life changed and the future suddenly trilling with giddy promise.

"Top-up?" she beamed.

When she suggested that he must take a peek at the cellar before he left, he knew he was home and dry.

It was dark and smelled of earth. In spite of the maze of struts and supports, the area was large enough to turn into another room.

"We'd thought of turning it into a games space."

Stannard nodded politely.

"Or maybe a wine cellar."

Stannard said nothing.

Mrs Foley gave a nervy laugh. "You probably have your own ideas."

He didn't comment.

She twitched a smile and crossed to the stone steps, up and out through the door and into the hall. Stannard followed, pausing by the entrance.

"Right," he said decisively. "I'll get my people to contact your people." He stretched out his hand and looked straight at her. When she thanked him she dropped her gaze and took an avid interest in her expensive shoes.

CHAPTER TWENTY-THREE

"And you believe him?"

We were in the kitchen. Music oozed through the speakers. Crowded House singing a depressing song about tears and slow turning pain.

I spread my hands. With the pressure off, and from the safety of my Devon nest, I endeavoured to view things through a less narrow perspective. I could afford to be magnanimous. I could feel sympathy for Stannard. A bit. I reckoned he was on the spectrum. Quite how far along, I wasn't certain.

Voice raised, arms crossed, Chris remained resistant. "The police are useless. We both know he won't give up that easily."

"We *don't* know anything."

Chris had been edgy and moody from the time I'd stepped through the door the previous evening. I'd tried to jolly him out of it and failed. This was the unattractive side of his personality that pissed off our friends and, frankly, me. I felt at a loss how to help, particularly as he appeared to be glued to his mobile when we were out and his laptop when we were in. It was as if there were three of us in the room, not two. Chris was not even sufficiently cheered by his purchase of a sleek black Mazda MX5.

"Look," I said, making one last attempt to get through to him, "I'm dazed. I want to believe it's all over. I need to have that faith, do you see? From your point of view it's not so easy."

"How so?"

"You haven't had time to catch up with the shift in events. I appreciate that," I pushed on. "In a way, I've got the advantage."

Chris fixed me with an unyielding expression. To deflect him, I did what I'd learned to do a long time ago: I smiled. Then I explained, "Because I've experienced all this first-hand." I also believed, but didn't say, that men were less able to process risk assessment when it came to their nearest and dearest. Either they were in hackles-up, full-on defence mode, or they were shooting the breeze, oblivious. As a child, I'd experienced fierce overprotectiveness and spine-tingling neglect.

"Have you forgotten how scared you were when you saw him?"

I clenched my jaw, felt a vein pulse in my neck. Seeing Stannard's face had given me an unwelcome insight into how others might view me. I shook my head.

"I can't get the sound of your fear out of my mind. You seemed so crushed, so very frightened. I've never heard you like it before."

"Did I? I don't think—"

"Have you any idea how crap that makes me feel, how powerless I am to protect you? He could come along at any moment, when he chooses, and I can't do a damn thing about it." Weary, he drew up a chair at the kitchen table and sat down. "Maybe you're right. I just . . ." His voice tailed off. Sleeves rolled up, he clawed at a bare arm. I caught his despondency and, for reasons I couldn't pin down, didn't think it was remotely connected to my stalker.

"What?" I reached over, stayed his hand.

He hooked me with his haunted eyes. "This is changing both of us. We mustn't let it. We have to get our lives back."

"And we can." I tried not to show fear. When bad things happen to couples or families it doesn't always unite. Sometimes it shatters. Dad had sought solace with other women, some who wanted me to call them mother. My brothers, that much older, had concentrated on exams and work and, in Luke's case, carving out a career. I could see how, rather than bonding us, this damn stalker had split Chris and me into different camps.

I gave his hand a gentle, hopeful squeeze.

His face relaxed into a smile. "We will be all right, won't we?"

"Of course." Tentative and faltering, I said, "Maybe now is the time to make changes — good changes, I mean." I couldn't discern whether Chris was still looking at me with apprehension or expectation. "Perhaps," I gabbled, "we've both got a bit too comfortable in our own spaces. Maybe we've become selfish and set in our ways, complacent even. I mean," I said, searching for the right words when all I could find were the wrong ones, "are we always destined to live like this?"

The silence screamed in my face. His expression was unfathomable and I didn't dare move. Then, as if remembering that he was supposed to respond, his face softened. He gave my hand a gentle tug. I got up and edged my way around the table, let him pull me down onto his lap. He wrapped his arms around me, buried his head into my neck.

Neither he nor I uttered a single word.

CHAPTER TWENTY-FOUR

"Crikey," Charlie exploded.

Claire looked stunned. "And it's all over?"

"Yes." It better be.

We were sitting in the shade on the small terrace outside the kitchen, overlooking the river. Blades of sunshine played off the water. Iridescent-looking insects hovered above the glassy-green surface. I'd opened champagne in a feeble attempt at celebration, my conversation with Chris, or rather lack of it, seriously undermining my confidence. I couldn't rule out the niggling fear that he didn't want me to move back on a permanent basis and it needled me.

We ate a light mousse of freshly caught Salcombe crab followed by crisply glazed duck breasts seared by my new culinary toy. I'd spent the afternoon getting the hang of using the blowtorch, sealing meat, skinning tomatoes and peppers, caramelizing sugar and fruit and anything else that moved. My childhood accident ensured an almost phobic fear of fire and heat, but it wasn't so bad as long as I could control it — gas flames on a hob were okay, likewise irons and fires in grates as long as there was a guard in front. I wouldn't venture near bonfires though, and the thought of burning buildings induced a panic attack. That afternoon, in the sanctity of my own kitchen, it took nerves of steel to conquer my intrinsic fear. But I did. From an early age, it was what had always been expected of me. "Get a grip" should have been my middle name.

Over coffee, Charlie and Chris discussed the merits of various cars, talking torque, electro-hydraulics and cylinders.

"Why didn't you tell me about him, Kim?"

I looked at Claire. "Stannard?"

"Yes."

I saw hurt in her eyes and Claire was the last person I'd ever wish to offend. "If I talked about him, I risked giving it oxygen. Besides, I didn't want to burden you."

She let out a sigh.

"What?"

"Nothing."

Nothing meant something. I attempted to force the issue, but Claire simply said, "I only wished you'd told me."

"I'm sorry."

"I knew something was up the night of the dinner party."

"Yes, but it's over now, thank God."

After a brief uncomfortable silence, Claire asked if I'd seen anything of Molly and Simon.

"I went round for dinner recently." It felt like a confession. After all, I'd discussed being stalked with them at some length. I decided to change the subject and asked after the Chadwicks.

"I received a thank-you phone call from Lottie and an invite to a drinks party next month. I think we were asked out of a sense of guilt," Claire confided with a laugh.

"Are you going?"

"You must be kidding. I'd rather walk barefoot through nettles. Anyway, I don't think I'll be feeling much in the mood." I observed the shy smile. There was something familiar in her expression. I'd witnessed it three times before.

"You're not . . ."

"Four months gone." Claire beamed.

"Oh, Claire." I reached over and kissed her on the cheek.

Charlie broke off from his conversation with Chris. "She's been suffering badly with morning sickness this time so we're hoping it might be a girl."

"Bound to be, they're always the source of trouble," Chris said, laughingly slapping Charlie on his arm. "You're building up quite a brood."

Claire wrinkled her nose in delight and looked lovingly at her husband. "We always wanted a big family, didn't we?"

I watched my friends with a stab of envy. They looked so content and serene in that rare way when two people are clearly meant for each other. Looking at Claire's face, soft and serene in the candlelight, I longed for what she had: a lasting relationship that was solid and stable with the man I loved. I glanced over to Chris and smiled. He met my eye, held my gaze then looked away.

* * *

Chris was already asleep by the time I showered and climbed into bed. I lay awake listening to his steady breathing, my mind returning to Stannard and the extraordinary effect of seeing him in the flesh, his twisted looks, the way his eyes shone like burning flames. I'd been afraid, almost to the point of paralysis and, yes, for a strand of time, I'd fallen under his spell. Dealt a tragic hand of cards, he must have been magnificent. I couldn't help but wonder about the story behind the random attack on him. Was it motivated by envy, malice or greed?

Stories. Every person had one. Not the *once upon a time* variety, or everyday tales of jobs and marriages and pursuits, but the *this is what happened that changed me* story. It might be a single event, tragic or otherwise, an important influence, a parent, lover or mentor. Every day I listened to my client's life histories, replayed them, interpreted, reworked, categorized and retold them: stories of loss and loneliness, of jealousy and false expectations, of bitter disappointments and crushed hopes. I heard the noise of crippling fear and rage.

But I hadn't listened to Stannard's story. I'd refused. I'd done what was expected of me. I'd done as I was told. Don't talk to him, they said. Don't engage. Walk away. And I had. But really I'd fled for my own reasons, because when I looked at Stannard's face, I recognized a piece of my own narrative. I saw a cruel reflection.

CHAPTER TWENTY-FIVE

Aroused by Chris's touch, I'd responded sleepily like I'd done many times before when we'd enjoyed slow, languid sex. But this time was different. This time there was desperation and recklessness. He pinned me down as if he needed to break flesh and bone. There was determination, no violence, but Chris fenced and parried my every move. Not like this, but like that. I felt as if I'd had an affair and been forgiven, and this was his way of repossessing me. Events blurred. Teeth clashed, limbs collided, nails tore, skin on sweaty skin. Stubble rasped against my chin. My lips itched and swelled and bruised. I didn't dare shut my eyes. I moved into another zone where words didn't count or matter, only acts.

He caught hold of me and forced me in front of a long antique mirror that had belonged to my father. Kicking my legs apart, I feasted my eyes on him as he went down on me. My legs trembled as he bent me over and fucked me from behind. Dazzled by our bodies, I felt revered and dirty, like an actress in my own porn movie. The computerized image flashed into my mind. I snuffed it out. Afterwards I lay there spent, letting the silence seep in.

"Like a drink?" Chris said.

Vodka, I thought. "Fruit juice," I said.

He pulled on a robe and went downstairs. At that moment I felt a million miles away from Stannard. No longer a nameless, unknowable, frightening entity, he was simply a disfigured man who, for a short period of my life, had shouted for my attention. Sex that morning had reset the boundaries. Like it always did.

I rolled over onto my stomach, one arm outside the bed, and heard the sound of voices punctuated by a sudden torrent of laughter. Mystifyingly, I caught a silvery female tone. I rolled out, pulled on a pair of knickers, threw on Chris's shirt and went downstairs.

Andy sat in the kitchen. A wide smile split his face. Self-conscious, I rolled up the collar, did up another button, and briefly wondered what they'd been laughing at, what I'd interrupted. Two men, one woman, I shivered, recalling the painting in my flat.

"I told him his timing was crap," Chris said in mock despair.

I exchanged a glance. "I didn't hear you arrive, Andy. No camper van?" Andy's mode of transport was a running gag between us.

"We cycled here."

"We?" I looked around the kitchen as though someone was about to pop out of a cupboard.

"Jen and me. She's in the loo."

"Must be mad," Chris said, handing me a tumbler of juice. "Haven't you got anything better to do at half past ten on a Sunday morning — newspapers to read, a car to clean, a woman to screw?"

"Leave Jen out of it, and how do you know what we were up to first thing?" Andy said with a grin.

"Leave Jen out of what?"

I followed the voice. Jen was exactly as Andy described and more: big eyes, big lips, sizeable curves. Andy carried out the introductions. I apologized for my state of undress.

"Don't worry about it, maid." Jen pulled up a chair close to Andy. "We're not bothered, are we, babe?" She squeezed Andy's thigh as if she were kneading dough.

"Coffee?" Tight at the intrusion, I smiled in a vain effort to conceal it.

Andy nodded.

"Shall I be mother?" Jen said, making to get up.

"Wouldn't dream of it." I swiped the kettle and filled it with water. Wasn't Jen's fault she used an expression I couldn't actually stand. My father had once had a fleeting relationship with a woman fond of the phrase. She was fond of him too and hadn't lasted five minutes.

Jen made herself at home. "Mine's black, two sugars."

Chris leaned back and linked his hands behind his head. "So, to what do we owe the pleasure?"

"We're having a drinks thing in the garden next Saturday," Andy said.

"You haven't got a garden."

Jen let out a screech of laughter. "He's right, And."

"Yard, then," Andy continued, unabashed. "We'd like you both to come."

I prayed Chris hadn't forgotten.

"Sorry, mate. We can't. It's Kim's birthday."

"Shit, I forgot, stupid of me."

"But that's brilliant," Jen said, eyes popping. "Come to ours on Saturday and we can make it a real party."

I turned away to mask the expression of frozen horror stamped on my features. Andy's bashes were surreal affairs — loads of alcohol and desperate people. Above the clatter of mugs, I heard Chris say four magic words.

"Made other plans, mate."

I glowed inside. What and where? I dealt four mugs of coffee on the table, like a croupier handing out chips.

Jen pouted her pink lips. I didn't know her well enough to spot whether it was mock disappointment or the genuine article. "We should go out for a girls' night."

"I'll check my diary." I hoped my enthusiasm was convincing.

"No such problem for me," Chris said. "Got the prospect of six weeks of unfettered freedom."

Andy grinned and made a passable stab at the chorus of Alice Cooper's "School's Out For Summer".

Jen gave his arm a playful slap and shrieked. "You're such a laugh."

I did my best to mentally turn down the volume control. "Andy said you teach at Totnes Leisure Centre, Jen."

"S'right, keeps me in shape."

"Certainly does that." Andy cast her a lascivious grin.

"You should try it, Kim." Jen's gaze locked on to my neck. "It's a good little confidence booster."

I froze. Feeling impossibly awkward, I questioned what on earth I was doing standing in my own kitchen in such a state of undress.

Maintain composure, I thought. "Well, I . . ."

"In the meantime we should definitely arrange a foursome."

"Fabulous," I lied.

* * *

After they left Chris let out a groan. "She was gruesome. Why on earth did you agree to go out with them?"

"I'd already batted her off twice. It was starting to look rude. I don't know how he manages to pick them. And that laugh."

"Don't you see? She's exactly Andy's type: no brains, curvy bod."

"Bit harsh," I said. "God knows what Andy must have thought of me this morning."

"Don't worry about him. He's almost part of the furniture."

"I'm sure he'd be very flattered by that description."

"Well, you know what I mean," Chris said with a grin. "Andy is . . ."

"Andy." I let out a giggle.

Chris suggested a picnic and we headed for Mill Bay on the Triumph — sea air in my face, the roar of the arrow sports exhaust in my ears. Predictably, the beach bustled with febrile activity. Despite this, something had shifted. I couldn't put my finger on it but my spirits soared. For the first time in a while I was determined to hope.

"You okay?" Chris said, putting a protective arm around me.

I peered from underneath the brim of my sunhat. "Yes, I think I am. Let's head back to the coastal path. There's that rocky outcrop round the corner. It will be quieter."

The rocks were black and shiny, like overlapping mussel shells. The waves caught against them and sent up a fine salt spray. I could taste it on my skin. We inched along close to where cormorants perched and the land fell away to the sea below. The air was thick and crusty with the smell of seaweed. While I paddled Chris laid out our towels side by side. Stretching out, a hard layer of shale resting against the small of my back, I tipped my hat over my face, determined to extinguish all thought of the drive back to Cheltenham the following morning. I wanted to rest in the moment, be still and snuggled in our private world. Later, we ate. In spite of the heat, I was insanely hungry. We bit into rolls filled with lettuce and salami and, between us, scoffed a big pack of posh crisps.

An hour or so passed. Half asleep, I felt serene and sorted.

When Chris announced he wanted to take a photograph of me I barely stirred.

"You know I loathe having my picture taken," I murmured lazily.

"Go on. I've only got one pic of you."

"The one where I look wasted." I'd been trying to avoid the flash. "You said you'd rip it up."

"No, *you* said." He laughed and playfully poked me in the ribs. "Go on, it won't take a moment. Look behind you and then turn back. That way it will look natural."

"Honestly, I'd rather not."

His jaw tightened. His expression darkened. I fled from that look and tried to pass off my refusal as a joke.

Desperate to please him, I stood up. "Go on, then."

He took the shot and lay back down, silent. I lay beside him, suddenly tense. What the hell was going on inside his head?

CHAPTER TWENTY-SIX

Olivia Mallory kissed her son full on the mouth. Her hands rested on his shoulders and she held him away a little with concern. "You look tired, darling."

Wearing his trademark sunglasses, Kyle tipped his head to one side. "I'm fine, mother. You worry too much."

She let her hands drop, linked her arm through his and walked him into the sitting room, where Gerald was waiting. The men exchanged restrained greetings. Gerald offered Kyle a glass of white wine. "Viognier," he said, as if it were something unusual.

At his mother's insistence, Kyle sat down in Gerald's favourite wingback chair. If Gerald was jealous, he didn't say so. He asked his stepson about business. Olivia excused herself to check on the meat's progress. As soon as the door closed, Gerald pushed himself forward in the chair, any pretence of civility gone.

"So what was it you wished to discuss?"

Kyle's mouth twitched. "There's this woman," he began, pausing to remove a fruit fly from his glass. "She's of interest to me. I don't really know her, but what I've seen, I respect . . . greatly." He noted a tick pulse in Gerald's neck. No matter. "She's got a good mind," he continued, "she could help me."

Gerald frowned. "Help you? How?"

"I need to talk to her. We share certain things in common."

"Like what?"

"Scars."

The pulse increased. Kyle watched with detached amusement. "Is she married?" Gerald said.

His mind went blank. The thought had never occurred to him. "I don't think so."

"Then what's the problem?"

"She alleges I've been calling her and sending her stuff. She even accused me of following her in the street."

"Kyle, for God's sake. Are you stalking her?"

He gave a short incredulous laugh. "Don't be ridiculous."

Gerald opened his mouth, as if to speak, and closed it. He took a long swallow of wine.

"Anyway, I went to view this flat for sale in Montpellier," Kyle continued. "Ground floor and smartly appointed. Before I knew what was happening, some copper picked me up and pushed me into the back of his vehicle for a chat."

"Jesus." A spit of wine dropped onto Gerald's beautifully pressed shirt. He rubbed a hand over his jaw and inched forward in his chair. "Let me get this straight. What were the police doing there?"

Kyle hiked one shoulder. "Haven't a clue. They said she lived in the block."

"She?"

"Keep up. The woman I told you about."

"In the flat for sale?"

"No." Kyle frowned in irritation. "She lives in the one above."

"And you didn't know?" Gerald's eyes narrowed with suspicion. "It's too much of a coincidence."

"Coincidences, like accidents, happen." Kyle thrust him a crooked smile and took a drink.

"You really expect me to believe that?"

"Believe what you like." His stepfather generally did. Kyle threw him a challenging look.

Gerald swallowed and drummed his fingers against the glass. "What did the police do?"

"Read me the riot act."

"You denied it?"

"Of course I denied it."

Gerald held Kyle's gaze. "They haven't charged you with anything?"

"No."

"No caution?"

"No."

Stony silence.

"I won't have your mother upset," Gerald said tightly.

"That's why I'm talking to *you* and not *her*. The thing is, I don't know why this woman is saying these things. We happened to chance upon each other in the street the other day. She waved, beckoned to me." His voice grew hard and bitter. "I thought we could talk, and then she does something like that. It's as if she's playing games."

"Then don't play."

"It's not that simple. She can help me, and she's drawn to me. I *know* it."

"In this country we have the Protection from Harassment Act and it has recently got more robust. However innocent your motive," Gerald said, giving Kyle a bloodless stare, "you must forget about her, forget about the flat too. You stay away. Do I make myself plain? You've already been in trouble with the law."

Kyle bit down hard. Don't think about it, he told himself. Get a grip. "I don't need reminding."

"It seems to me you do. Whatever this woman's problem with you, it won't look good. You've got history."

Kyle swept off his sunglasses, his eyes flat and cold. He knew that his stepfather could never bear to see the full extent of his disfigurement. "There was no evidence. The allegations were dropped."

"No smoke without fire."

Gerald drained his glass. Olivia appeared at the door. "Lunch is ready." She beamed radiantly at both the men in her lives and stretched out a hand to Kyle as if he were her toy-boy lover. Kyle got up and took it.

"You two seem to be getting on famously." She gave Kyle's hand a tender squeeze. "Have I missed anything?"

CHAPTER TWENTY-SEVEN

At about four o'clock, we walked back home and, pulsing with desire, took a shower. Chris kissed my mouth and held me as rivulets of water sprayed our faces. He flattened and entered me against the cool-tiled walls. Full-on sex. Blistering. Afterwards Chris insisted on cooking spaghetti. I watched as he chucked in butter, oil and wine.

"Are you trying to give me a coronary?"

He turned and grinned. "I don't remember any complaints about the picnic, Miss Slade. Sit there, shut up, sip your drink and look decorative. This is going to be fabulous, trust me."

And it was. After we'd finished off a bottle of plum-ripe Merlot, we watched a film, an action adventure with a high body count, guns blazing, tons of blood and an implausible plot line, but hey, what did I care? It was the perfect distraction; I loved it.

We went to bed early and I fell asleep and dreamed about the dead. Guy was outside in the darkness, his face half lit in the green glow of a bonfire, boasting like a latter-day Abednego that he could walk through it and not be hurt. I tried to stop him, but he laughed and touched the flames with his hand.

I woke up with a jolt, perspiration exploding across my brow, sheets drenched, mind whirring with thoughts of my imminent return to Cheltenham. It took me an age to go back to sleep and, when I finally awoke, I'd overslept.

Darting out of bed, I hurriedly washed and dressed, and crept over to Chris to wish him a silent goodbye.

Tentative rays of amber light splashed across his face. I bent down and kissed his mouth. He stirred and reached up, sliding a hand across the back of my head, his other moving my hair, exposing the scar tissue, tracing the ridge with a finger. His eyes were quite open now, studying me. It felt peculiar, as if he were mapping me, recording every detail, committing me to memory, like he was someone about to go to war and perhaps never come back. I tried to twist away — I was running hellishly late — but he held me fast. In other circumstances his grasp would have felt deeply inappropriate. Something in his eyes, like an apology, troubled me. I wanted to stay. I needed to ask a question that had been on my mind for far too long and that I hadn't yet properly processed.

"I have to go," I said, chickening out.

When he said goodbye it felt as if it were final.

* * *

I pulled into the nearest gateway and cursed. Already late, I'd got stuck behind a tractor for three tortuous miles and then, pulling out of Loddiswell, and taking the twisty and slow-travelling lane that led to the A38, the car started handling badly. I knew immediately what was wrong: a puncture.

I scrambled out, feet hitting the dry, dusty earth, the hem of my skirt snagging on brambles, nettles stinging my legs. Cursing, I examined the rear of the car and the extent of the damage. The nearside tyre was blown. It was nothing short of a miracle that I'd managed to manoeuvre it successfully off the road. I guessed providence was looking after me, but now what? I hadn't changed a wheel in an age and didn't relish the prospect of broken nails, and dirt and oil on my clothes.

I'd only ever practiced once: the first lesson my father taught me in a bad-tempered exchange after I'd passed my driving test. I ran through the motions in my mind. Make sure you're in a safe place — I was. Shove on the hazard lights. Put the car in first gear. Everything I needed was in the compartment in the boot. The first time, I'd done it in forty minutes, but if the wheel nuts were too tightly fixed, or I had trouble unlocking them, it would take longer. I pulled out my phone and called Cathy.

"Sorry, I'm going to be late."

* * *

I stared, absolutely floored. Chris was right and Grant was wrong. After the puncture on the way to work, this was turning into a really crap day.

The card had slipped through the net because Cathy thought it a birthday greeting. Coffin-shaped, black, there was no inscription. The design said it all. Sharp tears pricked my eyes. The happiness of the past forty-eight hours seemed nothing more than an illusion. Dragged emotionally one way, I was yanked back another. The man stalking me was in for the long haul.

Chill settled on me at the thought of Chris that morning, the question left unasked, the answer unspoken. *What if?* No, I absolutely refused to believe it. He'd planned a birthday surprise. We'd made love.

Reaching for the envelope and attempting to decipher the sorting office, I told myself to stop emoting and use my brain. Unfortunately, the postmark was blurred. All I knew: it was sent on Saturday, the day after Grant had spoken to Stannard.

Even with my professional experience, it wasn't always easy to predict human behaviour. Now what? Go back to the police? And what would they do? So I decided that if I could keep silent, stay safe, last out until Friday, I'd be all right. I could forget about my urban stalker and walk away. The idea appealed. In the meantime, maybe I *would* think seriously about changing my job, changing the trajectory of my career.

Jim stuck his head around the door. I stuffed the card away in a drawer and explained that the police had spoken to Stannard.

"That's a relief."

I flicked him a smile, muttered about punctures and running late. Undaunted, Jim loped in and perched on the edge of the desk. "I've come across numerous fascinating details."

"Really? Look, Jim, I've got a number of—"

"Apparently most stalkers have a history of failed relationships. Stalking is their way of taking back control, their chief motivation one of anger. I'd always assumed sex to be the dominant theme," he said, as if amazed by his lack of perspicacity. "Another interesting snippet is that it's not unusual for them to start late in life. You know the old adage: life begins at forty? Well, quite often so does stalking."

I'd already worked out Stannard's age: thirty-eight or thereabouts. Chris was also thirty-eight. Jim, however, was in his forties. Humour him, I thought, unsettled by the way my mind could so easily be derailed. "Quite often, you say?"

"Well, not exclusively, of course. There's always the exception to the rule when it comes to the human psyche. And," Jim said, working up to the finale, "stalkers will often rope in family members to defend their cause."

I hoisted an eyebrow. Jim spotted the heightened interest. From the spellbound look on his face, he was revving up for another pronouncement. "From the little you told me, Stannard's not your stereotypical oddball. He's a guy who saw you as a potential confidante and, when you weren't interested, got uppity —" he registered my exasperated expression — "his feelings of rejection a little extreme, I appreciate. I'm glad the police have sorted it so quickly. Apparently we're not that clever at curing the problem. Riveting stuff," he smiled. "So, you're all right, then?"

"Never better. Thank you," I added, the pitch forced, a little too bright, a tad too upbeat. My smile made my face muscles hurt. I looked pointedly at my watch.

"God, is that the time?" he said, sloping back out of the room.

CHAPTER TWENTY-EIGHT

Peeking into shop windows, looking out for a stranger's mirrored reflection, I took a less than obvious route to the flat. When a bloke shambled across the street and accidentally bumped me, unforgivably, I tore into him.

"For Chrissakes, watch where you're going."

"Sorry, love," he muttered in a twenty-fags-a-day voice.

Horrified to feel so brittle, I moved off, my fight-or-flight response jammed on alert: attack first and ask questions later. Walking quickly, mindful of being ambushed, I threw myself into the flat. Shutting the door fast, I dragged the chain across.

Everything looked comfortingly normal. No sign of break-in. No notes. No calls. Relieved, I prepared dinner and ate with a solitary glass of claret and a novel by Lisa Jewell. Against a background of classical music, a favourite piano piece by Debussy, I nibbled and drank and read, and endeavoured to create a sense of calm within. Only four days and four nights to go and I'd be in Devon, where I could regroup among my closest friends. Then the doorbell rang.

My pulse jittered. The doorbell rang again, more insistently. I stood up and spoke into the entry phone. No answer. I crossed the floor and looked out the window. No one. Creeping up to the spy hole, I peered onto the empty corridor. Drawing away, waiting a few moments, I did the same again: nobody.

Stomach flooded with acid, appetite abandoned, I reached for the phone and called Chris. The messaging service clicked in. Assuming he was monitoring his calls, I asked him to pick up. He didn't. I called his mobile — switched off. I wondered what he might be doing and decided he'd probably gone for a drink with Andy, or perhaps was engrossed in a film, either at home or at the local cinema, or . . .

Downhearted, I replaced the receiver and toyed with calling Luke in the States. He'd be at work and, knowing me so well, would pick up that something was wrong. He was bound to have a view though, something I didn't welcome. While growing up I'd been surrounded by older and, by inference, wiser siblings. It didn't matter if I was thirty or seventy, the dynamics would never change. I would always be the kid sister, not so bright, not quite cutting it. At least I'd elevated myself from being, as my dad once memorably told me, "no bloody good" to "not bad". At a loss, I called Molly. Simon picked up. Two sentences later, he insisted on coming round. I backed off.

"It's all right. I only want a chat." I hated being the centre point of drama.

"I'll be round in ten."

Seven minutes later he was sitting on my sofa. Wearing shorts and vest and running shoes, Simon smelled strongly of sweat. His legs were brown, smooth and hairless, at odds with his hunky build. His lashes looked unusually dark. It was an odd contrast.

"Just got back from a jog when you called," he explained.

I told Simon about the latest twist in what I feared was becoming a miserably boring saga and braced for a lecture. Simon would surely urge me to go back to the police. To my surprise, he didn't. He asked about Chris.

"It's difficult — for both of us. It's put quite a strain on the relationship but I think, or I thought, we were over the worst. I don't want to load him with any more."

"So he doesn't know about the card or the mystery caller?"

I shrugged my shoulders. That wasn't all he didn't know. "Probably someone ringing the wrong flat." Now that Simon was with me, I had a clearer perspective. "I called Chris a few minutes ago but he wasn't in."

Simon issued a straight look that reached into the core of my being. "How often have you tried to contact him and got no answer?"

"Not sure I understand what you're getting at." I did, but I wasn't travelling down that rutted path with Simon.

Simon's expression didn't alter. His gaze didn't shift. "Have you been noting times and locations when you think you've been followed?"

"Not literally. Mental notes, for sure."

He gave me a hard look.

"How long have you known me, Kim?"

"Got to be ten years," I replied, wary.

"We're good mates?" His expression was intense.

"I think so." I attempted a smile. "And Molly too," I added hastily. Something made me look at the door. How long would it take to yank it open and flee?

"So you trust that whatever I say, whatever Molly and I think, I'm only telling you because you're our friend."

I nodded vacantly. I didn't like the way this was shaping. He was going to say something horrible; I knew it. People got away with the most atrocious things when they used the *friend* line: *I don't mean to be nasty but, as a mate, your breath smells. Because you're my friend, I thought you should know that your husband is in grave debt, is having an affair, is gay, enjoys the company of prostitutes, and/or rent boys.*

"Stalkers rely on one thing to carry out their activities," Simon pronounced.

"A victim."

Simon remained straight-faced. "Time. It's like a job to them. They need to be either in part-time work or an occupation that allows them the freedom to move around."

I stifled a sudden surge of anger and didn't trust myself to speak.

"Hear me out. If Stannard was that intent, he'd have tracked you to Devon."

"What are you trying to say, Simon?" The scars on my neck felt scratchy. I wished that Simon would go away. Because if it wasn't Stannard, then . . .

Simon continued, unchecked. "Stannard is harmless, his intention born out of genuine interest."

"Have you forgotten the way he followed me, his threats, the way he tried to scare me witless?"

"Did he? Are you absolutely certain?"

"Not you as well?" My heart caught in my ribs. Was I having some kind of mental breakdown? Was I delusional? Was I gripped by paranoia? I gulped. Shouldn't I *know*?

"Sometimes things can get out of hand and be misinterpreted," Simon said. Or misunderstood, according to the police, I remembered. "He's an ambitious man, unhappy with taking no for an answer."

I threw back my head and laughed. It sounded staccato. "The hallmark of the stalker."

Undeterred, Simon continued, "He's got a reputation to uphold. Stannard wouldn't be so stupid."

"Stupidity doesn't figure. This is about obsession."

Simon shook his head. "A significant number of stalkers know their victims. They're often ex-partners—"

"So we're back to Phil again." I very nearly snapped with frustration.

"Hear me out, Kim. How well do you actually know Chris? You said yourself he's hardly ever at home."

And there it was. Out in the open. What I'd tiptoed towards and run like hell from, Simon had said out loud. Wasn't that why I clung to the belief that it was Stannard because it had to be him. *It had to be.* The alternative was too gross.

I tried to get a handle on the one or two specific times I'd called Chris and found that he was out. I tried to remember his timetable. He taught solidly every day. But then there had been that two-day visit to Huckham. No, I thought. It didn't tie in, didn't make sense. Stannard was already in the mix by then.

"Does Chris have the key to your flat?"

"Yes."

"The key to your car?"

"The spare as a precaut—"

"There rests my case."

I felt as if he'd hit me over the head with something heavy and then tied me up and gagged me. Entertaining something in your mind was one thing, somebody else breathing life into the thought quite another. Horrified, I couldn't formulate the words, couldn't speak. I thought of the weekend, Chris's mood, the heightened sex and new accord. I hadn't fully processed it. Part of me felt like a woman in jeopardy. The other . . .

"He doesn't seem committed to you," Simon said more gently.

"For God's sake, we're not joined at the hip. We both have careers." And I was prepared to give up mine for Chris, but he wasn't so enthusiastic. There was that whole criminal thing loitering in his background. And he was acting strangely, his moods as unpredictable as rip tides. I'd put it down to Stannard, but what if . . .

"You don't know him," I protested hotly. Shame on me, but at that precise moment I wished Simon would drop dead.

"Too right. Chris rarely ventures out of Devon. In four years, we've met him three times. He never wants to see your friends and he hardly ever stays with you in Cheltenham, even when he has his wonderfully long holidays. He's a loner. He's solitary. He's—"

"Stop!" I said, my voice unpleasantly shrill.

Simon didn't understand what living in Devon did to people. Seduced by the scenery and the illusion of the good life, people became extraordinarily insular. It took either ambition or boredom to effect a change. And it didn't matter whether you were born there or chasing a dream. Once cuddled up under the large, fluffy duvet of the South Hams, it was easy to be deceived. People found it difficult to escape. But sometimes they had to. Sometimes the illusion was revealed. Sometimes they got scorched living there. But Chris, with his history of broken homes and foster care, could be forgiven for digging in.

"It doesn't make him my stalker," I gasped, tears in my eyes.

CHAPTER TWENTY-NINE

How well do I know Chris? Answer: not very.

I edged myself into the day. I'd had one glass of wine the previous night but my mouth was dry and my eyes felt prickled, a clear case of psychology influencing physiology. I gobbled down a couple of painkillers and arranged for a guy to come and fit an alarm system at the flat, something I should have done sooner.

Next, I phoned Chris. No reply. Was he ghosting me? I ordered myself not to jump to the wrong conclusion and, in what I hoped was an immensely calm and unemotional voice, left a message for him to call.

Walking to work, I felt less contained. Consumed by questions, Simon's seed of doubt took root, bloomed and spread like Japanese knotweed. Where was Chris? Why hadn't he called? Was Stannard simply a misfit with appalling timing?

With a tight throat, I checked in with Cathy, who treated me as if I were returning after a spell of compassionate leave and gathered with a dozen other staff in the common room to "touch base", as Jim fashionably termed it.

Closed down, as far removed from the here and now as it was possible to be, I itched to get back to my room so that

I could phone school. Waiting for what seemed an interminable amount of time, I finally broke free and spoke to one of the secretaries, who confounded me with one sentence: "He's not in this week."

"Are you sure?"

"That's what it says here."

"Does it say why?"

"Personal reasons."

Feeling sick, I explained who I was. "Do you know who took the call?"

A muffled discussion took place between a number of people. "Sorry. Would you like me to find out?"

"Please, and could you ask Andy Johnson to give me a ring when he's free?"

I waited and waited, saw the last of the girls on my list for the morning session and, under the guise of entering up notes, pretended to work. I sharpened a pencil, poured a cold drink and spent a long time checking emails and news bulletins.

Personal reasons. So personal it didn't include me? *Or did it?*

I went to the loo, studied my face in the mirror, tipped my chin to the light, watching it play on my less-than-perfect skin. Faces held stories. Every line and groove, every fixed expression clues to the emotional history of the wearer. I thought of the girls I treated, some with faces wizened by self-inflicted abuse; those born with facial defects; victims of Cherubism, a rare condition resulting in bulging eyes and lengthened jaws; those who'd been disfigured through injury, or disease, or plain malice. Without warning, Stannard's weird, beautiful and crazy face loomed in front of my eyes. "Fuck you," I swore aloud and strode back to the office.

* * *

The phone rang as I tipped cheese into a risotto. Believing it was Chris I snatched it up.

"Kim."

One word. My name. Blood-freezing.

"Why did you tell the police a pack of lies?"

My jaw dropped with indignation.

"In the absence of an answer or an apology, I propose we start over again." No plea. An order.

God, he was good. Most blokes would have backed off. Not him. Stannard was coming on with a vengeance. I flashed with temper. "There's nothing to start. If you don't leave me alone, I'll go back to the police."

"Are you sure about that?"

"Is that a threat?"

"For a shrink you're remarkably quick to take offence."

"You're stalking me."

His response was cool and superior. "Do you actually know what that means?"

"Of course I damn well—"

"According to the Concise Oxford English Dictionary, it means to steal up to game under cover. I don't consider you as prey and all my actions have been quite open. Incidentally, if I was really stalking you, you could get the cops to slap a restraining order on me, not that it's always a good move. I understand from some of the legal circles I move in that it can sometimes inflame a situation."

Legal circles, I registered with a jolt. "You send me spooky cards. You take my car. You send a pornographic image to where I work. You hog my phone line. You pester me in person, *and it isn't what I think it is*?"

"Sounds like you have a heavy-duty problem."

"I do: *you*."

"You know perfectly well it's not me." The tone was patronizing.

"You're lying."

"Bullshit. Incidentally, I've got a perfectly good car of my own."

That much was true, according to Simon's information, but no way did it let Stannard off the hook. I would not allow this utter creep to beat me.

A telephone call apart, he could be right outside the flat. I peeped out of the window. No sign of him. Screw the rules. Time to turn the tables.

"Do you have family?" I said.

"Do you?"

"I asked first."

This seemed to amuse him. "Yes."

"You're in regular contact with them?"

"I visit my mother often."

Stalkers will often rope in family members to defend their cause. "Where did you grow up?"

"Kent. What about you?"

"Never you mind. Are you on medication?"

He issued a laugh. "A moderate amount of wine each day helps me sleep."

"You have a problem sleeping?"

"I'm an insomniac. I have bad dreams, day and night."

"By day?" I silently cursed my failure to conceal my professional interest.

"I imagine I'm in the middle of a crowd. There are literally hundreds of people cheering, the cream of society. They're all beautiful, gorgeously dressed, McQueen, Marc Jacobs, Armani, Chanel." His voice had taken on a strange intonation. "I can smell them."

Smell. One word and my alarm bells sounded. My lungs felt seared with acid. I knew what he meant. I *knew* . . .

Stannard sliced and diced my thoughts. "Are you superstitious?"

"What?"

"Cracks in the pavement, touching wood, magpies? One for sorrow, two for joy. Best thing to do is run over the bastards."

Christ, he was sprinting away with the conversation. I snatched it back. "Where did you go to school?"

"The local comprehensive."

"That's not where, that's type."

"Clever," he purred. Maddeningly, I felt flattered. "What you're really trying to find out is where I live now."

"Wellington Square." I bit my lip.

"Well, well. Who's stalking whom?"

"I like to know where the enemy is coming from."

"Tsk, Kim. I'm not your enemy."

Snookered, I adopted a less combative approach. "Do you live with anyone?"

"Your technique to extract information lacks finesse, if you don't mind my saying."

I did mind. "Why don't you talk to her, or maybe it's a him?"

"Neat try. Points for that." He issued a smug laugh.

"So?" I said, persistent.

"I'm straight and I live alone — like you." His voice slipped into a low, seductive tone. "How do I make you do what I want?"

If this wasn't some form of harassment, what the hell was it? "You can't browbeat people."

"Learned behaviour, darling. Sometimes it's the only way to get things done."

"I'm not your darling and I don't respond to being railroaded."

"Don't be haughty, Kim. It doesn't suit you."

Exhausted, I fell silent. The quiet stretched for at least thirty seconds, maybe longer.

"Hello," he said, "cat got your tongue?"

Temporarily refusing to engage, I said nothing. I needed to gather my mental resources.

"Are you still there?" he asked.

"I am."

"Good. I'll pay twice the going rate."

"Look, I understand your difficulties and I'm sorry, but—"

"I only want to talk to you, for God's sake. Where's the harm?"

"Kyle, I can't." Damn, should never have used his Christian name.

"What do you want me to do, beg?"

"I don't want you to do anything." I was weary of him, of his games, of everything. "I simply want you to leave me alone."

"Is that your final word?" He sounded as though he was giving me one last chance to change my mind and redeem myself.

"It is."

Silence stretched out like an empty road through the desert.

"Secrets and guilt." He articulated the words slowly.

"Pardon?"

"It's what you trade in. And I have to share mine with you."

Have to. "Why me?"

"Because we're both shot through with sadness."

The hairs on the back of my neck stood erect. "Like I said," I repeated, thick-tongued, "my expertise is in an entirely different field."

"You could treat me, if you wanted to. You could help me."

I rubbed at my eyes. "I can't. I'm the wrong person."

"You're exactly the right person. It's why you became a shrink, isn't it? The mind becomes so much more interesting when one's looks are compromised."

"Fuck off."

He let out a laugh. "I like that about you — no shit, straight to the point. It's quite a muscular trait, unusual in a woman . . ."

"That's—"

"Let me finish. It's rude to interrupt." It had been some time since I'd been told to shut up. "I haven't yet got past the point of feeling bitter," Stannard continued. "Naturally, it's not as bad as it used to be, thank God. At least I can function. It's a kind of trick, isn't it?"

"That's self-pitying rubbish. I wouldn't know."

"I think you do. I think you understand only too well. Were you burned a long time ago, Kim? Was it a tragic accident?"

I slammed down the phone.

* * *

I am seven years old and bubbling with excitement because it's Guy Fawkes Night. For a month, gales threaten to douse the entire occasion. Then the rain stops, replaced by a bitter winter chill.

Stepping outside, the breath punches out of me. My tiny feet feel numb. Ears tingling, they turn hot and itchy. My gloveless hands are red and raw. Daddy forgets things like that. Jackets too. I only clean my teeth and wash properly when I'm away at school. My brothers tease me about it. They taunt me about lots of things, grace before meals, deportment, elocution lessons and the *la-di-dah* accent to replace my slow Devon drawl, and what they call my new airs and graces. They view my going away to school as our dad's attempt to turn me into a lady and take every opportunity to rib me about it. I feel like a cuckoo, not quite fitting into either world. One alien environment with strict and incomprehensible rules, the other where there are no rules at all.

And therein lay the tragedy.

My adolescent brothers spent days hauling bits of dead tree and wood to build a bonfire. It stretches up to the sky as solid as a fortified castle.

We ransack Daddy's wardrobe and find one of his old jackets. It's made of sheep, they say, dung-coloured and stained. Then we find a frayed pair of trousers and a funny Russian hat, lined with fur, that he bought long before I was born. Luke persuades the gardener, who comes once a week — or maybe it's the cleaner, can't remember now — to sew the clothes together. I think Daddy will be very cross and I threaten to tell. The boys don't like that and accuse me of being a scaredy-cat. When I scream blue murder they give me sweets and crisps and pop to shut me up. Afterwards, they fill the guy with straw and throw him up onto the bonfire and wait for darkness to fall.

We all troop outside. Daddy cooks hot dogs. We eat them with fried onions and ketchup. I drink loads more pop. My tummy hurts and I feel sick.

Daddy lights the bonfire. I thought it would go off with a terrific whoosh but it doesn't. It crackles and spits and goes out. “Too much damp,” Daddy cries. The boys suggest putting petrol on it and get well and truly told off. Daddy chucks on dry wood and lights it again and, this time, the twigs crackle. At last, tiny yellow flames flicker into life, creeping slowly, tongues spreading fire, like a flowing river. I gaze, mesmerized, feeling the power and heat, watching the light play in my brothers’ eyes, seeing the blackened sky ignite.

I take a step forward and squeal as Daddy grabs hold and pulls me roughly back. He gives me a stern talking to, warning of the dangers of getting too close. Out of the corner of my eye I notice Guy smirk and he sticks out his tongue at me.

We start off with sparklers. I hold one in each hand, circling them, making pretty patterns. Daddy scurries across the grass, a taper in hand, lighting first one firework and then another. I don’t like the shouty jumping jacks and cracky bangers. I clamp my hands over my ears and screw my eyes up tight. I like Roman candles with their red and green stars best. Holding Daddy’s hand, watching the blaze of colour, I feel cosy inside. For once, I forget about my mummy.

Then the phone rings. It blares across the garden. Daddy grins. He looks pleased and excited. I think he is expecting a call from a lady friend. He bends down to light a rocket and calls to Luke to look after me. I turn and watch as he runs across the frosted grass and shoots inside the cottage.

Luke’s hand is hot and sticky in mine. Daddy has gone and so we fix our eyes on the firework. It’s huge with yellow and red stripes and it has a tail like a shark’s. A wispy tendril of smoke curls from its base. Naughty, it refuses to budge. We wait and stamp our feet on the frozen earth, but nothing happens.

“It needs relighting,” Guy says, patting his pockets. “Got any matches?”

“We should leave it,” Luke points out. “You know what Dad said. Never go up to a firework that hasn’t ignited.”

“Yeah, but this one’s gone out.” His voice sounds funny. Half boy. Half grown-up.

“You don’t know that.”

“Duh, stupid, yes I do.”

"Just leave it."

"You're scared." Guy's thin face looks mean in the moonlight.

Luke juts out his chin and squares up him. "Not."

"You are so."

Luke lets go of my hand and takes a swing. Guy, quicker and more agile, punches him in the face.

I scream and tell them to stop. They will be in *so* much trouble with Daddy. Blood pouring from his nose, Luke launches himself at Guy and brings him down. Dismayed, I watch them tangle into a mass of kicks, grunts and shouts. I try to haul them off each other but I'm not strong enough. A stray fist glances off the side of my head and sends me flying. It really hurts. Sprawled on the frozen ground, my hands are grazed and sore.

I cry and cry for Daddy, but he doesn't come. I cry and cry, but the boys don't notice. And it seems to me then like nobody ever did. I'm Little Miss Invisible.

Luke has Guy pinned down. His hand is raised, his fist balled. As little as I am, I sense that one of them is about to be badly hurt.

"I'm not scared," I yell, scrabbling to my feet. "Look, you two, it's easy." I run towards the rocket as fast as my stout legs will carry me. The rest is jumbled. There's a tremendous whoosh.

Flames.

A shrill scream.

Yelling.

Drum roll of boys running.

Shouts.

A sour smell of cooked flesh and burnt, acrid clothing.

Panting.

Utter indescribable pain.

Someone picks me up and rolls me in the frozen grass, then throws a coat over me. Daddy's voice, loud and unnatural, bellows. My small hands are peeled from my face. Searing. Screaming. Shattering. Heart-stopping. There is black stuff and gore in my hands — my melted skin, my flesh and blood.

CHAPTER THIRTY

I didn't believe Stannard's patter about *simply* wanting to talk. A talk would lead to more conversation. One meeting followed by another. Before I knew where I was, Stannard would think he was in a full-blown relationship with me. He'd be planning visits home to his mummy and wedding bells. Given time, he believed that his feelings would be returned. This was the make-up of Stannard's interior world. *Delusional.*

Over a second cup of tea, I pooled information. What was he really planning to talk to me about? His self-pity, his inability to come to terms with his disfigurement? His lack of courage? Something he didn't appear to be short of from where I stood. I scowled. It was no use trying to view him as I would a client. Stannard was driven by another agenda: *me.*

But that didn't necessarily make him my stalker, I was forced to admit.

I showered and dressed, phoned Chris and left another message. As Andy had still not returned my call, I caught him at home. He answered after three rings and sounded half-asleep. Irrationally, it made me testy.

"Didn't you get my message?"

"What message?"

"The message I left at school for you to ring me."

I heard him yawn. "Must have disappeared in the general swamp of administration."

I stifled a curse. "Never mind, have you seen Chris?"

"I've been working my bollocks off putting the finishing touches to a program for a local company. Had a bit of a time frame." Andy's moonlighting was a lucrative, if time-consuming, sideline. He made no secret of it and often talked about jacking in teaching and going into it full-time.

"When was the last time you saw him?"

"Last time I saw you — Sunday morning."

"You know he hasn't been at school this week."

"Uh-huh."

"Do you have any idea where he is?"

Uncomfortable silence.

"Andy, is there something you're not telling me, something I should know?"

"No." He sounded flat and, to my ears, evasive.

"I can't get a reply. I'm worried something's happened."

"Like what?"

"I don't know," I bluffed. "It's so odd that he hasn't returned my calls. Could you go over to the cottage? Give me a ring back?"

"Sure, but it's probably nothing."

I replaced the receiver and wondered why the sense of dread was so compelling. What was Chris trying to tell me that very last time? I visualized the scene, re-visualized the look of apology in his eyes. Was it connected to those damn messages on his phone and laptop? Impulsively, I dialled Claire's number but cut the call before it connected; she'd be knee-deep in children and the school run. There was nothing else to be done, I told myself and, if I didn't leave soon, I'd be late for work.

On the way out, Lizzie popped out of her flat, a look of simmering excitement on her face. "Ta-dah! We've had an offer."

"And you've accepted?"

"You bet. We couldn't refuse. Time to crack open the champagne."

I gave her a hug. "So what are my new neighbours like?"

"*Neighbour*. Single guy. I didn't get to meet him. Pete showed him around. Actually, he felt a bit sorry for him. Apparently the guy has some sort of facial disability, but he seems pleasant enough." The excitement fizzled out of her voice in response to my crumpled expression.

"Oh God, Kim, me and my big mouth, I didn't mean—"

"It's not tha . . ." Suddenly light-headed, I clapped a hand over my mouth. Breakfast worked its way up from my stomach to the back of my throat. I tried to swallow.

"What is it?" Lizzie asked in consternation.

Devastated, I tore outside and threw up on the steps. Lizzie followed me. "What's the matter? I'm so very sorry . . ."

I rummaged for a tissue, wiped my mouth. Vomit spattered my shoes. "Kyle Stannard's going to buy your flat, isn't he?" My voice came out thinner and squeakier than intended.

"You *know* him?" Lizzie's body stiffened.

I must have looked stricken. Lizzie grabbed hold of my arm to steady me and led me into her flat, sat me down and gave me a glass of water. Five rambling minutes later, I watched Lizzie's expression change from shock to disbelief to anxiety.

"Are you asking us not to sell?" Lizzie's face was tight and uncompromising.

"I don't know what I'm asking."

"Oh God, Kim, we've waited so long to get out of here." Lizzie ran her fingers distractedly through her hair.

"I know."

"Are you sure? Pete's a good judge of character. He said he was charming and polite."

What was the point in arguing? Lizzie and Pete wanted to move. This wasn't their problem, and it wasn't in their interests to take my side; I'd only complicated the issue.

Lizzie stood up and looked at her watch. "Leave it with me. I'll have a word with Pete." Her expression lightened. "There is an alternative."

I arched an eyebrow, weak and hopeful.

"You could always move instead."

CHAPTER THIRTY-ONE

Slow-burning chaos. My world was imploding.

I arrived late for work. Feeling third-rate, I winged it by sheer luck. At the first opportunity I changed my mind and phoned Claire, who knew nothing about Chris's movements. Sounding exhausted, Claire sweetly offered to go and check up on him.

"Andy's already taking care of it."

"Oh good," Claire said with obvious relief.

Unable to play down my grating unease, I said, "It's out of character for Chris not to contact me."

"I'm sure there's a simple reason. Maybe he's not well." It was good to hear the calm in Claire's voice. I so wanted to believe that everything would be fine, nothing more than a case of overreaction on my part. Under pressure, it's the simplest thing in the world to see sinister intent behind innocent actions. That's the way humans ticked. With shame, I recalled my anger towards Simon. Whatever he believed, he was looking out for me. Claire was still talking.

"Although we didn't think he seemed quite himself last weekend."

"Didn't you?" Simon's accusation did a double flip in my brain and landed with an awkward bump, like a gymnast fluffing a routine.

"Probably the strain of that bloke bothering you."

I agreed but wondered if I was wrong about the reason. In the past twelve hours, I felt as if all my judgements were flawed.

"Everything else all right?"

"Yes," I said hastily, not wishing to add to Claire's fatigue. "I'll see you at the weekend." With a distinct lack of enthusiasm, I remembered my thirty-sixth birthday.

I spent the lunch hour poring over books, trying to make a stab at what type of personality disorder Stannard suffered from. The more I read, the more questions arose. Was he fuelled by a desire to be loved, or was rejection the key to his behaviour? Was he driven by envy, viewing me as someone who had more than her fair share of happiness? Was it fury, or something entirely other? In spite of his modest claim to drink only in moderation, did he use drugs to crank himself up? Did he have a mother who was a sound influence or a colluding, cloying partner? Without talking to him, I'd never be able to discover the answers and yet contact was out of the question. I'd already strayed across the boundaries and done the verbal equivalent of throwing a firecracker in his face. Ironic.

Almost two in the afternoon, I stumbled across a fact that chilled. When it came to stalking, the victim wasn't the only person in danger. Those closest were also in peril. Partners and relatives ranked top of the list. My God, Chris, I realized. My instinct was to drive straight to Devon. Fortunately, Jim was easily persuaded.

"We can handle your workload for the rest of the day, and next week, if you like."

"I hope that won't be necessary."

"Of course, but the offer is there. Kim," he said, as I gathered up my things, "before you leave, phone the police. Tell them what's happened."

I blanched. "I don't know if anything's happened."

Jim flicked a tense smile. "Keep them in the loop is all I'm suggesting."

I didn't. I drove at lunatic speed. Angered by the volume of traffic, I wove in and out and switched lanes with naked aggression. Chris was the one barrier to my stalker's ambition and, if what I'd read contained a grain of truth, he was in real and imminent danger.

I was off the motorway and travelling along the A38 towards Kingsbridge when my mobile phone rang. Breaking the law, I picked up.

"He's not there," Andy said.

"Are you sure?"

"Well, I guess he could be hiding under the bed."

"This isn't funny."

"Sorry, you're right."

"What about the car?"

"Gone."

"Bike?"

"Still there."

"Right," I said, mouth drying. I didn't know if that made things better or worse. "Andy?"

"What?"

"Is Chris seeing someone?"

I heard a noise, the scuffling of dozens of pairs of feet, scraping of chair legs, school clamour and chatter.

"I've got year ten pouring in," he shouted above the din. "I'll have to go. Catch you later, yeah?"

I slowed down. I crashed gear changes and misjudged distances. I didn't remember any part of the journey to the cottage. An affair would explain everything, I thought. Better than Simon's alternative, but oh my God.

Cormorants Reach emerged swathed in sunshine, its thick, squat chimney poking up into an expanse of cloudless sky. It seemed exactly the same — cared for, attractive and welcoming. A lie.

On the mat, several envelopes — greetings cards, I supposed, to celebrate my forthcoming birthday. I scooped them up, scanned each one, relieved to match the handwriting to the sender, then entered the living room with its low ceiling and the chair near the window in which my father used to sit. A long-forgotten image of me in my short white socks assailed me. I sat next to my dad, my shoes not touching the floor. We had plates of congealed food on our laps, loneliness in our hearts.

In the early days, not long after my mother left, a cleaner used to cook our meals at lunchtime and leave them on the boiler for when my dad finished work and picked me up from whoever was looking after me. I hated those dinners. My adult aversion to gravy was a direct legacy of terrible meals eaten in strained silence.

Stifling the memory, I called out Chris's name, heard the shake in my voice, the sound sucked into empty space. Elsewhere, the room was neat and tidy, as Chris liked it. No mugs on the coffee table. No newspapers on the floor. The hearth cleared. Aggressively clean. Only the phone in the corner, the message light winking at me, disturbed the picture of order. I peered into the study, my private lair dark and womb-like, papers on the desk where I'd left them days before. Everywhere an eerie silence blunted my senses.

I walked down the two steps to the kitchen with its honey-coloured tiled floor, Belfast sink, the cross-paned windows that looked out over the terrace and river below. My heart briefly lifted at the sight of the spare keys to the motorbike hanging up where they should be. Worktops and the cherry wood kitchen table with its four chairs neatly arranged, fastidiously uncluttered. Against the beat of my heart, I heard the slow tick of the kitchen clock, the gentle purr of the freezer. Then I saw the envelope propped against the kettle, my name written on it, Chris's unmistakeable handwriting. Proof that he was safe, my heart gave a small lift of relief. Short-lived. The bunch of house keys next to it winded me.

I touched the envelope, which was white and narrow, and picked it up between thumb and forefinger. The flap had been folded inside and, as I pulled it out with trembling fingers, the paper felt cheap and flimsy.

I drew up a chair, sat down and read. A concession to his illegible handwriting, it was typed.

Dear Kim,
I know this will come as a shock but I'm leaving. I wanted to do this some time ago but then with the other business I didn't feel it right to abandon you when you so clearly needed me. The truth is there's someone else in my life and has been for a while. We've decided to go away together and start a new life. I wish you well, Kim. I hope, with time, you can forgive me. What we had together was good and special. I will always remember you.
Chris.

CHAPTER THIRTY-TWO

One note to kiss off four years.

The paper slipped from my fingers and onto the floor. My throat swelled and my chest contracted. *Can't be true*, I gasped, my sense of denial compelling.

Not again.

I bent down, snatched up the note, reread it, studying the flourish of his handwritten signature, digesting every word, looking for hidden meanings, searching for hope when there was none to be had, hating myself for feeling this desperate. I wanted to howl but was too blindsided. I'd so wanted a letter as evidence that Stannard's mind games were taking their toll, a plea for space, perhaps, a desire for thinking time. Not a sorry and goodbye. Not an ending. Not like this.

Worst of all, a part of me had known, had *always* known it would be this way.

In a bid to hold the wounded remains of myself together, I cursed his cowardice, swore at him for his weakness, criticized the note for being full of the stuff people trot out when they've made up their minds and already have a firm foot outside the door. Who was this bloody woman who had taken him? And how could I have been so wilfully blind?

With astringent clarity, I understood Chris's insistent desire for sex, a weird form of apology, one last service he could do for me. Either that, or he was making a last territorial attempt to stamp his identity on my body, preprogrammed to ensure he, as the dumper, felt better about ending the relationship with me, the dumpee. Even the photograph was nothing more than a trophy, a badge of fucking honour. I felt such a clown. The moods, the irritation, his obsession with private messages, that blasted phone call to the landline, were nothing more than symptoms of his conflicted desires, his damned affair.

I rushed upstairs to our tiny bedroom. Symbolic of our ending, the bed was stripped bare. I threw open the specially designed wardrobe that had been built into the eaves, pulled out the drawers. What few clothes Chris possessed were gone — shoes, possessions, the lot. The tiny bathroom told the same story. Shaving accoutrements, toothbrush, aftershave and aftersun all vanished. So it was true. I sat down hard on the floor, drew up my knees to my heaving chest and buried my face in my hands. A wave of tears engulfed me, déjà vu in its entire vile and vivid colour.

I didn't know for how long I sat there on the cool bathroom floor like a tethered, beaten animal. Grief slid into self-pity. Memories clamoured like angry ghosts: the difficulties of growing up in a household where public displays of emotions were rare and tears disapproved of, the day I'd started a period at home and didn't know how to get rid of the soiled sanitary towels, the energy devoted to being the best I could despite my best never being good enough.

Much later, I forced myself to return downstairs and opened the doors to the terrace to clear the musty air. I read the letter once more, my lover's rejection like bleach splashed over a beautiful painting, then, crushing it between my fingers, I sped outside and threw both letter and envelope into the water.

Pressing a fist to my mouth, I watched the paper curl and sink. Concern for him, worry about the impact of my stalker on his life and, all the time, Chris had been seeing, loving, having sex with another woman. Maybe even in *our* cottage. And, like a fool, I'd made it easy. I'd not been around to witness an increase in the number of showers he took, the greater attention paid to his appearance, the new clothes, old lies, those lengthy furtive conversations, all the hallmarks of infidelity. I felt the sudden heat of jealousy. Far greater: my intense sense of abandonment, and the obliterating realization that we fear most the things that have already happened to us.

I had few strong memories of my mother. I remembered the fragrance of her perfume, her enchanting smile, what I would now describe as her vivacity. There was nothing to suggest a heartless streak. That came later. I remembered her leaving only in the sense of feeling discarded.

My father had taken care of my daily needs in a rough-and-ready fashion. I was stoutly ignored if I asked when Mummy was coming back, discussion of the subject firmly discouraged. All he would say was that she'd gone away. One day I overheard him speaking to my older brothers. They were now a triumvirate, he said portentously. It sounded grand and important except I found out later that it was a Roman phrase of office meaning three, not four. The move to boarding school only served to confirm my feelings of rejection. There were two girls in my year whose mothers were dead. I envied them. There was something dramatic and sad and noble about their loss. And it was final. How could I explain that my mother had left me, didn't want me, was alive but unavailable. So I retreated into a different world, a world in which my mother was good and beautiful and loved me. Sometimes I thought she'd return. I wished it, willed it, prayed for it. But it never happened. I was fifteen when, unknown to my father, I decided to hunt my mother down. Guy, now twenty-two, supplied the information and arranged a clandestine meeting at a café in Exeter. I travelled for nearly two hours on a stuffy bus to get there, my heart bursting with excitement and trepidation. The café, or more accurately tearoom, was around the corner from the cathedral. White starched tablecloths graced the tables. Waitresses wearing bleached white aprons with black high-collared shirts paired with dark skirts, stockings and flat shoes served with unnerving civility. My mother sat in a corner near a window. She looked a great deal younger than my dad, pretty, maybe a little careworn. I felt thrown, not because she didn't square with the person of my dreams but because I saw how much I resembled her, similar eyes and nose. I didn't know it then, but afterwards I realized that, when my father rebuked me, he was really berating her.

There was an embarrassed exchange in which we awkwardly hugged. Did I imagine that she clung to me for a fraction of time? Without much preamble, she remarked on my face, offering condolences as if someone had died and, as if because of it, my life was forever blighted. I tried to ask the questions that had been dogging me for years, but she had a habit of deflecting them with platitudes and excuses while looking frequently out of the window. Perhaps she was nervous. Perhaps she felt guilty. I didn't know, but I knew she didn't really want to be there, that she couldn't wait to escape. In answer to the big question, the reason she left, she said:

"You're too young to understand, Kim. You'll probably never comprehend. Here," she said, pressing a ten-pound note into my hand, "I have to leave. I have a train to catch. Good luck."

I rose up and out of the café on a tidal wave of anger. It sustained and supported me, and gave me that brand of courage so highly spoken of and prized by others. Afterwards, I dedicated myself to a job requiring the compassion I'd missed out on.

Blinking away the memory, I remembered little of the next couple of hours. At some stage I wandered across the drive to the garage. Neither of us parked our cars inside, but the Triumph was exactly where we last left it, like a strange parting gift. Perhaps it didn't fit into his new life with his new woman, I thought, half-crazed.

Back in the cottage, I listened to my own increasingly desperate phone messages to Chris, moved stuff into the spare bedroom and set up camp there in a weak attempt to embrace single life again. Had I been at the Cheltenham flat, I'd have found it easier to kid myself. The cottage was *us*. Walk into any room, and I'd remember something Chris said. Sit in this chair or that and I'd recall a certain expression on his face. It was as if he'd died. Everywhere seemed inhabited by his ghost and the spooks that had fled before him.

Now I was really on my own, with nobody to hold or protect me, nobody who, in turn, I could love. My life had come full circle.

And Stannard was still out there. And, if not him, my stalker.

On my third glass of wine, it occurred to me that Andy had known all along. I swore, feeling the acuity of double betrayal. I wondered how many others knew, or how long it would take for the drums to beat and the whole community to hear. With Jen on the scene it would be all over the South Hams in moments. Claire had hinted at something in their last conversation. Had she been about to reveal all, but bottled? Could one of them be persuaded or coerced into telling me about the other woman? Did I really want to know, and what good would it do?

With tired resignation, I conceded that my friends were right, and I was wrong. Not only was I a hopeless chooser of men, which seemed odd given that I'd been brought up almost exclusively in their company, but I was also on a crusade for love, a quest that led me into all the wrong places. So what was stopping me from leaving this time? Why not give up the bolthole in Devon, sell the flat and start over, somewhere different . . . somewhere Kyle Stannard, or whoever, would never find me?

For the next hour, my overloaded mind grappled with what had happened. Sometime later, clarity returned and I picked up the phone to Luke and got through to him half past four in the afternoon, US time. I told him I was putting the cottage on the market, that I was perfectly fine, work was good and that nothing was wrong.

CHAPTER THIRTY-THREE

I drove into Kingsbridge the following morning, spoke to two estate agents, then drove round and parked the car in Salcombe, visited another and made appointments for a valuation with all three.

Ambling back past the boat-builders, and on towards Whitestrand and the main street, I felt coldly vengeful. A thirst for retribution was common in my clientele, usually when they were on the mend. I always counselled against it. Unproductive, I'd say. False judgement. People usually do the best they can even if they let you down. In the majority of cases, most bad actions are mistaken, not malicious. A hypocrite, I tried hard to take my own advice and failed. I mused how easy it would be to pin the blame for the breakdown of my relationship with Chris on Stannard. Unfortunately, I was forced to accept that, had it not been for Stannard, Chris would have long since departed. I felt no gratitude. Stannard was the bogeyman, the embodiment of everything bad. All had been well until he parachuted and crash-landed into my life uninvited.

I called in at a café awash with sunburnt holidaymakers and crying children, and ordered a cold drink. Melting into the crowd, I watched out for an offset face, glad not to find one. Afterwards, I walked outside and parked my rear on a castellated section of wall that overlooked the bay. I loved the sea and would miss it, but there were other seas to sail, other places to settle. Where exactly was anyone's guess. Blitzed by possibilities, I ruled nothing out and nothing in. Overnight, the cottage had ceased to be an intimate part of my history. It had never really belonged to me, in any case. It was, and always would be, my father's home. I was an impostor. Claire and Charlie and Andy, and all those people and faces I'd known and recognized since I was little would be dearly missed. To some, I'd promise to keep in touch, even visit, and yet I knew that, in time-honoured fashion, absence would extinguish even the closest relationship.

Resolve hardened, I drove back up the steep, narrow road from Salcombe, through Kingsbridge and Frogmore, over the river and wended my way towards Holset, finally making the steep descent to Goodshelter. Drawing near to Cormorants Reach, I scanned the gravel, looking for footprints or tyre marks, but there was nothing and nobody to see.

Inside the cottage there were no signs of disturbance, only silence and emptiness. I showered and changed and wandered about the house hating the bleakness of my surroundings. A sudden memory of Luke crying over Guy's death darted through my brain. Haunted and half insane with grief, I fled.

Along the tidal road, the car's wheels splashing in the shallows, I took the higher route up the winding hill to the church where my father and brother were buried. The next six miles were a blur of disjointed thoughts: Chris with another woman. Chris when I kissed him goodbye. Smiling Chris on the beach. Chris recoiling from my touch. Then there was Stannard the stalker, Stannard not the stalker. I shook my head. Had to be him. *Had to be.*

Or was Stannard right and I was the one with the obsession?

Every view, every building held a memory. I passed my old primary school in West Charleton, the cricket and rugby grounds in Kingsbridge where I'd cheered on the sidelines and watched the boys I fancied and who mostly didn't fancy me.

I remembered illicit beach parties and barbeques. The odd one out, I was the girl who didn't quite belong because I was not one of them, because my face, in every sense, didn't fit. Apart from Claire, the other local kids made it clear that I could never be part of their set, not with my posh accent and snotty-nosed, alien expressions and public school education.

With a shiver, I passed the stretch of road where Guy careered off on his motorbike and hit a tree, no other car involved. Not especially morbid, I hadn't thought like this in years and it rocked me. Well adjusted, psychologically stable — I'd had the assessments to prove it — I was a walking good-news story and yet, abandoned for a second time, I saw how much it was a lie.

I was a classic screw-up.

I was a fraud.

My stalker was in my hair, on my skin, in my blood, all conscious and unconscious thought manipulated by him. He was out to get me.

I had to get him first.

CHAPTER THIRTY-FOUR

"Don't you think Crozes-Hermitage smells of horse piss?" I thought it screechingly funny. Everything seemed hilarious. Even Chris bunking off with the games teacher amused me. It seemed so commonplace and predictable. I'd met the bitch once. Carolla Dennison. Unusual name. Great figure. Pretty face. No scars.

We'd drunk Andy's peace offering in record time and were three-quarters through the second bottle. The flowers were for my birthday, he explained. The party had been postponed — best mate gone, too many people away or unable to make it. Jen had opted for a girls' night instead.

"How long had it been going on?" We sprawled on the terrace in deckchairs, a couple of straw hats planted on our heads. Andy wore his lightly tipped over his face at a jaunty angle.

His mouth screwed into a frown. "Is it helpful to have a post-mortem?"

"Probably not but, as a shrink, I specialize in them."

He gave in with a grin. "I found out about six months ago. I think it had been going on for two or three months before."

"Long enough to have a baby." The length of time for which Chris had lied sobered me up. My fault because I wasn't there, I thought. Like an idiot, I'd handed the possibility of an affair to him on a plate. No wonder he didn't fancy me moving back. And that's why he'd bought a smart new motor, a means to impress his new love. In my inebriated state it all made perfect sense.

Andy was contrite. "I should have told you."

I shook my head. "It might have burned itself out and I'd have been none the wiser." Who was I trying to hoodwink? And, honestly, would that be any better?

"In spite of all the arsing about, I really believed you two were meant for each other. You seemed so good together." There was genuine regret in his voice.

I thought so too. I took a large gulp of wine to drown the sentiment. "Who else knows?" You couldn't do anything in Kingsbridge on the quiet. Relationships broke down and moved around as erratically as musical chairs. Adulterous liaisons were something of a spectator sport.

"It was kept pretty schtum. I expect the head put two and two together. To be honest, I was shocked to hell. Chris was my friend — a dark horse, I know, but I never expected this."

Tell me about it, I thought. "Do you know where they've gone?"

Andy averted his eyes. "He wouldn't say."

I struggled to sit up and abandoned the attempt. "Because he knew you'd tell me?"

He looked straight at me. "I tried to talk him out of it, Kim, honest."

I looked into Andy's wide, open face and saw the concern in his eyes. "Thanks." I rolled across and kissed his cheek.

He flashed a smile, lowered his voice as if letting me in on a great secret. "They were planning to go to the States. Carolla's mother lives there, Michigan or Massachusetts."

"Hell, Andy, there's a bit of a difference."

"Sorry, geography's not my strong point."

"Great admission for a teacher."

"Only if you're teaching geography," he countered, making me shriek. I drained my glass unsteadily. A drop of wine dribbled down my chin and plopped onto my shirt. Normally, I'd be embarrassed. I didn't give a fuck and wiped it away, poured out more and stared at the empty bottle. I wasn't drunk enough, not by a long way. "Perhaps we should drink a toast to the happy couple." I tipsily raised my glass.

Andy started, as though I'd poked pins in his eyes.

"Well, I've got to be grown-up about this," I said airily. "It's why I've decided to move away, go back to civilization." Straighten my head out and get on with my life. Fresh start.

Andy sat up, perplexed. "You can't be serious?"

I sniggered. "Deadly. I've visited three estate agents and they're all going to give me the benefit of their expert opinion."

"Christ, you don't hang around."

"That's my point. I've hung around for too long." And obsessed for too long. I was starting to sound like one of my own clients with an extra dash of paranoia. Not good. Not good at all.

I lurched to my feet and tottered towards the kitchen, bouncing off a wall as I negotiated my route to the wine rack.

"Bugger, things are getting serious. We're down to the last bottle." I opened it with a tremendous flourish and almost nutted myself. Brain and feet muddled, I headed back to the terrace.

"Don' look at me like that."

"Like what?"

"As though my knickers are caught in my skirt."

He laughed out loud. "I'm truly not, but do you think that's a good idea?" He eyed the bottle.

"Absolu . . . absolu . . ." For the life of me I couldn't think how the word finished. "Yeah," I said, merrily splashing fresh wine into our glasses. "Pity Jen's not here to share in the celebrations. You did well there, Andy. Looks like we'll have to put the foursome on hold."

He gave me an old-fashioned look.

"Did Chris tell you I've got a fan club? Very select. Jus' one member." I lunged towards him with a giggle and pressed a finger to my lips. "Shhh. Don' tell anyone, but I've got my very own personal stalker."

Andy gaped.

"You didn't know?"

He shook his head, astounded.

"'Course not. Dark horse. Chris tol' me not to tell anyone."

"You mean someone's following you?" he said in shocked disbelief.

"Not here." I gestured, waggling my thumb. "There."

"Cheltenham?"

"Yeah. Police have sorted him, 'cept he won' go away. Keeps on coming. Got to stop him, the bastard. Sen' me stuff, borrowed my motor, porn."

"You're not making too much sense, Kim."

I agreed with a smile. Things were getting blurry. There were now two Andys in the room and the sound of helicopter blades whirling above my head. Somewhere in my brain I registered that I was making an exhibition of myself. Or was that Daddy's voice? What the hell?

"This guy following you . . ." Andy said slowly.

"What about him?"

"Have you actually seen him?"

A cruel laugh sounded out of nowhere, took me a while to work out that it was coming from me. "Can't miss him. Got a face like mine. Well, bit of an exaggeration. One side's irresistible, the other . . . yuk."

"And you're sure it's him?"

"Positive." Well, I was, wasn't I? At least, I thought so. Booze had sharpened my wits, hadn't it?

Andy leaned towards me, a determined expression in his eyes. "I could sort him out for you."

"You're lovely." I patted his knee and did my level best to focus. "My knight in shining armour."

"God, you're pissed as a fart."

"I know."

Serious again, he said, "I mean it, Kim. If this guy bothers you, you let me know."

"No need. All taken care of. You're a sweetie, Andy, but you don' understand. Mr S. is in for the biggest shock of his life."

CHAPTER THIRTY-FIVE

I'd been sick — again.

Eyes pickled, tongue soldered to the roof of my mouth, brain in a tumble dryer, I reached for the painkillers. *Happy Birthday, Kim.*

I didn't recall what time Andy left. I had a dim memory of rambling about my dad giving me my first taste of alcohol when I was ten, a crème de menthe frappé, and instructing me never to eat spaghetti on a first date. Andy had coaxed me to eat a cheese sandwich and drink a pint of milk in a belated attempt to line my stomach and sober me up, not that it had done much good. The grease lay on top of the booze like an oil slick.

The conversation floated back in fragments. Chris. Games teacher. Stalker. Unlike on the previous evening, the idea of Chris falling in love with Carolla Dennison didn't seem the least bit funny. I felt humiliated.

As for my evangelical certainty about Stannard, I was no longer quite so sure. My moods seemed to swing like a pendulum and, with it, my judgement. Being stalked had taken a hell of a toll, stretching my cognitive functions to the limit. Getting through the day unscathed felt like a major achievement.

Trying to stem another tide of rising nausea, I showered gingerly, letting the cool water mingle with and wash away a fresh surge of salty tears. Then I dressed in a loose-fitting shirt and jeans and went downstairs.

I picked up the collection of envelopes, sat down at the kitchen table and opened them, smiling weakly at the particularly daft card from Luke. Halfway through a cup of heart-starting coffee, the doorbell rang. I put a hand to my pounding head and squinted painfully through the window. Claire stood on the doorstep. Beyond, I spotted her SUV parked in the drive, Charlie and the boys inside. When I opened the door I was immediately enveloped in a hug.

"Andy told us. I'm so sorry, Kim. Happy Birthday anyway." Claire wore a sleeveless dress, the outline of the child she carried visible beneath. Our two situations in life couldn't be more polarized.

"Do you want to come in?" I glanced at the car: Claire's boys bouncing furiously and impatiently inside, Charlie bellowing at them in an effort to retain order. Enough to fry even the most sober brain, which mine definitely wasn't.

Claire broke into a smile. "We want you to come out."

"Oh no, I don't think—"

"Birthday surprise." Serene and calm, Claire slipped her arm firmly through mine.

"I can't. I've got things—"

"It's no use," Claire said with a laugh, giving my arm a gentle tug.

"But I feel absolutely dreadful." Alcohol seeped out of every sweaty pore. My body felt as if my blood had reached boiling point, my stomach full of bleach. A sudden lurch signalled an urge to vomit again.

"You've looked better, I have to say." Her expression was one of maternal reproof.

"Had a bit of night of it with Andy."

"We know," she said with a laugh. "Fresh air is what you need, and a change of scene."

The decision was already made; I'd be rude to refuse. "All right, let me pop to the loo first, splash my face with water and get my bag."

* * *

"WICKED." Tommy gave an ear-piercing shriek as he emerged from the death-slide, button-brown eyes gleaming with raw excitement. I was feeling at that stage in my hangover where it could go either way. Food would be the deciding factor.

"Are you having a go, Auntie Kim?"

Auntie Kim felt more like chucking up again. "Don't think so, darling. I'm not sure my tummy would cope. You go again, if you want to."

We'd been on the water chute, the assault course and the nature trail. Super-dark sunglasses in place, I dragged myself along with the others, hot and shaky, wishing that I didn't feel quite so horrific. The aftermath of heavy drinking left me weepy. Anything set me off. Claire's stupendous efforts to give me a nice birthday, my favourite chocolates from the boys, a shiny, hardback, glossily illustrated cookery book on Italian cuisine from my friends, and all the time there was the desolation that was my personal life.

Claire spread out a red-and-white checked tablecloth. On it were plates of sandwiches, quiches, cold meats, savouries and salads.

"Hair of the dog, birthday girl?" With a sadistic grin, Charlie held aloft a bottle of chilled champagne.

I let out a long sigh and smiled weakly.

They toasted my birthday. Awkward yet loved, I let the burn of alcohol course down my throat. After an unfeasibly short time, my head magically cleared and I felt surprisingly better. I watched in wonderment as the boys fell upon the food, rogue hands snatching too much in one go.

Slightly cooler by the river, I settled back in the shade of a willow tree and watched the picnic with benign detachment.

I'd forgotten how good it felt to be part of a family, to have that sense of belonging. Temporarily, it made me feel safe, wanted and valued. *Why leave the place and the people who matter most?* I thought drowsily. Why the desperate need to challenge and confront my fears, to play out my blistering anger in the blind belief that I could change the past?

And then I saw him.

He walked down the path, head held high, sunglasses in place, newspaper in hand.

He looked oddly dressed — charcoal-grey pinstripe business suit. I wanted to say something to Claire and Charlie, but they were lost in domestic chatter, and the words refused to budge from my mouth. I slid down, flattening my body, hoping he wouldn't see me. Maybe if I kept very still he'd walk on by. Then little Harry got up and pointed to him. "Look, Dad. See the horrible man. What's wrong with his face?"

I held my breath, watched the hopeless look in Stannard's eyes, saw him turn and move towards me. He was calling now, shouting my name, yelling, steel in his voice . . .

"Kim, Kim!"

I sat bolt upright. Charlie had his hands tight on my shoulders. Claire was kneeling at my side. I looked around, feverishly scanning the woodland. No sign of Stannard. "Has he gone?" I felt extremely frightened.

"You fell asleep," Claire said soothingly. "You were dreaming, Kim."

"Was I?" I wanted so much to believe her.

"Honest." Charlie's brow was chiselled with lines. He offered me a drink of water. Taking a sip, I tried to make a joke of it. "Delirium tremens," I said, rubbing the tops of my arms. Heat spent, I felt icy inside.

Claire exchanged worried looks with Charlie. "The boys are in the playground," she said, pointing to an enclosed area nearby.

I felt cagey. Was this code for "we're going to talk"? I reached for a Scotch egg, nibbled at it.

"If it makes you feel any better," Charlie began, biting into a sandwich. "I never liked him."

"Who?" I said, bewildered.

"Chris."

"We went along with it," Claire said, "for your sake."

I stared at the pair of them not really knowing what to say. "I'm sorry, then," I said, numb. "I'd no idea." Like a wife who is the last to discover that her husband has been unfaithful, part of me closed down inside. These were my best friends and for four years they'd humoured me. Claire cast me an anxious look.

"He was secretive," Charlie said, stoutly defending his corner, "something not direct and honest about him. You never knew what he was thinking. Of course, now we know the reason why. Two-faced bastard."

Catching the mean expression in his eye, I wanted to get up and run.

"Ask him anything and he'd either be your best mate or go all mercurial and get bolshie and defensive." Charlie narrowed his eyes in a way that spooked me. "Inconsistent, if you ask me. Volatile, something missing."

I knew all this, and yes, Chris had betrayed me. He'd abandoned and hurt me deeply, but whatever I felt about Chris's behaviour, I found the way Charlie talked disturbing. If anyone should be slagging Chris off, it should be me. Nobody else had the right.

"We'd suspected for some time," Claire said.

Hurt, I rounded on her. "You're my friend. Why didn't you tell me?"

"Because it wouldn't have made a difference."

"It might have made a difference to me." My voice, against every intention, was raised, mainly because I knew I was wrong and she was right.

"We didn't know who the woman was for certain," Charlie said, clearly trying to take the heat out of the situation.

The afternoon suddenly spoiled, Claire called the boys back for birthday cake. I watched their shiny laughing faces as six token candles flittered in the sunlight. Out of steam, I blew them out after two attempts.

"Where's Chris?" Tommy said with a sly grin. Claire and Charlie exchanged uneasy glances.

"He's gone away." I thought how much I sounded like my father talking about my mother.

"Andy says you're selling up," Charlie said, once the boys were out of earshot again.

"I've got nothing to stay for." It sounded like a challenge. I supposed it was.

His pale blue eyes fastened on me. "You've got us."

Afterwards we packed up the picnic and wandered back to watch a creepy middle-aged clown. The kids ate ice cream. I passed on watching a young fire-eater and went back to the car to wait. Hopelessly adrift, I felt that my brief foray into family life was over.

Politely declining an invitation to go back to the farm, Charlie took me home after we'd first dropped off the boys and Claire en route. Conversation became stilted.

"I meant what I said, Kim."

"I know."

He looked across at me. "About you staying in Devon."

I looked straight ahead.

"If you're worried, I could always keep an eye on the place while you're away in Cheltenham."

"Thanks, but it's not necessary."

"Or, if you need any jobs done in the house . . ."

"Charlie," I pleaded, "please, let's just leave it. I can't think straight at the moment." When was the last time I'd done so?

He drove the rest of the way in silence. Pulling into Cormorants Reach, he asked when I was taking time off.

"Why?"

"Curious, that's all. Maybe we could all get together."

"All" didn't quite have the same resonance any more. I made a neutral non-committal response, said goodbye, clambered out and walked briskly inside.

Were the cushions on the sofa a little bit squashed? Slightly out of place? Imagination, I thought, nervously running my fingers over them, checking to see if they were warm. They weren't. I was definitely letting my mind run away with me.

Food holding no interest, I poured myself a glass of water, clasped it in my hands as if it were a crystal ball, and took it out onto the patio, where the heat felt more dissipated. Like a maggot in my brain, Stannard burrowed in and refused to shift. His face swam before my eyes. Good side. Bad side. The memory of his voice was strangely seductive to my ear, hypnotic even.

How, in God's name, could I get rid of it?

CHAPTER THIRTY-SIX

Sleep was so total and without dreams that, when I awoke early on Monday morning and reality kicked in, the realization that Chris had left cut through me like a sharpened blade.

When I swung my legs out of bed my stomach growled, my legs wobbled and my throat felt sore and dry, the aftermath of too much booze. Light-headed, I tottered downstairs, stood in the kitchen, munched a slice of bread and butter with disinterest, and washed it down with fruit juice. Everything and everywhere blared that I was single again.

Dressed in a pair of jeans and T-shirt, I collected several old removal boxes from the garage and started on the study. Books and papers not specific to my current work, all were whisked away. Moving on to the kitchen, I was shocked by the amount of gadgetry acquired. Milk frothers, slicing implements for every vegetable and fruit known to man, graters and separators, culinary machines, all came under close inspection. I mentally split things into three piles: stuff to be junked, non-essentials to be packed away, items to leave where they were. Feeling more ruthless than I thought possible, it occurred to me that to do my job required a modicum of toughness. Hard to confront, there were times when my efforts failed, and young women died.

After an hour and a half of clatter and bang, I lost interest and steeled myself for the onslaught of gushing and gung-ho responses from estate agents.

Yes, I knew the location was great. Yes, I knew that the property was *niche*. As a young lone female, I felt at a distinct disadvantage, talked at rather than talked to about anything from buoyant markets and profit margins to government policy. There was little consensus about the value of the property, the differential between the lowest and highest figure in the region of fifty thousand pounds. Out of the three, I decided to select the Salcombe agency because they had more flair, seemed to have better contacts outside the West Country, with a particular handle on the London market. The clincher was an open sense of humour — not particularly sound business principles but good psychology. I wished I could apply that same decisiveness to other areas of my life.

Galvanized by the departure of the last agent, I reached for my laptop, punched in stalking and, disappearing down several digital bunny holes, found myself immersed in a ton of cod-psychology. When I got to the important stuff my stomach plummeted to my toenails. Lifetime contact bans and restraining orders were routinely broken. One poor woman had been stalked for the best part of twenty years. Fuck, I thought, how does that even happen? According to some government spokesperson, a ton of money was being thrown into victim support in a bid to deal with "the problem". Fat lot of good that would do, I thought, bitterly. What women, and they were mostly women, needed was cast-iron protection. The way in which police handled the crime varied from "not bothered" to "weak" to "okay". Sentences in the 0.1 per cent of cases that led to conviction were derisory. Most striking of all, the terrible psychological toll it took on the victim. Under the intense onslaught, relationships crumbled and careers foreshortened. Having one's mind routinely taken apart reduced previously reasonable and rational individuals to ruins and shadows of their former selves.

I sat back, utterly powerless.

About to shut down my laptop, my eye caught sight of a police report of a missing woman from Exeter. Gaynor Lassiter had vanished without trace the year before. Alarming as this was, the suggestion that she'd been stalked prior to her disappearance made my eyes revolve inside my skull.

I read on: Gaynor was a thirty-five-year-old medical research assistant when she went missing on her way home from work one October evening. She was last seen wearing a fake fur coat with a long brown skirt and tan leather boots. She was described as having dark hair and of a medium build, whatever that meant.

Was there a link, or was I grasping at a connection that didn't exist? Exeter was scarily close, geographically speaking. The more I thought about it, the less certain I felt. What I needed was an expert eye. Scouring my address book, I picked up the phone and called a number I hadn't used in years.

"Professor Fallon?"

"Kim? What a lovely surprise."

"I wondered if we could talk?"

Unabashed by my sudden desire for contact, he said, "Of course. What are you doing now?"

Going crazy. "Not a huge amount."

"Got time for a late lunch?"

"Today?"

"Absolutely."

"I'd be so grateful."

"I'll tell Iris straightaway."

* * *

Skirting Exeter, I could not budge the disappearance of Gaynor Lassiter from my brain. No body had been found, so there was a chance she was still alive. Although, nine months is a long time to go missing. Maybe she'd done a runner, like Chris, except it didn't compute with the stalking aspect of her disappearance.

More than a little unsettled, I flew off the M5 at 11A and almost doubled back on myself to the capital of the Cotswolds, Cirencester. Shrouded in heat-haze, the countryside became more undulating as I approached the pretty market town.

Parking in the main car park, I walked through the square and down narrow streets in the direction of the Bathurst estate. Set back from the road, with hanging baskets and weeping figs, the Fallons' Cotswold stone cottage was distinct.

Robert Fallon opened the front door and ambled out to greet me. In his late sixties, a large man with soft benign features, he'd changed little since the days he'd lectured at Leicester University. Thinner on top, jowly, he still presented a commanding figure.

"Come inside out of the heat. Hope you don't mind eating salad. Iris thought it too hot for anything more substantial."

"Sounds lovely."

Sublimely cool inside, the Fallons' home smelled of geraniums. I gave Iris a pot of clotted Devon cream.

Like her husband, Iris Fallon was well built. She had remarkably unwrinkled features and soft blue eyes that peered through tortoise-shell spectacles. Her mouth was small and she wore peach-coloured lipstick.

"You're looking well, Kim," she said.

Unable to tell whether it was a genuine compliment or an icebreaker, I forced a smile.

Lunch was convivial, the conversation uncontroversial. After coffee, Fallon suggested we take a stroll in the garden.

"We can walk down to the brook. It's quite pleasant in the shade."

Iris tactfully said that she would stay to wash up, declining my offer of help.

The heat blasted us as we crossed the courtyard but once we were safely under a canopy of trees, the air felt fresher. This was my big moment. This was what I'd come for. I told him about everything that had happened to me, including Chris leaving. I told him about Stannard and being stalked.

"Stalking is still uncharted territory," Fallon began. "There is research but, as usual, it's difficult to find funding. There are exceptions, yet most stalkers are men. They tend to be devious and extremely intelligent. Although the reasons for the behaviour are varied, there's one common theme."

"What's that?"

"Rejection."

I lowered my head. Fallon didn't change step, didn't miss a beat.

"They fall roughly into three groups," he continued. "Former intimates who cannot accept that a relationship is over. The zealous type who's never met the object of his affection or has only come across her in passing, maybe a smile across a supermarket counter, or a brief exchange of conversation on the bus. Lastly, we have the deluded erotomaniac, who again has no prior relationship to his victim but is convinced that she's in love with him, or would be given the right circumstances. I don't need to tell you that human beings rarely fall neatly into any of these categories. There's some variation but, broadly speaking, that's the rough spec."

"Any evidence of personality disorders, psychiatric problems, schizophrenia, for instance?"

"Some, but not exclusively. Have you gone to the police, Kim?"

"I have. It didn't really help because of lack of evidence."

We carried on walking. The ground was pitted and dry and difficult to cross. Eventually the path curved gracefully as it made its slow descent to the brook.

"And you genuinely believe your stalker is this Stannard fellow?"

I spread my hands in frustration. "I can't see who else fits the profile."

"That doesn't necessarily mean he's your man."

I stopped in my tracks. "Surely, after all I've told you . . ." My voice tailed off into the lengthening silence. He touched me lightly on my back.

"It makes me so damned angry!" I burst out.

"Then you know how your stalker feels."

I flashed him a sharp look. Fallon smiled. "It wasn't a vindication. At heart this is a power struggle. Throw into the mix that he's both unpredictable and a fantasist."

"A fantasist?" I remembered Stannard's admission of daydreams.

"He wants to reduce and diminish you, piece by piece, until you become blank so that he can colour you in with all the attributes he finds attractive and appealing to him. He doesn't care if you crack up. It's a turn-on simply knowing that he can find ways to guarantee he's never out of your mind."

I let out a small gasp and told him about the woman who'd disappeared.

"Very unfortunate and, sadly, an all-too-common scenario. Most likely unconnected though."

"You think?"

"I'm not a betting man," he said cautiously, "but I'd say so. Quite understandable you're highly tuned in to such a situation, of course."

"But stalking *is* often a precursor to something worse, isn't it?" I said doggedly.

"In worst-case scenarios, it can culminate in abduction, rape, torture and murder. The flipside of love is hate. But you know this already, don't you, Kim?"

I nodded, humbled by his ability to see right through me, maybe the only person who ever had. "You're not making me feel any better."

When Fallon looked into my eyes his expression was grave. "I'm trying to make you see what you're up against."

Something awkward caught in the back of my throat. "There must be recognizable stages of behaviour." It was like facing a terminal disease, each level signifying a critical escalation.

"The deadly stage is when he realizes that he really can't have you."

"And when will I know he's made the transition?"

"He'll up the ante without warning."

And I will be prepared.

"You've come here to estimate your chances of success. Am I right?"

"I need to know if I can win."

"You can't," he said bluntly. "You have to hand control to those who can: the police."

It wasn't what I wanted to hear. Fallon sussed it. "Stannard, if that's who it is, presents you with the ultimate mind game and you're secretly fascinated by it . . ."

I almost stamped my foot. Hadn't Chris implied the same? "That's not true. I didn't seek this. I never encouraged it. I don't want it."

"You regard him as a challenge," Robert said, his voice stern.

"I've never run from anything in my life."

"I understand that, my dear."

Tears pricked my eyes. One trickled down my cheek. I pushed it away, hoping Robert hadn't noticed.

"*Don't* be seduced, Kim. If you go after your stalker in a blind attempt to convert him, you'll be playing straight into his hands. You already understand a little of what makes this man tick, but always remember, in his eyes, he's doing nothing wrong. It's all quite rational within the context of his personality. He's really quite impervious to any form of deterrence. He enjoys what he's doing too much."

"So where does that leave me?" To my annoyance, my voice came out as a pathetic cry. "Do I let him carry on? Do I change my life? Move away? What do I do? I can't stand by and fail to act. I *have* to stop him." *Crack him before he cracks me.*

"Deep down, you know that's impossible. Has it occurred to you that maybe you want payback, not for what he's done, but for everything else that's gone wrong in your life?"

I was open-mouthed.

"You're a victim . . ."

"Oh Christ, Robert, not that—"

He put up the flat of his hand. "And deserve to be listened to, but not by your stalker. Go back to the police before it escalates."

I laughed with derision. "They've dealt with the matter. It's closed. If I go back now, they'll say I'm making a fuss."

"Then talk to someone in higher authority; I could make some calls, pull strings."

I declined his kind offer. "Just suppose I go back to the police," I said, as if seriously considering the possibility. "And they nail him, then what?"

"The judiciary step in." He glanced away. I was quick to pick up on it.

"And do what exactly? Take him off the streets for six months?"

"Judges can and do hand out lengthy custodial sentences."

"Only if a stalker threatens violence. You know how it works, Robert. All the stalker has to do is appoint a sharp-thinking lawyer to defend his corner. Someone," I said, my brain hooked on Gavin Chadwick, "who will state that his client is innocent, misunderstood and a victim of miscarriage of justice."

Fallon's response was late. "I hear you, but don't, for God's sake, think that by speaking to Stannard, or whoever your stalker is, he'll go away."

Who said anything about talking to him? I thought darkly. I wanted to embarrass, shame and scare the living crap out of him. I wanted him to leave me alone.

CHAPTER THIRTY-SEVEN

I parked down a side street and arrived at the apartment block shortly after three thirty. Lizzie's door was resolutely shut. I contemplated the outcome of the discussions that had taken place behind it. No matter what Lizzie said, they'd sell. I couldn't blame them. As soon as Stannard moved in, I'd have to sell up too — unless I could coerce him to pull out.

Entering the flat, the stench hit me as if I'd been pushed head first into a cesspool. Suspicion wired me for sound. Reduced to its essence by the sweltering heat, the smell was sour, rotting and faecal.

Clapping a hand to my mouth, I searched for the one thing that was wrong, my eyes fixing on a thick dark fog of bluebottles. Beneath, parked on the hearth, a large black plastic bucket, the sort that might be used for coal or cleaning the car. Placed with precision, painting directly above, framed by the fake marble mantelpiece, it sat squat and glowering. I approached warily, thumb and finger pinching my nostrils. Flies lifted in unison and buzzed around my head in a frenzied cloud. Batting them madly away, I peered inside the bucket, my jaw tensed to stifle a cry. Filled to the brim, festering in the heat, glistening intestines, bones, blood, hair and, if I wasn't mistaken, shit. A single eye from a butchered cow stared up from the surface, like a macabre piece of conceptual art.

I sprinted to the bathroom, resisted the urge to be violently ill and splashed my neck and face with water. I wanted to be rid of his games, his twisted calling cards, HIM. Wrapping a towel around the lower half of my face as if about to run through fire, I tore back into the sitting room, picked up the bucket and, dashing back to the bathroom, threw the contents down the lavatory, flushing it three times.

Then gaped at what I'd done.

Anything he sends, bag it, Simon had told me in no uncertain terms, and in five fevered seconds I'd destroyed the best evidence I had, my instinct to wipe out the traces stronger than pragmatism. To do anything else seemed unthinkable, and what was I supposed to do? Hang on to it? *Oh, excuse me, officer, I've just had a bucket of guts delivered.* Hysteria nibbling at my brain, I laughed out loud.

I threw open all the windows, filled the bucket to the brim with hot water and disinfectant and walked round, checking the points of entry for signs of break-in. There was no escaping the fact that someone had gained access to my flat. He'd already set a precedent by driving my car. He could easily walk in again, do what he liked, when he liked, only this time when I was there.

I left the apartment, walked quickly at first, then, sure that I wasn't being followed, slowed down, sauntered almost, making sure that my movements did not betray my intention.

Cutting down an alley from Lypiatt Road, I crossed over into Tivoli and a short parade of shops that included two estate agents and a locksmith. Simmering anger gave in to eerie calm. Who the fuck had done this?

A locksmith promised to come out the next day. When Jim called I didn't state that I was in Cheltenham.

"Any news on Chris?" he asked.

"He left me."

"God, I'm sorry, Kim."

"No need."

"It wasn't what I was expecting."

What were you expecting? "It's fine."

"So you're on your own?"

Prickling with suspicion and hating myself for it, I said, "No."

"Good. This thing with Stannard . . ."

"Don't worry. He's back in the box."

"Really?"

"Yeah," and I hung up.

Crossing back into town, I decided on a process of elimination. To be sure about Stannard I had to test my theory to destruction.

I considered the weapons at my disposal, which were:

Observation: study the enemy in his environment.

Knowledge: find out everything about him, including his routines and who he hung out with.

But the most powerful trick in my armoury was one I'd studied for all my adult life. I knew its stressors and what drove it to breaking point. The human mind was indeed the deadliest weapon known to man. It was also the most vulnerable.

CHAPTER THIRTY-EIGHT

Following up on Simon's information I went online and discovered that Stannard's current home in Wellington Square was a Grade II detached villa and that Stannard Property Developments was situated adjacent to the town hall in Imperial Square, one of a row of three-storey buildings with both residential and commercial use.

Mid-afternoon, Stannard HQ looked like any other set of offices in Cheltenham with fine ironwork and Ionic-style columns.

The large window fronting the building was open and, from the street, I could see a decorative palm in a huge ornamental pot, a desk with a computer monitor, several smartly dressed figures moving around. It looked honest and respectable.

Shortly after five, Stannard and his trademark sunglasses emerged. From the municipal gardens opposite, I watched him pause, gather himself against the wall of heat, before trotting down the stone steps and turning right into Oriel Road and in the direction of the city centre. Brushing off the grass from my jeans, I stood up and followed.

Dropping back far enough so as not to seem conspicuous, letting my attention be caught every so often by a piece of architecture, I experienced a swell of power and wondered if Stannard felt that same lick of excitement when he'd followed me.

At no time did he look round or break pace, nothing to suggest he was suspicious. His destination was a bar off the high street near Cambray Place. I went into another opposite, ordered a soft drink and took a window seat. An hour later, Stannard emerged and I took up the chase at a distance as he retraced his steps to the office where he spent fifteen minutes pacing, small cigar in his mouth, phone stuck to his ear, before picking up his charcoal-grey Maserati from a reserved area behind the block. I made a note of the registration and, with the sense of a job well done, cruised back to the flat.

A fermented, cloyingly sweet odour clung to the room in spite of my efforts to eradicate it. Without the locks changed and the alarm system yet in place, I spent the night on high alert, mobile in hand, half of me waiting for a light to shine underneath the door, the redistribution of air, the smell of a stalker disguised as a stranger. I woke early, eyes grainy from lack of sleep.

At half past eight, the alarm was fitted and a guy with a port-wine stain on his face came to change the locks. I made him tea and we chatted, and I felt the fleeting comfort of having a human being to talk to about nothing in particular, nothing that mattered.

By quarter to ten, I was sitting in a low-grade car rental agency with a bloke called Bill booking a dark blue Ford Focus for the day. An hour later I'd parked four cars down from Stannard's beautiful vehicle, waiting for the great man to go out and about his business. Fifteen minutes later, my vigil was rewarded.

I pulled out of the parking lot and followed the Maserati as it headed through town towards Pittville, a leafy enclave with a park and lake and lovely houses. The centre was dense with traffic, aiding rather than impeding my progress; the much faster car could no more escape than the Focus. Eyes boring into the back of Stannard's head, I attempted to read his thoughts, wondering what his next move might be. He rarely, if at all, looked in his rear-view mirror, which suited me.

After half a mile or so, we passed the Pump Room, a surviving spa building with its green dome and colonnaded facade. The road opened up and the Maserati surged forward with a full-throttled, sophisticated growl. From the direction in which we were travelling, I estimated Stannard was heading for Prestbury, the site of National Hunt Racing, but the Massa veered off, making a sharp left, picking up speed, powering along a straight piece of road as though the Grim Reaper sat in the driving seat. About to stick my foot down I was cut up by a courier. A quick exchange of horns and hand gestures, and the Italian stallion had faded to a speck in the distance.

Facing a crossroads, no car in sight, not knowing which route to take, I tapped the steering wheel with frustration. To turn left would take me back towards town. Turn right, out of town altogether. Had Stannard clocked me? Had he deliberately led me astray?

He specializes in old houses, does them up, full architectural spec.

I pulled forward and onto the Evesham Road with its constellation of old properties, as polished and polite as a wealthy silver-haired pensioner. Scanning the driveways and restricted parking spaces, my hopes thinned. Depressed, I pulled over with the intention of getting out of the car and stretching my legs. That's when I noticed the *Property For Sale* sign half obscured by a neighbouring home's scaffolding, and Stannard's car parked in the drive. Called Rowanbank, the house, a fabulous specimen of faded glory, looked tired, the roof worn, the windows giving every appearance of throwing themselves out of the brickwork and into the unruly borders.

Suppressing a streak of triumph, I noted the agent and, picking up the Focus, made my way back to the centre. Dropping the car at the rental company, I returned to the place I called home.

Lizzie was coming out as I was going in. Her cheeks flashed the colour of fresh meat. I didn't need to ask for the decision. It was already clear.

"I've spoken to Pete. No dice, I'm afraid. We're desperate to sell. Sorry." Lizzie's voice was like a candle about to snuff out.

I nodded gravely. "When?"

"He wants an early completion." Lizzie shifted her weight from one foot to the other, her face tight. "What will you do?"

"I'm working on it." I flicked a confident smile. "I don't blame you in the least. Better go. Stuff to do." I spun on my heel, walked away, leaving Lizzie to the exciting prospect of a new start.

Back in the flat, I picked up the phone and called Fairweather and Co. They weren't particularly helpful. "Rowanbank is already under offer," a monotone voice explained.

"That's not what the board says."

"We haven't had a chance to change it yet."

"But until the property's sold it's still up for grabs, isn't it?"

A disgruntled sigh coursed down the telephone wire. "An offer has been accepted by Mrs Foley. To allow someone else to view at this delicate stage in the negotiations would be entirely improper."

I was getting the impression that Stannard was quite an important fish.

"Thanks for being so candid," I said, polite. I wondered what time would be best to catch Mrs Foley in.

CHAPTER THIRTY-NINE

Taking a deep breath, I knocked on Heather Foley's front door the next morning and stood back and waited. I felt supremely guilty for conning my way into the woman's home and reckoned I'd be given five minutes, tops, before being told to sling my hook.

A woman in her middle fifties, wide-hipped and of a stout build, opened the door. Her polite smile broadened then narrowed into a grimace as the blue eyes zoom-lensed onto my neck and the injured side of my face. For a second or two, Mrs Foley appeared unable to string a sentence together. I may as well have had the word *mutant* written on my forehead.

I took a step forward, threw her a bright smile. "Hope I'm not too early." I followed up with a firm handshake.

"Not at all," Mrs Foley stammered. She gestured to me to enter, walked halfway down a cavernous hall and turned on her heel as if she'd had second thoughts. "As I explained on the phone, Rowanbank *is* under offer . . ."

"But you said you're unhappy with the terms."

Heather Foley ran a manicured hand through her tastefully tinted hair and, suddenly weary and careworn, crumpled. I was oddly reminded of my mother at the tearoom.

"To tell the truth, I feel besieged, Miss Slade. It's not easy when you're a woman on your own." A lost look entered her eyes. "It's difficult to find people to talk to, people one can trust, which is why I decided to let you view. Most unethical, of course, but then I'm not too sure either my estate agent or my prospective buyer are quite as scrupulous as they would have me believe."

"You mean Mr Stannard?"

Heather Foley blinked in surprise.

"I'm afraid I wasn't as honest as I should have been when I called. I don't want to buy your house, Mrs Foley. I want to talk to you about Kyle Stannard."

I watched the woman's startled reaction. The mouth widened into an O, her head thrust forward, her hands clenched into fists. "What a damned cheek."

"I couldn't agree with you more," I said softly.

Mrs Foley's eyes narrowed. "Are you a police officer?"

"I'm a psychologist."

"Now you've lost me."

"Mr Stannard is causing difficulties for both of us. From what you've said, I think we could help each other. Naturally, anything you say would be treated in the strictest confidence."

Mrs Foley gave me an appraising look, her face masked by uncertainty. "All right," she said slowly. "You'd better come into the drawing room. I've a feeling I may need to sit down."

* * *

"Call his bluff," I said stoutly.

I'd spent the past hour listening to Heather Foley's story, her failed marriage, her loss of confidence, her desperate desire to rebuild her life, including her hope of a facelift "to give her a fresh start", and Stannard's miserable attempt to beat her down. Once she'd started unloading, she was unstoppable.

"I thought he was so nice. He had a lovely voice, especially with the damage to the left side of his mouth," she said, seemingly oblivious to my own sensibilities. "And he dressed *so* well," she said, barely pausing for breath. "Then I received a call from the estate agent with an offer that was, frankly, an insult. I've got visions of being trapped here for the rest of my days." Her eyes filled with tears. "I'm no good on my own. I absolutely hate it."

I empathized with her deep loneliness. From the torrent of words it was clear that this was the first time the woman had opened up about her abrupt change of circumstances to anyone — so much easier to confide all to someone you're unlikely to see again.

"Did Mr Stannard contact you directly with the offer?"

"Damian Fairweather, that's the estate agent," she explained.

"You've not heard another word from Stannard?"

She shook her head.

"What did your agent advise?"

"To accept the offer. I rather got the impression that he does good business with Mr Stannard."

No surprise there, I thought. "If you're unhappy, say you've changed your mind and ask Stannard to improve on it."

"But he might back out." Heather Foley twisted her hands.

"He might, but there will be other buyers, and if you're not entirely happy with Fairweather, bin him. This is estate agent city. You could try one of a dozen other agents in town." I immediately thought of Simon. "In any case, I think, from what you've said, Stannard is genuinely interested. You say he wrote a card."

"I've got it somewhere." Heather left the room briefly, her sharp footsteps reverberating down the hall. I got up and looked out of the window, admiring the row of wonderfully appointed houses on the other side. With a little TLC, Rowanbank could be magnificent. I couldn't fault Stannard's taste or business acumen.

Heather Foley reappeared, brandishing the postcard. On one side, a picture of a grand double-fronted house in Wellington Square, just as Simon had informed me, an address and phone number printed on the blank side, below a handwritten *thank you* message in black pen, large and fluid. I read it twice, salted it away and handed the card back. "He definitely wants it."

"But at a price," Heather said with frustration.

"At *your* price. Don't let him toy with you. You've already come down forty grand. He's trying it on, taking advantage of your situation. Don't let him."

Heather's eyes hardened. She sat up straight, bristling with new determination. "You're absolutely right. I'll speak to my lawyer today."

"This is your home, your future, your game," I insisted. "You set the rules."

Heather beamed. Her eyes radiated fun and youthfulness. She patted me on the knee, a clear expression of sisterhood.

"We must share a toast."

"It's a little early," I said, glancing at my watch: not yet eleven o'clock.

"Nonsense, I've had rather a nice Chardonnay chilling in the fridge for far too long." She got up, smoothed the creases in her skirt, her face flushed with excitement, and took two steps. Without warning, her face briefly clouded, a look of worry invading her features. "I'm so sorry. I seem to have done all the talking. It's such a relief, you see. You don't mind, do you?"

"Not in the least, and you have my word it won't go outside these four walls."

"I suppose you're used to it, people's confessions, their anxieties. You never did say how Mr Stannard upset you."

I looked up at her squarely. "I think we could do with that drink first."

* * *

I called Simon, explaining Stannard's method of operation, without making any specific reference to Rowanbank.

"He's not doing anything illegal."

"It's sharp practice."

"Name of the game, I'm afraid."

"Taking advantage of a vulnerable middle-aged woman?"

"Happens all the time. She doesn't have to accept." Simon sounded irritated. I wondered if I'd gone too far and cast a slur on his new profession. "In fact the vendor could be accused of encouraging gazumping," he added. When a vendor accepts a higher offer after already agreeing a sale price with a buyer, I registered. Reluctantly, I had to agree that Simon was right. "I'm sure Stannard knows what he's about," he continued. "His stepfather's Geoffrey Mallory."

"Who's he?"

"*The* criminal defence lawyer. He's a KC."

I gave a start. So that's what Stannard meant by *moving in legal circles*. No wonder he felt invincible. "Why didn't you tell me before?"

"I didn't know before. You're still convinced Stannard's your stalker?"

I hesitated. In my few sane and honest moments, I had to admit that Stannard wasn't ticking quite so many boxes. Weird and obsessive for sure, and it would be one hell of a coincidence if I had two men fixated on me, but maybe that's where the confusion lay.

"Kim?" Simon pressed.

"Jury's out," I said, evasive. "Where does Mr Mallory hang out?"

"Works in London, though I think it's more part-time these days. He's got a huge pile near Bourton-on-the-Water, at Great Rissington."

"What about Stannard's mother?"

"Haven't a clue."

I wondered what had happened to Stannard's blood father. Simon jabbed through my thoughts.

"You're barking up the wrong tree, Kim." Did Simon still have Chris in the frame, or did he have an ulterior motive? I needed to let Simon and Molly know that Chris had left me but, fearing a similar reaction to Claire and Charlie's, kept this aspect of my personal life private.

"Means I'll have to look elsewhere, then," I said, ending the call.

CHAPTER FORTY

I stood in the gated square opposite Stannard's home, an elegant villa with shutters and sash windows, and three stone steps and a painted balustrade leading to the teal-coloured front door. As soon as he left I crossed over to take a closer look at his habitat.

The air was close and sticky and gave every indication that the day would be swathed again in brilliant sunshine.

Rippling with nerves, I glanced around. A cat stretched in the morning sun. Nobody about. No noise of human endeavour, only the sound of birdsong. Emboldened, taking quick steps, I sped across the herringbone-patterned brick drive, trampled a border and peered inside a downstairs window. With minimal furnishings, no ornaments or keepsakes, no paintings adorning the wall, the vibe was Spartan. Crossing to the other side of the front door, I peered into another room, which housed an ultra-modern glass-topped table, eight chrome and leather-backed chairs and a light wood sideboard. Functional. Practical. No soul.

I slipped across the drive towards a wrought-iron side gate. Taking a swift look over my shoulder, I clambered over and dropped heavily onto a paved cutout, narrowly missing a Cheltenham wheelie bin. Thick bushes and hedges formed a natural boundary with the property next door. Beyond, a walled garden filled with borders, cascading rose bushes and fruit trees laden with apples, plums and pears.

A conservatory filled with rattan furniture jutted out from the main house. With double wooden doors obscuring the view further inside, I walked around the conservatory and tried the back door. Firmly locked, all windows closed.

Shielding my eyes with the flat of my hand, I squinted through a kitchen window, the glare of reflected sunshine temporarily distorting my vision. When I could finally see, breath exited my body in one great whoosh. The cradle of his obsession: dozens of photographs. I expected to see my own image among them, but only one subject mattered: Stannard. In black and white, and colour. Stannard as he once looked. Stannard with his amazingly symmetrical features. Stannard audacious, charismatic and powerful.

Shaken, I took a smart step back.

Something snagged my peripheral vision.

Heart rate quickening, I shot across the lawn and disappeared through a tangle of trees into a jungle of hedges and shrubs, my gaze fixed on the apex of a roofline almost invisible from the house. The closer I got, pieces of an architectural jigsaw took shape and form — an upper elevation, stone, glass, wood, until a small, perfectly conceived stone-built two-storey detached coach house emerged out of the foliage.

What secrets did it hold?

Pressing my face to the glass, my jaw slackened. Strikingly, the room was empty, its whitewashed walls naked apart from several large framed photographic prints that stole my breath away. Deep in my groin, I felt a stir, a suppressed feeling of arousal that shook me to the core.

On the farthest wall, Stannard was bare-chested. Breathtakingly sexy, eyes narrowed, looking into the sun. A second print depicted a mean and moody Stannard leaning against the bonnet of a Jaguar convertible. By squeezing myself into the corner of the window and twisting my head, I could make out the third: Stannard dressed in a suit, white open-necked shirt, head tilted back, throat exposed, mouth wide as if he were letting out a roar of laughter, his expression one of pure exhilaration. I could almost hear him and, in that sublime moment, I recognized his immense joy, his lust for life and blatant belief that he was invincible. It was like standing in a place of worship before a fallen angel.

I lost all sense of time. Cast under his spell, I was transfixed.

CHAPTER FORTY-ONE

As if I'd awoken from a coma, I took to my heels. Shooting over the gate, feet landing sure and firm, I fled across the road and narrowly missed an elderly woman with ruby-tinted cheeks and a painted mouth to match. A bony hand shot out and clamped onto my right elbow. Her gaze drilled into me.

"You were snooping."

"I don't know what you mean." I tried to extract myself from her fearsome grip. Her fingernails, like talons, dug deeper.

"I watched you. You were prying."

"I wasn't doing anything."

"Explain that to the police."

I froze. The old woman released her grasp, triumph in her eyes.

As I pounded out of the square, not looking back, her yell sounded over my head: "They're watching you."

I ran through streets bustling with humanity. Losing Stannard was not so easy. My brain exploded with his image. Stannard standing alone, solitary by nature, a guy who told the outside world that he was sexy, no pushover, fun. This was the nature of the man, the make up of his identity.

All twisted and crushed.

Embarrassed for dwelling on his former glory like a ghoulish voyeur, ashamed by my accusations regarding a man who had suffered so much, I was as certain as I could be that I'd read Stannard completely wrong. Speculation followed by assumption, fuelled by fear and paranoia, equals one hell of a mistake. And I knew exactly who I needed to see to confirm it: someone I should have spoken to before.

* * *

Kyle Stannard was in his car when he picked up the call from Mrs Foley via his hands-free. Damian Fairweather had assured him that the deal was in the bag and he greeted her warmly, a pleasantry that was not reciprocated.

"Your offer is not acceptable," she launched in. "Unless I receive the assurance of the full asking price, within the next twenty-four hours, I will assume that you are no longer interested in purchasing the property. After that, Rowanbank will no longer be on the market. Good day."

Astonished, he wondered what, or rather who, had changed her mind.

* * *

Cathy viewed me with surprise. "I thought you were in Devon."

"Splitting my time," I said breezily.

"Something wrong?" Cathy's expression pierced me.

I broke into a defensive smile. "No, not at all."

She looked unconvinced.

"Had to pop back to collect something." I bowled along, hoping that if I kept talking, the flimsiness of my excuse would stand up to scrutiny. "Is Kirsten around, only, as I'm passing, I'd like a quick word?"

Cathy's expression remained cautious. "I think so. Want me to go and see?"

I gave a no-rush shrug and waited. Minutes later, Cathy returned, Kirsten at her side, bloated with sullen disdain.

"Sorry to drag you away, Kirsten, but I wondered if we could have a chat? We could sit outside on the lawn." I looked to Cathy for approval. She gave a brief nod, her expression indecipherable.

Kirsten mumbled, "Whatever" and loped towards the door. She wore sunglasses and a long dress with flowing sleeves that concealed her bony limbs. I threw an awkward smile and followed. We walked past a bush of crimson-coloured flowers, towards a neatly trimmed lawn, where Kirsten sat down on the grass.

"Thought you were away." She drew her knees up to her chin and fixed her gaze on the lawn.

"I am, sort of." I knelt down opposite her. "How are you keeping?"

"All right."

"The thing is, Kirsten, I need your help."

The girl looked up slowly. It was impossible to read her eyes behind the shades.

"You must have met a lot of people when you were modelling — photographers, make-up artists, agents, other models."

"Some."

"Did you ever come across a male model by the name of Kyle Stannard?"

"No."

"You're sure?"

"Means nothing to me."

The words were clear, firm and loud. Kirsten's face showed no colour, no giveaway facial tic.

"Maybe if I describe him to you."

"Tall, dark and handsome, like thousands of others."

"So you *did* come across someone like him."

"All the time." Kirsten suppressed a yawn. I noticed the whiteness of the girl's knuckles, the way her fingers twisted the fabric of her dress. Brittle.

"This man was special," I said, emphatic. "Stood out from the crowd. He had presence and charisma."

Kirsten glanced away with a thin smile. "Have you any idea how many model agencies there are in London?"

"We're looking top end. Your notes state that you worked for Visage, one of the most select and successful modelling agencies in the country." From a professional standpoint, what I was doing was unforgivable. I was breaking every ethical code, yet I stood to lose everything if I didn't establish the truth. "He worked for Quartz. Are you sure you never came across him?"

"Positive."

"He's not the sort of guy you'd forget. He has an aura about him. Still does, even though he got his face kicked in."

Alarm careered across the girl's features. That got to her, I thought, not understanding how. "He's not in the game anymore. Works as a property developer in town."

"Here?" Kirsten's limbs tensed. Her face pinched. "You know him, then, this guy?"

"Kind of."

She fell quiet. The air hummed with heat. She pulled up a clump of grass then let it fall, pulled up another. "Did he say he knew me?"

"No."

The aloof expression quickly resumed. I studied the girl's shrunken features and saw the buttoned-down misery in her expression. I'd hardly tapped the surface of what was going on in Kirsten's mind. But Kirsten *was* hiding something, and secrets required a high degree of mental agility to conceal.

"Kirsten, I want to help you. But you have to trust me too. I get the impression that you're holding out on me, that there's something you're not telling, something you feel bad about, maybe something you haven't even told your parents." Unethical in every aspect, I knew that not only had I crossed a line, I'd travelled several miles on the other side.

Kirsten threw the handful of grass across the lawn, her lips parted and then she seemed to check herself and change her mind. She looked back at the Lodge. "There's nothing to tell and, if that's all, I'm due to see Jim. He doesn't like people being late."

CHAPTER FORTY-TWO

The phone rang. I picked up, Jim's voice at the other end of the line unusually frosty.

"I understand you came to see Kirsten this afternoon."

"Yes, I did."

"But you're on leave."

"Yes. I—"

"Would you mind telling me what was discussed?"

"We talked about Visage."

"The modelling agency she worked for?"

"That's right."

"Why?"

"Because it has a bearing on her current condition." I flushed at my own spin.

"We're all aware of that," Jim said, terse. "And?"

"I didn't get very far."

"How far?"

"I think she's hiding something."

"What exactly?" Jim's tone was highly critical. "Can you be specific?"

"I don't think the modelling agency was responsible for precipitating her weight loss."

"Then what was?"

"That's what I'm not sure about." I wanted to tell Jim about Stannard and the way Kirsten reacted, but it would be seen in a bad light. The bald truth was that I'd exploited my professional position and broken a professional code of conduct. And I'd underestimated Jim's sleuthing abilities.

"This wouldn't be connected to you, by any chance?"

"No, I—"

"I don't know what went on this afternoon apart from the fact that you hounded Kirsten about Kyle Stannard."

"Hounded?"

"What the hell did you think you were playing at?"

"Jim, please . . ."

"Whatever you said has had profound consequences."

This brought me up short and I stopped digging. "What sort of consequences?"

"Kirsten slashed her wrists half an hour after you left."

My heart somersaulted and leaped into my throat. "Oh my God, is she all right?"

"Fortunately, yes. Cathy got to her before she'd lost too much blood. She's in Cheltenham General in a fairly poor mental state. As you'd imagine, her parents are extremely concerned."

"Jim, I'm so terribly sorry. I don't know what else to say. Do you want me to talk to the Mathersons?"

"Christ Almighty, no."

"They have no idea I spoke to her?"

Jim deflected the question by asking another. "Why did you talk to her about Stannard?"

"I thought it might help," I said lamely, "what with them both involved in the modelling business."

"Help *you*," he hissed in a withering tone. "If you have a problem, you sort it out, understand? You're supposed to be taking a break. You're supposed to be getting your act together."

"That's not fair."

"Neither is what you did this afternoon." I fell silent, braced for the next body blow. "God alone knows what will happen. Did the word 'ethics' ever cross your mind? What are you trying to do, throw your entire career away?"

"I'm sorry." I was genuinely mortified.

"I don't know what personal axe you have to grind, or how you think your situation has any bearing on Kirsten's, but don't you dare involve and interfere with my patients. Have you got that?" he barked.

"It won't happen again. Will you let me know how she is?"

"I think it best you stay off the case." His voice was full of winter chill. "I'm sure that's what the Mathersons would want. There will have to be an internal inquiry."

"I understand." I felt bleak and guilty. Never in a million years did I ever imagine that I would breach the professional code for my own personal crusade, yet that was exactly what I'd done. "Will you be speaking to the team at Bayshill?"

"I've already been in touch."

My stomach gave a queasy lurch. "What was the reaction?"

"The one you'd expect." He cut the call.

I dropped down onto a chair. Stupid, stupid, stupid. What a terrible mess, and all my creation. Poor Kirsten. My crass approach had probably set the girl back weeks or even months. Understandably, my reputation was sunk and my job was on the line, but, measured against what I'd done to Kirsten, it was of little consequence.

I tried to focus, to analyse what Kirsten had said, and more importantly, to read what her silences signified.

Snippets of Stannard's conversation reverberated through my head. *Secrets and guilt.* But whose and what?

If their paths had crossed, and I was pretty sure they had, Kirsten would have been around fourteen or fifteen years old, Stannard considerably older. Kirsten, a gauche and impressionable teenager; Stannard, forceful, controlling and arrogant.

Now what? I'd wanted a conversation with Kirsten in the hope that it would reveal Stannard and the man behind the myth. Jim wanted an enquiry into my conduct, in the light of which Bayshill were bound to reconsider my contract. Meanwhile, my stalker was still out there. Somewhere.

Families were the best repositories for secrets. Stannard's ancestral family home in Great Rissington might yet hold a clue, but first I was going to London. I owed Kirsten that much.

CHAPTER FORTY-THREE

The Visage Modelling Agency lay behind a darkened glass exterior in smart SW7. I walked up and down the street several times, mentally cranking myself up to enter. By asking for help from an organization whose ethos I viewed as pernicious to the majority of my clients, I was selling out. Worse, I'd actually taken special care with my appearance. It's not what you look like that counts, I'd robustly maintain to clients, it's who you are. Yeah, right.

The vibe inside was plush and luxurious. Soft, caramel-coloured leather chairs rested against dark walls decked with starlets. The silence intimidated. I'd expected a place crawling with life. Maybe the inner sanctum was more vibrant.

A sultry-looking girl in her late twenties flicked her gaze up from behind a smart iMac. Poised and stately, she stared at my neck with something close to disbelief.

I counterattacked with a smile. "I wonder if you can help me." The girl responded by adopting a mask of impenetrability.

"You had a young model working for you a few years ago by the name of Kirsten Matherson."

No change in expression. No reaction.

"She would have been about fourteen or fifteen."

"I recall."

"You knew her?"

"Are you from the press?" Dark eyes thinned.

"No."

"Police?"

"No."

"So you are . . . ?"

"Kim Slade, I'm a clinical psychologist and I'm treating Kirsten." I shuddered at the lie. If Jim had his way, I'd have nothing more to do with her ever again. Because of my folly there was the serious possibility that I'd done untold harm to her. "Is it possible to talk to someone who knew her well?"

"You need to speak to Flick Sutherland."

"Thank you." I took a seat.

The girl resumed her duties. I waited, patient. She took out a pot of nail varnish and began to paint her nails. After a couple of minutes, she looked over at me. "Flick's no longer with the agency."

I stood up, affixed a smile to my mouth and said, "Any idea where I might find her?"

"No." Lights off, nobody in, shutters down.

"It's important," I said. "Kirsten's not at all well. She's in hospital right now. I could really do with some help here."

Clearly unhappy with having pressure applied, she blew on her nails, which were a deep shade of emerald. "Flick left London a couple of years back."

"And you've no idea where I can get hold of her?"

There was a fraction's hesitation.

"Please."

The girl scowled, drew out a pad and scribbled a note. "Decided to get out of the rat race," she explained, handing it to me.

I glanced at it, suppressed surprise and pushed the note into my bag. "Thank you so much, I really appreciate this."

The girl's expression slackened. "Is Kirsten really ill?" There was a tentative note of interest in her voice.

"She has anorexia. At the moment she's in hospital with her wrists slashed." *And it's my fault.*

"Bastard!"

"Excuse me?"

"That bastard's to blame." Her eyes gleamed with outrage.

"Who?"

"You don't know?"

"Know what?"

The girl's gaze travelled anxiously to the door. She leaned over the desk, lowered her voice, as if afraid someone might hear. "Kirsten was raped."

Astounded, my skin erupted with cold sweat.

The girl cocked an eyebrow. "Should help some with your therapy."

"Raped by whom?" My voice sounded distant and detached from me.

"A male model; he worked for another agency."

"You knew him?"

The girl shifted her gaze to the door again and shrugged. "Everyone knew him."

I steeled myself, hardly able to get the words out. "Was his name Kyle Stannard?"

For the first time the girl looked me straight in the eye, and nodded.

* * *

I headed for Gloucester Road tube-station in a daze. Stannard had raped Kirsten. Stannard had raped Kirsten. I murmured it over and over again.

Fallon's words blasted through my head: *In worst-case scenarios, it can culminate in abduction, rape, torture and murder.*

Kirsten's rape would play a massive factor in triggering anorexia. But, wait, why no mention in Kirsten's notes? Why hadn't the clinicians been informed? It didn't stack. Neither did it make sense that the police hadn't uncovered this important fact in their dealings with Stannard — unless they took the oh-so-reasonable point of view that he'd paid for his crime and was unlikely to reoffend. But surely they had a duty to warn me? With Kirsten underage, wouldn't he be on the sex offender's register? The only other explanation I could come up with: the crime was never reported.

Stannard's assertion, *People do as I say*, assumed new clarity. At the time I'd believed it was said to threaten me, but maybe he spoke the truth. His stepfather, the eminent Gerald Mallory, was in a perfect position to provide legal protection. Could there have been a cover-up?

In a daze, I got off and made my way to Paddington train station. A nasal-sounding announcement declared that the next train stopping off at Cheltenham was running late. Fed up, I went in search of a cup of tea, paid for it and took it back to the platform and waited.

When I finally climbed on board the train, I pulled out the note handed to me and called Flick Sutherland. An articulate youngster called Sky informed me that her mother was out and was not expected back until late.

"Can I get her to call you?"

"She won't know who I am, but if she wouldn't mind. Can you tell her it's in connection with one of her models?" Thanking Sky, I left my number.

As soon as I got back, I checked the flat, poured a glass of wine and took a long swallow. Normally, I would have called Chris. Except Chris had gone. I took another pull of wine, briefly toyed with phoning PC Grant and as quickly trashed the idea.

But if Stannard had raped Kirsten Matherson, people knew about it, and tomorrow I intended to find out exactly who they were and what they had done to shield him.

CHAPTER FORTY-FOUR

Waitresses and bar staff are invaluable funds of information. The crew at a local hostelry in Great Rissington proved no exception, the Mallorys' home swiftly located through a good-natured conversation with a genial barman.

I finished my Coke and stepped out into the car park. The sun was hot. Reflected in the Cotswold stone, it bathed the village in creamy yellow light. I drove down a street bordered by pretty cottages and gabled houses, and out onto open road.

Oakridge House was some three and a half miles away, hidden by a long tarmac drive that shared a right of way with walkers and ramblers. I parked the car on a wide verge near the entrance and began the steep walk down.

Dense woodland flanked my right. Signs indicated public footpaths and wildlife, and stark warnings for dogs to be kept on leads at all times. To the left, the land gave way to rich pasture where a couple of dozen sheep grazed. At my approach, they scattered.

My head buzzed with heat and doubt. Had it really been such a good idea to come? I was there alone. Nobody walked pets. No mother with her children. No one taking the air. Perspiration gathered in the small of my back. Anyone could take me here in the undergrowth. Hurling the thought aside, I placed one foot in front of the other, kept going.

Roughly three-quarters along the drive, a stagnant-looking lake, the surface a murky green scum. Winding around to the left and fenced by barbed wire, the way disappeared to a dirt track. There was no grass, only dense vegetation with little room for sunlight.

I kept to the main route, the drive wide enough to take a car, until I reached the entrance to Oakridge, which was marked by a fine set of gates. Open, they reclined against a bank of camellias and rhododendrons. I sneaked through, masking my arrival by staying close to the many bushes, flowering shrubs and trees.

The house itself was not what I expected. Colonial-looking with a wooden veranda that would immediately betray the sound of intruders, it was large enough for a family and an army of servants. The upstairs bedroom had white-painted shutters fastened back against the outside wall. A gabled porch fronted the house and, as I drew near, I could see a flat, perfectly cultivated lawn with croquet hoops. The place exuded grandeur and fine living. Neither breeding nor wealth insulated from personality disorders, I reminded myself.

Skin suddenly clammy, I twisted around, screwing my eyes tight, scanning a line of trees and holding my breath until I thought I might burst. From somewhere I heard the distant sound of traffic. Setting my face to the big house, a twig snapped and I let out a yelp of surprise.

"Impeccable timing," Stannard announced, with a half-smile. He wore tight jeans and an open-neck shirt, through which I glimpsed a dark line of hair. Fit and physically powerful, he was close enough for me to smell his distinctive aftershave, close enough to kiss him. The sheer magnetism of his presence shook me.

"We're about to sit down for lunch," he said. "I'm sure mother could squeeze in one more."

"Are you crazy?" I felt annoyed for using such an unprofessional phrase to describe someone whom I suspected was psychotic.

"From where I'm standing, I'd say you're the nutter. Was it you who scuppered my sale in Evesham Road?"

"I don't know what you're talking—"

"'Course you do. I'd no idea you could be so naughty. What a minx you are. Still, I forgive you." He gave my arm a tug.

"Come on, she won't bite. My stepfather's rather a grouch, but I'm sure you'll charm him."

I opened my lips in protest but my mouth went dry and Stannard's hold was firm. He didn't say another word, but his intention was crystal-clear. In his deluded way he was taking me home to meet the parents. I stumbled forward; Stannard, meanwhile, kept up a steady stream of chatter about the house and its architecture.

A set of golf clubs adorned the hall together with a selection of umbrellas, walking sticks and Wellington boots. A tall woman, gazelle-like, with classic bone structure, approached us. I estimated she was in her early sixties. As an older woman, she was extremely attractive. As a younger woman, she must have been very beautiful. I could see from where Stannard had inherited his looks, prior to the attack.

"This is Kim Slade, mother."

The woman looked vacantly from me to Stannard to me again.

"Olivia Mallory," she said. She did not extend a hand. Her mouth was a thin, disapproving line. I watched as the woman's deeply set eyes clamped onto my neck.

"She's my new friend," Stannard explained, casting me a cold-blooded expression.

Olivia Mallory nodded apprehensively. "It's rather unexpected. Kyle didn't say you were coming."

"What's this?" We all turned and followed the voice, which had travelled from an adjoining room. A tall man with a large girth stepped into the hall. Dressed in a pair of casual tan-coloured trousers and a short-sleeved shirt, he had thin, greying hair, heavily hooded blue eyes, and a jaw that was beginning to slacken and show the signs of age. The man took one look at me and paled. Undaunted, Stannard ran through the introductions for a second time. The air crackled with tension. Geoffrey Mallory shot out a hand as if he'd been hit with a cattle prod. I minutely shook my head and pressed my arms to my side.

"This isn't what it seems," I announced, my voice steely. The Mallorys viewed me as if I'd produced a gun. I chose my words with care. "Your son is following me."

Olivia Mallory let out a shrill cry.

Defiant, I stared at Stannard. He stared back, not with alarm, but with astonishing confidence. I suddenly felt as if I'd walked blindly into an ambush. "He's been phoning and threatening me."

"Then why are you here?" Geoffrey Mallory towered over me, the question asked in a forthright tone.

"Because I want it to stop."

"How dare you!" Olivia Mallory burst out. "How dare you come to our home and make false allegations."

"They're *not* false. Ask him," I said, tipping my chin in Stannard's direction. Geoffrey Mallory traded a look with his stepson, who let out a languid sigh.

"It's all nonsense. There's clearly been a huge misunderstanding."

Mallory stepped in like a hostage negotiator talking down a hijacker. "If this is so, Miss Slade, then I suggest you go to the police."

"Do you really want your stepson to go to jail?"

Olivia Mallory let out a dry sob. Visibly shaking, she cast her husband a desperate look that said, *For God's sake, do something.*

"Miss Slade," Mallory said, a stern edge to his voice, "think very carefully before you say something you may regret. Kyle has already spoken to me about you and your false allegations.

As you're probably aware, making such serious claims and wasting police resources could land *you* in the dock."

I reddened. They were obviously colluding with him. "So he's always been a good boy, has he? Always treated women and the girls in his life with respect and decency? What about Kirsten Matherson?"

Stannard's skin drained to the colour of wood ash. A vein pulsed in Mallory's temple. Olivia Mallory's eyes shrank to twin pinpricks of hate. "Are you going to let her stand there, Geoffrey?"

Mallory took a step towards me. "I think it's time you left."

I stood my ground. I wasn't finished yet. "Your stepson raped Kirsten Matherson and now she's starving herself to death."

"You stupid little bitch," Olivia Mallory exploded.

"Mother." Stannard's expression remained grim. He looked genuinely shaken.

"She was the start of it all," Olivia Mallory railed. "If it hadn't been for her and her pathetic lies . . ."

"*Her* lies?" I said. "Why is it that everyone, other than your precious son, is lying?"

"My son," Olivia gasped. "My son was beautiful, *really* beautiful. He was the best, at the height of his career, but that money-grabbing trollop came along to spoil—"

"Olivia," Mallory warned, but she was gone, lost in retaliation and rage.

"Look at him," she screamed. "His face is ruined, his career destroyed, and now you come along with your filthy accusations. I'll see you in hell before you hurt my boy." The slap came hard and fast across my face. Vicious and unexpected, it stole my breath away. Cheek stinging, I caught Stannard's expression of dismay and shock.

Geoffrey Mallory put an arm around his wife. "Get out," he ordered, "and don't come back."

I stumbled from the house and ran at breakneck speed down the drive. All I could hear was Olivia Mallory's shrieking voice ringing in my ears.

CHAPTER FORTY-FIVE

I wrestled with my conscience. I badly needed to hear Kirsten's version of events, but contact was impossible. Attempting to stay in the loop, I called Cathy on Sunday morning to get an update only to be told in wintry tones that Kirsten was *comfortable*.

Turning things over in my mind, I plucked up enough courage to risk ridicule and phoned PC Grant. He wasn't immediately available but I was assured he'd call back. I was making coffee when my entry phone rang. It was Jim. *Oh crap*, I thought, pressing the buzzer.

I let him in feeling like a sixteen-year-old capitulating to a parent after an almighty row. He looked grave and sad, and I feared the worst. I showed him into the sitting room. He examined my face in a way I recognized.

"If you've come about Kirsten, I can explain."

"It's not about Kirsten. It's about Kyle Stannard."

My chest tightened. Jim loosened the collar of his shirt. I noticed he was wearing a tie. It made him look strange and official. I invited him to sit down.

"When you told me that he was stalking you, you had my support and my sympathy," Jim began. "We were all behind you."

Were, I registered, picking up on the change of tense.

"Only now things are less straightforward. I've received a formal complaint from Geoffrey and Olivia Mallory. They came to see me first thing this morning. They maintain that you've been stalking their son."

"That's simply not true."

Jim continued, steadfast, "They say you followed him to their house and made a scene there. They've threatened to go to the police."

It was all I could do not to put my head in my hands and let out a long, low, keening howl.

"I've managed to deter them for the time being, although I can't give you any guarantees. Mallory is a hotshot barrister. He's not going to take this lying down. I take it from your silence that it's true."

Dumbstruck, I nodded. Could I trust Jim? That was the big one. Finally, taking a chance, I said, "Jim?"

"Yes, Kim."

"Would you like coffee?"

He broke into a daft smile. "Long story?"

"Interminable."

* * *

I told him everything. He listened intently. His expression stiffened when I confessed to following Stannard. When I told him about the rape, his eyes widened, then narrowed.

"Nothing more than vicious gossip and allegations."

"But what if it's true?"

"Where's your proof?"

"Kirsten Matherson."

Jim's laugh was hard and hollow. "Now I really think you've lost the plot. Has it ever occurred to you that Kirsten is highly suggestive, that what you were doing was wrong?"

"Yes."

"That you might be mistaken?"

"Yes." I wasn't infallible. I had doubts.

"Well then," Jim said.

"But everything leads back to him. Are you telling me that the receptionist at the modelling agency has fallen prey to malicious gossip? Everywhere I look, he's there with his irritating logic, his compulsion to grab my attention. He's like a jinx."

Jim took both my hands in his. "Chris would have left without Stannard's interference, Kim."

I drew away. I couldn't disagree. "What about Kirsten?"

He gave me a level look. "Something as massive as this would be in her notes."

"You're really not convinced?"

Jim waited a beat. "The truth is I don't know."

And neither did I. Not for certain. I could have been looking at two entirely separate issues. What I needed were hard, incontrovertible facts.

"In any case," Jim continued, "Kirsten's treatment is academic. The Mathersons want to move her back home as soon as possible."

I was despondent. The Mathersons lived on the wrong side of the Welsh borders, far away from an in-patient eating disorder unit. What would become of her? "How did you leave it with the Mallorys?"

"I promised to reprimand you, which I'm now doing. The real problem, Kim, is that the Mallorys have a point. Whether or not Stannard is your stalker, you've handed it to him on a plate."

* * *

The estate agents called shortly after Jim left to inform me of a viewing scheduled for the following afternoon. I was asked whether or not I'd be at Goodshelter.

An uncomfortable pull on my heartstrings; it was still a home of sorts. I told them I'd be there, and I'd no sooner put down the phone than it rang again. Taking precautions, I waited for the answering service to collect the call.

Flick Sutherland sounded as though she was calling from a party — loud music, people laughing, the clatter of glass and cutlery. I picked up.

"Sorry," Flick said, in a throaty mid-Atlantic drawl. "It's the kids. Got their friends round. Turn the music down, someone," she blared, half deafening me.

The volume decreased a little. "Sky said you're some kind of shrink."

I explained my credentials.

"You don't say. I went to a therapist once. Best thing I ever did. Helped me get in touch with myself. The real me." The music erupted again. "For Chrissakes," the real me roared. This time the music died down to a low bass burble. Unfazed, Flick said, "How can I help?"

"I need to talk about one of your girls."

"I'm no longer in the business, honey."

"That's not relevant."

"Okay, shoot."

"Kirsten Matherson."

I heard a match being struck, the sound of lungs pulling on a cigarette. "What about her?" The zip had bounced right out of Flick's voice.

"What's your connection?"

"I scouted her. What's yours?"

"Kirsten Matherson's one of my clients."

"Let me guess, eating disorder."

"Anorexia, unfortunately."

"No surprise with a mother like that."

Flick had my undivided attention. I waited for her to expand.

"Marie Matherson was always pushing the girl, nagging her, putting her up for any and every job. Kirsten had quite a look, popular at the time. Her mother wanted her to ride the wave while she had it. She insisted on as many castings as could be humanly fitted into a day."

"And Kyle Stannard?"

Flick's lungs drew heavily on the cigarette. I could almost taste the nicotine on my tongue.

"He was gorgeous and unique with good looks that last a lifetime. I'd have slept with him myself if I hadn't been pregnant."

I didn't need to muffle my surprise. After seeing those photographs in his house, I got it. "Tell me about him."

"He had the three Fs: flash, fun, fucking great in the sack, or so I have it on good authority. I lost count of the times girls cried on my shoulder because of Kyle. He was too damned charming for his own good."

Charming? "Did he have a temper, a bad side?"

"Sure he was bad," Flick gave a throaty laugh. "He had an exotic lifestyle with a taste for cocaine and young women."

"Underage girls?"

"Not knowingly," Flick said as though it wasn't that big a deal, which it most certainly bloody was. "Hey, we girlies love that bad boy stuff, don't we? It's kind of intoxicating and wild. Truth is, Kyle had a love 'em and leave 'em philosophy that ruffled lots of baby feathers."

I wondered uneasily whether the receptionist at Visage was one of them. "But was there a nasty side to him?" With every revelation, I was sucked a little deeper into Stannard's world.

"He was a perfectionist so he was quite capable of throwing a tantrum, but I never believed that stuff about him and Kirsten."

"You mean the rape."

"The *alleged* rape," Flick corrected me. "Kyle was the pinnacle of Marie Matherson's career plan for her daughter. That woman offered Kirsten to him like a sacrifice to the gods."

My heart thudded against my ribcage. "But she was only fourteen or fifteen."

"And looked a *lot* older."

"So what are you saying — that it was encouraged?"

I heard Flick exhaling. "Who knows what goes on behind closed doors? All I can tell you is that there was a ton of chatter, rumours flying around but, at the end of the day, the case was dropped."

"It never went to court?"
"Damn right."
"And afterwards?"
"Plain tragic."
"You mean Kyle?"
"Must have been seven or eight months afterwards," Flick said, sombre now. "Kyle was walking down the street at night and got jumped by muggers. They stole his wallet and watch. He put up a fight and they smashed his face in. Last thing I heard, he was having reconstructive surgery. I left London not long afterwards, moved to Cornwall."
"Because of what happened?"
"Nah, I had my own demons to flee."
We all have those, and mine were laughing in my face.

CHAPTER FORTY-SIX

Georgia wasn't keen. I couldn't blame her. Risking everything, I'd be finished if I were caught. By implication, Georgia would bear a heavy share of responsibility.

"I only want ten minutes," I said. "Ten minutes when I can talk without her parents coming in and blowing me out."

"Remember what happened last time?"

"You'll be there. You can monitor it."

"What about Jim?"

"He won't know unless you tell him."

Georgia stuck her hands in her pockets and said nothing — default position, exasperated.

"Kirsten's in denial," I pointed out, "and it's not going to go away. She can will herself to starve but can't will away the past. She won't get better unless she confronts it."

"That's your professional opinion?"

"Yes."

Georgia shook her head. "Insight isn't always a cure, as well you know. It's too risky."

"So is doing nothing."

Stony silence.

"Please, Georgia."

"Kim, this is about you," she hissed. "It sure as hell isn't about Kirsten."

"It's about *both* of us. Come on, Georgia, my career's on the line, but Kirsten's life is in the balance."

Georgia's face darkened. She looked at the wall then looked back at me. "You really reckon this Flick woman knows what she's talking about?"

"I do."

"Ten minutes?" Georgia said at last.

"Tops." I beamed. "And thank you."

"Don't thank me," Georgia glowered. "This is probably the most stupid decision I've ever made in my life. I swear to God, if you go one second over . . ."

"Got it," I said.

* * *

Kirsten Matherson's bandaged arms rested in her lap. She sat on a wicker chair, her face tilted towards a window revealing an artistically arranged garden. Entranced by sparrows taking a bath in an ornamental trough, she didn't move as we entered the room.

Georgia took up a position by the door like a minder protecting his gangland boss. She spoke first, gently reminding Kirsten of my visit. Kirsten gave an imperceptible nod as I sat down next to her.

"I'm so very sorry for what happened," I began. "I never meant to upset you." A faint smile played on the girl's bloodless lips. "Are you feeling better?" I asked.

"A little."

"All right if we talk about stuff?"

Kirsten's bony shoulders relaxed. "I guess."

"Your parents are right to be angry," I said.

"It's my dad. He's protective of me."

"As all good fathers should be," Georgia cut in lightly, catching my eye.

Kirsten twitched a smile. "Yeah," she said, dreamy. I wondered how much medication she'd been given.

"Tell me about him," I said.

The girl shrugged. "He's great. He's a bit strict, but he looks after me, and my mum. They both want the best for me."

"And you've got two older brothers, Robert and Stephen, that's right, isn't it?"

Kirsten braced, big-eyed. "What about them?"

"Nothing. I have two of my own," I smiled. Always would have, to my mind, despite the fact that Guy was dead. "Sometimes it's a pain being the only girl, don't you think?"

"I suppose. I don't see much of them," Kirsten said briskly. "They're working out in Australia."

"Visit much?"

"Once, not lately." A sudden, hunted look appeared on Kirsten's face. Her limbs tensed, shoulders bunched up.

"Are you getting tired, Kirsten?" Georgia broke in, throwing me a warning look.

"A bit."

"One last thing, and I know it's hard," I said, avoiding Georgia's furious expression. "We talked about Kyle, remember?" I held my breath in an agony of frustration. "You knew him, didn't you?"

Kirsten looked past me to a faraway point that only she could see. "How is he?"

"He's fine."

"I'm glad."

Georgia traded a baffled glance with me.

"Can you tell me what really happened?" I said softly.

"I fell in love," she whispered.

"With Kyle?"

Kirsten nodded.

"And he broke it off?"

"He broke my heart." Kirsten's eyes glistened.

So that was it. I wished I could put my arms around her and give her a hug. "And then what?"

"It was my mother's idea." Kirsten's expression was pleading. "I knew it was wrong but I was so hurt, so broken. You've no idea what he was like. He was funny and wonderful and kind. When I was with him I felt like a princess." She spoke as if her voice had harnessed all the energy from her body. "All the other girls were jealous of me. Then . . ." She stumbled, big tears in her eyes. "When he told me it was over, I thought I'd die. You've no idea how it feels to be crushed and rejected."

I smiled sadly, laid a hand on Kirsten's arm and recalled Flick's account of Marie Matherson's ambitions for her daughter, ambitions that were thwarted. "So your mother came up with the rape story in revenge?"

Georgia's eyes shot wide with surprise. Kirsten looked down, licked the corner of her mouth. "It seemed a good idea at the time," she said unconvincingly. "I didn't know what would happen. Mum made me promise not to breathe a word, especially not to my dad."

"What was his reaction to the alleged rape?"

"He went ballistic. There was so much pain in the house. I felt swept along by it. Will I get into trouble?"

"No," Georgia cut in. "This isn't your fault."

Kirsten looked anguished. "Once you make up a lie, you need another to back it up. I kept changing my story to keep ahead of the game. In the end it was my word against Kyle's."

Your lie against his truth, I realized with a jolt.

"There was no physical evidence," Kirsten shivered, "and it got more and more difficult. I was warned what might happen in the witness box and I thought then that no matter what my mother said I couldn't go through with it, not for my sake but for his. The worst that could happen was that Kyle could be done for underage sex. In the end, I refused to press charges, and the case was dropped."

"But mud sticks," I said.

"Yes." And with deep sadness in her voice, she added, "And my dad never forgave him."

* * *

I left the hospital. The thread of evidence on which I'd tugged had unravelled and exposed a grave mistake. Mine. No wonder the Mallorys were furious.

I replayed events in my head, thinking back to the time I hung back outside the bookstore. I'd raised my hand to get a signal for my phone. Was that what Stannard mistook for a wave? His cold denials, his justified horror at yet another false allegation, and I'd been deaf, dumb and blind to them.

I didn't doubt that Stannard had been all of the things Flick Sutherland described. And yes, he'd bugged me, pursued me with relentlessness, eager to talk out his fears and obsessions, but he was not the man who'd turned my life upside down. This was a guy who'd been set up, his reputation destroyed and then, when life was returning to normal, mercilessly beaten. Life had indeed dealt him a bad hand of cards, and, as I considered this, I discovered that, although he'd complicated my life to a terrible degree, my compassion for him and my empathy ran deep. How could I have been so morally bankrupt?

It left one last question wide open: if I was so off-beam, so out of whack, who was the real scary bastard?

CHAPTER FORTY-SEVEN

With no appetite either for food or retail therapy, feeling as if the proverbial rug had been well and truly ripped from underneath my feet, I idled in the direction of Bath Road — Cheltenham's very own Left Bank and the centre of bohemia — and bumped into Molly.

"Kim, you look dreadful."

I supposed I did. My friends considered me crazy. I'd lost credibility at work. I'd lost faith in my own sense of morality and judgement. I planned a move to God knows where to a place my face, no doubt, would be gawped at. I had no idea who my stalker was, other than it wasn't Stannard. No pressure.

Molly linked an arm through mine and propelled me in the direction of Moran's Eating House. Grabbing a table for two, Molly ordered for both of us and under her merciless interrogation, I told her enough edited highlights to satisfy my friend's curiosity. Molly's eyes grew wider with each revelation.

"My God, you poor thing, how absolutely awful for you."

"I'm selling up. I've got a viewing at the cottage tomorrow afternoon."

Molly's shock translated to disapproval. "Do you think it wise to sell? You're quite safe there. After all, the nutter following you has no idea about your other home, your other life."

What other life? "Only a matter of time."

Molly slipped out a lipstick and compact from her bag. "I'll have a word with Simon."

"About what?"

"Your house sale, silly."

"I've made up my mind, Moll, and I've appointed a local estate agent."

"You can be so stubborn." Molly applied a generous coat of lipstick. "You should listen to good advice." She snapped the compact shut.

We paid and walked back through town together. Pausing to go our separate ways, Molly kissed me on both cheeks. "Sorry about Chris," she said. "We never really . . ."

"I know," I jumped in.

Molly threw an awkward smile, told me to take care and left.

My heart flipped with surprise at finding Grant and Cunningham waiting for me back at the apartment. Grant's face was set like weathered granite. "We've received a complaint about you."

* * *

"So you freely admit it?" Grant said, once we were inside.

"Yes." No point in denial.

"You entered his property?"

I felt only a moment's contempt for the old lady who'd grassed me up. I was in no position to take the moral high road. Chastened, I said, "I was strung out and frightened. I was wrong. I made a mistake."

Grant slowly shook his head in disbelief. "What if you'd been right? Do you realize the risk you were running?"

I bit my lip. Risk, to me, meant doing nothing.

Grant glanced at Cunningham in irritation.

"Has anything else happened, Miss Slade?" Cunningham asked.

"Nothing." I could have told them about the threatening card and the bucket of maggoty flesh and shit, but it would only sound dubious in the current circumstances. They'd think I was making it up. Best to admit to what I'd done and take the rap. "What happens now? Do I receive an official caution?"

"Not this time. Consider this a reprimand," Grant said, steely-eyed. "If anything else happens, you report it to us first. You do *not* try to take the law into your own hands. Got it?"

I nodded obediently.

Once they'd gone, I took a shower. Standing in the kitchen later, I opened a tin of tuna and mechanically ate the contents. When the phone rang around quarter to nine, I listened, heard the click, the recorded message followed by the sound of breathing. I went over to the window and looked at people slipping by. The phone went several times, each time the caller staying on the line for around ten seconds, no more, no message left.

He didn't give a damn.

CHAPTER FORTY-EIGHT

I arrived at Cormorants Reach at midday. My feet halted almost before my body at the sight of the front door ajar. Theoretically, I should have called the police, but after the frosty exchange with Grant and Cunningham, I was reluctant. Besides, the cottage was in a dead zone for mobile coverage.

Briefly looking around for something to use as a weapon, I stole back to the car. Opening the boot, I took out the wheel brace, returned to the house and eased the door gently open. It protested with a loud, complaining whine.

Grinding with nerves, I waited a beat then zipped across the living room floor, peered into the study and moved soundlessly down the steps into the kitchen.

There, I saw him. He had his back to me. I swung the wheel brace. He turned, eyes wide and white.

"Charlie," I gasped. "What the bloody hell do you think you're playing at?"

Both his palms shot up. "Are you going to put that thing down?"

"Not yet." I ground my jaw so hard I thought my teeth would crack.

"Simon asked me to look in."

"Simon?" This was getting more bizarre by the second.

"He said you'd got someone viewing your house this afternoon. He thought it would be a good idea if a bloke was with you."

Molly must have told him. "Then why didn't you phone?"

"I didn't think it would be such a big deal. God, Kim, you don't seriously think—"

"Where's your car? Why isn't it in the drive?"

"Because," he said, his voice loud, "I came in the Land Rover and the handbrake's not that clever. It's parked down at the river where it won't roll away."

Eyeing him, I backed off, awkwardly laying the wheel brace down on the kitchen table, within reach. Every part of me was on high alert and primed for a fight.

Charlie sat down hard on the nearest chair. I smelled the fresh tang of farmyard on his clothes.

"I think Simon has a point," he snapped. "You need protecting from yourself."

I glared at him. "You still haven't explained how the hell you got in." *Keys*, I thought, in alarm. Charlie would have had ample opportunity to "borrow" my car keys and clone them.

He expelled an exasperated sigh. "The door was already open."

"Impossible."

Charlie scowled. "Are you absolutely certain you locked it when you left? You do seem to be in a fair old state." His voice was caustic.

"Which is why I'm very careful about my security."

He locked eyes with me, as if saying *screw you*.

"There's really no reason for you to be here," I continued. "The agent is accompanying the viewing."

"What the hell's got into you? I'm trying to help."

"I don't need your help," I bit back.

"If that's the way you feel about it." Ugly-faced, he clambered to his feet.

Yes, I did. I didn't trust him. I didn't trust anyone anymore. They were all featuring way too heavily. They were all too damn close.

Charlie marched past. I followed him out. He suddenly turned, his weathered face pale with anger and close to mine. "From what Simon's told me you're sailing pretty close to the wind. It won't bring Chris back, you know. He's gone for good. Can't say as I blame him."

* * *

The viewing was a pointless exercise. To be fair, the agent acted with suave sophistication, talking the cottage up, throwing in the odd amusing anecdote, using the right amount of carrot and stick. I guessed the viewers were a second marriage. The husband was old and dishevelled in spite of the effort to dress in a trendy fashion — trousers with spanner pockets and a baseball hat; the wife was young, skittish and strident, as were their two little girls. Within minutes, the children were left to roam and wreck. While Mummy and Daddy amused themselves by comparing the small rooms with the *much larger* proportions of a property they'd seen earlier, I spent my time deterring Tamsin and Lily from throwing themselves into the river.

"Why are you leaving such a glorious place?" the husband asked.

"Personal reasons," I answered evasively. *Personal* covered every crisis under the sun. Chris had cited the same excuse, I remembered bitterly.

"That went well," the agent said, as we watched the family disappear in their pearl-white Tesla.

I issued a brief, cynical smile. "They won't be back." About to return to the cottage, I heard the crunch of tyre on gravel. I looked at the agent. "Did you schedule someone else?"

He shook his head.

Two men stepped out of a BMW. I ran through the stock list of possibilities — Jehovah's witnesses, evangelicals, door-to-door salesmen, lost tourists — and found myself coming up empty. Something staged in the way they approached chimed with a grim and distant memory of police officers bearing the worst kind of news: *There's been an accident, Mr Slade.*

The older of the two, a lean, wiry individual with close-cropped sandy-coloured hair, walked a couple of paces behind the other, his line of vision scoping the cottage and its surroundings with a professional eye. The younger, tall, blonde and with a heavier build, was, by contrast, entirely purposeful. His gaze locked on with a kind of ruthless determination. He flashed a warrant card announcing he was Detective Sergeant Martin Hatchet. The older man gave a curt smile and introduced himself as Detective Inspector Malcolm Darke.

"Are you Kim Slade?"

I nodded, a sudden sensation of dread crushing the centre of my chest. Hatchet eyeballed the estate agent.

"Is there somewhere we can talk in private?"

"I was on my way out." The agent's expression was one of febrile curiosity. I imagined he'd have a lot to gossip about in the office on his return. "Speak to you later, Miss Slade," he threw over his shoulder with a little too much swagger.

My mind racing, I took them inside and showed them into the sitting room. I'd hoped that the business with Stannard was officially cleared up. *Oh God,* I thought, *the Mallorys.* Even so, it seemed a ridiculous waste of police resources for two detectives to come all the way to Devon to charge me, or maybe these were local boys. I guessed they were going to do me for harassment. How ironic.

"I understand you lived with Chris Beech," Hatchet said.

Confused, I looked from one to the other. Darke's blue eyes remained steady, though I could see, by the way Hatchet leaned forward, my response carried significance. "We split up."

Hatchet regarded Darke. I saw the tightening of the jaw. I could smell impending disaster. "What is this? Is he in some sort of trouble?"

"I'm afraid we have bad news for you, Miss Slade," Darke said. "Chris Beech is dead."

CHAPTER FORTY-NINE

Someone had done the equivalent of chucking me onto a rollercoaster ride and thrusting the gear in reverse. After an initial, "Oh my God, oh God," I was clean out of words. Body rigid, heart twisted, I tried to concentrate. Beads of sweat pocked my brow. Blood pounded in my head. Everyone and everything felt blurred and indistinct. Without warning, my legs buckled and gravity took its toll.

Later, a glass of water was pressed into my hand followed by a mug of sugary tea. I took an eager sip. Time coalesced. Darke was talking and talking, his words far away and obscure as though he were speaking from an underwater and long-forgotten city.

"Are you feeling better?"

How could I answer a question like that? I sat and stared but focused on nothing.

"His body was found by walkers yesterday," he said gently. "On the moor."

"Dartmoor?"

"In a remote forested area, near Sittaford Tor."

"I don't understand. What was he doing there?"

"That's what we're trying to find out."

"Some kind of accident?" I tried to strike the hopeful note from my voice. Accident was comprehensible, something else wasn't.

Darke lowered his gaze. "I'm afraid not."

I gasped. "Are you sure?"

"Yes."

Slow tears rolled down my face.

"Chris was found in his car. Some effort had been made to set it alight."

Involuntarily, I gagged and clasped a hand to my neck, shielding the skin. These are old burns, I wanted to tell them, unconnected.

"Probably as a means to cover the crime," Darke explained.

"Lucky not to have set the entire area ablaze," Hatchet added blackly.

I could barely bring myself to ask, but ask I did. "How did he die?"

"Can't say," Darke replied. "There will be a post-mortem and lab reports."

"And this happened when?"

Hatchet and Darke exchanged glances. Darke answered, "Time of death is uncertain due to the prevailing high temperatures. There was some putrefaction."

I stared incredulously. I wanted to reel the footage back, to discover that it was all a mistake, anything to deflect the desolation. Chris had betrayed me. He was never going to return, but this . . . I clutched the mug tightly with both hands. My nose streamed and slow tears splashed down my face. Darke handed me a tissue.

They waited as I made a not entirely successful attempt to pull myself together.

"So when did you last see him?" Hatchet asked casually.

I frowned. So much had happened. "It's hard to say exactly. Must have been two weeks ago." Was it? I honestly couldn't remember. "Yeah, a Monday morning," I added more confidently. "I was on my way back to Cheltenham. If I look on the calendar I can find the date."

"Later will do. What were you doing in Cheltenham?"

"I work there. I'm a clinical psychologist."

"And Chris?" Darke interposed.

"An English teacher."

"Where?"

I wondered why he'd asked the question. Surely they'd discovered that already. Maybe it was a method of getting me to talk, to cross-reference and corroborate facts.

"At the secondary school in Kingsbridge."

"How did Chris seem on that Monday?" Darke enquired.

I didn't want to remember. Somehow I managed to force an answer. "He was half-asleep."

"And over that weekend?"

"A little pensive, thoughtful."

"In what way?"

"I don't know."

Hatchet made a note. It put me on edge. I wanted to slink away, dig a hole and hide in it.

"And the last time you saw him, was that also the last time you spoke to him?"

"Yes." I looked from Darke to Hatchet. "I phoned Chris as usual when I arrived in Cheltenham but he didn't answer."

Darke glanced around the room. "You phoned him here?"

"And I tried his mobile, but it was switched off. I was worried so I contacted the school and discovered he'd phoned to say he wouldn't be in."

Hatched looked up. "When did he make the call?"

"The same day I left."

"Any idea of time?"

"Before lessons, I presume."

"But he didn't tell you of his intention?"

"No."

"Was he ill?"

"Not that I knew of."

Darke nodded for me to continue.

"So I came back," I explained.

"When?"

I told him.

"And that was unusual?" Hatchet's face was without expression.

"Very. I left several clients in the lurch."

"Go on."

"Chris wasn't here. He'd cleared out. He'd left me."

Darke's eyebrows drew together. "Left you?"

I nodded, unable to hold my distress at bay. He looked genuinely sorry. "Do you need a break?"

I shook my head, wiped my nose furiously. "I want to help. I do, but I can't believe it's happened. I can't think who would do this to him." Except, I could. Blood rushed through my head like a flash flood. Should I tell them about the stalking? Would they believe me now that I'd been so utterly discredited by the police in Cheltenham?

"Take your time," Darke said. "How long have you known Chris?"

"We'd been living together for almost four years."

"What was he like?"

Spun out, I bit my lip. I wanted to do the best by Chris, but it wasn't simple. I let out a breath, fudged the question. "He was very private. Hard-working, well-liked by colleagues." God, it sounded like the sort of stuff people put in CVs.

"Friends?" Darke pressed.

"He didn't have a huge circle. My friends were his friends." My nerves tightened. "There were people he went drinking with from school. His best mate's Andy Johnson, another teacher. Andy's known him longer than me."

"It would be helpful if you could provide us with a list of associates," Hatchet said, tapping the tip of the pen on his pad.

"Of course."

"What about family?" Darke said.

I shook my head. "He was put into care. Spent much of his early life in foster homes." My voice sounded halting, false and businesslike. I didn't want to tell them about his black moods, his brush with criminality. Anyway, if it were recorded, they'd find it without my help.

Hatchet clicked his tongue. "Not what you'd call an idyllic upbringing."

Darke threw him a reproachful look. "Did he have any enemies, Miss Slade?"

"None that I can think of." I thought of Simon and Molly, Charlie and Claire, their barely concealed dislike.

"He wasn't in debt or had any drink or drug problems?"

"No."

In the briefest of silences, I sensed that they were regrouping.

"The split, was it completely out of the blue?" Darke leaned forward a fraction. His eyes locked onto mine. "Did you see it coming?"

"No, no I didn't." I briefly shut my eyes, braced for the inevitable.

"So you don't know why." There was an upward inflexion in Darke's voice.

I gathered the remains of my pride and looked straight at him. "He left me a note. There was another woman. He . . ." I stopped. They now had a motive. Nobody said anything for a moment.

"The identity of the other woman." Darke dropped the remark delicately into the conversation.

I made eye contact with him. "Chris didn't say." I wasn't sure why I used the truth to conceal a lie.

"Do you have the note?" Hatchet said.

"I threw it in the river." To my own ears, I sounded dodgy.

"Have you got the pad it was written on?"

"It was typed on a computer. Chris had appalling handwriting," I explained.

"But he signed it?"

"Yes."

"You're sure it was his signature?"

"Yes." Unmistakeable.

"Do you have a computer here?" Hatchet's expression was penetrating.

"In the study, but Chris rarely used it. He had his own laptop for work."

"We'll need to search your home," Hatchet told me, "and remove any digital equipment for analysis. We'll also need to take a formal statement from you."

I rubbed the top of my arms although I wasn't cold. "I understand."

Darke returned my gaze with a searching expression, his eyes two black orbs. "You said during the last weekend you spent with Chris he was troubled."

"I said pensive."

"Because of his extracurricular relationship?" Hatchet said, smart with it.

"I assume so."

"And you had no idea?"

"I already said. None."

Hatchet scribbled some more, head down. "Any idea what time you left the house that morning?"

"I was running late. I'd overslept. I suppose it must have been around half past seven. I don't really remember exactly."

"So you arrived in Cheltenham at what time?"

"Around quarter to twelve."

Hatchet's eyes shot up to meet mine. "Four and a half hours?"

"Traffic was slow and I had a puncture," I protested.

Looking into his face, I had the horrible realization that the timing was deemed a game-changer.

"Where?"

"Outside Loddiswell."

"What did you do?"

"Changed the tyre."

Hatchet raised his pale blonde eyebrows in disbelief. "You didn't call Chris?"

"Why would I? I believed he was going to work. I'm perfectly capable of changing a wheel." It came out mighty defensive. I tried to cover it with a laugh that only made it worse. "I called Cathy," I said, a light pinging on in my head.

"Cathy?"

"Cathy Whitcombe at Ellerslie Lodge, where I work. I told her I was going to be late. You can check."

"How long did it take to sort the puncture?" The question sounded clipped.

"I don't recall. Forty-five minutes, maybe."

Hatchet's eyes fixed on mine once more. "Anyone see you?"

"I don't think so. I was concentrating on what I was doing. Look, do we have to do this now?" I said, suddenly drained. I understood they had a job to do. I genuinely wanted to help but I wasn't ready for being shoved under a microscope yet. Most importantly, I needed to think, to process the horrible news.

Darke was more solicitous. "Is there a friend you can call?" I immediately thought of Claire and wished I'd been more civil to Charlie. "You'll need to vacate the house for two or three days. We'll be sending a team round to carry out a search of the property and you'll also be assigned a family liaison officer."

I imagined a load of people in white zipped-up suits, kitted out with gloves and special footwear, poring through and ransacking my things. Numbed, I nodded. "I'll sort something out."

"And we'll need you to come to the police station tomorrow to formalize things, take a video-recorded statement," Hatchet said, "and resume our discussion," he added pointedly.

Oh God, I thought. "What time?"

"Eleven."

"Where?"

"Plymouth, Charles Cross."

They took my contact details. I walked with them to the door. Darke paused. "I see you have the cottage on the market. How long has it been for sale?"

"Not long."

I didn't dare analyse the expression on his face.

I watched from the window as they drove away. They'd need to reach the top of the hill before they'd get a mobile signal. The second they did the whole machinery of a murder investigation would swing into operation. And I was a major cog in its wheel.

I slid down onto the floor.

To die like that . . .

The grim thought made me crawl inside.

Fire. The word, alone, conjured up a primitive and elemental fear. I knew its strength. I understood the terror it engendered, the pain it caused, its ability to scorch and disfigure. Mystical and sexual, it symbolized both death and rebirth. For arsonists it was a turn-on, the ultimate power, and a means to create impact. Whatever the reason for setting Chris's body alight, I doubted it was simply a means to cover the evidence. There was a message in the murder.

A warped love letter meant for me.

And the cops were hunting Chris's killer in the wrong place.

CHAPTER FIFTY

I packed a bag and phoned Claire. Initially, her voice was strained, not like Claire at all, which was understandable. Then I told her about Chris.

"Oh my God, Kim. I don't know what to say."

I explained I needed somewhere to stay for a few days.

"Of course, not a problem," she said, "and for as long as you like. Come whenever you're ready."

Before I'd got out of the door, the phone rang with messages of condolence from Chris's midweek drinking pals and colleagues. I fielded them as best I could, wondering who knew about Chris's affair, and shot out of the cottage before I lost my composure.

Andy lived in one of a row of cottages in Eastern Backway in Kingsbridge. Situated in the cleft of a steep road, the little home vibrated with the permanent sound of cars slowing down and changing gear. The front aspect looked out onto a park and a fire station.

As soon as I saw Andy, I knew he'd heard. No cheeky grin. No off-colour joke. Red-rimmed eyes accentuating his pale skin, he held his arms out to me. We fell into each other. He gave a low groan. I'd no idea how long we stood there, propping each other up.

Eventually, we went inside. Mess as usual. The only area that looked sane was around the computer. On the floor, next to the sofa, two orderly piles of newspapers beneath a tidy desk.

The jumble resumed as we walked through to a kitchen that stank of Chinese takeaway. Jen was at the sink, rubber-gloved, tackling an awesome pile of washing-up. She twisted round at my arrival.

"Hiya, want a cuppa? That's all I've done since we heard the news. Terrible, isn't it? Everyone's talking about it. They're saying it's murder. Sugar, milk?" she said, coming up for air.

"Tea, no sugar, thanks." I'd wanted to speak to Andy alone, without interference. We retreated to the sitting room and sat down together on the one available sofa, covered in cat hairs.

"How did you hear?" I asked him.

"Heart Radio. Wasn't specific at first, but it didn't take long to work it out. Half the school is in shock. He's going to be badly missed."

"Have the police seen you?"

"Not yet. It's true, then?" Andy's voice cracked.

I took his hand in mine. "I'm sorry, Andy." Without warning, a wave of tears erupted. He put his arms around me. I buried my face in his shoulder, soaking his shirt. He stroked my hair.

"That's right, you have a good cry," Jen said, emerging from the kitchen. "It's what my mum says. No point in keeping it all in."

We pulled apart. I felt Andy bristle beside me, Jen blundering through our grief like a cheerleader at a funeral service.

"There you go. A nice cup of tea and a plate of biscuits."

"We're not hungry." Andy spoke for both of us.

"Got to keep your strength up at times like this," Jen said. "So, what's the craic?"

"Fuck's sake, Jen," Andy exploded. "Just listen to yourself. Will you stop fucking talking — *please*?"

Her heavily made-up eyes shot wide with hurt. "Sorry. I always talk too much, especially when it's serious. It's me. Mum's always telling me to button it. I didn't mean—"

"It's all right, Jen." I gave a tired smile.

Andy cast Jen a meaningful look. "Why don't you go and buy a pint of milk or something?"

Grateful for a reprieve, she reached for her bag. "Anything else you want? Sweets, newspaper, magazine?"

"No!" Andy snapped. "Take as long as you need," he added more gently.

We fell silent while the door opened and shut.

"She's completely doing my head in. I wish I had a remote to switch her off."

"She's trying to be helpful, that's all." We were overwrought. Jen couldn't help being an emotional illiterate.

"I know," he said, apologetic. "We were supposed to be going off in the camper van together today, but this has changed everything." He took a drink of tea. "So, what actually happened?"

"Andy I'm not—"

"I need to know."

I told him.

"Christ Almighty." He put his hands to his face.

"And the police think I had something to do with it."

He looked as if I'd handed him a gift wrapped in razor wire.

"The police know that Chris left me for someone else."

"What's that got to do with anything?" He was indignant.

"*Crime passionnel*, revenge. Don't you see? It looks like I have a motive."

"That's bollocks." He gave me a sharp look. "You think Carolla Dennison was involved?"

"Definitely on a sexual level." I failed to push the bitterness and resentment out of my voice. I knew Chris. I knew his needs. "God, you don't think . . ."

Andy shook his head slowly. "I wouldn't put Carolla Dennison down as a murderer."

"But she might provide a lead." I didn't spell it out. We both knew I was talking about my stalker. "Is there any way I can get hold of her?"

"Is that wise?"

"I only want to talk. She might have seen Chris with someone who had it in for him."

"Right, I see where you're going with it."

"Where does she live?"

"She was renting somewhere in Thurlestone but I'm not sure she's still there, or whether they'll give a forwarding address. Pat Emerson might be a better contact but he's on holiday."

Of course, the head was bound to know how to get in touch. "What about other work colleagues?"

Andy brightened. "She was quite pally with Jo Sharpe. She lives in Saffron Park."

"Number?"

"Can't remember . . . Wait," he said, putting a hand to his temple, "the house is called Fallowfields."

CHAPTER FIFTY-ONE

"Are you Jo Sharpe?"

Small with fair hair, green eyes and a deeply freckled face, the woman nodded and got up from the border she was weeding. I introduced myself.

"Chris Beech's girlfriend?" The green eyes gleamed in apprehension.

Not really. Not anymore. Is there a term for bereaved ex-significant other? "That's me."

"Christ," Jo let out.

"Can we talk?"

Jo tilted her head, looked at the sky, as if she'd thought about such a moment but never believed it would happen. "I don't know. I'd rather not get involved. I'm Carolla's friend," she said in response to my searing expression. "I know she behaved badly, but in the end no one got hurt."

I checked a verbal response and stared in astonishment. Embarrassment flooded Jo's freckled features.

"You don't know what's happened, do you?" I said. "You don't know about Chris."

Jo wrinkled her nose. "Know what?"

"He's dead. The police think it was murder."

* * *

We sat in Jo's cramped kitchen. Tension either makes you talkative or clam up. Jo was a natural gabber.

"I don't know how much you know about Chris and Carolla. I can guess what you're thinking, but it really wasn't like that. Not far off, I know. More like having sex with all your clothes on."

"Frottage," I said. Hell, what a comfort.

Jo looked blank.

"Having sex with . . . oh, never mind."

Jo gave another mystified nod. "See, there was a group of us who'd meet up midweek for a drink after work, usually at the Hermitage. It got to be quite a regular event. We'd drink far too much and end up at the Balti House."

"Who exactly?"

"Carolla, me, Paul Hammond . . ."

"The history guy?"

"That's the one. Faye Hannaford, the new chem teacher, Andy and his new squeeze, Jen, Chris . . ."

I briefly tuned out. Chris the loner, Chris the friendless, Chris who liked his own company best of all, Chris the man I barely recognized.

"They used to go to the cinema a fair bit."

"What, Chris and Carolla?"

"Yeah, she complained to me once that she didn't like his choice of films. She was more into comedy, romance, you know the thing?"

Crawling inside, I nodded. I'd thought films were *our* thing.

"Anyway it was never going to happen with you on the scene. Sure, there was a deep attraction there right from the off. Any fool could see that. You'd only have to walk into a room and you could sense the sexual tension, but it came to nothing."

"How do you know?"

"He felt too guilty. You were the stronger pull, I guess. Not that Carolla told me every little detail. I mean, she wouldn't, would she? My God, I wonder if I should tell her. She'll be devastated."

She has no bloody right to be devastated, I railed inside. "You said it came to nothing."

Jo tilted her head. "Shouldn't you be at home or something?"

"I need to know the truth."

"Why torture yourself?"

Because the alternative is too horrible to contemplate. "How much did Carolla really tell you? Did she tell you that Chris was leaving me? Did she tell you that he was going to fly with her to the States?"

Jo's denial was more a shout of alarm.

"I don't think you know your friend as well as you think," I barked.

* * *

I drove slowly out to the farm.

Truth was such a flexible commodity; it all depended on whose truth I believed.

Nothing to write home about, Jo would have me believe, yet even she'd been forced to admit to the existence of stolen kisses, secret meetings, simmering phone calls, sexual fucking tension. So it wasn't all a one-way street, then. And in the end Carolla had won, not me. The final goodbye letter proved it.

Obsessively, I wondered why Carolla hadn't reported Chris missing if they were such an item? Even if I spoke to my love rival, I'd only be scratching the surface and getting Carolla's sanitized version of events. But whatever I did now, I couldn't afford to make the same mistakes again. This time there could be no assumptions, no emotions, only facts. I needed to apply Gavin Chadwick–proof rules if I were to establish cast-iron evidence. My stomach lurched.

As if on cue, my phone rang. Detective Sergeant Fiona North introduced herself as my family liaison officer. Condolences out of the way, she asked me where I was staying. I gave her Claire and Charlie's address.

"How are you holding up?" she asked.

"Like you'd expect."

"A tremendous shock, I'm sure."

"Yes."

"You're understandably deeply upset, Kim, but I'm here to help. Look on me as a bridge between you and the police side of things."

"Right. Thanks."

"Alright if I drop round first thing tomorrow?"

A rhetorical question, I agreed. "The police mentioned a formal interview in Plymouth."

"That's correct. We can go together. Try to get a good night's sleep, Kim."

I thanked her for her concern and ended the call as I pulled onto the rutted mile-long drive to Badger's Leap, a long, low traditional Devon longhouse and the Lidstone's farm. Claire was outside to greet me. Of Charlie, there was no sign.

"Cleaning out the combine and balers to reduce the fire risk," she explained. "It's been that hot and dry."

Rude to Charlie and potentially a murder suspect, I was grateful for the lie. "Did Charlie mention our last meeting?"

"He did."

"I shouldn't have bitten his head off," I mumbled. "Bad habit. I'm sorry."

"You threatened him, Kim."

"Claire, I really didn't. I was frightened. He was in my home unannounced, for goodness sake."

"We've put you in the annexe," she said, speedily moving the conversation to a less contentious footing. "Thought you'd like some privacy."

"Don't you need it for guests?"

"We had a cancellation." Another glance away, another lie, even though it was whiter than white.

"Let me pay you the going rate — please."

"Wouldn't dream of it."

Uncomfortable, I followed her across a yard to what used to be a cow shed. Charlie and Claire had done a cracking job of converting it to a cosy, modern one-bedroom dwelling.

"The fridge has all the basics plus a bottle of wine," she said, with a smile that reminded me of the old Claire, the friend I had before my world turned dark. "Of course, you must eat with us tonight," she said briskly.

I shook my head. "Think I'll have an early one."

"If you're sure?"

I smiled, praying the warmth in my expression would assure her that this was for the best. "You won't even know I'm here."

She reached out and touched my arm. "Are you all right, Kim?" How often she'd asked that same question, usually after one of my frequent and distressing trips to hospital, or when another of my father's women breezed in and took over.

"I'm okay." The answer had been my default position for as far back as I could remember. Claire searched my face with concern.

"You know I'll always be here for you."

"I know," I said humbly.

"Is there anything else you need?"

"Gavin Chadwick's home phone number."

"God, are you sure that's a good idea?"

"I haven't had a better one." If his lawyerly expertise was as robust as his debating skills, he no longer seemed like a rubbish bloke to have onside.

"If you're sure," she said doubtfully.

"I am."

"It's on my phone. I'll WhatsApp it across."

After Claire left I set down my bag, unpacked my things and poured myself a drink. Taking out my phone in readiness, I noticed a message from the estate agent: *No offers, but endeavouring to get more punters round.* I swallowed a mouthful. *Better not*, I thought, making a mental note to cancel all viewings. Murder puts people right off.

CHAPTER FIFTY-TWO

Fiona North was not what I expected. Slim, with blonde hair that she wore clipped back into a low ponytail, she had baby-blue eyes and, in her casual trousers and shirt, looked about nineteen and too young to be dealing in murder.

Barely eight in the morning, I scratched my head, wondering why on earth she needed to arrive so early. I hated anyone seeing me without my make-up on. It made me feel exposed and vulnerable. Maybe that was the point. I gave myself a silent ticking off. She's doing her job. No need to be cranky about it.

"Come in," I said. "I'm not fully functioning yet."

"Don't worry. I'll make us a pot of tea, or would you prefer coffee?"

"Well, I . . ."

"I'll put the kettle on while you think about it." North headed straight for the kitchen area with practiced calm. "How are you feeling? Sleep all right?"

"Not really." I sat down, studied the grain of the kitchen table and listened to the clatter of someone else taking over my life.

North rested her back against the worktop. "We could have a word with your GP. Maybe he could prescribe something."

I winced. I didn't like *we*. Neither did I like the fact that I felt as if I were sitting in *her* kitchen. "Thanks but no, I'm not keen."

The baby-blue eyes didn't waver. She explained that the Major Crime Investigation Team dealt with all murder cases and the team dealing with Chris's murder were based at Plymouth. "If there's anything you want to tell me, or anything you don't understand, or something you wish to ask, then fire away. I want you to see me as a friend. Call me Fiona, please."

Mentally, I thought, *spy*. I nodded and forced a smile. "Fine."

Fiona beamed, glad, it seemed, to have got the lowdown out of the way. "Tea or coffee then?"

I settled for coffee and expected a torrent of questions or at least to be actively pumped for information. Instead we talked about Fiona's background and the years spent growing up in Solihull. It's what I would call finessing. When I found myself talking about my own family, I realized that Fiona was smarter and more experienced than she looked.

"So you've not seen your mother since?" Fiona said.

"No."

"You don't miss her?" Fiona's expression failed to conceal her fascination.

I looked at the wall. I missed the fact that I'd had nobody to shop with, to discuss clothes with, to talk to or confide in when I was growing up. Had my mother stuck around, I doubted I'd have been cast into a boarding school. I hoped that she might have defended me, stuck up for me, girls together, understood me. With her on my side, I suspected that my life would have turned out quite differently. Who knows, I might have escaped the perils of the bonfire. For me, the big heartache was that it didn't matter how many people were in the house, there was always one missing, always a grave sense of loss. I didn't say this. I gave Fiona a highly edited answer.

She listened, hand under her chin. She wasn't taking notes exactly, but I could see the information being stored behind those kind eyes, slotted in and measured against the evidence.

"It must have been difficult."

"Let's not overstate it."

"But you must have felt lonely and rejected."

Her observation didn't come close. As soon as the words left her mouth, I could almost see a light flash on in Fiona's head. She was making the link between the earlier abandonment of my mother and then my lover. Sharpened emotions and powerful feelings equal crime of passion. Added to my gaff with Stannard, I felt practically convicted already.

"What will happen to Chris?" I asked, trying to shift the focus.

"There'll be an inquest. His body can't be released for burial yet because of the investigation."

"Are they still running tests?"

"There are certain procedures."

I cleared my throat. "And what are the mechanics of the police investigation, or aren't I allowed to know?"

Fiona flicked a reassuring smile. "We need to establish timelines."

"You mean when Chris was last seen, time of death?"

Fiona nodded and took a sip of coffee, every movement full of grace, feline.

"How do they establish that?"

"Forensics. Witness statements. House-to-house enquiries."

"There are no houses. My nearest neighbour is the other side of the river." The fact that the population was in constant flux would hardly help.

Fiona looked at her watch. "You remember we're due at the police station at eleven?"

"I haven't forgotten," I said with the ghost of a smile.

"I'll drive," she said, businesslike.

I'm being hustled, I thought.

* * *

Darke thanked me for coming. Wearing a lightweight navy suit, pale blue shirt and red tie, he looked smarter than the day before. I wasn't sure if it flagged something significant, whether I was going to be treated less as a victim and more as a suspect. My scant knowledge of police interview techniques based on television dramas, I worried that I might be in for an aggressive line of questioning. As it turned out, I had nothing to fear. Not at first.

I was shown into a sparse interview room with moulded plastic chairs. It reminded me of consulting rooms in poorly funded regional hospitals. Darke explained the proceedings while waiting for Hatchet to join us. When he arrived I was told this was a voluntary witness video statement and I was asked to run through much the same ground covered the day before. Darke smiled sympathetically. It occurred to me that he wanted to be liked and trusted, which wasn't difficult. He gave the impression that we were working together, part of a team, although I'd stop short of suggesting that he was batting for me. I didn't feel threatened, which was why I decided to expand one of my answers. I took a deep breath. If I didn't tell them now, they'd find out later and then it would look even spookier.

"Yesterday, when you asked me about Chris's state of mind, I said that he was pensive."

Hatchet jumped in. "Because of the other woman." Darke's reproving look connected and glanced off his police colleague.

"Because I was being stalked."

Darke did his best to look matter-of-fact. His eyes gave him away. They glinted.

"The police in Cheltenham know all about it," I said. "If you talk to PCs Grant and Cunningham, they can fill you in."

"This person stalking you," Darke began.

"I don't know who it is but, don't you see, the person stalking me could be Chris's murderer." I looked at both of them, waiting for them to make the link.

Hatchet exchanged a look with Darke, who shrugged.

"Have you experienced problems in Devon?"

"Well, no."

"So whoever was stalking you in Cheltenham knew nothing of your life here?"

"I don't know. Assume nothing, surely?"

There was a brief silence, broken by Darke. "Thanks for being so candid."

Is that it? No more questions? No new leads? Cold assailed me in spite of the stuffiness of the room. Was it possible that I was suffering from false memory syndrome? Had I made everything up, my disordered home life with my dad and brothers screwing with my brain? I pressed my hands underneath my thighs, dug the nails into the soft flesh to prove to myself that I was real, that I existed.

Darke stroked his chin, casual. "Does the name Carolla Dennison mean anything to you?"

I struggled to recover and keep my gaze steady. "She's a games teacher at the school where Chris worked."

"Have you met?"

"Briefly. I don't recall."

"For how long did you know she was the other woman?"

"I only found out very recently."

"You didn't mention her *yesterday*," Hatchet said with heavy emphasis. His blue eyes felt as if they were boring into me, mining for buried secrets. "You didn't tell Fiona," he added, his voice laced with accusation.

I blindly wondered whether Jo Sharpe had told the police of my visit. If she had, oh my goodness . . .

"Didn't you?"

"No."

"And *now* we all know," Hatchet said slowly, "how does that make you feel?"

I looked from one to the other. "Betrayed."

"By Chris," Darke said, with emphasis.

"But not enough to kill him, if that's what you're driving at."

CHAPTER FIFTY-THREE

I had the motive. Because of that silly puncture, I had the opportunity. And they'd caught me in a lie. Worse, the police seemed unsurprised by my disclosure of a stalker. Had they done their homework? Had they already discounted my theory? If the police weren't going to make the connection between Chris's murderer and my stalker, I'd have to do it for them.

"Did it go all right?" Fiona asked after I'd staggered out of the interview room and we were back in the car.

"Mostly." My voice was flat.

Fiona gave me a quick, sideways glance. "What do you want to do now?"

Prove I'm innocent. Find Chris's murderer, who I was certain — as certain as I could be — was my stalker. Nail him.

"Lovely day for an amble along the beach," she said.

God, I was tired to my bones. After my bruising encounter with Darke and Hatchet, I wanted to go back to the annexe, climb into bed and pull a sheet up over my head.

"It will be packed with people," I protested. Some I'd know or would know me. I didn't relish the pitying looks, the tongue-tied words and the suspicion.

"Not where we're going." She grinned, almost playful.

I had to admit, despite everything, I rather liked her.

Fiona was right. High brambly hedges, zigzagging road, no passing places or ice cream vans — an unlikely place for the modern tourist.

She parked the car in one of only a dozen possible places and we got out and walked. It took ten minutes to reach the raised beach at Prawle Point. There, we found a family of adders sunning themselves on rocks.

Fiona very smoothly manoeuvred the conversation round to Chris. I saw it coming, watched the moves, the seeming indirectness, and rapidly readjusted my earlier take on the baby-faced liaison officer. This was one smart woman.

In answer to her questions I told her the truth. Why not? If Fiona were sophisticated, she'd recognize that no relationship is perfect, that there are flaws beneath even the most successful partnerships. I didn't play down Chris's moods, his ability to irritate others, his mercurial manner.

"Did he gaslight you, Kim?"

Her directness blew me away. Shaken, I denied it.

"Did he make enemies?" Fiona probed.

"Not that I knew of. But he didn't make friends easily either." Except, was that strictly true? Jo had given a different impression. What about all those people he hung out with and who phoned to express their sympathy?

"Apart from Andy?"

She'd obviously been well briefed. "Andy's outgoing, happy, brash really. I guess it's a case of opposites attract

"And there was no one from Chris's past?"

"It's possible," I said, reflective. "Before coming to Devon he'd worked in London in an inner-city school where teachers were regularly threatened by parents and pupils. I guess it might be a line of enquiry worth looking into."

We pottered about, stepping over rocks, throwing stones, the tang of sea air briefly lifting my spirits.

"You should eat," Fiona pronounced, at last.

"I'm not hungry."

"But I am."

Back at the car, I scrunched myself up in the seat, trying to make myself as small and inconspicuous as possible. Nothing was said for the next mile. I didn't even register in which direction we were driving.

She pulled up outside the Cricket Inn at Beesands. The place was rammed inside and out with couples with shiny-faced toddlers, families wading through seafood platters and ploughmans, and gaggles of teenagers larking about, stuffing chips. I dodged a swarm of wasps attracted by a shoal of sticky empty glasses. Somehow Fiona managed to commandeer a table outside, with a perfect view overlooking Start Bay.

Ten minutes later, I had a glass of white wine in my hand, Fiona a soft drink.

I half closed my eyes, tipped my face to the sky, letting the sunshine fall on the good side. Might as well come out with it. "They think I did it." I opened my eyes and looked straight at Fiona to better gauge her reaction.

Fiona took a sip. "They have to pursue all lines of enquiry, Kim. You're only a strand."

"More like a thick piece of rope."

The blue eyes suddenly went very pale, very cool. "Did you do it?"

"No."

Fiona waited. I held her gaze. "You're bound to feel under the spotlight," she said with a level look. "Unfortunately, nearest and dearest always come in for special scrutiny. It's a sad fact that most murders are committed by people known to the victim."

"Then why not investigate Carolla Dennison?"

Fiona shrugged. No quickening of interest.

"What about the guy stalking me?" I locked on, read the same dull reaction in her eyes. "I get it. You don't believe my story."

"It's not about belief. It's about evidence."

I frowned. "What aren't you telling me?"

"Nothing." Fiona's face had a closed expression.

I took another cautious sip of wine. "So, how did you get into all this?"

"All what?"

"The police."

"By accident." Fiona's features loosened. A smile hovered on her lips. This was easier terrain for her, her expression intimated. "After my degree I wasn't sure what I wanted to do. There were several avenues I could have taken but none of them felt quite right. On a whim I applied for the police service. They were having a major drive on recruiting graduates at the time. It seemed like an attractive package. There were incentives."

"Fast-tracking?"

"Uh-huh."

"So what was your degree in?"

Fiona smiled sweetly. "Psychology."

CHAPTER FIFTY-FOUR

It took two days before I could go back home.

Superficially, the cottage looked pretty much the same. No obvious evidence of disturbance. Only when I opened drawers and cupboards did I find things put back in the wrong place, or not put back at all. The boxes carefully packed in preparation for a move were unpacked, the computer gone.

Fiona stated that she would pop in sometime the following day though she didn't specify when, a ploy no doubt to keep me on my toes. I thought about calling Jim but didn't have the energy to explain I was at the centre of a murder investigation — still less deal with his reaction. Instead, I phoned Andy. He sounded flat and depressed. I invited him round but he said Jen was popping in to see him. I didn't know whether this pleased him or not.

"I'm glad you've got company."

"I feel rotten for being horrible to her. She's trying her best to be supportive, but I wish she wouldn't fuss so much. I'm bloody drowning in caffeine."

"She means well."

"I know. She's a decent, salt-of-the-earth Devon girl."

"Don't knock it."

Neither of us spoke for a few seconds.

"So what's the latest, Kim?"

"I've given a statement. The police have searched the cottage. Standard procedure," I said, skirting the nitty-gritty. "How about you, have the police called?"

"You mean the body snatchers, Darke and Hatchet?"

Trust Andy to make a joke. Another time I'd have found it amusing.

"They asked all the usual guff," he continued. "Wanted to know when I'd last seen Chris. How he seemed. How we got on. How long we'd been mates. What I knew about his relationship with Carolla Dennison — precisely zilch. About you . . ."

I gave a start. "Oh."

"It's all right," Andy said, a trace of humour in his voice, "I didn't tell them you were weird or anything."

"Andy, it's no joke."

"Sorry, my way of dealing with it, I guess." He let out a gale of a sigh. "He was my best mate, Kim — my only mate, if I'm honest. I feel bloody frozen inside. Part of me hasn't really taken it in. What about you?"

"Desolate." Yet determined, if that were possible.

In the awkward silence that followed, a question needled the back of my mind. "Andy, did you speak to the cops about the stalking business?"

"Yeah, I did."

"When did they come and see you?"

I heard him drumming his fingers. "God, not sure . . . Yep!" he said, his voice spurting with sudden energy. "Same day you last saw me. An hour or so after you left."

Shit. That explained their less-than-enthusiastic reaction. They already knew.

"Did I do the wrong thing?"

"It doesn't matter." But I wished it were me who had told them first.

* * *

I cleaned, scrubbed, polished and hand-washed a pile of clothes that lay in a dirty heap in the spare bedroom, the standard woman's response to emotional turmoil. I lumped kitchen gadgetry together and boxed it all up, stacking cardboard containers side by side on the work surfaces. I changed sheets, moved round furniture and tried to watch television. A police procedural flashed onto the screen — art imitating life. I switched it off, answered a call from Molly and got caught up in a three-way conversation. Once the basics were covered, I found myself on the end of an interrogation. Yes, I answered, the cops had paid a visit, asked lots of questions, the place had been searched, and I was "cooperating with the enquiry".

"Do they know about the stalker?" Simon said.

"It's irrelevant to the investigation."

"Did they say that?" I couldn't tell whether he was surprised or something else.

"They acted it."

"You know you're a bloody fool to go after Stannard."

"Simon!" Molly burst in.

"Well, it puts her in a helluva bad light."

"*Her* is quite aware of that," I said, crestfallen.

"Sorry, Kim," Molly said. "I'll kick him for you."

It was lovely talking to Molly. I missed the familiarity, the rough and tumble.

"So do the cops have any idea who did it?" Simon asked, relentless.

"Yes, me."

"Absurd," Molly snorted. "You're having us on." There was a nervous feathery ring to her voice.

"I wish I was. I had the motive. I had the opportunity."

"But you couldn't . . ." Molly's voice faded.

"In theory, she could," Simon said frankly.

"Thanks for the vote of confidence," I said with a jittery laugh.

"I'm simply stating that the police are only doing their job. They have to explore every possibility, every avenue."

"Even if they're peering down a no-through road and I'm at the end of it?"

Simon didn't offer any reassurance. "Who do you think it is?"

"It could have been the woman he was having a fling with," Molly interrupted. "A long shot, maybe, but *cherchez le femme*, I say."

Simon didn't say anything at all.

CHAPTER FIFTY-FIVE

Carolla Dennison.

Was it possible?

I half slept. Part of my brain tuned to the sound of a latch dropping, the creak of footsteps on the wooden stairs. A tawny owl had taken up residence outside across the river, hooting a warning. Foxes screamed in rapture. At last, plunging into unconsciousness, I was disturbed by a loud rapping at the door.

I stumbled out of bed, grabbed a robe and went downstairs. Making sure the chain was secure, I opened the door a crack. Fiona North stood on the step with a large bag of shopping in her hand.

Dispirited, I let her in. Fiona looked more corporate in a cream-coloured short-sleeved shirt and matching skirt. Her legs were shapely, smooth and lightly tanned. The sandals looked Italian, not too high. Nice. I wondered anxiously whether the businesslike image came with a businesslike message.

"What time is it?" I asked, my words slurred with sleep.

"Time you were up."

"Has something happened?" I was alert now, cued by the edge in Fiona's voice.

"Darke wants to see you."

"Should I have solicitor with me?"

"Up to you."

My choice. No sweat. In my head, appointing one made it seem as if I had something to hide, as if I were guilty. I decided to hold off from contacting Gavin Chadwick just yet.

"I'm not dressed or anything," I protested.

"That's why I brought breakfast with me," Fiona smiled, a checkmate expression on her face. She emptied the bag onto the kitchen table. Croissants, a pot of jam, butter and a litre of fresh grapefruit juice spilled out. "You go and shower. I'll warm these up."

Over croissants and coffee, Fiona mentioned her current boyfriend. I spotted it as a warm-up to find out about any of my previous relationships. Sure enough, the question was slipped into the conversation. Glad to be one step ahead, I gave Fiona a brief resume, mainly because any past serious liaisons, apart from Phil, were few. After a while it dawned on me where Fiona was going with it; she wanted to explore whether my disfigurement was a bar to members of the opposite sex. Failing to elicit an enlightening response, Fiona came straight out with it.

"I noticed you have a scar on your neck. How did you get it?"

Not subtle enough and none of your business. "A childhood accident. I'll go and give my teeth a clean." I smiled, firmly concluding the conversation.

We arrived at the police station shortly after half past ten. This time I was asked to take a seat in a waiting area.

Darke entered. His smile was a grimace. He invited me to follow him. I was shown into an incident room. This time there were more people. Hatchet was already seated. A young police officer stood by the door. I sat down, drew my chair close to the table rather than sitting isolated away from them. I wanted to create an impression of full cooperation and civic responsibility.

Darke went through his usual routine then turned to me with a strained smile, which I found faintly worrying.

"The post-mortem report suggests that Chris suffered extensive head injuries; the damage was caused by something heavy, maybe a hammer."

"God," I burst out, "so the fire was definitely a cover-up, a means to destroy evidence?"

"It would seem so. We've been trying to establish timelines. We know that friends of yours, the Lidstones, had dinner with you on the Saturday evening you were last in Devon with Chris. We're also aware that Andy Johnson popped in to see you the following Sunday morning. We know Chris made the call to school at seven fifty a.m. on Monday."

"Shortly after I left."

"Yes," Darke agreed. "After that the trail goes cold. We can only conclude that you were the last person to see him alive."

Instantly, I realized its significance. "What about Carolla Dennison, the woman he left me for?"

"He didn't, Kim." Darke's voice was marshmallow soft.

"What do you mean?" I sensed that they were holding something back.

"Carolla was already in the States."

"In America?" I said, as if I were thick.

"Carolla Dennison boarded a flight to New York that same Saturday," Hatchet stated, loud and slow, as though I were deaf. "She travelled alone and was already in the air by the time you sat down for your main course."

So Chris never left with her, I thought incomprehensibly.

"There was no ticket registered in Chris's name either," Hatchet added.

"Then why the note?" I said in angry confusion. "Why the hell did he tell me he was leaving with her?"

"Maybe he changed his mind," Darke suggested.

"Or was using her as an excuse," Hatchet said.

"But the affair," I said.

"Depends how you define it. Miss Dennison firmly denies they ever had a serious relationship."

"You've spoken to her?"

"We have."

"Sexual equals serious, doesn't it?"

Neither police officer responded.

"Sexual tension. Her best friend said so. Everyone said so," I flared.

Darke exchanged the type of glance with Hatchet that suggested I was unhinged. Maybe he was right.

"Where's the evidence? People gossip. You know what this place is like."

Before I could respond, Hatchet said, "Were you jealous?"

You bet. "Maybe you should be asking her that question."

Darke frowned. "Would you like to explain?"

"Maybe Carolla was stalking me."

The lines in Darke's brow deepened. I could tell he simply didn't buy it.

I'd no idea how many minutes passed, or if they were mere seconds. I was asked if I was prepared to continue. I agreed, although I would have preferred to request an adjournment.

Hatchet took up the story. "We've spoken to PCs Cunningham and Grant at the Gloucestershire constabulary."

Believing this to be good, I nodded.

"They say that the person stalking you was never identified."

"That's correct."

"But you had an idea who it was. Did you believe it to be Carolla Dennison?"

I shifted position. This was getting worse. I wished I'd never mentioned Carolla. "I thought it was someone else, actually. It turned out I was wrong, a dreadful mistake."

"We know that," Hatchet said briskly.

Darke thrust him a warning look and picked up the thread. "When we were downloading information from your home computer we found the note from Chris to you."

"*My* computer? But Chris never used it." And I only used it on rare occasions, relying more heavily on my laptop.

I looked from one stern face to the other, tumbling to exactly what they were thinking.

"We also found something else," Darke said. "You remember the anonymous letter you received after your car was taken?"

I gripped the seat, anchoring myself, as if preparing for a tornado.

"We found that on your computer too."

"But that's not possible. That would mean Chris was my stalker."

"Or you wrote the letters yourself," Hatchet said.

CHAPTER FIFTY-SIX

"That's plain ridiculous!"

"Which — Chris stalking you, or you writing the letters?" Darke's voice was metallic.

"Both," I responded with fury.

Hatchet pushed a sheet of paper towards me itemizing the times and dates when the letters were written. I studied them, breaking into a thin smile, and pushed the sheet back.

"I can prove categorically that I was in Cheltenham. You can check with the Bayshill Clinic, check with the Lodge."

"What are your technical skills like on a computer?" Hatchet said, unstinting.

"Not good enough for what you're suggesting."

"Still doesn't rule Chris out," Hatchet said doggedly.

"Yes, it does," I insisted. I didn't know whether I felt relieved the spotlight had shifted from me or not. "Psychologically it makes no sense."

"A high proportion of stalkers are ex-partners."

"The crucial word is *ex*. We were still together." Only technically, I realized with a thud. Hatchet's shrug confirmed as much. Darke opened his mouth to speak.

"Wait," I said, brain electric. "The timeline."

"What about it?"

"When did Chris die?"

Darke answered, "At the moment we've got the date Chris was last seen and heard, and the date he was found dead. You recall we mentioned putrefaction."

How could I possibly forget? I nodded grimly.

"To try and pin down a more accurate time of death, we brought in a specialist," Darke continued. "Scientific deduction points to the fact that Chris was killed at least ten days before his body was found."

"That's your working theory?"

"It is."

"Then he couldn't have delivered a bucket of crap to my flat in Cheltenham." My heart roared with excitement.

"A bucket of crap?" Hatchet's eyebrows met in the middle.

"Flesh and faeces."

"Flesh?" Hatchet's reaction was visceral. He paled, his disgust clear.

"Animal not human," I said pointedly. "Like from an abattoir, or a butcher's shop."

"When was this?" Hatchet said, rallying.

"After I discovered Chris had bailed."

"Perhaps it was already there," Hatchet said. "Perhaps he planted it."

It was difficult not to eye him with disdain. "I think I'd have spotted it."

"We only have an estimation of time of death," Hatchet pounded back. "It's not absolutely certain."

I glared at him. Hatchet's nasty tendency to cherry-pick pieces of so-called evidence to suit his argument made it virtually impossible for me to counter his accusations.

"Did you report the incident?" Darke said.

I coloured up and confessed that I'd chucked the contents down the lavatory. They both looked at each other, the unspoken exchange revealing to me that they were dismissing it as another unlikely tale cooked up by a desperate and guilty woman. Darke took hold of the reins of the conversation once more.

"As a psychologist you must be aware of the dynamics that govern relationships?"

"We all play games to a lesser or greater degree," I conceded.

"What kind of a relationship did you have with Chris?"

"An equal one." We both had emotional wreckage stuffed into our closets.

"Which one of you was more dominant?"

I locked eyes with his. What the hell had Fiona told him? Her gaslighting remark shot across my mind. "I've stated it was equal."

Darke glanced away for a moment. "Your career is obviously important to you."

"It is."

"But you were prepared to jeopardize it."

"I don't understand," I swallowed. Except I did. What the hell had Jim told them about Kirsten, about Stannard, about Geoffrey Mallory's complaint? I was flailing and they knew it.

"Was Chris jealous of your work?" Hatchet asked.

Had there been an undercurrent? "Absolutely not."

"So he wasn't a jealous man?" He eyed me with contempt.

"Not in the least," I said, my jaw grinding.

* * *

They let me go. I'd no idea why. After the grilling I thought they'd detain me. Perhaps it was a case of too much circumstantial evidence, not enough of the hard stuff. I said nothing on the way home to Fiona and was relieved when she left.

In my absence the post had arrived. At a glance I could tell there were a number of sympathy cards and put them to one side to be opened later.

I made strong coffee and took it into the dining area, an alcove off the kitchen separated by an ornate and battered Chinese screen. It was dark and quiet inside. The view from the single low window extended to the smudge of trees opposite. One of Chris's favourite places, he would often hive himself off there to mark papers.

Setting the coffee down, I found a notepad and pen and returned.

The police had two theories, both undeclared: I had fabricated the stalker story and killed Chris; Chris was my stalker and I'd found out and killed him. Lose–lose.

Tiptoeing up to the possibility, I recognized that our separate lifestyle gave Chris the perfect opportunity to hound me, but what about the logistics? I was sure the timing was off. Chris simply couldn't have been responsible for all those incidents, not without exhausting himself or clocking up enormous mileage on the car. With a jolt, I remembered that he'd got rid of the old one to buy the Mazda. He'd made a joke of it. Maybe it was to cover his tracks. Then again, maybe he'd used the Triumph.

Back to square one.

I tore off a sheet of paper and started another. It still didn't answer the question: who had murdered Chris? *Most murderers are people we know.* And the people Chris knew were my friends. I couldn't imagine any of them killing him. Not like that. Not by stoving his head in. Not by fire. So what about people at work? There was Andy — absurd idea. Pat Emerson — hardly. Other teachers — professional jealousy, perhaps. Or what about pissed-off parents, pathological pupils? *No, no, no.*

The call to the school office was the last official sign of Chris alive. Sometime during the next twelve hours, he was killed. But what happened in between?

I tried to put myself in his shoes. Maybe he felt conflicted, regretting his choice to stay, sad even at Carolla leaving. It would explain his constant need to check his phone for messages. He'd also feel guilty for treating me so shabbily. So what would he do? Go for a walk, wander down to the beach, get some sea air in his lungs, feel the wind in his hair. Along the way he meets someone. No, it wouldn't work for one very simple reason, I realized. There were literally scores of people crawling the lanes in high summer. He would have been seen and, more importantly, whoever was with him would have been seen too.

A pain gnawed at my right eye. I got up, rolled my shoulders to break the accumulated tension in the muscles, stretched my arms above my head and caught sight of something askew on top of the dresser. Pulling out a chair, I stood on it and reached down a spiral-bound photograph album. A little scuffed, clearly handled by unseen hands, my name written in capitals on the front in Chris's writing. Below, a photograph of me aged about three. I had a crooked goofy grin and a cute look on my face that proclaimed I was not camera-shy. I marvelled at the perfect skin, plump and smooth, and felt an intense pang of loss.

I flipped the front cover, the page faintly creased, presumably by a crime scene officer. Then my jaw slackened, eyes widening at a photograph of myself holding hands with a young and pretty woman. I'd never seen it before, and God alone knew how Chris had got hold of it, but I recognized from the set of the eyes and mouth that the young woman was my mother.

Dropping down into the nearest chair, I ran my fingers over the print, riveted by the story unfolding in front of me. I turned the pages. Pictures of me gap-toothed with Guy and Luke scoffing ice cream with our father on holiday in Bournemouth, school photos where I looked sullen and afraid, a birthday party in a garden at Claire's mum's, me on a pony, me proudly wearing a gown and hat, holding my degree. There was even the photograph that I made Chris promise to destroy with a *Sorry!* scrawled next to it. On the very last page there was . . . nothing. I stared at the empty space for ages, my heart leaping with hope. If I'd stumbled across a scrapbook of crude and jumbled images, Darke's theory would be conclusive, but this book, this wonderful gift, was hardly the work of a man who hated and wanted to control me. This was the work of a man who had loved me, who wanted to say that he was sorry, that he'd been a fool, that in the end, even after temptation and struggle, he'd chosen me.

I went back to the beginning of the album and journeyed through my life story for a second time. As I came to the final, empty page, I realized what was missing: the day on the beach when I'd stretched out on the rocks and felt radiantly happy.

Without considering the time, I called my big brother. I should have called him and told him absolutely everything before.

CHAPTER FIFTY-SEVEN

I drove up the motorway, half expecting a police car to scream up behind, siren wailing. Nerves shredded, I'd received the mental equivalent of a smack round the head.

According to Luke, Chris had phoned a couple of months previously and told him about his novel idea for my birthday.

"I'd clean forgotten about it when you called," Luke said. "I guess I was too shocked. I thought the break-up was a blip and that he'd come back."

If only. "So when did you send him the photographs?"

"Must have been a week after that. He phoned to thank me. He was really made up by them."

The same time he was supposed to be stalking me.

I switched into the faster-moving outer lane and arrived back at the flat in Cheltenham around half past five. Up the stairs, boldly unlocking the door, I scoured the carpet for a note or an envelope, ears straining for the beep of the answering service. Nothing.

Into the sitting room, I expected to find something amiss. I sniffed the air. No foul smell. No unusual fragrance. No graffiti or writing on the wall. The kitchen told the same story. I peered inside the fridge and opened the cupboards.

God alone knew what I expected to find, only that I needed to find something, *anything* that would convince the police that my stalker was alive and well and functioning.

I checked the bedroom and bathroom. Only when I was really, really certain, I slumped into the nearest chair.

Whoever was stalking had stopped. I'd waited and waited for such a moment, longed for it, but now that it had, I felt a stab of cruel disappointment.

If I went to the police with my latest finding, I knew what they would say, that the album was an elaborate subterfuge, a cover for his criminal activities, that Chris was my stalker after all. With his death, his stalking activities were finally over.

Lids heavy, I closed my eyes. Drifting, it was like looking into polluted seawater. You think you see something then it disappears, lost in the murky depths.

Robert Fallon had talked of a critical period when the ante was upped. Chris's murder fitted the pattern. It marked the beginning of the endgame.

My eyes opened and fell on the painting. There are three: stalker, love object, rival. Two men. One woman. Both want her. So one destroys the other. Then what? Game over. Winner takes all. Except, he doesn't. He can't, I realized with shock. That's not what he wants. His goal is annihilation. Hers. He wants to crush her. He wants to reduce her to a nothing. So he leaves her out in the cold. He *frames* her. He lets her take the rap for a crime he committed. Destruction complete.

I waited, half hoping the phone would ring, but it didn't. Five minutes later, I made a call I never thought I'd make and explained as best I could my situation.

"Sounds as though you're in a rather a mess," Gavin said, in answer to my request. "I was going to dig up the garden tomorrow — not that I've a clue what I'm doing. Lottie's the one with the green fingers. I'm the hired hand. How about I come to Cheltenham, away from the scene of the crime, so to speak?"

"You don't mind?" Aghast at his kindness, I streaked with shame for being so horrible about him.

"One can have too much of the country lifestyle," he assured me. "Once you've seen one cow, they pretty much all look the same."

* * *

Chadwick's smile had long disappeared. "A pity you didn't think to bring me in sooner."

"I thought it would seem like an admission of guilt."

He shook his head in disbelief and made another note. "Have the police had the results back from the search of the property?"

"If they have, they haven't informed me. Does it make a difference?"

"It depends whether Chris was killed at the cottage or not."

My blood froze. "He was killed in his car."

"Did the police state that?"

"Well, no. It's what I assumed."

"Assume nothing." Chadwick's expression remained grave.

"If he was," I said, "it looks bad for me, doesn't it?"

"Not necessarily," Chadwick said, a bit too airily, I thought. "Forensics may shine a new light on an enquiry, but it has to be a part of the process."

"But my DNA will be all over the place."

"True, but they're looking for solid evidence, causal links. If they find blood in the cottage, they'll have to first establish whether it belongs to Chris. If that's the case, the cottage will become a crime scene and—"

"I'll be their prime suspect."

Chadwick held my gaze, unflinching. "Yes."

"Meanwhile the murderer goes free."

He didn't say anything, gave me a searching look. "Tell me about the stalker again."

I ran through the lot, blow by blow, including my own shabby part in following Kyle Stannard.

He frowned. "Not very wise."

I agreed.

"And the police are convinced Chris was your stalker?"

"Or I fabricated the whole thing."

"And the letters on your computer?"

"I can prove that I was in Cheltenham when they were written."

"That's a start," Chadwick said crisply. "And you're not being stalked anymore?"

Embarrassed, I dropped my gaze to my hands. "I know how it looks."

Chadwick tapped the side of his nose with his fountain pen. "Setting aside the identity of the stalker, what do *you* think happened to Chris?"

"I genuinely don't have a clue about the chain of events, but I'm sure my stalker and his murderer are one and the same."

He nodded silently. For the first time I felt as if someone was actively considering my theory. It felt good.

"The police appear to believe that Chris was killed on the same day you returned to Cheltenham, right?"

"Yes," I said.

"Reason?"

"Putrefaction."

"Which can be open to interpretation." He nodded for me to continue.

"Someone stoved his head in with a heavy instrument, a hammer odds-on favourite."

Chadwick's eyes fastened on me. "Did they tell you that?"

"I think so. Yes, I'm sure they did."

"Which part of the head?"

"I don't know. Does it matter?"

"Rather. Was he sneaked up from behind or was it a full-frontal assault?"

"I don't know." If it were full on, Chris would have defence injuries, and bits of the murderer's DNA would be underneath his fingernails. I felt a rush of euphoria as if, after struggling for days, I'd found a piece of jigsaw that fitted into one of the numerous pieces of sky. "If full on, it's less likely to be me."

"But if the reverse were true . . ." The question hung in the air like a kite on the breeze. Was this the point, I thought, where a lawyer entertains ideas about his client's guilt in spite of knowing that he has to defend them? My newfound confidence evaporated.

Chadwick got up, walked over to a window. "You say you had a puncture that morning. Did anyone see you pulled over?"

"I was so busy struggling with the wheel nuts I didn't notice."

He drew breath in through his nose and let out a long sigh. "As I see things," he said, "the evidence so far is circumstantial. There is no smoking gun. One of the easiest traps detectives can fall into is developing a theory about what happened and forcing the facts to fit. A lot depends on what, or if, they find conclusive evidence at the cottage. As far as the police are concerned, you had the motivation. Hell hath no fury, et cetera."

"So even if Chris wasn't the stalker, I'm still in the frame?"

He turned sharply towards me. "You're still convinced of Chris's innocence?"

I bent down, pulled the photo album from my bag and handed it to him. "Does that look like a man hellbent on destroying me?"

While Chadwick was flipping through, my mobile phone rang.

"Where are you?" Never have three words sounded more accusing.

"In Cheltenham."

"You can't take off without telling me."

I pictured the soft, flattering contours of Fiona North's face sharpen into a tangle of angry lines. "I'm sorry, I was in a meeting with my lawyer."

"Good, you may need to bring him with you. Darke wants to see you at two. Don't be late."

CHAPTER FIFTY-EIGHT

I had visions of Chadwick stepping in every five minutes with a cauterizing remark or the immortal line, "My client is under no obligation to answer that question." It didn't work like that.

There was no sign of Hatchet. This time, I'd given a DNA sample and the interview was conducted under caution, although I was assured I was not under arrest.

I shook hands with a bottle-blonde woman in a sharp suit and heels. "I'm Detective Chief Inspector Hayley Niven," she announced. You didn't have to be a shrink to work out that the inquiry had stepped up a gear. I felt relief I'd got Chadwick batting for me.

Niven ran through a rough summary of events as described by me on the morning I last saw Chris. I nodded my way through so comprehensively that I almost missed the trick question.

"So you didn't return for anything?" Niven said.

"No."

Niven gave an easy-going smile. She had a large number of teeth crammed into a small mouth, an orthodontist's nightmare. "How did you feel about Chris breaking off the relationship?"

"As one would expect," I replied evenly. "Upset."

"It must have been especially difficult believing that there was a third party involved."

Here we go, I thought, a show of female solidarity to suss out whether my tears were for Chris or for myself. Aware of Darke and Niven looking at me, and the need to say something, I muttered in agreement.

"It would be natural for you to feel angry," Niven said.

"I was distressed."

"But you *were* angry?" Niven leaned forward a little. Her eyes were cold-rolled steel. I met her gaze, knowing that I was being given a get-out clause. I could write the script. *Perfectly normal to feel anger and betrayal in the circumstances. Quite understand how you lost your temper and lashed out.* Except, I didn't.

"I said I was distressed," I said as evenly as I could. "There's a difference."

Niven gave me a cool stare. "I see your cottage is on the market. Is that a recent decision?"

It would be easy enough to check with the estate agents. "As I already told DI Darke, yes."

"Rather sudden, isn't it?"

"It's not unusual to make a hasty decision after a traumatic event."

Niven raised an eyebrow. "Traumatic?"

"Divorce, bereavement, losing one's job can all be classed as life-changing events, as can the break up of a major relationship, with or without marriage."

Niven smiled agreement, glanced down at her notes. "You've been married before, I see."

"Yes."

"What happened?"

"It didn't work out."

"And did you wish to marry Chris?" Niven inclined her head.

"It was never discussed."

"But was marriage something you—"

"I fail to see where this is leading," Chadwick intervened, his voice piercing the air like an arrow in flight. "I would remind you that my client has already covered similar ground in an earlier interview."

Niven fixed him with a cold-blooded look. "I'm merely suggesting—"

"That I was distraught enough to kill him," I said with horrible calm.

"And were you?" Niven locked eyes with me.

"I was not."

Darke shuffled. Niven waited. Chadwick tapped a finger on the table. First round over.

"For the last couple of months you were under a great deal of pressure." Niven's tone was more solicitous.

I didn't say yes, or no.

"Could you tell us about the period of time during which you allege you were stalked?"

"I've already given a detailed account to the police in Cheltenham."

"We'd like to hear it again from you."

I gave as full a picture as possible.

"When was the last time you were harassed?"

I appealed to Chadwick. "I've already been through this."

"It will help clarify things for me," Niven said, as if asking a favour. Chadwick conceded with a small wave of his hand.

"When someone left a bucket of crap in my flat."

Niven remained unfazed, stone-faced. "Yet you failed to mention this particularly abhorrent incident to the police in Gloucestershire." She looked down at her notes. "It says here that you received a number of silent phone calls, a pornographic image was sent to a computer at work and your car was moved."

"Yes."

"Why no mention of the bucket? Seems a very odd thing to forget," Niven said, glancing up.

"I didn't forget. I wasn't sure of the response, that's all."

Niven locked eyes again. I felt my cheeks flood with colour. "We have reason to believe that Chris was killed in another location, his body dumped later the same day at Sittaford Tor. Forensics suggest Chris was killed by several blows to the head," she continued effortlessly. "He sustained no defence wounds and, from the trajectory of the injuries, the blows were delivered from behind."

I felt Chadwick bristle beside me. I maintained eye contact with Niven. "By someone taller than me."

"How do you know?"

I addressed Darke. "How tall are you?"

"Er . . . six two?"

"Stand up."

Darke looked at Niven, seeking permission. She let out a weary sigh and motioned for him to stand. I stood behind him. Niven described the action for the benefit of the tape. I made a fist and reached up. "Even with a hammer in my hand, my blows would have fallen on top of your shoulders, or neck. To hit Chris, I'd have had to be standing on a box." I sat back down.

Niven issued a smug smile. "Unless he was sitting or bending."

"No doubt a pathologist will be able to confirm," Chadwick said.

"Already has," Niven said. "Chris was bending over."

Stunned, I did my best not to appear rattled. Chadwick asked for a break. I nodded blindly, then, as if I'd snapped out of a hypnotist's trance, demanded, "Where?"

Niven flashed confusion.

"Where was he bending over?" I persisted. "At the cottage, or at Sittaford Tor?"

"We thought you could answer that."

"I can't."

"Can't or won't?"

Anger balled in my stomach. I swallowed, did my utmost to control my voice and stop it from shaking. "You've done a search of the cottage, what did *you* find?" I looked from Niven to Darke, seconds grinding. The air crackled. I could hear Chadwick breathing in anticipation beside me.

Niven forced a thin smile. "We found nothing, Miss Slade. Nothing at all, which is why we'll be examining your car."

CHAPTER FIFTY-NINE

I watched my Mini being secured onto a low loader. Fiona offered to run me back home. I declined. Chadwick gallantly stepped in. He looked pleased with himself, sly even, though I couldn't think why. As the hunted, it was me who'd made the running.

"Forensics is playing in your favour," he said, with a self-congratulatory smile. "They've got nothing on you, Kim. No bloodstains at the cottage. No DNA under Chris's fingernails."

"They'll keep on trying," I said with heavy resignation.

"To be honest, they can afford to take their time. Bloodstains are not easy to remove. Obviously, if there was any attempt to clean the inside of a vehicle, or sell it, the police are going to pay it very serious attention."

"Thanks for the advice," I said, sober.

He inclined towards me in a confidential tone. "I gather there are other lines of enquiry." Did he really know or was he making a presumption? "They certainly don't have anything near enough to charge you with," he assured me.

We arrived at Cormorants Reach. It was hard to describe my feelings of relief. I couldn't bear the place I'd known as home to be a violent scene of death. It would have been a gross violation.

The house phone was already ringing as I crossed the drive. Immediately on alert, I charged for the door, thrust the key in the lock, threw it open and listened hard. On hearing Jim's voice, I snatched up the receiver. He ran through a standard *how are you bearing up and everyone sends their best* routine.

Once that was over he told me about the visit he'd received from the police. "It would seem they have an agenda."

"In their eyes I had the motive and opportunity."

I hoped he'd protest strongly. He didn't. He asked if they'd found the murder weapon.

"Not that I know of."

"Let's hope they do," he said. "It might put you in the clear."

Might? "Only if it has a big label attached to it saying *this was not handled by Kim Slade.*" Pathetically, I tried to sound funny. He gave a snort of mirth, which he quickly stifled.

"Jim, what's the news on Kirsten?"

"She's gone home. No lasting physical damage." He lowered his voice. "You have enough to worry about without piling on any more. About coming back to work," he said briskly.

"Yes?"

"Unfortunately, the press have got hold of the story, and that's not good for the clients or the clinic."

"I'm sorry. I should have anticipated—"

"We therefore think it appropriate to suspend you."

My world turned several shades darker. "For how long?"

"I really can't say."

* * *

I went for a walk to clear my head and meandered up a narrow, secluded track flanked by fields and woodland. The air smelled earthy, a hint of autumn in the summer sun. I tried very hard to be lost in the moment and enjoy my surroundings. I didn't want to speculate, to guess what Jim was really thinking, to fog my already overloaded brain with thoughts of hammers and motives and people.

I heard the definitive sound of a branch cracking behind me. Jumpy, I spun round, expecting to see a man with a dog, a couple hand in hand, a family returning, hot and sweaty and bad-tempered from a day on the beach, but no one was there. I peered through the trees. Nothing and nobody.

I dry-swallowed, turned back and hurried on.

Had he come?

Was he here?

In Devon?

No longer a beautiful piece of scenery, the leafy track joined a farm trail. By the time I reached it, my muscles screamed and I had a stitch. Rather than cross and rejoin the woods, I took the wider and longer route out onto the road and passed through Rickham. That way, there were houses and more chances of being seen by a random driver or a farmer ploughing a field.

Back inside the cottage, I searched the downstairs and upstairs rooms, took a shower, dressed and poured a cold drink. It took mental strength to resist pure, unadulterated terror. Trees *did* make a noise, breeze or no breeze. Twigs snapped. Could have been a stoat or a fox. He'd come all right, but not yet. The timing was off.

Cooler at the front of the house when the sun moved around, I opened the door and sat on the step, legs stretched out. When the phone rang it didn't freak me. I refused to let it. I got up slowly, with determination, and walked into the study.

"Hi, is that Kim Slade?" The voice was breathy, female, transatlantic.

"It is."

"This is Carolla Dennison."

I reached for a chair and sat down with a thump. "I appreciate the call."

"I shouldn't really be talking to you. It's not allowed," Carolla rushed on. "But I wanted you to know how sorry I am."

I prickled. For what exactly?

"When Jo told me I felt so bad. It really is the most devastating news. Chris was such a great guy. I can hardly find the words to explain how terrible his death is. I'm so very sorry for your loss, especially after, well . . . you know."

I did know. That was the problem.

"I, or rather we . . . oh dear, I don't know how to describe what happened."

Every time she opened her mouth it was like a lash across my back. "What exactly are you trying to say, Carolla?"

"Chris and me, it wasn't what you think."

That's what Jo had said, I recalled. Seemed like the pals were reading from the same script. "Look, I don't know why you phoned." *Spare me the bleeding-heart routine* was what I really wanted to say. "I don't need protecting. I don't want my sensibilities respected. I simply want to know whether you're aware of anyone approaching Chris, anyone odd, anyone you noticed hanging around and he didn't."

"No," Carolla said. "Can't say I did."

"Are you absolutely certain? Did he mention anything that was strange, an incident, something not quite right?"

She seemed to think about it. "No," she said, finally, "he never mentioned anything like that."

"Right," I said, in a way guaranteed to finish the call.

"I thought you'd want to know the truth," Carolla said.

"What truth?"

"About us, about our fling."

I felt as if someone had shot me. I'll be all right, I told myself. A fling was nothing, sex without love, that's all. Happened all the time.

"We only slept with each other half a dozen times."

Only? "Why are you telling me this? What the fuck do you want — absolution?"

"I don't blame you for being angry. I'm ashamed to admit it but I was ruthless in trying to take him off you. I bombarded him with texts and messages, pretty much *stalked* the poor guy, even after he'd finished it." Had I not been sitting down, my legs would have buckled. "And, yeah, he got tempted to run away, but in the end Chris broke it off."

"And that's supposed to make me feel better?" I was rabid with rage and pain. "He broke off with me too, and it was your fault."

"But he said he couldn't give you up," Carolla said in astonishment.

My brain felt full of porridge. Nothing made sense. "Did he tell you that he was leaving me?"

"No way."

"He never said he wanted to go away with you and start a new life?"

She hesitated. My heart creased with pain. "In the first flush of lust, sure he did," she said. "Later, no."

"And you told the police this?"

"Yes."

"Did he ever talk about *another* woman?" My mind thrashed about with possibilities — the more outlandish, the more appealing.

"Are you crazy? He adored you. And do you have any idea the kind of hours the guy worked?"

"So there was no room for anyone else in his life other than you and me?" I had to be absolutely certain.

"Only you."

About to speak, I swore a shadow moved across the front window. *Fool*, I cursed under my breath. I'd failed to take the most basic of precautions and now someone was loitering outside the cottage. Someone uninvited. If it were a friend, they'd surely call out. I cut the call and grabbed the poker from the fireplace. The shadow moved.

Flattened against the wall, banking on the element of surprise, I listened and heard whoever it was quite clearly now. Footsteps and small shallow gasps punctuated the air. Mine. This was the someone who'd followed me, the someone who—

The door flew open. I lunged. Heavy arms grabbed me. Thrown face down on the carpet, skidding across the pile, my cheeks burned with friction. The poker tumbled from my grasp. Gripped by one wrist, I let out a terrific scream and lashed out. A hand released me almost immediately and I struck out hard with a fist.

"It's me. It's me, Simon," he said, pinning me down.

"Let go," I struggled. "Get off me, you fucker."

His arms fell to his sides. He shot back on his haunches and scrabbled to his feet. "I didn't mean to startle you."

"Are you out of your tree?" I rolled onto my knees and, one hand flat on the floor, pushed upright. "What the hell are you doing here?" I tried to blot out the intense pain in my arm, my stinging face. I didn't want to put a foot wrong. It seemed that this bloke, my friend, an ex-soldier, could quite easily kill me.

"I came to make sure you're all right."

I stared, open-mouthed.

Simon suddenly paled. "Jesus, you think I came to hurt you?"

"You gave a damn fine impression."

He spread his hands, brow furrowed, a pained expression in his eyes. "Kim, surely you can't think that of me?"

Yep, I could. Whether or not I was right was another matter. Lately, anything was on the cards. "Like a drink?" Nice and easy.

"Good thinking."

We moved into the kitchen. He scoped the room in a professional manner.

I made a play of going through the motions, finding the bottle, locating the corkscrew, popping the cork at the same time as pinpointing the extension phone and putting myself within easy reach. I also slipped out one of the new knives from the kitchen block and slid it under a tablemat, in case.

I handed Simon a glass and watched his eyes. This is an old friend, I reminded myself, taking a long swallow. *Someone close.*

"So you're all right, then?" He eyed me over the rim of his glass. I didn't care for it.

"Yes."

"You haven't been harassed?"

"Do the police count?" I said, making a weak attempt at humour.

"That bad?"

"I've got nothing to measure it by. At least I've found a decent lawyer."

"Sounds like a contradiction."

I smiled clumsily and snatched at my drink. "Simon," I said, treading with caution, "you did rather overreact."

His eyes connected with mine. "Instinct. It's what I'm trained to do. I see someone coming at me with a knife—"

"A poker," I corrected him.

He flashed a brilliant smile. "And off I go. Is your arm okay?"

"It isn't broken or anything," I said drily.

"Sorry." He tugged at his drink.

"Is something wrong?"

"Astute as always."

Something fragile ripped inside me. I inched closer to the tablemat.

"Things aren't working out, Kim." His expression was straight and direct.

"No?" I measured the distance between the blade and me.

"Since leaving the regiment, my life has lost all meaning. I know this sounds awful but your bit of bother, well, it's about the first time for a while I've actually felt alive."

"And how does murder score on the excitement scale?"

He visibly cowered and hung his head in shame. "I'm really sorry, Kim, crass of me."

Hot air escaped through my nostrils. My life has been turned upside down. He finds it a turn-on. Terrific. I did my best to haul the conversation back on track.

"I thought you were doing fine. You seemed happy enough last time we spoke. Job going well . . ."

"Do I *look* like an estate agent?"

"No, no, not really," I said, surprised by the sudden burst of aggression.

"Sorry." He ran a hand over his stubbly chin. "Shouldn't have spoken to you like that. I didn't mean to be short, not with you of all people, not after everything you've been through."

Is this him? Is this the real Simon or is he an impostor?

"Does Molly know you're here?" I tried to make it sound casual, as if it were no big deal either way.

"Sure."

"Shouldn't we give her a call?"

"Go ahead."

I crossed the floor and picked up the kitchen phone. If Simon had another agenda, he wouldn't be keen on me contacting his wife. Molly answered after two rings. "Is my lovely husband with you yet?"

"He is." I kept my eyes firmly on Simon. Lovely, he was not.

"Are you all right, Kim?"

"I guess so."

"We're worried about you, honey, what with Chris and everything. Simon thought you were such a frigging nutcase going after Stannard. He's concerned he might come looking for you — you obviously bring out my hubbie's protective instinct," Molly said, clearly finding it endearing.

"Sweet," I said with a fixed grin.

"You know Simon," Molly said proudly, "he can't resist the lure of danger. I sometimes think he misses the old days. Shall I have a quick word?"

I gratefully passed the phone over.

"Hello, sweetie," Simon said.

Simon continued to chat with his wife, and I watched and listened and felt raw inside. I didn't enjoy suspecting my closest friends.

After a couple of minutes Simon put down the phone and broke into a cheeky grin. "She says I mustn't lecture you."

"Good for Molly. Have you eaten?"

"No, and I'm starving."

While I cooked, Simon offered to check the security. "It's actually rather good," he pronounced. "Water one side, good solid door on the other, and the locks are quite sturdy. The only problem you've got is that you're quite cut off should he manage to get in."

We ate omelettes filled with bacon, mushrooms and cheese, and a side salad of freshly picked sorrel and tomatoes. We talked about the old days, Simon's chequered career path and his hopes for the future. One hour lapsed into another. I began to relax.

"Don't you have any sort of counselling or advice before you come out of the Forces?" I asked.

His laugh, in reply, was dull. "The nearest you get to psychology is eight pints of lager followed by whisky chasers. Supper was lovely, by the way," he said appreciatively. He stretched in a way that was faintly reminiscent of Chris.

"Coffee?"

"Please. Then I ought to be heading back. Where's your car?"

"The police are examining it."

"Bloody hell, Kim."

"Standard procedure," I assured him, embarrassed and wondering why he wanted to know.

"Hope they don't leave any nasty marks. Your Mini is a gorgeous set of wheels."

"Yes . . ." I stopped, mind scrabbling for a mental foothold. I'd heard the phrase before. No, not heard, *seen*. "What did you say?"

"Your car. It's a smart piece of kit."

"That's not what you said." I prickled with alarm.

"Didn't I?"

"You called it a gorgeous set of wheels."

"So I did. What are you like? It's a popular saying, Kim." Then he broke into a sudden, intoxicating smile and put his hand on my bare arm. "You look like someone's walked over your grave."

"I . . ."

"It's okay, Kim, you don't have to explain. Not to me."

He left forty minutes later. Craning his head out of the car window as I hovered on the porch, he said, "Don't waste energy stressing about me, will you? I'll figure it out. Maybe I'll take up flying or extreme sports or something."

I double-locked the door, the smell of burning rubber all that was left of his Audi TT as it vanished from sight.

CHAPTER SIXTY

I couldn't sleep so I got up, made tea and took it upstairs. Creeping back into bed, I closed my eyes and lay ramrod still. My mind refused to shut up. I felt as if I were splitting into numerous personalities: Kim the professional psychologist, Kim the bereaved lover, Kim the murder suspect. Events were speeding up uncontrollably and I felt pushed towards some horrible endgame. Cheltenham was only the playground in which my stalker chose to amuse himself. Devon was the place he'd play hardball. He'd come. It was simply a question of when.

At some stage, I fell asleep.

The next morning I phoned Andy first thing and brought him up to speed with edited highlights of the investigation. I kept the lousy allegation that Chris was my stalker to myself.

"I'm stuck here at the moment because the police are examining my car."

"Bloody hell, Kim."

"It's okay, there's nothing to find."

"I should think not."

"Don't suppose you fancy coming over for supper? I'd be really glad of some company."

"Can't tonight."

"Tomorrow?" If I hadn't been taken into custody, or whatever they did, by then.

"Alright if I bring Jen?"

Jen no longer seemed such a big deal. She'd been immensely kind to both of us.

"Fine," I said. "The truth is, Andy, I could do with you guys around."

"You haven't had any more trouble . . . you know, with that bloke?"

"Nothing to report."

"Thank fuck. I'll let Jen know about dinner. Want us to bring anything — wine, chocolates?"

"Just bring yourselves."

I'd barely ended the call when the landline rang.

"Can you be ready in half an hour?" Fiona North asked.

"Why?"

"We need to discuss a few things at the station."

Discuss what, precisely? "I'll call my lawyer." I phoned Gavin Chadwick straightaway, explaining the situation.

"Probably a new development," he said with authority. "I'm in Totnes at the moment but I can drive over afterwards."

I thanked him and waited for Fiona to arrive. She looked the same. She seemed different. More contained, somehow. Less like an intermediary and more like a police officer. We drove the entire journey in silence — a bad omen.

Darke and a couple of other officers were already outside waiting. They looked all business, like a bunch of gangsters at a Mafia convention. For a horrible moment I feared I was under arrest and tipped up on the balls of my feet, furiously casting around the car park for Chadwick. There was no sign of him. Trying to look relaxed, I walked over and offered an easy smile.

Darke was courteous. "Thanks for coming in. This won't take long."

"What won't?"

"There are issues we want to discuss."

"Issues?"

Darke looked evasive. "Things you should know."

"But my lawyer isn't here yet."

"We can wait."

Then it really was serious, I thought. We hung around for almost forty minutes. Fiona made small talk. Someone gave me a plastic cup of hot coffee that burned my fingers and tasted vile.

Chadwick phoned. "My car's broken down — something to do with the alternator. I've got the AA guy with me now."

"How long will you be?"

"Not entirely sure. What's the latest?"

"They've got new information."

"No sign of the DCI?"

"Haven't seen her."

"Then I'd better speak to Darke."

I called him over, explained and handed him my phone. He took it. I could hear Chadwick's voice booming from the other end. Darke muttered an affirmative, turned on his heel and walked off a little. Then he returned, a sheepish look on his face, and handed the phone back to me. Chadwick was still on the line.

"It's all good. Go and get some lunch. I'll be with you quick as I can."

"Thank you." I wasn't hungry.

* * *

Hair freshly cut and coloured, DCI Niven sat next to Darke. She wore a sober, pale grey suit with a white shirt that made her look like a conference delegate. She offered Chadwick and me a brief smile and gave a limp wave of her hand, indicating for us to take a seat.

"Thanks for coming in, Kim."

Interesting use of Christian name, I thought — could be a softening-up tactic or, wildly optimistic, I was viewed as less of a suspect.

"We've had detailed analysis back on Chris's car. Bloodstains were found in the engine compartment. It would seem that he was bending over as one does to check the oil—"

"He wouldn't need to check the oil. It was a new car," I pointed out, ruining her opening gambit.

"I'm simply giving an example." Niven's smile was cold. Her teeth glittered like specks of ice. She waited a beat. "Would it be true to say you're a woman who lives on the edge?"

Niven's incisive assessment contained more than a grain of truth. Still it winded me. I opened my mouth, but no words emerged. Fortunately, Chadwick did the talking for me.

"I really must protest."

Niven continued unabated. "As you are aware, Kim, we've already established Chris was hit from behind. The initial blow would have been enough to knock him off his feet, pitching him forward. The second and third blow would have rendered him unconscious."

Without waiting for me to digest it, Darke fired a question.

"You were born and brought up in the South West, weren't you?"

"Yes."

"Would you say that you have a fairly good geographical grasp of the area?"

"Yes."

"Do you know the area around Sittaford Tor?"

"Not intimately."

"But you've been there?"

"Yes."

Niven leaned forward. Her hands were clasped, not tightly, but in a relaxed fashion. "I understand that Charlie Lidstone is a friend of yours."

"That's right." This was a hell of a switch in the conversation and I dreaded where it was heading.

"Known him for long?"

"About . . ." *Goodness*, I thought, *has it really been that long?* "Fifteen years or so."

"Good friends, then?"

"I'd say so."

"Yet only days ago you threatened him with a wheel brace." Niven cocked an accusing eyebrow.

Chadwick twitched beside me. "That's not strictly true." Claire's accusation that I'd threatened her husband clattered through my head.

"Which bit isn't true, Kim?"

Sod, I wish she'd stop calling me by my Christian name. "I didn't threaten him."

"You deny it?"

"Strongly," I protested. "He was in my house, uninvited. I was protecting myself. He could have been an intruder."

"Ah, back to the stalker."

"You make it sound as if I'm fabricating it." My voice shook. I wanted to run and run and run. Sensing it, Chadwick shot out a steadying hand.

"You were afraid?" Niven said evenly.

"Yes."

"Because you've been stalked?"

"Yes."

Her coral-coloured lips twitched into a barbed smile. "Did you get the stalking idea from the internet?"

My eyes shot wide. "I'm not sure I follow you."

Niven looked to Darke, who spoke. "Your search history suggests that you've spent time looking at stalking cases."

"Well, yes." Dizzy, I thought the floor might suddenly rush up to meet me.

"Gaynor Lassiter, in particular."

"I wanted to find out if there were any similarities." I looked helplessly at Gavin, who looked perplexed. I should have told him about Gaynor, I realized, only now seeing its relevance.

"Mrs Lassiter was allegedly stalked before her disappearance," Darke said.

I shot forward. "Exactly. It can't be a coincidence. There has to be a connection," I insisted, ignoring the fact that Robert Fallon had dismissed it.

Niven frowned. "A connection?"

"To me," I said, exasperated. "Geographically speaking." I looked from Niven to Darke, begging them to grasp what I was saying.

"There's no evidence whatsoever," Niven said, stony.

I cringed inside. They had me down for a fantasist.

"But what if there was?"

Niven lowered her gaze and crossed her legs. Darke shifted in his seat, tapped the point of his pen on the table. He knew something. *They* knew something. What the hell was it?

"Do you approve of taking the law into your own hands?" The barbed smile returned. We were back to my alleged threat to Charlie.

"No, of course not," I said, exhausted, "but, last I heard, it's perfectly acceptable for householders to defend themselves from intruders."

"I was referring to your conduct with Kyle Stannard."

I took a breath, trying to resist rising to Niven's bait. "It wasn't like that," I said as pleasantly as I could.

"We understand you were quite zealous in your pursuit of Mr Stannard. You went to his parents' home, isn't that right?"

"No comment."

"You also tried to interfere in his business dealings."

I swallowed hard. "It was a mistake." Chadwick's eyes bored into the side of my head.

Niven paused for effect. "Would it surprise you to know that we've identified the weapon used on Chris?"

An alarming switch of emphasis, I thought. "You've found it?"

"Not yet, but we know from the type of injuries what was used."

"You said it was a hammer."

"Did we? I thought we said it was something *like* a hammer."

Chadwick's gaze intensified.

"Maybe," I said, bullish. "I don't remember for certain."

"Are you sure you don't remember? You see, it was a wheel brace, Kim, exactly the type of weapon with which you threatened Mr Lidstone."

Chadwick immediately asked for a break and whisked me off to a side room.

Once inside, his gaze hardened. "They're giving you an opportunity to change your story."

"I don't want to change my story." Desperate, on the verge of tears, I tried not to cry. "I used the brace to change the wheel on my car. I grabbed it when I thought I had an intruder. I did *not* use it to kill Chris."

Chadwick's cool eyes fused on mine. "Tell me more about Gaynor Lassiter."

"I hardly know anything about her. In desperation, I researched stalking cases and she came up out of the clear blue."

Chadwick nodded in the way people do when they dismiss a theory. Sledgehammered, I was on a knife edge.

"And Charlie?" he asked.

Surprised, I told him what happened.

"Do you reckon Charlie laid it on thick to the police?"

"I've no idea." I really didn't want Charlie getting into trouble. They'd been good to me, allowing me to stay at the annexe free of charge.

Chadwick tapped the side of his nose, a perplexed expression on his face. He didn't say anything immediately. "What was Charlie doing in your house?"

"He came to sit in when I had a viewing. I'd no idea he was going to show up, so it was rather a shock."

"Did he have a key?"

"The door was open."

"Who said?"

"He did."

Then I gabbled on about Simon, his reference to my car as a gorgeous set of wheels, how it fitted with the anonymous note. As I ran out of steam I noticed a strange expression on Chadwick's face, as if he were saying, *All these men, the random disappearance of a stranger, they're all red herrings.*

"You don't think Simon's choice of words significant?" I was practically pleading with him.

The way he was looking there was a distinct possibility that a psychiatrist would be invited to rock up and section me.

Chadwick sliced through my thoughts. "They won't find anything incriminating in the car, will they?"

"Not unless someone's planted evidence." I meant my stalker. I didn't mean the police. Unfortunately, Chadwick didn't see it that way. His eyes darkened. His voice was sharp. "This is real life, Kim, not an episode of *Murder, She Wrote*." He opened the door, popped his head round, intimating that we were ready to resume. "Leave me to handle this," he warned under his breath as we hurried back inside.

"My client feels there's nothing to add to or retract from her original statement," Chadwick said, like a KC summing up for the defence. "I think it's fair to say that my client's professional life is exemplary. Her work, specializing in eating disorders, is highly regarded both by her peers and patients alike. She has a livelihood and a reputation at stake." With a rush of guilt, I remembered Kirsten Matherson.

"I would also point out that she has roots in this community and is therefore not likely to flee."

He's persuading them not to arrest me, I thought, my eyes trained on Niven's inscrutable face.

Darke looked at Niven, who looked at me. With a ruthless smile, she said, "Surrender your passport and you're free to go."

CHAPTER SIXTY-ONE

I asked Fiona to drive me to an off-licence. In preparation for the following evening, I bought a mixed case, South African white, French and Chilean red, and a pack of lager because Andy preferred it to wine. A concession to responsibility, I also bought two litres of water — one still, one sparkling. I hardly spoke on the drive back to the cottage, deflecting any question with a monosyllabic answer.

The police had maintained that there was no link to Gaynor Lassiter. Niven had been adamant, but her body language gave her away. Darke's obvious discomfort also spoke of something else. What were they hiding?

We arrived home and I carried the case of drink to the door. With one foot on the step, I stopped. Fiona, behind, barrelled into me.

"What's up?"

"Listen."

She took a step forward, put her ear to the door. "Music playing."

"Yes."

"You must have left it on."

"No."

"Are you sure?"

"Certain."

"You wait here. Give me the keys." Fiona unlocked the door and walked inside. I rested the box down and sat on the step, waiting for something but not sure what. Seconds later, the cottage fell silent. Fiona reappeared. "Coast's clear."

I followed her in.

"It was on a loop. Do you recognize it?" Fiona held up a CD.

Of course I did. U2's "Love Is Blindness". Three-in-the-morning drunk, lyrics sucking me in, sexy riffs epitomizing a dark, obsessive theme. I didn't know my stalker's identity but I knew now what drove him. Therein lay the fear and the anger. And I knew about that too. Mine.

I looked at Fiona squarely. "Dead men don't stalk."

"What do you mean?"

"He's back. He's here. Like I always knew he would be."

"But Chris . . ."

"*Not* Chris," I insisted. "Here, let me show you." I led Fiona to the dining room and showed her the photo album.

"We've already looked at it," Fiona said, dismissive.

"But you didn't realize its significance. This is the real Chris. Don't you see, psychologically speaking, this can't have been the man stalking me?"

I watched Fiona's pensive expression. "Maybe it's the impression he wanted to create," Fiona said. "To come across as the attentive, caring lover, but underneath something else was at play."

I shook my head, vehement. "*What* was at play? *What* motivated him? He had an affair. He had an exit strategy already lined up and then changed his mind and decided to stay. He wanted to celebrate my birthday with a very personal gift because he loved me."

Neither of us spoke. Fiona touched the album lightly with her fingers. There was hesitation in her manner. I picked up on it. She was weakening and coming round to my point of view. I pressed home my advantage.

"Chris was already dead when someone entered my flat in Cheltenham and left a revolting calling card. Now this." I glanced in the direction of the CD player.

"You say your brother, Luke, can verify that Chris called him?"

"Yes."

"How do you explain the letters?"

"The computer can't tell you the identity of the letter writer."

"What about the dates? What about his signature?" The blue eyes filled with concern.

"They must have been forged." To my mind, Fiona was outgunned, but she still didn't look convinced.

"Would you like me to stay?" she said as if to appease me.

"No, I want you to go." It won't end unless you do.

CHAPTER SIXTY-TWO

I put the lager and two bottles of white wine in the fridge then walked to the top of the drive where I could get a signal. Holding my phone aloft, I reread the piece on Gaynor Lassiter. Scrolling down, my eyes hooked on the wrongful arrest of her husband, Ivan, a lecturer of molecular microbiology at Exeter University. No wonder Darke had looked shifty.

Only Gaynor's husband could confirm that his wife was being stalked. The very nature of stalking meant things often happened in secret and only held significance for the victim. Perhaps the police had been as sceptical of Gaynor's stalker as they had of mine. I felt for Ivan Lassiter. If anyone knew what this nightmare was like, he did.

Checking out the university website, I found his name in a list of biosciences staff, under the Faculty of Health and Life Sciences. My pulse quickened at the sight of an email address and phone number. A long shot was better than no shot, I reasoned. The number rang and rang and I was about to hang up when a gruff male voice answered: "Lassiter."

Halfway through my staggered pitch, he said, "Look, I'm really sorry, but I've got nothing to say. I've had enough press and people hounding me for information to last a lifetime."

"Please," I begged, "I understand why you don't want to talk, and I genuinely don't want to rake it all up, but I'm desperate, Mr Lassiter. The police are trying to arrest me for a crime I didn't commit. You're the only person who understands, who can help."

The line went quiet. I could practically hear him breathing. I wasn't running out of options. I'd hit a brick wall.

"How soon can you be here?" he asked.

I screwed my eyes up tight and suppressed a groan. Why the hell did I live in the arse end of nowhere? "Hour and a half."

He gave me an address. "I can spare you precisely twenty minutes."

I exchanged my sandals for a pair of sturdy ankle boots, my thin jacket for leather. I scrunched back my hair into a ponytail. It wasn't a style I liked because it exposed too much the damaged side of my face, but it was practical.

Snatching my crash helmet from the cupboard, Chris's keys from the drawer, I went outside and crossed the gravelled drive to the garage. Chris's metal-grey bike sat inside, ready for a fast exit. I let out a low moan and a rush of grief stormed me as I remembered better times. When the worst was over I pushed aside the illegality of what I was about to do and, with both hands on the high handlebars, swung onto the saddle. Flicking the kickstand up with my boot, I stabbed the key into the ignition. Immediately the dashboard lit up, the neutral light glowing green. As Chris's ghostly voice whispered the moves in my ear, I punched the kill switch, pulled the clutch in, pressed the starter button to fire up the engine, then flexed the twist grip and short-shifted through the gearbox, as Chris had shown me, one down and five up through the six-speed gearbox, the accompanying growl from the non-baffled exhaust providing the bass rhythm for the roar in my heart. I'd no idea if I could handle such a powerful machine. I'd only ever test-ridden the Tiger on lonely country lanes; a motorway was a very different story.

Before I lost my nerve I shot out of the drive and headed straight to Kingsbridge, concentrating hard on not taking the bends too fast. From there, I tore along the A38, the bike opening up enough to set my jeans on fire.

I arrived in Exeter around seven in the evening. Ivan Lassiter lived in a large historic-looking building close to the university, where he now taught. I looked up at the vast expanse of red brick and arched windows, solid and dependable, and prayed that my journey had not been in vain.

Parking in the visitors' slot, I sneaked in as a young foreign student came out and found myself in a vast communal hall with high ceilings and echoey wood-panelled walls adorned with portraits of eminent scholars. A wide staircase ran up two sides of the building. It reminded me of school. Armed with only a name and number, I took the right set of stairs, travelled to the third and highest floor and rapped on the front door of Ivan Lassiter's apartment.

The door opened and in the entrance stood a serious-looking man with tinted spectacles, thick sideburns and thin lips. Around Chris's height, he carried less weight, as if he devoured books instead of food. His clothes were rumpled, his trousers loose and ill-fitting. His scrawny neck reared up from a frayed shirt collar and reminded me of an ostrich. Everything about him revealed that he was a man who lived alone and wished he didn't. From somewhere deep inside, I heard a snatch of Vaughn Williams.

"*Fantasia on a Theme by Thomas Tallis*," I said. Shamelessly, I turned my less attractive side towards him. I couldn't read the expression behind the lenses, but he stood stock-still. We both did. An unspoken acknowledgement of something I didn't yet fully understand passed between us. When he invited me in I realized I'd been holding my breath.

We sat in a sitting room with terrific views over the city.

He glanced at my crash helmet. "How far have you travelled?"

I told him.

"You must be thirsty. Can I get you a drink?"

"Water would be lovely, thank you."

While he was gone I looked around me. Everything was grey — the sofa, chairs, carpet and walls, even the granite-topped coffee table. I wondered if it had always been so. Had everything lost its vivacity and colour when his wife disappeared?

My gaze fell onto a framed photograph on the window ledge. I got up, crossed the room and picked it up. It was a shot of a younger, more rounded and better-dressed Ivan. The woman with him was laughing. They both were. A palm tree behind them suggested that it was a holiday snap. I studied her face. She had lovely hazel-coloured eyes, a neat nose and a mass of dark brown hair, but this was not what caught my attention. Briefly, and with a jag to my heart, I wondered if I were dreaming.

"That's Gaynor," Ivan said, handing me a glass, to which he'd added ice and a slice of fresh lime. "She was a gifted musician."

"Professional?"

"No." He took the photograph from me and placed it back on the sill.

"She's very pretty," I said tentatively. "I couldn't help but notice . . ." I let the rest of the sentence drift.

"The birthmark on her face," he said.

Maybe Gaynor's facial disfigurement was deliberately held back from the public and press so that it wouldn't elicit a load of calls from cranks and hoaxers. Perhaps to reference it was deemed ghoulish and in bad taste.

"I'm afraid I only half listened to what you told me on the phone," Ivan said. "Do you mind running through it all again?"

I told him about my stalker, about Chris, about the police and my fears.

When I finished he leaned back into the sofa, clasped his fingers together and touched his chin, thoughtful. For the first time, here was someone who understood and who'd listened to my story without cynicism, hostility, ridicule or disbelief.

"I thought coming to see you was a long shot," I said. "After seeing the photograph of your wife, I'm more certain than ever that her stalker is mine."

"Which would explain why the police turned up at my door yesterday."

Niven's response to me was not personal, I now realized. She wasn't being a cow. She was reacting to the situation. Not that it made me feel better.

"At last they seem to be joining the dots."

"If belatedly." Ivan's expression was rueful. "So much of what happened to Gaynor could be explained away as fantasy or false memory, or getting things muddled up. To be fair, it didn't help that my wife wasn't keen to make a fuss and ditched anything that could have provided the police with a lead. She thought if she ignored it, it would stop."

I understood only too well. "What form did the stalking take?"

"Her car was moved at work." I did my best to keep my expression steady. "The phone would ring," he continued. "If I picked up, the caller would hang up. If Gaynor picked up, he'd stay on the line. We did all the usual stuff, reported them as nuisance calls, tried to call back, but the calls were untraceable and the best the phone company could do was offer to change the number."

"Did the police check out her phone records?"

"As part of the investigation, but they never managed to trace the caller."

"Anything else?"

"She had gifts sent to her at work."

"Cards, chocolates?"

Ivan nodded, twitched a smile. It seemed as if it was a relief for him too, to talk to someone who'd experienced something of what his wife had suffered.

"And you never had a clue who it was?"

He pressed his hands to his face, tipping the spectacles up onto his head and rubbed one eye. "No." The glasses flicked back down. "The energy we expended trying to find out was astonishing."

"And exhausting. It turns your life upside down and inside out."

He nodded, his expression bleak. "Our lives and minds were comprehensively dismantled."

"So what happened in the end?"

"She didn't come home." He looked as mystified and hurt as he must have done at the time. "She went to work. We were supposed to be meeting for a drink afterwards and she never arrived."

"I am very sorry." I waited a beat. "You think she was abducted?"

"I'm convinced of it."

I fell into a respectful silence.

"It's been nine months," he murmured mournfully.

"I'm sorry to ask but when exactly in October did she disappear?"

"The twenty-sixth."

Ignoring the stuttering inside my chest, I stayed perfectly still.

"Deep down, I know she's gone. But the only way I keep going is thinking she's alive, that we still have a life together. Does that make sense?"

"It does," I said softly, my mind shooting off in unpleasant directions not travelled before.

"That's why I couldn't cope with the press intrusion. Every time I had a knock at the door or a message shoved underneath it with invitations to sell my story, I knew we'd moved from missing wife to murder victim. I still get the odd phone call from journalists, one in particular, but with nothing like the same intensity."

A light went on in my brain. "Who?"

"Josh Brodie, *Western Morning News*."

"I'd like to talk to him."

Anxiety etched Ivan's face. "Are you sure? Do you realize what you might unleash?"

Too late to worry about that. "I'll take my chances. I don't suppose you happen to have his number?"

Reluctantly, Ivan said he did. "Give me a moment, then."

He disappeared and reappeared with a business card. I gave it a glance, thanked him and pocketed it.

"One last thing: did Gaynor ever receive anything strange on her computer?"

"No."

"Are you certain?"

"Positive. It was mostly out of commission during that period. She had repeat problems with the hard drive, an absolute pain. The computer was constantly booked in for repair."

"But the police did take a look at it?"

"Yes."

I couldn't think of anything else to ask. "I'm sorry to have taken up so much of your time."

I got up and Ivan walked me to the door. "Apologies for earlier. Will you let me know how you get on?" he said.

"I will."

We both hovered awkwardly by the entrance, neither of us sure how to say goodbye. Impulsively, I gave him a hug. "Thanks for relenting."

Ivan's smile was ringed with sadness. "The anxious expression in your eyes reminded me of my wife. How could I not?"

CHAPTER SIXTY-THREE

I called Josh Brodie's mobile number. A voice answered, "Yep."

"Are you Josh Brodie?"

"The one and same." His raspy voice indicated a serious nicotine habit. In the background I could hear the noise of glasses clinking, conversation at full throttle.

I explained who I was. "I've just spent the past hour with Ivan Lassiter. He—"

"Gaynor Lassiter's husband?"

"Yes."

"Go on."

"I've got information that might interest you."

"Yeah?" The phone crackled. I assumed he was walking to somewhere quieter. "That's better," he said.

"It would be best if we met."

"Maybe," he said, not sounding that committed. "Are you in Bristol?"

"Down the road, Exeter."

"I don't have my diary on me."

"What are you doing now?"

"I'm at an awards ceremony in town. Can't duck out, I'm afraid."

I glanced at my watch. It was seven forty-five. I could be with you by nine-fifteen. How about afterwards?"

"That won't work for me. It could be an all-nighter."

"Mr Brodie, my boyfriend has been murdered. Gaynor Lassiter was being stalked and so am I. I think the same person who abducted her is out to get me."

He went awfully quiet.

I felt perilously close to meltdown. "Are you still there?"

He didn't answer my question but posed another. "I know this sounds strange, but have you got any marks on your face?"

"Will scars do?"

"Perfect," he said. They were the reason Ivan Lassiter had let me into his life, and now Brodie was doing the same. "Meet me at the Marriott on College Green as soon as you can. Ask for me at reception. I'll brief them that I'm expecting you."

CHAPTER SIXTY-FOUR

I navigated my way past a group of smokers, sped up the stone steps to the hotel, a grand Victorian building, and entered through a revolving door that opened out onto a wide foyer smelling of polish and fresh flowers. As I approached reception, I heard a ripple of applause from deep within and, close by, the sound of a bar working at full pelt. I gave my name, stated I was meeting Josh Brodie and was asked to take a seat, which I did in an alcove by a window. Minutes later, a man I assumed to be Brodie strode towards me. His bowtie was undone James Bond style, and he had an eager look in his hangdog eyes. He was younger than I'd imagined, nearer forty than fifty. He had short dark hair spiked upright with gel. He wore trainers, a trendy addition to his dinner suit.

I stood up to greet him. To my consternation, he crooked one finger under my chin to better examine my face, studying it as if it were a fine work of art. When I'd met with his approval, he invited me to sit down, which I did.

"Drink?" he said.

I shook my head. "I'm driving, but don't let me stop you."

"No, I can wait."

I cut straight to the chase. Josh was already three-quarters of the way there with my story. All I had to do was fill in the detail. Like a true hack, he interrupted when he wasn't quite clear and went over a couple of things, like timing and the computer image, the latter betraying no prurient interest. He also asked me about Stannard even though I'd discounted him.

"You've obviously followed the Exeter case," I said finally. "What I need to know is whether there are any other similarities, something else I've missed, a seemingly minor detail, anything else that connects me to Gaynor."

He studied me for a moment, as if weighing something up, then took out a fresh pack of cigarettes and pulled off the wrapper.

"Mind if we go outside? I think better when I smoke."

"Not a problem," I said.

Fortunately, other smokers had left so it was just the two of us parked beneath a spot-lit stone balustrade. I waited patiently while Josh went through the ritual of lighting up. He took a deep drag and a thin stream of smoke puffed out into the night.

"Better," he said, happy now. "How are the police dealing with it?"

I let out a giddy laugh. "They have me down for a murderer and believe I made up the stalking story to deflect from my guilt."

"I'm surprised they haven't banged you up."

"It's only a matter of time."

"Got a good lawyer?"

"I believe so."

Josh took another drag. "What you have to remember is that the police hate linking cases, particularly if it involves other constabularies. It goes against their Plod DNA," he added irreverently.

"Other cases? Other constabularies?" I asked with a shaky laugh.

His expression was nothing short of grave.

"Gaynor Lassiter, who disappeared in Exeter; Anita Finch from Birmingham; Melanie Simpson from Presteigne,

Wales; Deborah Lyons from Land's End; or Chrissie Taylor, who committed suicide in Holmes Chapel."

"Suicide?"

"According to her mother, she was being stalked by an anonymous stalker and couldn't take it anymore."

My heartbeat didn't quicken, it careered. "And were they *all* stalked?"

"Can't confirm in the case of Melanie Simpson, although I think it highly likely."

"And who was the first?"

"Chrissie."

"And she screwed up the grand plan by killing herself," I said thoughtfully.

"That's my guess."

"How did she do it?"

"Pills. Died of a massive overdose."

"When?"

"Four years ago."

Which meant he's been improving his game for some time. "And what do you think bonds us together?" I knew, but I wanted Josh to spell it out.

"Every single girl had some kind of facial defect."

The confirmation of what I most feared.

"Sick, huh?"

I nodded, rolled my neck and shoulders in a doomed attempt to stave off a shiver.

"Chrissie had badly scarred skin as a result of teenage acne," Josh explained. "Anita had a port-wine stain on her right cheek. Melanie Simpson suffered from a rare skin condition. Deborah had corrective facial surgery following injuries sustained in a road accident. Gaynor—"

"A large birth mark." I remembered the raised cluster of brownish marks on her face — congenital nevi, at a guess.

Josh nodded. "And then there's . . ."

"Me," I said. "Have you spoken to the police about your findings?"

"I gave up. To be fair, families were not always supportive. Can't say as I blame them," he said without rancour.

Assuming journalists put the story ahead of sensitivities, I was refreshingly surprised. "Are there any other similarities? You appeared to take an interest in the computer image."

"In two cases the girls had answered classified ads for computer recycling."

"Which girls?"

"Chrissie and Melanie."

And then there were Gaynor's computer repairs, I remembered. "What's your take on the perpetrator?"

"Someone who has the freedom to travel," Josh said. "Could be a lorry driver, a sales representative, someone with plenty of time on his or her hands."

I grimaced. "Her?"

"Statistically, it's more likely to be a male, I grant you. The victims are all female, and disappearing folk is a masculine pursuit, but, I don't know, it's such a weird one, maybe a woman is responsible. Women are more concerned with their appearance than men, aren't they?"

I lapsed into silence. I had to confess the argument had merit and was an angle I'd not considered. Josh punctured my thoughts. "Would you let me interview you? We could strengthen your case."

"I don't know. I haven't thought it through. It's not what I came here for." Irritation crackled behind his eyes. As far as he was concerned, I was an exclusive and, now that I'd got what I came for, I had no further use for him. Keen not to disappoint, I said, "Give me twenty-four hours to think about it."

"Fair enough. What's your number?"

I hesitated. The last thing I needed was a crime correspondent hounding me.

"In case I think of anything else," he said with a slack grin.

I relaxed, told him and watched as he shambled back inside followed by a wispy trail of cigarette smoke.

CHAPTER SIXTY-FIVE

The journey back was fraught. In spite of the halogen driving lights, I was unaccustomed to travelling in the dark on a motorbike and found myself constantly misjudging distances. On the outskirts of Exeter, the low-fuel light shone and I worried that it could have been on for some time. To try and conserve what petrol I had, I decreased speed and rode in the slow lane. It felt as if I'd painted a bull's-eye on my back. I fully expected the traffic police to rock up and signal for me to pull over.

By the time I reached the cottage, it was well into the early hours. Every muscle and sinew hurt. My eyes practically bled with strain. As the tyres crunched across the gravelled drive, I experienced a profound sense of dread. Was someone lurking inside, armed for my return?

As it turned out, nobody was there. Nothing was amiss.

Impossibly wired, it took me a long time before I dropped off to sleep. Sometime later, loud rapping at the front door roused me from unconsciousness. I shrugged off the duvet, dragged on a robe and sleepwalked to the open window. Pushing back the curtain, a shaft of bright sunlight prised open my eyelids. My bleary, stumbling gaze focused on Fiona North, who was looking straight up at me.

"Sorry, were you asleep?"

I mumbled a reply to the effect that I was. Her secret smile inferred that she was pleased — meant that I was in no fit state to argue.

"Your passport," she said. "I should have collected it already."

"I'll be right down."

"No hurry."

I took her at her word and took a detour. After having a pee, I splashed water over my face and went downstairs to let her in.

"What time is it?" My mouth was furred with fatigue.

"Lunchtime." She glanced at her watch. "Ten minutes past one, to be precise."

I'd slept for almost nine hours straight and had to check myself from saying so.

"Are you all right? You look peaky."

"Tired," I burbled. I asked Fiona to hang on while I fished out my passport from a drawer in my desk. Handing it to her, I said, "That it? No more interviews?" I guess I sounded facetious because her responding expression was cool and professional. "Not today." Which meant tomorrow.

"I've been thinking," I said, wrapping my dressing gown tightly around me. "Perhaps he's done it before. Perhaps there are other victims."

"Why do you say that?"

"Chris's murder infers a different type of offender."

"Go on," she said.

"Someone who has gradually worked his or her way up the criminal ladder, someone who might have started out with harassment or stealing, or—"

"Her?"

"It's possible, isn't it?"

She shrugged. "You appear to be suggesting that the alleged individual is a serial offender?"

"Yes."

Fiona looked sceptical.

"Chris's murder is almost incidental. It's not the point of it all, don't you see?"

From the look on her face, she didn't.

"Gaynor Lassiter had a birthmark on her face," I blurted out.

Her eyes narrowed. "How do you know?"

"Does it matter?"

"That's confidential information."

"And now it isn't." It came out as borderline snarky. I was just so very tired of hacking my way through an undergrowth of secrets and lies.

"All right," she said slowly. "So there's a tenuous connection to you."

"It's not tenuous. The stalker and murderer is driven and turned on by disfigurement. That's his bag. It's what grabs his attention." Other than that, I had little idea about the exact psychopathology.

"That's highly speculative."

I shook my head in an agony of frustration. "What if there were other victims?"

"What others?" She looked genuinely taken aback.

I reeled off the list. Fiona looked at me as if I'd announced I was about to set light to myself.

"Where on earth did you get this?"

"I contacted a journalist whose been working on the Lassiter case. He . . ." I stopped. Fiona's expression said it all. Journalist equals trial by media, resulting in utter garbage.

I grabbed the sleeve of her shirt. "Will you pass on what I've told you?"

She patted my hand and framed her mouth into a smile. "Of course I will. Shall I make you a nice cup of tea? You could take it up to bed."

Defeated and resenting being treated like an elderly patient with dementia, I smiled back, obedient. "That would be lovely — thanks."

I let Fiona faff about and promised to rest. When she offered to stay I said, "I'll only be asleep, no point." I had to send her away. I couldn't flush out my stalker unless I was alone. I was putting my life at risk, but without taking it to the limit, the game would never be over, never won.

As soon as Fiona left I showered and dressed and carefully put on my make-up. My mind was electric, consumed by the thought of the other women, what they had endured, the depths of their despair, the twisted way in which the stalker, abductor and now murderer was turned on by our physical imperfection. Next, I thought about me. *Gorgeous set of wheels*, Simon had remarked. *You're sailing pretty close to the wind*, Charlie had accused. *You're shot through with sadness*, Stannard had said. His perspicacity had amazed me. Was my stalker also turned on by my fragility, the sense that for all the show I had not quite transcended the consequences of an unfortunate accident and lonely childhood? And what about the other thought I'd entertained when Ivan mentioned the day that Gaynor had disappeared?

Then it clicked.

Purposeful, I picked up the phone and called Carolla Dennison's close friend, Jo Sharpe. There was something I needed to check.

CHAPTER SIXTY-SIX

Andy arrived sooner than planned. Wearing a cream linen shirt and stonewashed jeans, he looked smart and clean and together.

I squinted over his shoulder. "No Jen?"

"She got as far as my place then threw up on the sofa."

"About time you had a new one."

"Ha bloody ha!"

"Poor woman — what was it, something she'd eaten?"

"A dodgy prawn sandwich at lunchtime."

"Not nice."

He chucked his jacket, a lightweight sailing affair in navy blue, onto a chair and handed me a bottle of wine and a box of chocolates, oblong-shaped and gift-wrapped in a harlequin design. "Don't open them now," he said. "They're for later."

I thanked him. "I thought we'd have a drink on the terrace." I took hold of the corkscrew. "Wine or lager?"

"Wine."

I popped a cork and poured out.

"I feel guilty," he said.

"Why?"

"Here we are about to share a lovely meal and Chris is dead."

"Survivor guilt," I said. "Best cure is to make this a celebration of his life."

"I'll drink to that," Andy said. "To Chris." We chinked glasses.

"Are you hungry?" I asked him.

"Not especially."

"Good. I'll cook later — promise not to get drunk," I added with a knowing smile that made him laugh.

We went outside. I was glad of the fresh air. Andy sat down and spread his feet apart. I subsided into the nearest chair. I hadn't had time to properly take on board what Jo had said. Something that had appeared impossible for thirty different reasons was now credible. I gazed across the water, listened to the sound of birdsong.

"You look preoccupied."

I twitched a smile. "I've been thinking a lot about when I was growing up, places I visited, people I knew, family," I said. "I guess that's what happens when someone dies. You start looking at your life in a different way. You see the constant themes, the things you should have changed but never quite got around to, what you should have said or, more often, kept quiet about. Sorry," I said, "I'm dribbling on."

"No, you're all right. You said you wanted to talk."

"Yes, I did."

"About?"

My pulse rate stammered. I fell momentarily silent.

"Kim?" he prompted.

"About you."

"*Me?*" He tossed his head back and laughed. "You're so damn enigmatic. Is that the right word?"

"Probably." I forged a smile, took a drink. I ought to listen.

"Nothing to tell that you don't already know." His grin was off-centre. Fleetingly, he reminded me of Stannard.

"There's lots of stuff I don't know about you."

"Like what?"

"What your parents do for a living."

Andy's grin split wider. "My dad's a retired accountant. My mum's a homemaker and a world-class bore."

"See, I don't know everything." I took a sip, eyes fixed on the silvery water. "You're an only child, right?"

"Yeah, but I wasn't spoiled."

I chuckled, sharing the joke. "Didn't you move from Cheshire to Plymouth?"

"Yes."

"Ever go back to Cheshire?" *Holmes Chapel, in particular,* I thought.

"Why would I?"

"No reason."

"We hadn't always lived there," he said.

"Really?"

"My dad had a job in Kingsbridge, would you believe? We lived at Stentiford Hill for a short time."

"How old were you?" I took a drink to cover my sly gaze.

"Why?"

"Getting my bearings."

Andy blinked rapidly. "Twelve, thirteen, I forget."

"We might have gone to the same school if I hadn't been sent away."

"And I hadn't moved back to Middlewich," he reminded me.

"When was that?"

"When I was almost fifteen."

"Odd time to leave," I said. "You must have been in the middle of exams."

Darkness entered his expression.

"This is your cue to rattle on about your school days." It was meant to sound harmless.

There was no return smile. His look was stark. I recognized common ground. "I was bullied. It's why we relocated."

This was big news to me. "Yet you came back and now you teach in the same school."

"Payback," he said abruptly. "Walking the same corridors where I was teased and taunted gives me a sense of triumph, of power. I've mastered my demons." A strange light crept into his eyes. I couldn't distinguish whether it was the slant of the evening sun or if it came from deep within.

"Did Chris know?"

"No one knows."

"Except me."

"Except you."

He took out a pack of cigarettes and unwrapped the cellophane. "Something else only you now know about me," he said with a rakish smile. "Does it bother you?"

"We're outside. Go right ahead." He plugged his mouth with a cigarette and, taking out a silver-plated lighter, lit up, slowly, methodically, ritually, some might say pedantically. I thought of smoke in the night, the figure standing in the lamplight outside my flat.

"Seems like neither you nor Chris confided too much in the other."

Andy blew out a plume of smoke, dismissive.

"So, who *do* you confide in, Andy?"

"About what?"

"Things that bother you."

"I'm not the neurotic type."

"I didn't say you were. What about Jen?"

"What about her?"

"Do you two talk?"

He snickered, took another drag, another drink. "Fuck's sake, Kim, give it a rest."

I looked out across the river at the shivering light, the way the vegetation disappeared into the shadows. I was protected here, so Simon said, unless the person with malice in mind had already breached Cormorants' natural borders.

"Did you always teach design technology?"

Andy shook his head and blew out a thin wisp of smoke. "My degree is in mathematics. Design technology was a natural progression — both subjects require logic."

"You don't find it dull dealing with machines instead of people?"

"Machines are way easier to manage."

"And repair."

"Well, yeah."

"And control," I murmured.

"Saves a lot of hassle." He flicked some ash.

"Is that how you view people — as a lot of hassle?"

"Can be," he said, clipped.

"Doesn't that make life lonely?"

"I've got loads of friends. You missed some great nights at the Hermitage, by the way."

"So Jo told me." I took a drink for courage. "Is that your story, Andy?"

"What?" He smiled, but his glinting eyes didn't match the set of his jaw.

"Lots of friends, no deep relationships."

"I'm not sure Jen would be happy with your assessment."

"Ah, the elusive Jen, I was forgetting."

"She's sick for one night and she's elusive? What are you like?"

"It's okay," I said. "Not everyone is ready to settle down."

"Nothing wrong with that."

"I agree. We're all different. We each have our individual characteristics." I flicked a lock of hair back from my face, giving him the full effect. Did I imagine a facial tic, a tiny shudder? "Every one of us has a different story to tell. We all have our skeletons and demons."

"Not me." He drained his glass. "Got any lager?"

I got up, went inside, cracked open a can and handed it to him.

"As you were Chris's friend, his *best* friend, his *mate*," I said, with blood-freezing clarity, "I thought I'd test out a theory on you."

He looked at me with a faintly amused expression. "Go on, then. Entertain me."

CHAPTER SIXTY-SEVEN

"The police believe Chris was my stalker."

Andy's eyes widened in disbelief. "You're joking. That's impossible."

"Yes, it is."

"Poor Kim." His face was a picture of pity. "But what about that guy you were telling me about?"

"I was wrong. It landed me in a hell of a lot of trouble, but that's another tale." I leaned dangerously towards Andy. "Don't you see? The guy stalking me is the same person who killed Chris."

Rock-solid Andy didn't move a muscle.

"I've often wondered about him, what he's like, whether he's some pathetic creep, no friends, a loner, you know the type. I thought there was a fair possibility that he was mentally ill, but lately I've come to feel differently about him. He's sophisticated, manipulative and smart. Systematic in his approach, he has what you'd call a methodical and logical mind."

Andy's eyes glistened. "I'd guess you'd know."

I waited, watched his hands, hands that might kill. "I also think he's done it before. Possibly many times."

He wore an expression of pure shock.

"A woman in Exeter disappeared last year during half-term week. Her name was Gaynor Lassiter. She'd been stalked. Vile, isn't it?"

"Christ, Kim, you don't—"

"She had a raised birthmark on her cheek, quite visible. An odd similarity with me, don't you think?"

He took a drink by way of a reply.

"Remember when I came to your place to break the news of Chris's death?"

"How could I forget?"

"It was in a terrible state."

"You know how it is, a guy on his own," he said with a grunt. "Jen says I ought to get a cleaner."

"Don't apologize. It was quite telling really."

Andy's brow furrowed. "I don't understand."

"The thing about mess is that it makes it easy to pick out the part that's tidy. You had a neat, clutter-free zone near your computer."

Andy threw an indulgent smile. "That's because it's crucial to my work, duh!"

"And I noticed two piles of newspapers."

The smile stretched wider, the teeth whiter than white. I should have been terrified. Instead, I felt triumph, vindication, justice all rolled into one.

"I didn't spot it at first," I continued. "I didn't know you read the *Cheltenham Standard*."

Initially, Andy's face was blank, then puzzled, then annoyed. "For God's sake, Kim, are you implying what I think?"

"You tell me. Before you get cocky it was open at the piece on me and Ellerslie Lodge."

"Because I know you, idiot-brain."

"That's not the reason why." *Say it, you creep.*

"No, not the *only* reason. I pick up the local rag because I have clients in Cheltenham."

"Ah, your bit of moonlighting. Which client?"

"I'm currently putting a program together for a group of agricultural machinery specialists. Like many budding industrialists, the main man has a holiday home here in Devon, which is how I managed to get the business in the first place. Honestly, Kim." He shook his head in exasperation. "It's a good job we're mates otherwise I'd do you for slander or defamation of character or something. Now, if you've finished grilling me," he said with a wide grin, "perhaps we could think about dinner. I'm quite peckish."

Andy appeared to have a convincing answer. Doubt lodged in my throat. I did my best to swallow it and jumped to my feet, returning inside, giving him every impression that he was off the hook. Andy followed and watched as I took fresh lamb, red peppers and tomatoes out of the fridge and laid them out on two chopping boards. I handed him another can and he pulled up a chair.

Resting the small of my back against the work surface, I said, "The day Chris was killed you were teaching."

Andy rolled his eyes and tugged back the ring pull. It gave a small hiss.

"How many kids in your class?" I persisted.

"Thirty-three. Boys outnumber girls."

"Is that the way you like it?"

"It's the way it is."

"So, thirty-three alibis."

"If you want to put it like that."

"What time do lessons begin?"

"Nine-twenty. Are you going to put down that knife, or are you going to keep waving it around?"

I looked at the blade in my hand, placed it near the meat, somewhere close, somewhere I could easily reach it.

"The call from Chris came through at seven fifty," I said. "If you were passing through the office, you could have overheard."

Andy's eyes were like chisels. "You must be joking. One: I never roll into school at that ungodly hour. Two: I don't go in the office. It's full of women."

"But you like women, Andy. You're secretly fascinated by them, isn't that right?" Especially if they have defects. "None of it matters, of course, because you might as easily have been lying in wait, stalking prey."

"Know what? You're starting to piss me off. You're fucking cracked."

"Isn't that the objective?"

The air throbbed. The kitchen clock ticked then chimed. This was my home, my territory. Knives to the left. Meat cleaver to the right. The place teemed with domestic weaponry and, if provoked, I would have no hesitation in using it.

Andy let out a sudden sigh, his expression softening. The hard note in his voice melted away like snow in sunshine. "C'mon, Kim, this is all bollocks and you know it. We don't want to fight. We're both stressed out to the eyeballs. I know you have to examine all possibilities. I understand that, really I do. But even if I knew about Chris's call, how long do you think it takes to get from school to Goodshelter and back again? Oh, and fit in a murder?" He hooted with derision.

"Too long."

"There you are, then." He drained the can.

"Except that day wasn't normal. It was an intensive IT session that started first thing and didn't finish until the bell went for lunch." At least, that's what Jo Sharpe had told me.

"I still have to be there, you clown."

"That's the point, you don't," I said. "Today's kids have a high level of proficiency born out of endless hours on tablets, PlayStations, Xboxes and computers. You can set reams of stuff for pupils to be getting on with in your absence. How long did it take, Andy? How long for you to play the sympathetic friend, suggest a spin in Chris's new car to take his mind off his problems and then, under the guise of blokes being blokes, you ask to take a peek at his shiny new engine. Is that when you smashed his head in?" I was breathless. My chest hurt. So did the skin on my face and neck. I hadn't even got started on the forged letter, the anonymous messages and the porn. His stupefied reaction suggested that I'd confessed to a monstrous crime. The rap on the door made us both jump.

Andy cocked an eyebrow. "Are you expecting anyone?"

"No." Let it be Fiona, I prayed.

"We'll continue this later." He spoke in the way a teacher speaks to a recalcitrant teenager. He definitely didn't seem bothered. "You stay there. I'll go."

I snatched up the landline to make the call to the police and was surprised to see a message left on the answering machine. I pressed play: *Josh Brodie here. Something I should have told you: a camper van was seen in the vicinity of two abductions.* Startled, I almost choked at the sound of male voices inside the cottage, one Andy's, the other hauntingly familiar. Next, footsteps, deliberate and slow, then a face appeared. In a split second, two worlds crashed head on and I was crushed in the middle.

CHAPTER SIXTY-EIGHT

"What the hell are you doing here?"

Stannard arched a quizzical eyebrow and spread his hands. "*You* wanted to talk."

With the reminder of Brodie's message, the fog in my brain cleared. "Where do you park your camper van?"

"You are one crazy bitch. Do I look like the kind of guy who drives one of those aberrations?"

No, he didn't, but Andy did. Then what the hell was Stannard doing in my home?

"Your brother phoned this morning, Kim. He said you wanted to straighten things out."

"What things?" Andy stood squat and belligerent, chest straining underneath his shirt.

"Who are you, her minder?" Stannard sneered.

I saw Andy's fist ball. Confusion gripped me. Stannard's bellicose stance remained. He glared at Andy. "He said Kim wanted a meeting here at the cottage. As we left on —" Stannard glanced at me — "dubious terms, I believed him."

"Luke wouldn't do something like that," I said.

"Luke? It wasn't Luke. It was Guy."

"Guy?" I felt as if a thermobaric bomb had gone off and all my organs had been sucked out of my body.

"It was definitely Guy who called," Stannard insisted.

"You fucking bastard. My God, you've done your homework." So this was it. Stannard *was* my stalker. I made a face at Andy in apology.

"You're dead, mate."

Andy lunged. There was a loud crunch of bone as two bodies collided and crashed onto the tiled floor. Fists flew. Chairs overturned. Drawers wrenched out. Cutlery cascaded. A lamp smashed, shattering into jagged pieces, both men rolling in the broken shards, the air full of grunts and moans. Blood spattered cupboards. Bigger and heavier, Andy had the advantage. Transfixed, my knuckles pressed to my mouth, I remembered my brothers' fight and my rotten decision. *Got to get help*, I thought, heading for the phone.

"Kim!" Andy shouted breathlessly. "Fetch a rope, or something we can tie him up with."

I ran into the small utility room, grabbed a length of thick cord, a leftover from my father's sailing days, and handed it to Andy. He looked spent. His left eye ballooned. His lip was split and there was a nasty cut above his right eyebrow. Panting, he stood over Stannard, dripping sweat. Stannard, meanwhile, was barely conscious.

Andy hauled him onto a chair. Blood gushed from Stannard's nose. His lip, too, was swollen. The two sides of his face seemed to meld into each other, the good side less distinguishable from the disfigured. He let out a low moan.

Andy roughly pulled Stannard's hands back and tied them together, letting the twine trail onto the floor.

"You can't leave him like that."

"Why not?"

"He might choke or something with all that blood."

"After what he's done, I wouldn't worry."

Stannard let out another groan.

"I'll mop up the worst," I said, swooping up a tea towel, plunging it under the cold tap, simultaneously reaching for the extension phone. "We should phone the police."

"Leave it, Kim." Andy's voice was as cold and empty as a freshly dug grave.

CHAPTER SIXTY-NINE

Fear slashed a hole in my chest. Every trace of geniality had vanished; Andy's eyes were cruel. A glance at Stannard extinguished all possibility of help. He was too much out of it.

"This is all very nice and tidy." Swiping the wet towel from me, Andy dabbed at his wounds. "Quite a little party."

My mind flashed to the painting: two men, one woman. "You tricked Stannard."

"A willing dupe. Swallowed my tale like the proverbial hook, line and sinker. There's definitely something of the stalker about him. He's clearly obsessed with you."

"And you're clearly obsessed with disfigurement."

"Broken beauties." He shivered and walked slowly towards me. "The ultimate turn-on." Andy reached out, traced the jagged line of scar tissue, his alcoholic breath hot on my face. I didn't flinch, didn't move. "Time to open your present, Kim."

I glowered.

"Don't be so ungrateful. Go on, it won't bite."

I snatched up the box from the kitchen table, ripped off the paper and stood with my mouth open.

"Can't have a party without fireworks, can we?" Andy said. "I *love* rockets, don't you? I thought we'd have a display over the water. After that, we'll have a bonfire. You've got quite a lot of petrol in that old garage of yours. By the time the fire engines turn out, the cottage should be well and truly ablaze. Tell you what," he said, advancing, "Stannard can be our Guy Fawkes."

"You sad, pathetic bastard."

The blow split my lip. I put a hand to my face, tasted blood.

"*You* need to learn some manners."

"Is this how you treat Jen?"

"Stupid bitch. Not even a decent shag."

"You doctored the letters, didn't you? You made it look as if Chris wrote them."

Andy shrugged. "His signature was a doddle."

"Why Chris?" I flared. "He was your friend. What the hell happened to you?"

"There you go," Andy mocked, "looking for some deep psychological motivation. The truth is, I wasn't abused. My childhood was ordinary and painfully dull. I had a secure upbringing in a reasonably well-off family, no brothers and sisters to bug me or give me a complex, and my parents, poor suckers, offered pure, unconditional love."

Andy's moist red lips were almost on my face. I forced myself not to recoil. "Fucks up your psychobabble, I'd say." His eyes contracted into two straight lines. "But you," he said, tipping my chin up with the crook of his index finger, "*you* were always special to me.

"I know you better than you think," he goaded. "You smile for the camera, but it's an act. At heart, you're as false and as bitter and twisted as me."

My eyes swam with tears. I wanted to scream.

"I saw you once, a long time ago, coming out of the local surgery. I asked my mum who you were. She told me you were the girl who got burned. Fascinating."

I shrank inside. Was I the cradle of his obsession? Had I been the trigger, the start of it all? "But Chris, where did he fit—"

"Nowhere." Andy leaned in close, pressed his lips onto my face. His fat tongue darted out and flicked my ear. "I killed him because he was precious to you. I killed the others because . . ." His eyes glazed. Unexpectedly, he shot a hand out, groped my crotch.

Stannard groaned. Blood congealed under his nose. His chin slumped onto his chest, breathing laboured. It looked as if the chair alone propped him up.

"Enough conversation," Andy said. "I'm ravenous. Let's eat."

"Screw you."

Andy thrust me a look that would make a rattlesnake recoil. "Cook, or I'll gut him — right here, right now."

Cold crawled all over me. "I need a knife," I said, reaching for the nearest.

"'Course you do, but not that one," Andy said, taking it from me. "Way too small. This sharp enough for you?" He picked another out of the block. I trembled as he ran it down between my breasts. "I prefer a wider blade myself," he said, eyes panther black as he handed it to me. "Try anything —" he jerked his chin in the direction of Stannard — "I'm sure the police will be happy to believe you killed him."

Thinking and thinking, I cut the meat, sliced the peppers, a clove of garlic. I tossed olive oil into a frying pan, stir-frying the lot until the peppers were almost translucent and the meat cooked. I added wine and seasoning, brought it to the boil, reducing the liquid to a rich, dark, glossy sauce. In another pan I boiled basmati rice, adding a stick of cinnamon and a twist of nutmeg. I made a green salad and tossed it in vinaigrette. I'd prepared it all a hundred times before. I did it without thought, hands working automatically, independent of my mind. He'd be expecting scalding water, a knife or boiling hot food. All it took was one act to inflict maximum damage.

With one chance to shock and annihilate, I flicked my eyes right and left and caught sight of a packing box next to the kettle, the top open. I wondered whether Andy had clocked it. I focused my entire concentration on finding the right moment, the exact time, and all the while Andy, a monologue of self-congratulation, kept talking, prattling, liking what he said and saying what he liked.

"You got me started, Slade. Did you know that? 'Course, I didn't realize it at the time, but then when Chrissie came into my life . . ."

"The girl in Holmes Chapel?"

"Yeah, it was all going so well. Had her wound up a treat, but then," he said, face darkening, "she went and fucked things up by topping herself. Never got the chance to make her mine."

"And the others?" I didn't want to stop him, had to keep him engaged. Once the conversation ceased, the violence began.

His features dissolved into a warm, smug glow. "I'd perfected the art by then. Really got them dancing to my tune. By the time I closed in for the kill, they were glad. Did I ever tell you about my selection process, Slade?"

I shook my head, tried to prevent my teeth from chattering, my hands from shaking, desperate to keep him relaxed.

"See, every man and his dog is in the computer repairs business, but I offered exceptional rates, ads everywhere up and down the country." He took a slurp of lager. "Then when I had a female punter, I'd check them out on the internet — easy and as quick as sending an email — all those social networking sites, all those self-aggrandizing work portals."

"That's how you picked them," I murmured, as if in agreement.

"The amazing power of technology. Everyone leaves a communication footprint. Anita had her face pasted on Twitter — brave girl. Mel and Gaynor on work sites."

My stomach lurched. Isn't that how I'd tracked down Ivan?

"Neat, huh?"

I laid the table under his precise instruction. Tablecloth, knife, fork, peppermill and saltcellar. Each arranged just so.

I served the food on a large white plate, side salad separate. Andy drew up a chair. When he demanded more lager I played servile, humiliated, under his thumb. He seemed to have forgotten about Stannard altogether. Catching sight of him, I caught the gleam in his good eye, the tightening of his jaw, the wriggling motion of one hand.

Andy pulled back the tab and drank straight from the can, wiping his mouth. "Sit down, bitch."

I stood, defiant, blocking his view.

"Suit yourself." He ate, gobbling quickly, a dribble of sauce running down his chin. His eyes never left mine.

"You won't get away with it. The police know I'm here. I'm expecting an officer at any moment. One sign of trouble and they'll be all over the place."

"We'll see, or rather I will. This is very good, by the way," Andy said, jabbing at the air with a fork. He looked down fractionally to shovel up another mouthful. I shifted stance, twisting towards Stannard, and caught the expression, the almost imperceptible nod. I'd no idea what he was planning but I recognized that he was asking me to trust him. The man I'd never been able to trust.

"More?" I said to Andy.

"Yeah, that would be good." I went to turn. "Don't move. *I'll* get it," he said, shooting out of the chair. "Don't want you flinging saucepans at me."

Stannard, freed, struck like a viper. The rope flew over and looped around Andy's neck. I grabbed a saucepan and clouted the side of his head. It sounded like a paperweight dropped onto a marble floor. The impact reverberated up my arm. Blood trickling from his temple, Andy thrashed and bucked like a shark on a line. Stannard clung on. I made a grab for the extension, hit speed dial and got through to Fiona's number, gabbling for help.

Incomprehensibly, in that short passage of time, Andy had seized the advantage, Stannard fast losing his grip against the bigger and stronger man. Dropping the receiver, I leaped at Andy. A vicious jab from his elbow made me gasp and spun me across the floor and into the wall. Pain shot through my side and nausea gripped my internal organs. I staggered upright, watched helplessly as Andy delivered several blows into Stannard's already battered body. As Stannard collapsed Andy followed up with a swift kick to Stannard's head and then his back. The rope was now looped around Stannard's neck.

"How does it feel to watch a man die, Slade?" Andy hauled it tight.

Stannard's face went very red, the eyes bulged, a rattling sound ejected from his throat.

Desperate, I swooped on the open box, reached and grabbed the blowtorch. Hitting the ignition, I came at Andy.

The oh-so-pale skin blistered, bubbled and peeled. His hands shot up and became raw flesh. His screams ricocheted off the kitchen walls as he cowered from the intense heat.

Stannard pushed himself to one knee, coughing and retching, and staggered to his feet. With one hand on his throat, the other reached out to me and dragged me away from what I'd done, from what I'd been forced to do.

CHAPTER SEVENTY

We emerged from the cottage like fleeing civilians after a drone strike. I reeled at the pain I'd inflicted. Horrendous, it was beyond comprehension.

We kept moving up the steep, narrow road towards Holset, Stannard urging me on, hauling me forward until I felt my lungs would pack up. The sound of sirens wailed in the distance. Eventually, where the road bent and widened, he allowed me to stop. Stannard took off his jacket and wrapped it around my shoulders.

There were two police cars and two ambulances. Darke and Hatchet got out and ran towards us.

"Andy Johnson's in the cottage," I panted, dazed. "He's burnt. I burned him," I said quietly. "I did it."

"He tried to kill both of us," Stannard rasped, his voice a protest.

Darke instructed Hatchet to go to the cottage along with one of the ambulances. "You need medical attention," he told Stannard and immediately signalled for help.

"I'll be all right," Stannard croaked. He looked at me with desperate eyes. Andy was right in one sense. Stannard *was* obsessive.

"Go and get checked out, at least," I said kindly.

"Won't I have to make a statement?" Stannard muttered to Darke.

"We can take it later."

Stannard looked at me as if unwilling to let me out of his sight.

"Go," I told him.

With reluctance, he consented. Two paramedics in green uniforms approached and helped Stannard into an ambulance.

Darke took a call from Hatchet. I watched his face stiffen. Were they going to charge me with attempted murder?

We went to the nearest police station. Chadwick was summoned. I told my side of the story, repeated everything Josh Brodie had told me, pointing out Andy's fixation with disfigurement. "According to Brodie, a camper van was sighted close to two of the abductions. Odds on, he kept trophies of his kills, either there or at his home."

"When are you speaking to Andy Johnson?" Chadwick asked the police.

"As soon as he's fit enough to talk," Darke replied. "The burns to his face and hands are severe and extensive. He may lose the sight in one eye."

I lowered my head, mortified. "What if he doesn't confess? What if he presses charges?"

"Let's wait and see," Chadwick said.

"We're going to recheck his alibi," Darke said. "We're carrying out a search at his house. If your hunch is correct it'll provide the evidence we need."

CHAPTER SEVENTY-ONE

The wait was interminable. Finally, Darke, Fiona North at his side, broke the news.

"We've got him," he announced, triumphant. "We found his secret hideaway in the attic, plain sailing."

"An entire wall covered in photographs," Fiona said, animated, "a shrine to you and the other women, his fixation unmistakeable."

"They're all dead, aren't they?" I said, suddenly bleak.

Fiona looked to Darke. "It doesn't bode well," he admitted.

I thought about Ivan Lassiter, how he'd no longer be able to cling to the hope that his wife was still out there, alive and wanting to come home. I felt unspeakably sad for him.

"There were pictures of where you worked, your flat in Cheltenham, people you visited," Fiona said.

"And one of me on a beach?" The very last snap taken by Chris when I'd stretched out on the rocks and felt radiantly happy. In my mind's eye I pictured me with my hat pulled down, sunshine lighting my face, sea in the distance.

"I'm sorry, Kim," Fiona said.

It was what I'd expected. "And Stannard?"

"He also appeared in Andy's Hall of Fame," Darke said. "The real clincher came when we found Chris's belongings, including a bloodstained jacket and camera."

"What about the murder weapon?" I asked.

"Not exactly the sort of thing we'd expect Johnson to hang onto but we'll keep looking."

"And Kyle? How's he doing?"

"Discharged himself, gave a statement to the boss and went back home."

"He's gone?" I said, perplexed.

Fiona rummaged in a large brown leather handbag and handed over an envelope. "He said to give you this."

I'd screened my post for so long my first reaction was *don't open it.*

"Aren't you going to read it?" Fiona said, expectant.

"Later."

CHAPTER SEVENTY-TWO

Secrets and guilt.

Kyle hadn't deserved his fate. He hadn't deserved to be plagued by flashbacks and nightmares, and a face that repelled. I reread and folded up the letter again, slipping it into my jacket pocket.

Three days later, I was standing outside the Mathersons' home, a modern house that lay deep in the Welsh countryside. Set back from a winding road, it looked as if every brick, piece of gravel and blade of grass was arranged for a purpose.

Frank Matherson opened the door. Instantly recognizing me, his eyes narrowed to two incisions. "What the hell did you come here for?"

"To talk." I took a calm step towards him.

"You've got to be joking. Have you any idea of the damage you've done?"

"What about the damage *you* did?"

Frank Matherson looked as if someone had fired at him with a stun gun. "I don't know what you're talking about."

"No, you don't, which is why you're going to let me in so I can tell you." Other men would have slammed the door in my face. Something in my determined manner got to him. He shrank back and stood aside. I strode in and turned left, only because the door happened to be open, and found myself in a sterile-looking sitting room. Cushions plumped. No dust on the furniture. No marks on the carpet. No sign of homely clutter.

"Marie and Kirsten are out." His eyes darted. In spite of his earlier bravado, he looked pathetic and afraid.

I didn't tell him that I already knew, that I'd watched and waited, stalker style. "May I sit down?"

"I suppose so."

Matherson sat too. I eyeballed him. "I want *you* to talk about when Kirsten worked for Visage."

He rested his big hands on his thick thighs as if to anchor them. "Do you have children, Miss Slade?"

"No, I don't."

"Then you wouldn't understand."

"I understand a father's grief."

He met my eye, unsure what to do with that piece of information.

"Kirsten is special to me," he began in a hoarse voice. "She's my only daughter. My sons, Robert and Stephen, Kirsten's brothers, are fine young men, but it's a different type of relationship.

"I never wanted Kirsten to go into modelling. I hated the idea, but Marie thought it too good an opportunity to miss. I suppose a part of her felt she'd liked to have been given the same opportunity." He glanced at the floor. "Kirsten was striking, a beautiful-looking girl. Still is, to me," he murmured. "It was all right in the beginning. I thought as long as Kirsten was enjoying it and it wasn't interfering with her school work it couldn't do any harm, might even give her some experience. I was right there," he said mournfully, the fight gone from his voice.

"Kyle Stannard," I said.

Frank Matherson's dark dolorous eyes fixed on me. "He raped my daughter."

"And you couldn't forgive him."

He gasped in disbelief. "Tell me a father who could."

"What if I was to tell you that he didn't?"

He let out a shout. "That's not true."

"But what if he didn't? What if it was a lie?"

"You've seen what's happened to Kirsten," Matherson growled, unyielding. "The rape changed her. She became anorexic. Stannard did that to her. He almost killed her."

"If the rape was significant, why didn't you tell her GP when she first started to lose weight? Why didn't you inform Jim Copplestone? Why conceal it?"

Matherson stiffened. "Because we took care of it."

"We?"

"*I* took care of it."

"No, you didn't. You make a lot of noise, but at heart you're a coward. It's why you asked Robert and Stephen to administer the beating."

Matherson pitched forward, rubbed his face with his hands. When he looked at me his lips were drained of colour, almost white, and his eyes told me that he knew the game was up.

"It wasn't hard, was it?" I said, biting back my anger. "They felt as aggrieved as you. All you had to do was encourage them, pump them up. You made it look like a mugging that had gone wrong. It was easy because you knew Stannard, being the arrogant man he was, would fight back. Maybe you were there to make sure they didn't go too far in their punishment. You didn't want Stannard dead. You wanted him maimed. You wanted to crush his spirit. Afterwards you arranged for the boys to go to Australia. Am I right?"

He didn't answer. His coarse, hairy hands pulverized the fabric of his trousers.

"Your daughter became sick because she buried a secret, a secret she and her mother have concealed for too long."

He looked at me sharply. "I don't understand what you're saying."

"The rape was a story made up to discredit Stannard in a pure act of revenge." I let the thought hook into his mind and hang there.

"Made up by whom?"

"Your wife."

His jaw jacked open. Spittle crouched in the corner of his mouth. He broke into an ugly smile. "That's a disgusting thing to say. Marie spent hours with Kirsten, slept in her room for months. She comforted her as only a mother can."

"Did you ever speak to Kirsten?"

"It wasn't my place."

"Why do you think Kirsten dropped the charges?"

"Because she couldn't face the ordeal of the witness box."

"Because she knew it was a *lie*. She fell in love, Mr Matherson. Yes, Stannard treated her the same way he treated all his women but he didn't rape her. When he finished the relationship, a relationship your wife had encouraged from the start," I added, "Kirsten felt hurt and rejected and angry. It was easy for Marie to manipulate her. But your daughter is a fine young woman. She has a conscience. She knew that what she was being asked to do by her mother was wrong."

Matherson put his hands to his face. "No," he said wretchedly. "Marie's a good woman. She wouldn't make up a tale like that. She wouldn't lie to me. Not for all this time."

"She *had* to. You took the law into your own hands. You set your two sons on Stannard. If Marie told you the truth, you'd know that your sons had disfigured an innocent man."

His face caved in with dismay.

"And Kirsten's had to bear the guilt of that ever since," I finished quietly.

"Can't be," he said in a frail and frightened voice.

There was a movement by the door. Kirsten stood in the entrance, her face wan, her eyes blazing with conviction. "It's true, Dad. She's telling the truth."

CHAPTER SEVENTY-THREE

We arranged to meet on neutral territory in a nearby park. Stannard waited by the entrance. For the first time in my life I was not afraid to see him. "You fled pretty smartly."

"To convince you my interest is based purely on your professional expertise," he said with a sideways look, unexpected amusement in his eyes. I broke into a laugh and he laughed with me. It made me think of Stannard's photograph, his head tipped back, no cares in the world, joy in his heart. How I wished I could turn back the clock for both of us.

"Shall we walk?" he said.

We followed a tarmac path, past a wooden hut and a group of lads playing football on the grass.

"Your letter," I began.

"I wanted to put the record straight about Kirsten," Stannard said. "I wasn't kind to her. She was very young and I took advantage. Sure, I was a bastard but I never raped her."

"I know."

"But all those things you said and believed."

"I didn't know the truth then. I was hopelessly wrong and I'm sorry. Has your mother recovered from my visit?"

"She wouldn't want to, even if she could," Stannard said with dry humour.

We carried on walking.

"You wrote about being mugged and the resulting flashbacks."

"That's where I'd hoped you'd come in." His voice quickened. "You see I've started remembering, not in detail, not yet at any rate. With your skill—"

"The point is," I interrupted him, "there are certain things you should know."

He turned, apprehensive, as if he feared I was going to give him the brush-off again. I quickly cast around. "Shall we find somewhere to sit down?"

We found a bench underneath a weeping willow that overlooked a pond. A family of water rats darted from the undergrowth and plopped belly first into the water.

I told him about my visit to the Mathersons. Stannard listened, sat quite still, face bowed. When I finished he remained silent. I asked him what he was going to do.

"I don't know."

I viewed him with surprise.

"It doesn't change anything for me, does it?"

"I'm afraid not."

He gave a heavy sigh, weary, as if all his efforts had come to nothing. "Kirsten's brothers would need to be extradited."

"Shouldn't you at least attempt to bring them to justice?"

Stannard looked out across the surface of the pool. "Justice or revenge, Kim? They're exiled. The family's split apart . . ."

"They have their freedom."

"Do they?" His smile was serene yet bittersweet. He sat and stared into the middle distance. "I could only remember fragments of the attack, and that's what was bugging me. I was desperate to unlock the key. I never thought beyond, how I might feel once I discovered the truth. And now I do . . ." He broke off, wretched, and turned towards me, genuine pain in his eyes. "Perhaps by letting it go," he said, "by losing, it will make me a better human being."

I reached out and rested my hand on his. A better person than me, I thought. "I really think you should consider—"

"You don't understand." He smiled sadly. "The life I had is gone. I don't deny I mourn its loss. It's been," he said, his voice halting, "a deeply sobering experience. It made me realize exactly how much we're judged for the way we look. I still have days when I can barely face the world, when I feel eaten up with bitterness for my condition, when I want to spit in the face of fortune, but I'd be a liar if I didn't admit that I'd had a good run, better than most. I squandered and abused most of it. Sex, drugs and rock and roll," he said, glib. "Once, I had it all."

Unexpectedly, my eyes filled with tears. He seemed so unbearably alone. I blinked them back.

"You didn't deserve what happened to you, Kyle."

"You don't believe in divine retribution?"

"No, I don't."

We sat, not talking, watching a water rat poke its head out from underneath a bush, scurry across the path and join its brothers.

"When did you start remembering?" I said, breaking the silence.

"After I'd watched that TV programme you were on." He flashed a smile. "You became my Holy Grail."

"You thought I could put the pieces together."

"In a way, you did."

"Then you don't need me anymore."

We got up and walked back across the park. "What will happen to Kirsten?" Stannard said.

"I have a sneaking feeling that she'll be all right. She's approaching nineteen now. Her parents can't put her in a clinic unless they invoke the Mental Health Act. I reckon she's stronger than all of them put together. Now that the secret's out, there's every chance she'll feel more in control of her life."

"She could make a full recovery?"

"I'd say so."

"And what about you?"

I viewed him with surprise. This was the man who appeared not to give a damn about anyone, who threatened and bullied to get what he wanted, and then I remembered the words of the women who'd known and loved him. Flick had described him as charming. Kirsten had said he was funny and wonderful. "I'll survive. I'll be fine." *One day*, I thought.

"I wanted to thank you for what you did," he said. "You saved my life."

"Oddly enough, we saved each other."

We were back by the entrance.

"When do you move into the flat?" I asked.

"It's on hold at the moment. I've that large project on the Evesham Road that's swallowing up most of my time." He turned his good side towards me, tilting his lips, mischievous.

"I'm sorry about that."

"No need. You did Mrs Foley a favour. Are you going ahead with the sale of your cottage?"

What was I supposed to do? Chris was gone. Andy had all but destroyed me. I didn't know where I belonged anymore. "Why? Are you interested in buying?" I asked, gamely.

"Too many memories," he said with a shudder. He glanced across the street. "I guess this is it. Maybe we could meet up for a drink or something."

I flashed a warm smile. In my heart, I thought it unlikely. Not knowing what to do next, I held out my hand formally, part of me unwilling to simply say goodbye and walk away. Stannard stole the moment. He bent down, tipped my chin up and kissed me once, slowly, full on the lips.

"Goodbye, Kim."

I shivered and turned to go.

"Kim?"

I turned back. "Yes?"

"No more sadness."

CHAPTER SEVENTY-FOUR

I tried hard to take Stannard's advice.

There was talk about Andy pressing charges. In the end nothing came of it. Chadwick kept me informed of legal proceedings. Darke stayed in touch on the police side. So did Fiona North, who informed me that Andy's mother had undergone an operation to correct a cleft palate in childhood, the scar remaining. I took small comfort from the fact that, as Andy had led me to believe, I had not "got him started". Somewhere, deep down, his mother held the key to his Pandora's box of obsession. Specialist teams had been dispatched to Wales to search an old quarry, another to waste ground in the Midlands. Traces of Gaynor Lassiter's DNA had been found in Andy's camper van. Inexplicably, he refused to confess where he'd disposed of her body.

With Fiona's help, I organized Chris's funeral. He was buried at the same church as my father and brother. I invited everyone, including Ivan Lassiter and Josh Brodie. My friends welcomed me back into the fold like a conquering hero. After that, and with my suspension lifted, I immersed myself in work. I gave Josh the interview he'd asked for. The cottage refused to sell and I spent no time there. I made few plans.

One cold day in late October, almost a year on from Gaynor Lassiter's disappearance, when the light was still and clear, I was walking through the Suffolks in Cheltenham. A woman's voice called my name. I turned and saw Heather Foley on the other side of the road, frantically waving. She had a man with her, one arm linked through his. He was portly, grey-haired and clean-shaven. I crossed over.

"I had to let you know our little plan worked," Heather beamed. Her skin shimmered. There was an incredible radiance about her so that I wondered what kind of cosmetic surgery she'd had. "Mr Stannard phoned me back within twenty minutes of my make-your-mind-up call and apologized unreservedly. His lawyers were apparently at fault. Oh, forgive me, this is Des Overton," Heather said, introducing us. He had kind eyes, I thought, and an honest and open face. "We haven't seen each other in years and we're having a splendid time," Heather chattered, giving his arm a tender squeeze, utterly loved up, it seemed. Des returned the compliment with a look of undiluted adoration.

"I'm glad," I smiled.

Heather dropped her voice. "I didn't bother with the facelift."

"You don't need it, darling," Des said.

You've got him instead, I thought. When you're loved and liberated, happiness makes us all beautiful. Heather Foley was living proof.

"Are things all right with you, dear?"

"Yes, they are."

"No more problems?"

"None."

"Well, lovely to see you," Heather said, giving Des's arm a tug. "Cheerio."

I stopped off at a café and watched the faces of passers-by from the window. I studied the young and the old, the couples and the singles, the beautiful and the not so beautiful, as if trying to unlock the secret of their success. Stannard talked of losing as if it were something positive, something from which he could grow, something that held the potential to make him a better human being. I guessed it was the old maxim about a glass half full rather than half empty. He'd taken me by surprise. I thought him too bitter and twisted by what had happened to see any light in the darkness. It was humbling. Maybe I could learn from him. I'd once been beautiful to the man I loved. Maybe I could be beautiful again.

THE END

ACKNOWLEDGEMENTS

As ever, massive thanks to my agent, Broo Doherty at DHH Literary Agency, who believed in the story right from the start, and to David Headley for his consistent support over a number of years.

I always knew my nomadic lifestyle would come in handy for something other than conveyancing solicitors, and I'm delighted to draw on two locations, Cheltenham and South Devon.

Thanks to S. P., who advised me on locational and jurisdictional matters regarding the murder investigation. Initials are used to protect his undercover status. Any errors made, either for dramatic purposes or otherwise, are mine alone. Also thanks to Kate Bendelow, scenes of crimes officer for Greater Manchester police, who gave specific advice on the length of time needed to process Chris and Kim's cottage in Devon — and reduced my worst fears about potentially lengthy timelines!

To gain a better insight into the mind of a stalker, I'm grateful to Richard Gallagher for his book *I'll Be Watching You*. Changing Faces is a charity that offers support to those living with facial disfigurement. The website offers help and advice and gives a terrific understanding of what it's like to live with this type of disability.

Finally, I'm indebted to my editor, Kate Lyall Grant, as well as Jasper Joffe and, indeed, the wonderful team at Joffe Books for making this happen — again. Thank you.

THE JOFFE BOOKS STORY

We began in 2014 when Jasper agreed to publish his mum's much-rejected romance novel and it became a bestseller.

Since then we've grown into the largest independent publisher in the UK. We're extremely proud to publish some of the very best writers in the world, including Joy Ellis, Faith Martin, Caro Ramsay, Helen Forrester, Simon Brett and Robert Goddard. Everyone at Joffe Books loves reading and we never forget that it all begins with the magic of an author telling a story.

We are proud to publish talented first-time authors, as well as established writers whose books we love introducing to a new generation of readers.

We have been shortlisted for Independent Publisher of the Year at the British Book Awards three times, in 2020, 2021 and 2022, and for the Diversity and Inclusivity Award at the Independent Publishing Awards in 2022.

We built this company with your help, and we love to hear from you, so please email us about absolutely anything bookish at feedback@joffebooks.com

If you want to receive free books every Friday and hear about all our new releases, join our mailing list: www.joffebooks.com/contact

And when you tell your friends about us, just remember: it's pronounced Joffe as in coffee or toffee!

ALSO BY E.V. SEYMOUR

STANDALONES
MY DAUGHTER'S SECRETS
THE PATIENT

Printed in Great Britain
by Amazon

18171223R00212